DECADENCE FROM DEDALUS

LÀ - BAS

(Down There)

J.K. Huysmans

LÀ - BAS

(Down There)

with an introduction and chronology by
Robert Irwin

Dedalus /Hippocrene

Published in the UK by Dedalus Ltd,
Langford Lodge, St Judith's Lane, Sawtry, Cambs, PE17 5XE

UK ISBN 0 946626 85 5

Published in the USA by Hippocrene Books Inc,
171, Madison Avenue, New York, NY10016

US ISBN 0 7818 007 2

Distributed in Canada by Marginal Distribution,
Unit 103, 277 George Street, Peterborough, Ontario, KJ9 3G9

Publishing History
First published in France in 1891
First published in England in 1925
Dedalus European Classics edition 1986
Decadence from Dedalus edition 1992

Introduction copyright © Robert Irwin 1986

Printed by Billings Book Plan Limited,
Hylton Road,Worcester,WR2 5JU

A C.I.P. listing for this title is available on request.

Dedalus would like to express its gratitude to David Blow for his help in originating
the Decadence from Dedalus series.

Also by J. K. Huysmans

En Route
The Cathedral
Des Esseintes Song (in The Second Dedalus Book of
Decadence)

IS SPIRITUAL WARFARE SILLY?

AN INTRODUCTION TO HUYSMANS'S 'LÀ-BAS'

Huysmans's early novels were written in the shadow of the realist movement and are bleak anti-romantic depictions of the struggle of humble folk to bear up under the twin curses of heredity and environment. In this Huysmans was much influenced by the novels of Emil Zola. **A Rebours,** however, marked a new departure, for in this study of decadent sensibility, Huysmans redeployed realistic techniques to new subject matter (and Là-Bas would take this further yet). **A Rebours** is at one and the same time a fantastic flight from boredom and a blueprint for the refinement of boredom. Huysmans, like Baudelaire, was writer driven by the limitless, obsessive and dementing power of boredom. As Baudelaire put it 'L'Ennui, fruit de la morne incuriositè,/Prend les proportions de l'immortalitè'. Though Huysmans's later novels will point the way to Christian salvation, **A Rebours** and **Là-Bas** have a common source in Baudelairean spleen. In the course of **A Rebours,** Des Esseintes and his creator Huysmans discover that if you push life to its limits you will find it very limited. Huysmans's next novel was to be a renewed attempt to escape from tedium and vulgarity.

Casting around for new subject matter Huysmans provisionally fixed on Naundorffism as a promising topic. As every schoolboy knows, Charles Naundorff appeared in Paris in the 1830's claiming to be the Duke of Normandy and son of the guillotined Louis XVI. His claims received some support from a fringe of the Bourbon legitimist movement and were enthusiastically taken up by certain occult groups. In particular Vintras, a prophet who had acquired a large following by repeatedly performing the miracle of the Bleeding Host in a cardboard box factory, took up the cause of Naundorff's legitimacy. Links between Bourbon royalism and occultism were multifarious in the 1890's and have remained so to the present day. Was the French Revolution masterminded by Freemasons? Did Marie Antoinette die as a martyr to redeem her contemporaries? Did the centuries old curse of the Order of the Knights Templar take Louis

XVI to the scaffold? Are there occult clues to lost royalist treasure in France? These and similar daft questions continue to vex the minds of cranks. In the end Huysmans decided not to make Naundorffism the subject of his next novel, but in the course of his researches into these queer folk he had met Oswald Wirth, a committed Naundorffist and the designer of the first occult tarot pack. Huysmans had also learnt something of the Abbé Boullan, the self-styled spiritual successor to Vintras.

Huysmans's father had been a lithographer and painter of some talent. It was perhaps from his father that Huysmans acquired his keen visual sense. (He was one of the first and most articulate of the supporters of impressionist painting). Through study of the techniques and subject matter of the Flemish Primitive painters of the fifteenth century, he had come to realise that a realistic technique was not incompatible with very bizarre or highly spiritual subject matter. Through intense study of Grunewald's famous grim painting of the Crucifixion, he had further come to realise that an intensely realistic depiction of physical suffering could yet be used to point to something beyond the material world. So Huysmans decided to redeploy the realistic techniques pioneered by Zola in order to study the world of occultism.

'It is just at the moment when positivism is at its zenith that mysticism rises again and the follies of the occult begin' as Huysmans observes, and indeed it is doubtful whether the relationship between **fin de siècle** occultism and science should be regarded as one of outright opposition. Huysmans's muddled half-understanding of the invisible powers of electricity, mesmerism and cholera bacilli only encouraged him to plunge yet further into the astral fog. In France a widespread enthusiasm for occultism went hand in hand with an introduction to the wonders of electric lighting and early experiments in cinematography. Victor Hugo experimented with seances and table tapping. Rimbaud studied alchemy. Almost all the symbolist painters steeped themselves in Rosicrucian and Theosophical doctrine.

So Huysmans plumped for subject matter that was both fashionable and colourful. But behind the conflict between good and evil, between the Satanist and the exorcist in **Là-Bas**, a more profound struggle is going on that actually has more reality for Huysmans — a struggle to find some alternative to vulgar everyday reality. 'Literature has only one excuse for existing. It saves the person who makes it from the disgustingness of life.' Huysmans viewed the imminence of the **belle époque** with a bilious eye. General Boulanger and the Eiffel Tower epitomised the modern vulgarities of politics and science. 'I believe, alas, that a dotard heaven maunders over an exhausted earth.'

Huysmans was one of those people who like to lead an interesting life so that they can be sure that they have enough material for their books. All Huysmans's novels are autobiographical, painfully so. **Là-Bas** is more of an autobiographical document than a shaped and contrived piece of fiction. Durtal in this and subsequent novels stands in for Huysmans and when he speaks of his loneliness and fear of women, or rages against the failings of modern science, or abuses the vulgarity of the present age or lays down the law about what good cooking should be, he stands in for Huysmans — and what Durtal witnessed of the obscenities of Satanism was seen also by Huysmans.

So **Là-Bas** is a **roman à clef** and Durtal is Huysmans and his investigations into the life and times of the fifteenth century sadist and child murderer, Gilles de Rais, were actually carried out by Huysmans. Carhaix, the bellringer, is based on a certain M. Contess who actually performed that function at St. Sulpice. Gevingey, the astrologer in the novel is based on the Parisian astrologer Eugene Ledos. Charles Buet, a Catholic historian provided the model for M. Chantelouve. Madam Chantelouve in the novel owes a great deal to Berthe Courrière, a mistress of the literary critic Remy de Gourmont who subsequently became Huysman's mistress and who may have taken him to a black mass. She seems to have been somewhat unbalanced, obsessed with the idea of sex with priests and keen on feeding consecrated hosts to animals. Indeed she was eventually incarcerated as a madwoman. But another woman, Henriette Maillat, ex-mistress of the Archmagus Sar Péladan, also provided material for the love affair between Durtal and Mme Chantelouve. In particular their bizarre correspondence is reproduced in the novel fairly faithfully.

The fictional Satanist Docre is based on gossip that Huysmans had heard about a Belgian Abbot, Van Haecke. Van Haecke was supposed to have crosses tattooed on the soles of his feet so that he could continually trample upon them. Huysmans may also have seen Van Haecke attending a black mass in Paris, but this is by no means certain. More supporting material about succubi, spiritual warfare, the profanation of the Host, etc. was provided by the professedly disinterested Abbé Boullan. The good Doctor Johannes, the exorcist who fights the evil forces of Satanism, is a thinly fictionalised rendering of Abbé Boullan — as Huysmans saw him at the time. In fact, as Huysmans was to learn only after Boullan's death, Boullan was at best a morally ambivalent figure engaged in very dubious occult operations. Boullan was an adulterer, possible child murderer and defrocked priest. Sar Péladan and Oswald Wirth who claimed that Boullan was a black magician were probably closer to the truth than Huysmans. Sex played a large part in the rituals of Boullan's coterie of followers. Sexual intercourse was a religious act by which one could raise one's own spiritual status (if one was having sex with a superior being) or the status of others (if one was spiritually slumming it). This sexual assault course to the peaks of spiritual enlightenment was not restricted to human beings. In the eyes of the congregation of Boullan's Church of Carmel bestiality could be viewed as a peculiarly spiritual form of kindness to dumb animals. Boullan and his followers also experimented in astral sex with incumbi and succubi and Boullan was supposed to have coupled with half-human creatures on the astral plane in order to raise them to a fully human form. After an attentive reading of Huysmans's novel, it is hard to avoid the conclusion that sex with succubi has much in common with the more ordinary experience of masturbation and the guilt arising therefrom.

Là-Bas should not be confused with the later sanitised adventure fantasies of Dennis Wheatley. In this novel Huysmans has given us real spit-and-sawdust Satanism. His black mass and its aftermath still has the power to shock. As must be apparent from what has been said already, Huysmans seems to have got everything exactly wrong, conferring a sinister glamour on figures who were probably innocent, while exculpating the one man who almost certainly was not. Those of us who have actually attended a black mass will know how chaotic such affairs can be and how easy it is to make mistakes.

Boullan had warned Huysmans that after the publication of **Là-Bas** he would be subjected to occult attack by the enemies of the Church of Carmel, and, indeed, once the book was published Huysmans experienced cold chills several times, and alone in his bedroom the novelist would engage in 'spiritual fisticuffs' with unseen presences. Surely Boullan's Rosicrucian enemies Sar Pèladan and Oswald Wirth were behind all this? Here was clear evidence of the existence of Evil. It certainly made life more interesting for a junior civil servant in Paris. Having realised that the Devil must exist — if only to rescue Huysmans from the tortures of boredom — it is only a short step to the conclusion that God must also exist. 'With his hooked paw, the Devil drew me towards God.' And in fact Huysmans was to take the path that had already been mapped out for him by the writer and critic, Barbey d'Aurevilly, in 1884. 'After **Fleurs du Mal**, I said to Baudelaire "nothing logically remains for you but to choose between the muzzle of a revolver or the foot of the Cross"; but will the author of **A Rebours** make this choice?' Huysmans's road to the foot of the Cross is charted in his later novels **La Cathédrale** and **L'Oblat**, but it started in **Là-Bas**. Though Boullan was a hyper-sexed charlatan and ultimately recognised as such by Huysmans, nevertheless Huysmans retained and developed something that is implicit in the teachings of the old fraud, the doctrine of redemptive suffering, the belief that it was possible through conscious acceptance one's own physical and spiritual sufferings to take some of the burden of sin and suffering from others. As Christ on the Cross substituted himself for the whole of humanity, so, on a small scale, the hard task of mystical substitution can be taken on by the spiritually enlightened on behalf of the poor, the sinful and the ignorant.

Huysmans's re-evaluation of the Middle Ages has proved to be one of the most important and influential aspects of **Là-Bas**. To take one example and a most important one, Johan Huizinga's famous study **The Waning of the Middle Ages**, first published in 1924, owes almost everything to **Là-Bas**. In **Là-Bas** and in **The Waning of the Middle Ages** we find the same flight from comfortable nineteenth century bougeois values, the same hard edged vision aiming to reproduce in words what the Van Eycks had created in paint and the same preoccupation with the extremes of sensibility and experience. Indeed Huizinga's masterly work can be read as an extended if oblique commentary on the later novels of Huysmans. Few intelligent men growing up in western Europe in the 1890's were unaffected by Huysmans's vision of the world and what lay beyond the world. Another unlikely intellectual beneficiary of Huysmans's time was the famous Arabist and anti-colonialist campaigner, Louis Massignon, and it was Louis Massignon, whom Huysmans had prayed for in his death agonies, and Massignon who would interpret the doctrines of mystical suffering and redemtive suffering to the next generation of Catholic intellectuals. So from a ghastly **fin de siècle** stew brewed from the chatter of literary poseurs, occult charlatans and **demi-mondaines** emerged an ultimately profound vision of Christian suffering.

BIBLIOGRAPHY

Robert Baldick, **The Life of J.K. Huysmans** (Oxford, 1955).

Jean Benedetti, **Gilles de Rais, The Authentic Bluebeard,** (London, 1971).

James Laver, **The First Decadent: Being the Strange Life of J.K. Huysmans.** (London, 1954).

Christopher McIntosh, **Eliphas Levi and the Occult Revival,** (London, 1972).

Pierre Mariel (ed.), **Dictionnaire des Sociètés and Secrètes en Occident,** (Parish, 1971).

M. Praz, **The Romantic Agony,** (London, 1933).

James Webb, **The Flight from Reason: The Age of the Irrational,** (London, 1971).

La Tour Saint Jacques, (vol 10, 1957), numèro special sur J.K. Huysmans.

Cahiers de l'Herne, (vol 47, 1985), **Huysmans.**

CHAPTER I

"You believe pretty thoroughly in these things, or you wouldn't abandon the eternal triangle and the other stock subjects of the modern novelists to write the story of Gilles de Rais," and after a silence Des Hermies added, "I do not object to the latrine; hospital; and workshop vocabulary of naturalism. For one thing, the subject matter requires some such diction. Again, Zola, in *L'Assommoir,* has shown that a heavy-handed artist can slap words together hit-or-miss and give an effect of tremendous power. I do not really care how the naturalists maltreat language, but I do strenuously object to the earthiness of their ideas. They have made our literature the incarnation of materialism — and they glorify the democracy of art!

"Say what you will, their theory is pitiful, and their tight little method squeezes all the life out of them. Filth and the flesh are their all in all. They deny wonder and reject the extra-sensual. I don't believe they would know what you meant if you told them that artistic curiosity begins at the very point where the senses leave off.

"You shrug your shoulders, but tell me, how much has naturalism done to clear up life's really troublesome mysteries? When an ulcer of the soul—or indeed the most benign little pimple—is to be probed, naturalism can do nothing. 'Appetite and instinct' seem to be its sole motivation and rut and brainstorm its chronic states. The field of naturalism is the region below the umbilicus. Oh, it's a hernia clinic and it offers the soul a truss!

"I tell you, Durtal, it's superficial quackery, and that isn't all. This fetid naturalism eulogizes the atrocities of modern life and flatters our positively American ways. It ecstasizes over brute force and apotheosizes the cash register. With amazing humility it defers to the nauseating taste of the mob. It repudiates style, it rejects every ideal, every aspiration towards the supernatural and the beyond. It is so perfectly respresentative of bourgeois thought that it might be sired by Homais and dammed by Lisa, the butcher girl in *Ventre de Paris.*"

"Heavens, how you go after it!" said Durtal, somewhat piqued. He lighted his cigarette and went on, "I am as much revolted by materialism as you are, but that is no reason for denying the unforgettable services which naturalism has rendered.

"It has demolished the inhuman puppets of romanticism and rescued our literature from the clutches of booby idealists and sex-starved old maids. It has created visible and tangible human beings—after Balzac—and put them in accord with their surroundings. It has carried on the work, which romanticism began, of developing the language. Some of the naturalists have had the veritable gift of laughter, a very few have had the gift of tears, and, in spite of what you say, they have not all been carried away by an obsession for baseness."

"Yes, they have. They are in love with the age, and that shows them up for what they are."

"Do you mean to tell me Flaubert and the De Goncourts were in love with the age?"

"Of course not. But those men were artists, honest, seditious, and aloof, and I put them in a class by themselves. I will also grant that Zola is a master of backgrounds and masses and that his tricky handling of people is unequalled. Then, too, thank God, he has never followed out, in his novels, the theories enunciated in his magazine articles, adulating the intrusion of positivism upon art. But in the works of his best pupil, Rosny, the only talented novelist who is really imbued with the ideas of the master, naturalism has become a sickening jargon of chemist's slang serving to display a layman's erudition, which is about as profound as the scientific knowledge of a shop foreman. No, there is no getting around it. Everything this whole poverty-stricken school has produced shows that our literature has fallen upon evil days. The grovellers! They don't rise above the moral level of the tumblebug. Read the latest book. What do you find? Simple anecdotes: murder, suicide, and accident stories copied right out of the newspaper, tiresome sketches and wormy tales, all written in a colorless style and containing not the faintest hint of an outlook on life nor an appreciation of human nature. When I have waded through one of these books its insipid descriptions and interminable harangues go instantly out of my mind, and the only impression that remains is one of surprise that a man can write three or four hundred pages when he has absolutely nothing to reveal to us—nothing to say!"

"If it's all the same to you, Des Hermies, let's speak of something else. We shall never agree on the subject of naturalism, as the very mention of it makes you see red. What about this Mattei system of medicine? Your globules and electric phials at least relieve a few sufferers?"

"Hmph. A little better than the panaceas of the Codex, though I can't say the effects are either lasting or sure. But, it serves, like anything else. And now I must run along. The clock is striking ten and your concierge is coming to put out the hall light. See you again very soon, I hope. Good night."

When the door closed Durtal put some more coke in the grate and resumed a comfortless train of thought aggravated by this too pertinent discussion with his friend. For some months Durtal had been trying to reassemble the fragments of a shattered literary theory which had once seemed inexpugnable, and Des Hermies's opinions troubled him, in spite of their exaggerated vehemence.

Certainly if naturalism confined one to monotonous studies of mediocre persons and to interminable inventories of the objects in a drawing-room or a landscape, an honest and clear-sighted artist would soon cease to produce, and a less conscientious workman would be under the necessity of repeating himself over and over again to the point of nausea. Nevertheless Durtal could see no possibilities for the novelist outside of naturalism. Were we to go back to the pyrotechnics of romanticism, rewrite the lanuginous works of the Cherbuliez and Feuillet tribe, or, worse yet, imitate the lachrymose storiettes of Theuriet and George Sand? Then what was to be done? And Durtal, with desperate determination, set to work sorting out a tangle of confused theories and inchoate postulations. He made no headway. He felt but could not define. He was afraid to. Definition of his present tendencies would plump him back into his old dilemma.

"We must," he thought, "retain the documentary veracity, the precision of detail, the compact and sinewy language of realism, but we must also dig down into the soul and cease trying to explain mystery in terms of our sick senses. If possible the novel ought to be compounded of two elements, that of the soul and that of the body, and these ought to be inextricably bound together as in life. Their interreactions, their conflicts, their reconciliation, ought to furnish the dramatic interest. In a word, we must follow the road laid out once and for all by Zola, but at the same time we must trace a parallel route in the air by which we may go above and beyond. . . . A spiritual naturalism! It must be complete, powerful, daring in a different way from anything that is being attempted at present. Perhaps as approaching my concept I may cite Dostoyevsky. Yet that *exorable* Russian is less an elevated realist than an evangelic socialist. In France right now the purely corporal recipe has brought upon itself such discredit that two clans have arisen: the liberal, which prunes naturalism of all its boldness of subject matter and diction in order to fit it for the drawing-room, and the decadent, which gets completely off the ground and raves incoherently in a telegraphic patois intended to represent the language of the soul—intended rather to divert the reader's attention from the author's utter lack of ideas. As for the right wing verists, I can only laugh at the frantic puerilities of these would-be psychologists, who have never explored an unknown district of the mind nor ever studied an unhackneyed passion. They simply repeat the saccharine Feuillet and the saline Stendhal. Their novels are dissertations in school-teacher style. They don't seem to realize that there is more spiritual revelation in that one reply of old Hulot, in Balzac's *Cousine Bette,* 'Can't I take the little girl along?' than in all their doctoral theses. We must expect of them no idealistic straining toward the infinite. For me, then, the real psychologist of this century is not their Stendhal but that astonishing Ernest Hello, whose unrelenting unsuccess is simply miraculous!"

He began to think that Des Hermies was right. In the present disorganized state of letters there was but one tendency which seemed to promise better things. The unsatisfied need for the supernatural was driving people, in default of something loftier, to spiritism and the occult.

Now his thoughts carried him away from his dissatisfaction with literature to the satisfaction he had found in another art, in painting. His ideal was completely realized by the Primitives. These men, in Italy, Germany, and especially in Flanders, had manifested the amplitude and purity of vision which are the property of saintliness. In authentic and patiently accurate settings they pictured beings whose postures were caught from life itself, and the illusion was compelling and sure. From these heads, common enough, many of them, and these physiognomies, often ugly but powerfully evocative, emanated celestial joy or acute anguish, spiritual calm or turmoil. The effect was of matter transformed, by being distended or compressed, to afford an escape from the senses into remote infinity.

Durtal's introduction to this naturalism had come as a revelation the year before, although he had not then been so weary as now of *fin de siècle* silliness. In Germany, before a Crucifixion by Matthæus Grünewald, he had found what he was seeking.

He shuddered in his armchair and closed his eyes as if in pain. With extraordinary lucidity he revisualized the picture, and the cry of admiration wrung from him when he had entered the little room of the Cassel museum was re-echoing in his mind as here, in his study, the Christ rose before him, formidable, on a rude cross of barky wood, the arm an untrimmed branch bending like a bow under the weight of the body.

This branch seemed about to spring back and mercifully hurl afar from our cruel, sinful world the suffering flesh held to earth by the enormous spike piercing the feet. Dislocated, almost ripped out of their sockets, the arms of the Christ seemed trammelled by the knotty cords of the straining muscles. The laboured tendons of the armpits seemed ready to snap. The fingers, wide apart, were contorted in an arrested gesture in which were supplication and reproach but also benediction. The trembling thighs were greasy with sweat. The ribs were like staves, or like the bars of a cage, the flesh swollen, blue, mottled with flea-bites, specked as with pin-pricks by spines broken off from the rods of the scourging and now festering beneath the skin where they had penetrated.

Purulence was at hand. The fluvial wound in the side dripped thickly, inundating the thigh with blood that was like congealing mulberry juice. Milky pus, which yet was somewhat reddish, something like the colour of grey Moselle, oozed from the chest and ran down over the abdomen and the loin cloth. The knees had been forced together and the rotulæ touched, but the lower legs were held wide apart, though the feet were placed one on top of the other. These, beginning to putrefy, were turning green beneath a river of blood. Spongy and blistered, they were horrible, the flesh tumefied, swollen over the head of the spike, and the gripping toes, with the horny blue nails, contradicted the imploring gesture of the hands, turning that benediction into a curse; and as the hands pointed heavenward, so the feet seemed to cling to earth, to that ochre ground, ferruginous like the purple soil of Thuringia.

Above this eruptive cadaver, the head, tumultuous, enormous, encircled by a disordered crown of thorns, hung down lifeless. One lacklustre eye half opened as a shudder of terror or of sorrow traversed the expiring figure. The face was furrowed, the brow seamed, the cheeks blanched; all the drooping features wept, while the mouth, unnerved, its under jaw racked by tetanic contractions, laughed atrociously.

The torture had been terrific, and the agony had frightened the mocking executioners into flight.

Against a dark blue night-sky the cross seemed to bow down, almost to touch the ground with its tip, while two figures, one on each side, kept watch over the Christ. One was the Virgin, wearing a hood the colour of mucous blood over a robe of wan blue. Her face was pale and swollen with weeping, and she stood rigid, as one who buries his fingernails deep into his palms and sobs. The other figure was that of Saint John, like a gipsy or sunburnt Swabian peasant, very tall, his beard matted and tangled, his robe of a scarlet stuff cut in wide strips like slabs of bark. His mantle was a chamois yellow; the lining, caught up at the sleeves, showed a feverish yellow as of unripe lemons. Spent with weeping, but possessed of more endurance than Mary, who was yet erect but broken and exhausted, he had joined his hands and in an access of outraged loyalty had drawn himself up before the corpse, which he contemplated with his red and smoky eyes while he choked back the cry which threatened to rend his quivering throat.

Ah, this coarse, tear-compelling Calvary was at the opposite pole from those debonair Golgothas adopted by the Church ever since the Renaissance. This lockjaw Christ was not the Christ of the rich, the Adonis of Galilee, the exquisite dandy, the handsome youth with the curly brown tresses, divided beard, and insipid doll-like features, whom the faithful have adored for four centuries. This was the Christ of Justin, Basil, Cyril, Tertullian, the Christ of the apostolic church, the vulgar Christ, ugly with the assumption of the whole burden of our sins and clothed, through humility, in the most abject of forms.

It was the Christ of the poor, the Christ incarnate in the image of the most miserable of us He came to save; the Christ of the afflicted, of the beggar, of all those on whose indigence and helplessness the greed of their brother battens; the human Christ, frail of flesh, abandoned by the Father until such time as no further torture was possible; the Christ with no recourse but His Mother, to Whom—then powerless to aid Him—He had, like every man in torment, cried out with an infant's cry.

In an unsparing humility, doubtless, He had willed to suffer the Passion with all the suffering permitted to the human senses, and, obeying an incomprehensible ordination, He, in the time of the scourging and of the blows and of the insults spat in His face, had put off divinity, nor had He resumed it when, after these preliminary mockeries, He entered upon the unspeakable torment of the unceasing agony. Thus, dying like a thief, like a dog, basely, vilely, physically, He had sunk himself to the deepest depth of fallen humanity and had not spared Himself the last ignominy of putrefaction.

Never before had naturalism transfigured itself by such a conception and execution. Never before had a painter so charnally envisaged divinity nor so brutally dipped his brush into the wounds and running sores and bleeding nail holes of the Saviour. Grünewald had passed all measure. He was the most uncompromising of realists, but his morgue Redeemer, his sewer Deity, let the observer know that realism could be truly transcendent. A divine light played about that ulcerated head, a superhuman expression illuminated the fermenting skin of the epileptic features. This crucified corpse was a very God, and, without aureole, without nimbus, with none of the stock accoutrements except the blood-sprinkled crown of thorns, Jesus appeared in His celestial super-essence, between the stunned, grief-torn Virgin and a Saint John whose calcined eyes were beyond the shedding of tears.

These faces, by nature vulgar, were resplendent, transfigured with the expression of the sublime grief of those souls whose plaint is not heard. Thief, pauper, and peasant had vanished and given place to supraterrestial creatures in the presence of their God.

Grünewald was the most uncompromising of idealists. Never had artist known such magnificent exaltation, none had ever so resolutely bounded from the summit of spiritual altitude to the rapt orb of heaven. He had gone to the two extremes. From the rankest weeds of the pit he had extracted the finest essence of charity, the mordant liquor of tears. In this canvas was revealed the masterpiece of an art obeying the unopposable urge to render the tangible and the invisible, to make manifest the crying impurity of the flesh and to make sublime the infinite distress of the soul.

It was without its equivalent in literature. A few pages of Anne Emmerich upon the Passion, though comparatively attenuated, approached this ideal of supernatural realism and of veridic and exsurrected life. Perhaps, too, certain effusions of Ruysbroeck, seeming to spurt forth in twin jets of black and white flame, were worthy of comparison with the divine befoulment of Grünewald. Hardly, either. Grünewald's masterpiece remained unique. It was at the same time infinite and of earth earthy.

"But," said Durtal to himself, rousing out of his revery, "if I am consistent I shall have to come around to the Catholicism of the Middle Ages, to *mystic* naturalism. Ah, no! I will not—and yet, perhaps I may!"

Here he was in the old dilemma. How often before now had he halted on the threshold of Catholicism, sounding himself thoroughly and finding always that he had no faith. Decidedly there had been no effort on the part of God to reclaim him, and he himself had never possessed the kind of will that permits one to let oneself go, trustingly, without reserve, into the sheltering shadows of immutable dogma.

Momentarily at times when, after reading certain books, his disgust for everyday life was accentuated, he longed for lenitive hours in a cloister, where the monotonous chant of prayers in an incense-laden atmosphere would bring on a somnolence, a dreamy rapture of mystical ideas. But only a simple soul, on which life's wear and tear had left no mark, was capable of savouring the delights of such a self-abandon, and his own soul was battered and torn with earthly conflict. He must admit that the momentary desire to believe, to take refuge in the timeless, proceeded from a multitude of ignoble motives: from lassitude with the petty and repeated annoyances of existence, quarrels with the laundress, with the waiter, with the landlord; the sordid scramble for money; in a word, from the general spiritual failure of a man approaching forty. He thought of escaping into a monastery somewhat as street girls think of going into a house where they will be free from the dangers of the chase, from worry about food and lodging, and where they will not have to do their own washing and ironing.

Unmarried, without settled income, the voice of carnality now practically stilled in him, he sometimes cursed the existence he had shaped for himself. At times, weary of attempting to coerce words to do his bidding, he threw down his pen and looked into the future. He could see nothing ahead of him but bitterness and cause for alarm, and, seeking consolation, he was forced to admit that only religion could heal, but religion demanded in return so arrant a desertion of common sense, so pusillanimous a willingness to be astonished at nothing, that he threw up his hands and begged off.

Yet he was always playing with the thought, indeed he could not escape it. For though religion was without foundation it was also without limit and promised a complete escape from earth into dizzy, unexplored altitudes. Then, too, Durtal was attracted to the Church by its intimate and ecstatic art, the splendour of its legends, and the radiant naïveté of the histories of its saints.

He did not believe, and yet he admitted the supernatural. Right here on earth how could any of us deny that we are hemmed in by mystery, in our homes, in the street,—everywhere when we came to think of it? It was really the part of shallowness to ignore those extrahuman relations and account for the unforeseen by attributing to fate the more than inexplicable. Did not a chance encounter often decide the entire life of a man? What was love, what the other incomprehensible shaping influences? And, knottiest enigma of all, what was money?

There one found oneself confronted by primordial organic law, atrocious edicts promulgated at the very beginning of the world and applied ever since.

The rules were precise and invariable. Money attracted money, accumulating always in the same places, going by preference to the scoundrelly and the mediocre. When, by an inscrutable exception, it heaped up in the coffers of a rich man who was not a miser nor a murderer, it stood idle, incapable of resolving itself into a force for good, however charitable the hands which fain would administer it. One would say it was angry at having got into the wrong box and avenged itself by going into voluntary paralysis when possessed by one who was neither a sharper nor an ass.

It acted still more strangely when by some extraordinary chance it strayed into the home of a poor man. Immediately it defiled the clean, debauched the chaste, and, acting simultaneously on the body and the soul, it insinuated into its possessor a base selfishness, an ignoble pride; it suggested that he spend for himself alone; it made the humble man a boor, the generous man a skinflint. In one second it changed every habit, revolutionized every idea, metamorphosed the most deeply rooted passions.

It was the instigator and vigilant accomplice of all the important sins. If it permitted one of its detainers to forget himself and bestow a boon it awakened hatred in the recipient, it replaced avarice with ingratitude and re-established equilibrium so that the account might balance and not one sin of commission be wanting.

But it reached its real height of monstrosity when, concealing its identity under an assumed name, it entitled itself capital. Then its action was not limited to individual incitation to theft and murder but extended to the entire human race. With one word capital decided monopolies, erected banks, cornered necessities, and, if it wished, caused thousands of human beings to starve to death.

And it grew and begot itself while slumbering in a safe, and the Two Worlds adored it on bended knee, dying of desire before it as before a God.

Well! money was the devil, otherwise its mastery of souls was inexplicable. And how many other mysteries, equally unintelligible, how many other phenomena were there to make a reflective man shudder!

"But," thought Durtal, "seeing that there are so many more things betwixt heaven and earth than are dreamed of in anybody's philosophy, why not believe in the Trinity? Why reject the divinity of Christ? It is no strain on one to admit the *Credo quia absurdum* of Saint Augustine and Tertullian and say that if the supernatural were comprehensible it would not be supernatural, and that precisely because it passes the faculties of man it is divine.

"And—oh, to hell with it! What's it all about, anyway?"

And again, as so often when he had found himself before this unbridgeable gulf between reason and belief, he recoiled from the leap.

Well, his thoughts had strayed far from the subject of that naturalism so reviled by Des Hermies. He returned to Grünewald and said to himself that the great Crucifixion was the masterpiece of an art driven out of bounds. One need not go far in search of the extra-terrestrial as to fall into perfervid Catholicism. Perhaps spiritualism would give one all one required to formulate a supernaturalistic method.

He rose and went into his tiny workroom. His pile of manuscript notes about the Marshal de Rais, surnamed Bluebeard, looked at him derisively from the table where they were piled.

"All the same," he said, "it's good to be here, in out of the world and above the limits of time. To live in another age, never read a newspaper, not even know that the theatres exist—ah, what a dream! To dwell with Bluebeard and forget the grocer on the corner and all the other petty little criminals of an age perfectly typified by the café waiter who ravishes the boss's daughter—the goose who lays the golden egg, as he calls her—so that she will have to marry him!"

Bed was a good place, he added, smiling, for he saw his cat, a creature with a perfect time sense, regarding him uneasily as if to remind him of their common convenience and to reproach him for not having prepared the couch. Durtal arranged the pillows and pulled back the coverlet, and the cat jumped to the foot of the bed but remained humped up, tail coiled beneath him, waiting till his master was stretched out at length before burrowing a little hollow to curl up in.

CHAPTER II

Nearly two years ago Durtal had ceased to associate with men of letters. They were represented in books and in the book-chat columns of magazines as forming an aristocracy which had a monopoly on intelligence. Their conversation, if one believed what one read, sparkled with effervescent and stimulating wit. Durtal had difficulty accounting to himself for the persistence of this illusion. His sad experience led him to believe that every literary man belonged to one of two classes, the thoroughly commercial or the utterly impossible.

The first consisted of writers spoiled by the public, and drained dry in consequence, but "successful." Ravenous for notice they aped the ways of the world of big business, delighted in gala dinners, gave formal evening parties, spoke of copyrights, sales, and long run plays, and made great display of wealth.

The second consisted of café loafers, "bohemians." Rolling on the benches, gorged with beer they feigned an exaggerated modesty and at the same time cried their wares, aired their genius, and abused their betters.

There was now no place where one could meet a few artists and privately, intimately, discuss ideas at ease. One was at the mercy of the café crowd or the drawing-room company. One's interlocutor was listening avidly to steal one's ideas, and behind one's back one was being vituperated. And the women were always intruding.

In this indiscriminate world there was no illuminating criticism, nothing but small talk, elegant or inelegant.

Then Durtal learned, also by experience, that one cannot associate with thieves without becoming either a thief or a dupe, and finally he broke off relations with his confrères.

He not only had no sympathy but no common topic of conversation with them. Formerly when he accepted naturalism—airtight and unsatisfactory as it was—he had been able to argue esthetics with them, but now!

"The point is," Des Hermies was always telling him, "that there is a basic difference between you and the other realists, and no patched-up alliance could possibly be of long duration. You execrate the age and they worship it. There is the whole matter. You were fated some day to get away from this Americanized art and attempt to create something less vulgar, less miserably commonplace, and infuse a little spirituality into it.

"In all your books you have fallen on our *fin de siècle*— our *queue du siècle*—tooth and nail. But, Lord! a man soon gets tired of whacking something that doesn't fight back but merely goes its own way repeating its offences. You needed to escape into another epoch and get your bearings while waiting for a congenial subject to present itself. That explains your spiritual disarray of the last few months and your immediate recovery as soon as you stumbled onto Giles de Rais."

Des Hermies had diagnosed him accurately. The day on which Durtal had plunged into the frightful and delightful latter mediæval age had been the dawn of a new existence. The flouting of his actual surroundings brought peace to Durtal's soul, and he had completely reorganized his life, mentally cloistering himself, far from the furore of contemporary letters, in the château de Tiffauges with the monster Bluebeard, with whom he lived in perfect accord, even in mischievous amity.

Thus history had for Durtal supplanted the novel, whose forced banality, conventionality, and tidy structure of plot simply griped him. Yet history, too, was only a peg for a man of talent to hang style and ideas on, for events could not fail to be coloured by the temperament and distorted by the bias of the historian.

As for the documents and sources! Well attested as they might be, they were all subject to revision, even to contradiction by others exhumed later which were no less authentic than the first and which also but waited their turn to be refuted by newer discoveries.

In the present rage for grubbing around in dusty archives writing of history served as an outlet for the pedantry of the moles who reworked their mouldy findings and were duly rewarded by the Institute with medals and diplomas.

For Durtal history was, then, the most pretentious as it was the most infantile of deceptions. Old Clio ought to be represented with a sphinx's head, mutton-chop whiskers, and one of those padded bonnets which babies wore to keep them from bashing their little brains out when they took a tumble.

Of course exactitude was impossible. Why should he dream of getting at the whole truth about the Middle Ages when nobody had been able to give a full account of the Revolution, of the Commune for that matter? The best he could do was to imagine himself in the midst of creatures of that other epoch, wearing their antique garb, thinking their thoughts, and then, having saturated himself with their spirit, to convey his illusion by means of adroitly selected details.

That is practically what Michelet did, and though the garrulous old gossip drivelled endlessly about matters of supreme unimportance and ecstasized in his mild way over trivial anecdotes which he expanded beyond all proportion, and though his sentimentality and chauvinism sometimes discredited his quite plausible conjectures, he was nevertheless the only French historian who had overcome the limitation of time and made another age live anew before our eyes.

Hysterical, garrulous, manneristic as he was, there was yet a truly epic sweep in certain passages of his History of

France. The personages were raised from the oblivion into which the dry-as-dust professors had sunk them, and became live human beings. What matter, then, if Michelet was the least trustworthy of historians since he was the most personal and the most evocative?

As for the others, they simply ferreted around among the old state papers, clipped them, and, following M. Taine's example, arranged, ticketed, and mounted their sensational gleanings in logical sequence, rejecting, of course, everything that did not advance the case they were trying to make. They denied themselves imagination and enthusiasm and claimed that they did not invent. True enough, but they did none the less distort history by the selection they employed. And how simply and summarily they disposed of things! It was discovered that such and such an event occurred in France in several communities, and straightway it was decided that the whole country lived, acted, and thought in a certain manner at a certain hour, on a certain day, in a certain year.

No less than Michelet they were doughty falsifiers, but they lacked his vision. They dealt in knickknacks, and their trivialities were as far from creating a unified impression as were the pointillistic puzzles of modern painters and the word hashes cooked up by the decadent poets.

And worst of all, thought Durtal, the biographers. The depilators! taking all the hair off a real man's chest. They wrote ponderous tomes to prove that Jan Steen was a tee-totaler. Somebody had deloused Villon and shown that the Grosse Margot of the ballade was not a woman but an inn sign. Pretty soon they would be representing the poet as a priggishly honest and judicious man. One would say that in writing their monographs these historians feared to dishonour themselves by treating of artists who had tasted somewhat fully and passionately of life. Hence the expurgation of masterpieces that an artist might appear as commonplace a bourgeois as his commentator.

This rehabilitation school, today all-powerful, exasperated Durtal. In writing his study of Gilles de Rais he was not going to fall into the error of these bigoted sustainers of middle-class morality. With his ideas of history he could not claim to give an exact likeness of Bluebeard, but he was not going to concede to the public taste for mediocrity in well- and evil-doing by whitewashing the man.

Durtal's material for this study consisted of: a copy of the memorial addressed by the heirs of Gilles de Rais to the king, notes taken from the several true copies at Paris of the proceedings in the criminal trial at Nantes, extracts from Vallet de Viriville's history of Charles VII, finally the *Notice* by Armand Guéraut and the biography of the abbé Bossard. These sufficed to bring before Durtal's eyes the formidable figure of that Satanic fifteenth century character who was the most artictically, exquisitely cruel, and the most scoundrelly of men.

No one knew of the projected study but Des Hermies, whom Durtal saw nearly every day.

They had met in the strangest of homes, that of Chantelouve, the Catholic historian, who boasted of receiving all classes of people. And every week in the social season that drawing-room in the rue de Bagneux was the scene of a heterogeneous gathering of under sacristans, café poets, journalists, actresses, partisans of the cause of Naundorff,[1] and dabblers in equivocal sciences.

This salon was on the edge of the clerical world, and many religious came here at the risk of their reputations. The dinners were discriminately, if unconventionally, ordered. Chantelouve, rotund, jovial, bade everyone make himself at home. Now and then through his smoked spectacles there stole an ambiguous look which might have given an analyst pause, but the man's bonhomie, quite ecclesiastical,

---

[1] A watchmaker who at the time of the July monarchy attempted to pass himself off for Louis XVII.

was instantly disarming. Madame was no beauty, but possessed a certain bizarre charm and was always surrounded. She, however, remained silent and did nothing to encourage her voluble admirers. As void of prudery as her husband, she listened impassively, absently, with her thoughts evidently afar, to the boldest of conversational imprudences.

At one of these evening parties, while La Rousseil, recently converted, howled a hymn, Durtal, sitting in a corner having a quiet smoke, had been struck by the physiognomy and bearing of Des Hermies, who stood out sharply from the motley throng of defrocked priests and grubby poets packed into Chantelouve's library and drawing-room.

Among these smirking and carefully composed faces, Des Hermies, evidently a man of forceful individuality, seemed, and probably felt, singularly out of place. He was tall, slender, somewhat pale. His eyes, narrowed in a frown, had the cold blue gleam of sapphires. The nose was short and sharp, the cheeks smooth shaven. With his flaxen hair and Vandyke he might have been a Norwegian or an Englishman in not very good health. His garments were of London make, and the long, tight, wasp-waisted coat, buttoned clear up to the neck, seemed to enclose him like a box. Very careful of his person, he had a manner all his own of drawing off his gloves, rolling them up with an almost inaudible crackling, then seating himself, crossing his long, thin legs, and leaning over to the right, reaching into the patch pocket on his left side and bringing forth the embossed Japanese pouch which contained his tobacco and cigarette papers.

He was methodic, guarded, and very cold in the presence of strangers. His superior and somewhat bored attitude, not exactly relieved by his curt, dry laugh, awakened, at a first meeting, a serious antipathy which he sometimes justified by venomous words, by meaningless silences, by unspoken innuendoes. He was respected and feared at Chantelouve's, but when one came to know him one found, beneath his defensive shell, great warmth of heart and a capacity for true friendship of the kind that is not expansive but is capable of sacrifice and can always be relied upon.

How did he live? Was he rich or just comfortable? No one knew, and he, tight lipped, never spoke of his affairs. He was doctor of the Faculty of Paris—Durtal had chanced to see his diploma—but he spoke of medicine with great disdain. He said he had become convinced of the futitlity of all he had been taught, and had thrown it over for homeopathy, which in turn he had thrown over for a Bolognese system, and this last he was now excoriating.

There were times when Durtal could not doubt that his friend was an author, for Des Hermies spoke understandingly of tricks of the trade which one learns only after long experience, and his literary judgment was not that of a layman. When, one day, Durtal reproached him for concealing his productions, he replied with a certain melancholy, "No, I caught myself in time to choke down a base instinct, the desire of resaying what has been said. I could have plagiarized Flaubert as well as, if not better than, the poll parrots who are doing it, but I decided not to. I would rather phrase abstruse medicaments of rare application; perhaps it is not very necessary, but at least it isn't cheap."

What surprised Durtal was his friend's prodigious erudition. Des Hermies had the run of the most out-of-the-way book shops, he was an authority on antique customs and, at the same time, on the latest scientific discoveries. He hobnobbed with all the freaks in Paris, and from them he became deeply learned in the most diverse and hostile sciences. He, so cold and correct, was almost never to be found save in the company of astrologers, cabbalists, demonologists, alchemists, theologians, or inventors.

Weary of the advances and the facile intimacies of artists, Durtal had been attracted by this man's fastidious reserve. It was perfectly natural that Durtal, surfeited with skin-deep friendships, should feel drawn to Des Hermies, but it was difficult to imagine why Des Hermies, with his taste for strange associations, should take a liking to Durtal, who was the soberest, steadiest, most normal of men. Perhaps Des Hermies felt the need of talking with a sane human being now and then as a relief. And, too, the literary discussions which he loved were out of the question with these addlepates who monologued indefatigably on the subject of their monomania and their ego.

At odds, like Durtal, with his confrères, Des Hermies could expect nothing from the physicians, whom he avoided, nor from the specialists with whom he consorted.

As a matter of fact there had been a juncture of two beings whose situation was almost identical. At first restrained and on the defensive, they had come finally to *tu-toi* each other and establish a relation which had been a great advantage to Durtal. His family were dead, the friends of his youth married and scattered, and since his withdrawal from the world of letters he had been reduced to complete solitude. Des Hermies kept him from going stale and then, finding that Durtal had not lost all interest in mankind, promised to introduce him to a really lovable old character. Of this man Des Hermies spoke much, and one day he said, "You really ought to know him. He likes the books of yours which I have lent him, and he wants to meet you. You think I am interested only in obscure and twisted natures. Well, you will find Carhaix really unique. He is the one Catholic with intelligence and without sanctimoniousness; the one poor man with envy and hatred for none."

CHAPTER III

Durtal was in a situation familiar to all bachelors who have the concierge do their cleaning. Only these know how a tiny lamp can fairly drink up oil, and how the contents of a bottle of cognac can become paler and weaker without ever diminishing. They know, too, how a once comfortable bed can become forbidding, and how scrupulously a concierge can respect its least fold or crease. They learn to be resigned and to wash out a glass when they are thirsty and make their own fire when they are cold.

Durtal's concierge was an old man with drooping moustache and a powerful breath of "three-six." Indolent and placid, he opposed an unbudgeable inertia to Durtal's frantic and profanely expressed demand that the sweeping be done at the same hour every morning.

Threats, prayers, insults, the withholding of gratuities, were without effect. Père Rateau took off his cap, scratched his head, promised, in the tone of a man much moved, to mend his ways, and next day came later than ever.

"What a nuisance!" thought Durtal today, as he heard a key turning in the lock, then he looked at his watch and observed that once again the concierge was arriving after three o'clock in the afternoon.

There was nothing for it but to submit with a sigh to the ensuing hullabaloo. Rateau, somnolent and pacific in his lodge, became a demon when he got a broom in his hand. In this sedentary being, who could drowse all morning in the stale basement atmosphere heavy with the cumulative aroma of many meat-stews, a martial ardour, a warlike ferocity, then asserted themselves, and like a red revolutionary he assaulted the bed, charged the chairs, manhandled the picture frames, knocked the tables over, rattled the water pitcher, and whirled Durtal's brogues about by the laces as when a pillaging conqueror hauls a ravished victim along by the hair. So he stormed the apartment like a barricade and triumphantly brandished his battle standard, the dust rag, over the reeking carnage of the furniture.

Durtal at such times sought refuge in the room which was not being attacked. Today Rateau launched his offensive against the workroom, so Durtal fled to the bedroom. From there, through the half open door, he could see the enemy, with a feather duster like a Mohican war bonnet over his head, doing a scalp dance around a table.

"If I only knew at what time that pest would break in on me so I could always arrange to be out!" groaned Durtal. Now he ground his teeth, as Rateau, with a yell, grabbed up the mop and, skating around on one leg, belaboured the floor lustily.

The perspiring conqueror then appeared in the doorway and advanced to reduce the chamber where Durtal was. The latter had to return to the subjugated workroom, and the cat, shocked by the racket, arched its back and, rubbing against its master's legs, followed him to a place of safety.

In the thick of the conflict Des Hermies rang the door bell.

"I'll put on my shoes," cried Durtal, "and we"ll get out of this. Look—" he passed his hand over the table and brought back a coat of grime that made him appear to be wearing a grey glove—"look. That brute turns the house upside down and knocks everything to pieces, and here's the result. He leaves more dust when he goes than he found when he came in!"

"Bah," said Des Hermies, "dust isn't a bad thing. Besides having the taste of ancient biscuit and the smell of an old book, it is the floating velvet which softens hard surfaces, the fine dry wash which takes the garishness out of crude colour schemes. It is the caparison of abandon, the veil of oblivion. Who, then, can despise it—aside from certain persons whose lamentable lot must often have wrung a tear from you?

"Imagine living in one of these Paris *passages*. Think of a consumptive spitting blood and suffocating in a room one flight up, behind the 'ass-back' gables of, say the passage des Panoramas, for instance. When the window is open the dust comes in impregnated with snuff and saturated with clammy exudations. The invalid, choking, begs for air, and in order that he may breathe the window is *closed*.

"Well, the dust that you complain of is rather milder than that. Anyway I don't hear you coughing. . . . But if you're ready we'll be on our way."

"Where shall we go?" asked Durtal.

Des Hermies did not answer. They left the rue du Regard, in which Durtal lived, and went down the rue du Cherche-Midi as far as the Croix-Rouge.

"Let's go on to the place Saint-Sulpice," said Des Hermies, and after a silence he continued, "Speaking of dust, 'out of which we came and to which we shall return,' do you know that after we are dead our corpses are devoured by different kinds of worms according as we are fat or thin? In fat corpses one species of maggot is found, the rhizophagus, while thin corpses are patronized only by the phora. The latter is evidently the aristocrat, the fastidious gourmet which turns up its nose at a heavy meal of copious breasts and juicy fat bellies. Just think, there is no perfect equality, even in the manner in which we feed the worms.

"But this is where we stop."

They had come to where the rue Férou opens into the place Saint-Sulpice. Durtal looked up and on an unenclosed porch in the flank of the church of Saint-Sulpice he read the placard, "Tower open to visitors."

"Let's go up," said Des Hermies.

"What for! In this weather?" and Durtal pointed at the yellow sky over which black clouds, like factory smoke, were racing, so low that the tin chimneys seemed to penetrate them and crenelate them with little spots of clarity. "I am not enthusiastic about trying to climb a flight of broken, irregular stairs. And anyway, what do you think you can see up there? It's misty and getting dark. No, have a heart."

"What difference is it to you where you take your airing? Come on. I assure you you will see something unusual."

"Oh! you brought me here on purpose?"

"Yes."

"Why didn't you say so?"

He followed Des Hermies into the darkness under the porch. At the back of the cellarway a little essence lamp, hanging from a nail, lighted a door, the tower entrance.

For a long time, in utter darkness, they climbed a winding stair. Durtal was wondering where the keeper had gone, when, turning a corner, he saw a shaft of light, then he stumbled against the rickety supports of a "double-current" lamp in front of a door. Des Hermies pulled a bell cord and the door swung back.

Above them on a landing they could see feet, whether of a man or of a woman they could not tell.

"Ah! it's you, M. des Hermies," and a woman bent over, describing an arc, so that her head was in a stream of light. "Louis will be very glad to see you."

"Is he in?" asked Des Hermies, reaching up and shaking hands with the woman.

"He is in the tower. Won't you stop and rest a minute?"

"Why, when we come down, if you don't mind."

"Then go up until you see a grated door—but what an old fool I am! You know the way as well as I do."

"To be sure, to be sure. . . . But, in passing, permit me to introduce my friend Durtal."

Durtal, somewhat flustered, made a bow in the darkness.

"Ah, monsieur, how fortunate. Louis is so anxious to meet you."

"Where is he taking me?" Durtal wondered as again he groped along behind his friend, now and then, just as he felt completely lost, coming to the narrow strip of light admitted by a barbican, and again proceeding in inky darkness. The climb seemed endless. Finally they came to the barred door, opened it, and found themselves on a frame balcony with the abyss above and below. Des Hermies, who seemed perfectly at home, pointed downward, then upward. They were halfway up a tower the face of which was overlaid with enormous criss-crossing joists and beams riveted together with bolt heads as big as a man's fist. Durtal could see no one. He turned and, clinging to the hand rail, groped along the wall toward the daylight which stole down between the inclined leaves of the sounding-shutters.

Leaning out over the precipice, he discerned beneath him a formidable array of bells hanging from oak supports lined with iron. The sombre bell metal was slick as if oiled and absorbed light without refracting it. Bending backward, he looked into the upper abyss and perceived new batteries of bells overhead. These bore the raised effigy of a bishop, and a place in each, worn by the striking of the clapper, shone golden.

All were in quiescence, but the wind rattled against the sounding-shutters, stormed through the cage of timbers, howled along the spiral stair, and was caught and held whining in the bell vases. Suddenly a light breeze, like the stirring of confined air, fanned his cheek. He looked up. The current had been set in motion by the swaying of a great bell beginning to get under way. There was a crash of sound, the bell gathered momentum, and now the clapper, like a gigantic pestle, was grinding the great bronze mortar with a deafening clamour. The tower trembled, the balcony on which Durtal was standing trepidated like the floor of a railway coach, there was the continuous rolling of a mighty reverberation, interrupted regularly by the jar of metal upon metal.

In vain Durtal scanned the upper abyss. Finally he managed to catch sight of a leg, swinging out into space and back again, in one of those wooden stirrups, two of which, he had noticed, were fastened to the bottom of every bell. Leaning out so that he was almost prone on one of the timbers, he finally perceived the ringer, clinging with his hands to two iron handles and balancing over the gulf with his eyes turned heavenward.

Durtal was shocked by the face. Never had he seen such disconcerting pallor. It was not the waxen hue of the convalescent, not the lifeless grey of the perfume- or snuff-maker, it was a prison pallor of a bloodless lividness unknown today, the ghastly complexion of a wretch of the Middle Ages shut up till death in a damp, airless, pitch-dark *in-pace*.

The eyes were blue, prominent, even bulging, and had the mystic's readiness to tears, but their expression was singularly contradicted by the truculent Kaiser Wilhelm moustache. The man seemed at once a dreamer and a fighter, and it would have been difficult to tell which character predominated.

He gave the bell stirrup a last yank with his foot and with a heave of his loins regained his equilibrium. He mopped his brow and smiled down at Des Hermies.

"Well! well!" he said, "you here."

He descended, and when he learned Durtal's name his face brightened and the two shook hands cordially.

"We have been expecting you a long time, monsieur. Our friend here speaks of you at great length, and we have been asking him why he didn't bring you around to see us. But come," he said eagerly, "I must conduct you on a tour of inspection about my little domain. I have read your books and I know a man like you can't help falling in love with my bells. But we must go higher if we are really to see them."

And he bounded up a staircase, while Des Hermies pushed Durtal along in front of him in a way that made retreat impossible.

As he was once more groping along the winding stairs, Durtal asked, "Why didn't you tell me your friend Carhaix —for of course that's who he is—was a bell-ringer?"

Des Hermies did not have time to answer, for at that moment, having reached the door of the room beneath the tower roof, Carhaix was standing aside to let them pass. They were in a rotunda pierced in the centre by a great circular hole which had around it a corroded iron balustrade orange with rust. By standing close to the railing, which was like the well curb of the Pit, one could see down, down, to the foundation. The "well" seemed to be undergoing repairs, and from the top to the bottom of the tube the beams supporting the bells were crisscrossed with timbers bracing the walls.

"Don't be afraid to lean over," said Carhaix. "Now tell me, monsieur, how do you like my foster children?"

But Durtal was hardly heeding. He felt uneasy, here in space, and as if drawn toward the gaping chasm, whence ascended, from time to time, the desultory clanging of the bell, which was still swaying and would be some time in returning to immobility.

He recoiled.

"Wouldn't you like to pay a visit to the top of the tower?" asked Carhaix, pointing to an iron stair sealed into the wall.

"No, another day."

They descended and Carhaix, in silence, opened a door. They advanced into an immense storeroom, containing colossal broken statues of saints, scaly and dilapidated apostles, Saint Matthew legless and armless, Saint Luke escorted by a fragmentary ox, Saint Mark lacking a shoulder and part of his beard, Saint Peter holding up an arm from which the hand holding the keys was broken off.

"There used to be a swing in here," said Carhaix, "for

the little girls of the neighbourhood. But the privilege was
abused, as privileges always are. In the dusk all kinds of
things were done for a few sous. The curate finally had the
swing taken down and the room closed up."

"And what is that over there?" inquired Durtal, perceiving, in a corner, an enormous fragment of rounded metal,
like half a gigantic skull-cap. On it the dust lay thick, and
and in the hollow the meshes on meshes of fine silken web,
dotted with the black bodies of lurking spiders, were like a
fisherman's hand net weighted with little slugs of lead.

"That? Ah, monsieur!" and there was fire in Carhaix's
mild eyes, "that is the skull of an old, old bell whose like is
not cast these days. The ring of that bell, monsieur, was like
a voice from heaven." And suddenly he exploded, "Bells
have had their day!—As I suppose Des Hermies has told
you.—Bell ringing is a lost art. And why wouldn't it be?
Look at the men who are doing it nowadays. Charcoal
burners, roofers, masons out of a job, discharged firemen,
ready to try their hand at anything for a franc. There are
curates who think nothing of saying, 'Need a man? Go out
in the street and pick up a soldier for ten sous. He'll do.'
That's why you read about accidents like the one that happened lately at Notre Dame, I think. The fellow didn't
withdraw in time and the bell came down like the blade of a
guillotine and whacked his leg right off.

"People will spend thirty thousand francs on an altar
baldachin, and ruin themselves for music, and they have to
have gas in their churches, and Lord knows what all besides,
but when you mention bells they shrug their shoulders. Do
you know, M. Durtal, there are only two men in Paris who
can ring chords? Myself and Père Michel, and he is not
married and his morals are so bad that he can't be regularly
attached to a church. He can ring music the like of which
you never heard, but he, too, is losing interest. He drinks,
and, drunk or sober, goes to work, then he bowls up again
and goes to sleep.

"Yes, the bell has had its day. Why, this very morning, Monsignor made his pastoral visit to this church. At eight o'clock we sounded his arrival. The six bells you see down here boomed out melodiously. But there were sixteen up above, and it was a shame. Those extras jangled away haphazard. It was a riot of discord."

Carhaix ruminated in silence as they descended. Then, "Ah, monsieur," he said, his watery eyes fairly bubbling, "the ring of bells, there's your real sacred music."

They were now above the main door of the building and they came out into the great covered gallery on which the towers rest. Carhaix smiled and pointed out a complete peal of miniature bells, installed between two pillars on a plank. He pulled the cords, and, in ecstasies, his eyes protruding, his moustache bristling, he listened to the frail tinkling of his toy.

And suddenly he relinquished the cords.

"I once had a crazy idea," he said, "of forming a class here and teaching all the intricacies of the craft, but no one cared to learn a trade which was steadily going out of existence. Why, you know we don't even sound for weddings any more, and nobody comes to look at the tower.

"But I really can't complain. I hate the streets. When I try to cross one I lose my head. So I stay in the tower all day, except once in the early morning when I go to the other side of the square for a bucket of water. Now my wife doesn't like it up here. You see, the snow does come in through all the loopholes and it heaps up, and sometimes we are snowbound with the wind blowing a gale."

They had come to Carhaix's lodge. His wife was waiting for them on the threshold.

"Come in, gentlemen," she said. "You have certainly earned some refreshment," and she pointed to four glasses which she had set out on the table.

The bell-ringer lighted a little briar pipe, while Des Hermies and Durtal each rolled a cigarette.

"Pretty comfortable place," remarked Durtal, just to be saying something. It was a vast room, vaulted, with walls of rough stone, and lighted by a semi-circular window just under the ceiling. The tiled floor was badly covered by an infamous carpet, and the furniture, very simple, consisted of a round dining-room table, some old *bergère* armchairs covered with slate-blue Utrecht velours, a little stained walnut sideboard on which were several plates and pitchers of Breton faience, and opposite the sideboard a little black bookcase, which might contain fifty books.

"Of course a literary man would be interested in the books," said Carhaix, who had been watching Durtal. "You mustn't be too critical, monsieur. I have only the tools of my trade."

Durtal went over and took a look. The collection consisted largely of works on bells. He read some of the titles:

On the cover of a slim parchment volume he deciphered the faded legend, hand-written, in rust-coloured ink, *"De tintinnabulis* by Jerome Magius, 1664"; then, pell-mell, there were: *A curious and edifying miscellany concerning church bells* by Dom Rémi Carré; another *Edifying miscellany,* anonymous; a *Treatise of bells* by Jean-Baptiste Thiers, curate of Champrond and Vibraye; a ponderous tome by an architect named Blavignac; a smaller work entitled *Essay on the symbolism of bells* by a parish priest of Poitiers; a *Notice* by the abbé Baraud; then a whole series of brochures, with covers of grey paper, bearing no titles.

"It's no collection at all," said Carhaix with a sigh. "The best ones are wanting, the *De campanis commentarius* of Angelo Rocca and the *De tintinnabulo* of Percichellius, but they are so hard to find, and so expensive when you do find them."

A glance sufficed for the rest of the books, most of them being pious works, Latin and French Bibles, an *Imitation of Christ,* Görres' *Mystik* in five volumes, the abbé Aubert's *History and theory of religious symbolism,* Pluquet's *Dic-*

tionary of heresies, and several lives of saints.

"Ah, monsieur, my own books are not much account, but Des Hermies lends me what he knows will interest me."

"Don't talk so much!" said his wife. "Give monsieur a chance to sit down," and she handed Durtal a brimming glass aromatic with the acidulous perfume of genuine cider.

In response to his compliments she told him that the cider came from Brittany and was made by relatives of hers at Landévennec, her and Carhaix's native village.

She was delighted when Durtal affirmed that long ago he had spent a day in Landévennec.

"Why, then we know each other already!" she said, shaking hands with him again.

The room was heated to suffocation by a stove whose pipe zigzagged over to the window and out through a sheet-iron square nailed to the sash in place of one of the panes. Carhaix and his good wife, with her honest, weak face and frank, kind eyes, were the most restful of people. Durtal, made drowsy by the warmth and the quiet domesticity, let his thoughts wander. He said to himself, "If I had a place like this, above the roofs of Paris, I would fix it up and make of it a real haven of refuge. Here, in the clouds, alone and aloof, I would work away on my book and take my time about it, years perhaps. What inconceivable happiness it would be to escape from the age, and, while the waves of human folly were breaking against the foot of the tower, to sit up here, out of it all, and pore over antique tomes by the shaded light of the lamp."

He smiled at the naïveté of his daydream.

"I certainly do like your place," he said aloud, as if to sum up his reflections.

"Oh, you wouldn't if you had to live here," said the good wife. "We have plenty of room, too much room, because there are a couple of bedchambers as big as this, besides plenty of closet space, but it's so inconvenient—and so cold! And no kitchen—" and she pointed to a landing where, blocking the stairway, the cook stove had had to be installed. "And there are so many, many steps to go up when you come back from market. I am getting old, and I have a twinge of the rheumatics whenever I think about making the climb."

"You can't even drive a nail into this rock wall and have a peg to hang things on," said Carhaix. "But I like this place. I was made for it. Now my wife dreams constantly of spending her last days in Landévennec."

Des Hermies rose. All shook hands, and monsieur and madame made Durtal swear that he would come again.

"What refreshing people!" exclaimed Durtal as he and Des Hermies crossed the square.

"And Carhaix is a mine of information."

"But tell me, what the devil is an educated man, of no ordinary intelligence, doing, working as a—as a day labourer?"

"If Carhaix could hear you! But, my friend, in the Middle Ages bell-ringers were high officials. True, the craft has declined considerably in modern times. I couldn't tell you myself how Carhaix became hipped on the subject of bells. All I know is that he studied at a seminary in Brittany, that he had scruples of conscience and considered himself unworthy to enter the priesthood, that he came to Paris and apprenticed himself to a very intellectual master bell-ringer, Père Gilbert, who had in his cell at Notre Dame some ancient and of course unique plans of Paris that would make your mouth water. Gilbert wasn't a 'labourer,' either. He was an enthusiastic collector of documents relating to old Paris. From Notre Dame Carhaix came to Saint Sulpice, fifteen years ago, and has been there ever since."

"How did you happen to make his acquaintance?"

"First he was my patient, then my friend. I've known him ten years."

"Funny. He doesn't look like a seminary product. Most of them have the shuffling gait and sheepish air of an old gardener."

"Carhaix will be all right for a few more years," said Des Hermies, as if to himself, "and then let us mercifully wish him a speedy death. The Church, which has begun by sanctioning the introduction of gas into the chapels, will end by installing mechanical chimes instead of bells. That will be charming. The machinery will be run by electricity and we shall have real up-to-date, timbreless, Protestant peals."

"Then Carhaix's wife will have a chance to go back to Finistère."

"No, they are too poor, and then too Carhaix would be broken-hearted if he lost his bells. Curious, a man's affection for the object that he manipulates. The mechanic's love for his machine. The thing that one tends, and that obeys one, becomes personalized, and one ends by falling in love with it. And the bell is an instrument in a class of its own. It is baptized like a Christian, anointed with sacramental oil, and according to the pontifical rubric it is also to be sanctified, in the interior of its chalice, by a bishop, in seven cruciform unctions with the oil of the infirm that it may send to the dying the message which shall sustain them in their last agonies.

"It is the herald of the Church, the voice from without as the priest is the voice from within. So you see it isn't a mere piece of bronze, a reversed mortar to be swung at a rope's end. Add that bells, like fine wines, ripen with age, that their tone becomes more ample and mellow, that they lose their sharp bouquet, their raw flavour. That will explain—imperfectly—how one can become attached to them."

"Why, you seem to be an enthusiast yourself."

"Oh, I don't know anything about it. I am simply repeating what I have heard Carhaix say. If the subject interests you, he will be only too glad to teach you the symbolism of bells. He is inexhaustible. The man is a monomaniac."

"I can understand," said Durtal dreamily. "I live in a quarter where there are a good many convents and at dawn the air is a-tingle with the vibrance of the chimes. When I was ill I used to lie awake at night awaiting the sound of the matin bells and welcoming them as a deliverance. In the grey light I felt that I was being cuddled by a distant and secret caress, that a lullaby was crooned over me, and a cool hand applied to my burning forehead. I had the assurance that the folk who were awake were praying for the others, and consequently for me. I felt less lonely. I really believe the bells are sounded for the special benefit of the sick who cannot sleep."

"The bells ring for others, notably for the trouble-makers. The rather common inscription for the side of a bell, *'Paco cruentos,'* 'I pacify the bloody-minded,' is singularly apt, when you think it over."

This conversation was still haunting Durtal when he went to bed. Carhaix's phrase, "The ring of the bells is the real sacred music," took hold of him like an obsession. And drifting back through the centuries he saw in dream the slow processional of monks and the kneeling congregations responding to the call of the angelus and drinking in the balm of holy sound as if it were consecrated wine.

All the details he had ever known of the liturgies of ages came crowding into his mind. He could hear the sounding of matin invitatories; chimes telling a rosary of harmony over tortuous labyrinths of narrow streets, over cornet towers, over pepper-box pignons, over dentelated walls; the chimes chanting the canonical hours, prime and tierce, sexte and none, vespers and compline; celebrating the joy of a city with the tinkling laughter of the little bells, tolling its sorrow with the ponderous lamentation of the great ones. And there were master ringers in those times, makers of chords, who could send into the air the expression of the whole soul of a community. And the bells which they served as submissive sons and faithful deacons were as humble and as truly of the people as was the Church itself. As the priest at certain times put off his chasuble, so the bell at times had put off its sacred character and spoken to the baptized on fair day and market day, inviting them, in the event of rain, to settle their affairs inside the nave of the church and, that the sanctity of the place might not be violated by the conflicts arising from sharp bargaining, imposing upon them a probity unknown before or since.

Today bells spoke an obsolete language, incomprehensible to man. Carhaix was under no misapprehension. Living in an aërial tomb outside the human scramble, he was faithful to his art, and in consequence no longer had any reason for existing. He vegetated, superfluous and demoded, in a society which insisted that for its amusement the holy place be turned into a concert hall. He was like a creature reverted, a relic of a bygone age, and he was supremely contemptuous of the miserable *fin de siècle* church showmen who to draw fashionable audiences did not fear to offer the attraction of cavatinas and waltzes rendered on the cathedral organ by manufacturers of profane music, by ballet mongers and comic opera-wrights.

"Poor Carhaix!" said Durtal, as he blew out the candle. "Another who loves this epoch about as well as Des Hermies and I do. But he has the tutelage of his bells, and certainly among his wards he has his favourite. He is not to be pitied. He has his hobby, which renders life possible for him, as hobbies do."

CHAPTER IV

"How is Gilles de Rais progressing?"

"I have finished the first part of his life, making just the briefest possible mention of his virtues and achievements."

"Which are of no interest,'" remarked Des Hermies.

"Evidently, since the name of Gilles de Rais would have perished four centuries ago but for the enormities of vice which it symbolizes. I am coming to the crimes now. The great difficulty, you see, is to explain how this man, who was a brave captain and a good Christian, all of a sudden became a sacrilegious sadist and a coward."

"Metamorphosed over night, as it were."

"Worse. As if at a touch of a fairy's wand or of a playwright's pen. That is what mystifies his biographers. Of course untraceable influences must have been at work a long time, and there must have been occasional outcropping not mentioned in the cronicles. Here is a recapitulation of our material.

"Gilles de Rais was born about 1404 on the boundary between Brittany and Anjou, in the château de Machecoul. We know nothing of his childhood. His father died about the end of October, 1415, and his mother almost immediately married a Sieur d'Estouville, abandoning her two sons, Gilles and René. They became the wards of their grandfather, Jean de Craon, 'a man old and ancient and of exceeding great age,' as the texts say. He seems to have allowed his two charges to run wild, and then to have got rid of Gilles by marrying him to Catherine de Thouars, November 30, 1420.

"Gilles is known to have been at the court of the Dauphin five years later. His contemporaries represent him as a robust, active man, of striking beauty and rare elegance. We have no explicit statement as to the rôle he played in this court, but one can easily imagine what sort of treatment the richest baron in France received at the hands of an impoverished king.

"For at that moment Charles VII was in extremities. He was without money, prestige, or real authority. Even the cities along the Loire scarcely obeyed him. France, decimated a few years before, by the plague, and further depopulated by massacres, was in a deplorable situation.

"England, rising from the sea like the fabled polyp the Kraken, had cast her tentacles over Brittany, Normandy, l'Ile de France, part of Picardy, the entire North, the Interior as far as Orléans, and crawling forward left in her wake towns squeezed dry and country exhausted.

"In vain Charles clamoured for subsidies, invented excuses for exactions, and pressed the imposts. The paralyzed cities and fields abandoned to the wolves could afford no succour. Remember his very claim to the throne was disputed. He became like a blind man going the rounds with a tin cup begging sous. His court at Chinon was a snarl of intrigue complicated by an occasional murder. Weary of being hunted, more or less out of harm's way behind the Loire, Charles and his partisans finally consoled themselves by flaunting in the face of inevitable disaster the devil-may-care debaucheries of the condemned making the most of the few moments left them. Forays and loans furnished them with opulent cheer and permitted them to carouse on a grand scale. The eternal *qui-vive* and the misfortunes of war were forgotten in the arms of courtesans.

"What more could have been expected of a used-up sleepy-headed king, the issue of an infamous mother and a mad father?"

"Oh, whatever you say about Charles VII pales beside the

testimony of the portrait of him in the Louvre painted by Foucquet. That bestial face, with the eyes of a small-town userer and the sly psalm-singing mouth that butter wouldn't melt in, has often arrested me. Foucquet depicts a debauched priest who has a bad cold and has been drinking sour wine. Yet you can see that this monarch is of the very same type as the more refined, less salacious, more prudently cruel, more obstinate and cunning Louis XI, his son and successor. Well, Charles VII was the man who had Jean Sans Peur assassinated, and who abandoned Jeanne d'Arc. What more need be said?"

"What indeed? Well, Gilles de Rais, who had raised an army at his own expense, was certainly welcomed by this court with open arms. There is no doubt that he footed the bills for tournaments and banquets, that he was vigilantly 'tapped' by the courtiers, and that he lent the king staggering sums. But in spite of his popularity he never seems to have evaded responsibility and wallowed in debauchery, like the king. We find Gilles shortly afterward defending Anjou and Maine against the English. The chronicles say that he was 'a good and hardy captain,' but his 'goodness' and 'hardiness' did not prevent him from being borne back by force of numbers. The English armies, uniting, inundated the country, and, pushing on unchecked, invaded the interior. The king was ready to flee to the Mediterranean provinces and let France go, when Jeanne d'Arc appeared.

"Gilles returned to court and was entrusted by Charles with the 'guard and defence' of the Maid of Orleans. He followed her everywhere, fought at her side, even under the walls of Paris, and was with her at Rheims the day of the coronation, at which time, says Monstrelet, the king rewarded his valour by naming him Marshal of France, at the age of twenty-five."

"Lord!" Des Hermies interrupted, "promotion came rapidly in those times. But I suppose warriors then weren't the bemedalled, time-serving incompetents they are now."

"Oh, don't be misled. The title of Marshal of France didn't mean so much in Gilles's time as it did afterward in the reign of Francis I, and nothing like what it has come to mean since Napoleon.

"What was the conduct of Gilles de Rais toward Jeanne d'Arc? We have no certain knowledge. M. Vallet de Viriville, without proof, accuses him of treachery. M. l'abbé Bossard, on the contrary, claims—and alleges plausible reasons for entertaining the opinion—that he was loyal to her and watched over her devotedly.

"What is certain is that Gilles's soul became saturated with mystical ideas. His whole history proves it.

"He was constantly in association with this extraordinary maid whose adventures seemed to attest the possibility of divine intervention in earthly affairs. He witnessed the miracle of a peasant girl dominating a court of ruffians and bandits and arousing a cowardly king who was on the point of flight. He witnessed the incredible episode of a virgin bringing back to the fold such black rams as La Hire, Xaintrailles, Beaumanoir, Chabannes, Dunois, and Gaucourt, and washing their old fleeces whiter than snow. Undoubtedly Gilles also, under her shepherding, docilely cropped the white grass of the gospel, took communion the morning of a battle, and revered Jeanne as a saint.

"He saw the Maid fulfil all her promises. She raised the siege of Orléans, had the king consecrated at Rheims, and then declared that her mission was accomplished and asked as a boon that she be permitted to return home.

"Now I should say that as a result of such an association Gilles's mysticism began to soar. Henceforth we have to deal with a man who is half-freebooter, half-monk. Moreover——"

"Pardon the interruption, but I am not so sure that Jeanne d'Arc's intervention was a good thing for France."

"Why not?"

"I will explain. You know that the defenders of Charles

were for the most part Mediterranean cut-throats, ferocious pillagers, execrated by the very people they came to protect. The Hundred Years' War, in effect, was a war of the South against the North. England at that epoch had not got over the Conquest and was Norman in blood, language, and tradition. Suppose Jeanne d'Arc had stayed with her mother and stuck to her knitting. Charles VII would have been dispossessed and the war would have come to an end. The Plantagenets would have reigned over England and France, which, in primeval times before the Channel existed, formed one territory occupied by one race, as you know. Thus there would have been a single united and powerful kingdom of the North, reaching as far as the province of Languedoc and embracing peoples whose tastes, instincts, and customs were alike. On the other hand, the coronation of a Valois at Rheims created a heterogeneous and preposterous France, separating homogeneous elements, uniting the most incompatible nationalities, races the most hostile to each other, and identifying us—inseparably, alas!—with those stained-skinned, varnished-eyed munchers of chocolate and raveners of garlic, who are not Frenchmen at all, but Spaniards and Italians. In a word, if it hadn't been for Jeanne d'Arc, France would not now belong to that line of histrionic, forensic, perfidious chatterboxes, the precious Latin race—Devil take it!"

Durtal raised his eyebrows.

"My, my," he said, laughing. "Your remarks prove to me that you are interested in 'our own, our native land.' I should never have suspected it of you."

"Of course you wouldn't," said Des Hermies, relighting his cigarette. "As has so often been said, 'My own, my native land is wherever I happen to feel at home.' Now I don't feel at home except with the people of the North. But I interrupted you. Let's get back to the subject. What were you saying?"

"I forget. Oh, yes. I was saying that the Maid had

completed her task. Now we are confronted by a question
to which there is seemingly no answer. What did Gilles do
when she was captured, how did he feel about her death?
We cannot tell. We know that he was lurking in the
vicinity of Rouen at the time of the trial, but it is too much
to conclude from that, like certain of his biographies, that
he was plotting her rescue.

"At any rate, after losing track of him completely, we
find that he has shut himself in at his castle of Tiffauges.

"He is no longer the rough soldier, the uncouth fighting-
man. At the time when the misdeeds are about to begin,
the artist and man of letters develop in Gilles and, taking
complete possession of him, incite him, under the impulsion
of a perverted mysticism, to the most sophisticated of cruel-
ties, the most delicate of crimes.

"For he was almost alone in his time, this baron de Rais.
In an age when his peers were simple brutes, he sought the
delicate delirium of art, dreamed of a literature soul-search-
ing and profound; he even composed a treatise on the art
of evoking demons; he gloried in the music of the Church,
and would have nothing about his that was not rare and
difficult to obtain.

"He was an erudite Latinist, a brilliant conversationalist,
a sure and generous friend. He possessed a library extraordinary for an epoch when nothing was read but theology and
lives of saints. We have the description of several of his
manuscripts; Suetonius, Valerius Maximus, and an Ovid
on parchment bound in red leather, with vermeil clasp and
key.

"These books were his passion. He carried them with
him when he travelled. He had attached to his household
a painter named Thomas who illuminated them with ornate
letters and miniatures, and Gilles himself painted the enamels
which a specialist—discovered after an assiduous search—
set in the gold-inwrought bindings. Gilles's taste in furnishings was elevated and bizarre. He revelled in abbatial stuffs,

voluptuous silks, in the sombre gilding of old brocade. He liked knowingly spiced foods, ardent wines heavy with aromatics; he dreamed of unknown gems, weird stones, uncanny metals. He was the Des Esseintes of the fifteenth century!

"All this was very expensive, less so, perhaps, than the luxurious court which made Tiffauges a place like none other.

"He had a guard of two hundred men, knights, captains, squires, pages, and all these people had personal attendants who were magnificently equipped at Gilles's expense. The luxury of his chapel and collegium was madly extravagant. There was in residence at Tiffauges a complete metropolitan clergy, deans, vicars, treasurers, canons, clerks, deacons, scholasters, and choir boys. There is an inventory extant of the surplices, stoles, and amices, and the fur choir hats with crowns of squirrel and linings of vair. There are countless sacerdotal ornaments. We find vermilion altar cloths, curtains of emerald silk, a cope of velvet, crimson and violet with orpheys of cloth of gold, another of rose damask, satin dalmatics for the deacons, baldachins figured with hawks and falcons of Cyprus gold. We find plate, hammered chalices and ciboria crusted with uncut jewels. There are reliquaries, among them a silver head of Saint Honoré. A mass of sparkling jewelleries which an artist, installed in the château, cuts to order.

"And anyone who came along was welcome. From all corners of France caravans journeyed toward this château where the artist, the poet, the scholar, found princely hospitality, cordial goodfellowship, gifts of welcome and largesse at departure.

"Already undermined by the demands which the war had made on it, his fortune was giving way beneath these expenditures. Now he began to walk the terrible ways of usury. He borrowed of the most unscrupulous bourgeois, hypothecated his châteaux, alienated his lands. At times he was reduced to asking advances on his religious ornaments, on his jewels, on his books."

"I am glad to see that the method of ruining oneself in the Middle Ages did not differ sensibly from that of our days," said Des Hermies. "However, our ancestors did not have Monte Carlo, the notaries, and the Bourse."

"And *did* have sorcery and alchemy. A memorial addressed to the king by the heirs of Gilles de Rais informs us that this immense fortune was squandered in less than eight years.

"Now it's the signories of Confolens, Chabanes, Châteaumorant, Lombert, ceded to a captain for a ridiculous price; now it's the fief of Fontaine Milon, of Angers, the fortress of Saint Etienne de Mer Morte acquired by Guillaume Le Ferron for a song; again it's the châteaux of Blaison and of Chemille forfeited to Guillaume de la Jumelière who never has to pay a sou. But look, there's a long list of castellanies and forests, salt mines and farm lands,"said Durtal, spreading out a great sheet of paper on which he had copied the account of the purchases and sales.

"Frightened by his mad course, the family of the Marshal supplicated the king to intervene, and Charles VII, 'sure,' as he said, 'of the malgovernance of the Sire de Rais,' forbade him, in grand council, by letters dated 'Amboise, 1436,' to sell or make over any fortress, any château, any land.

"This order simply hastened the ruin of the interdicted. The grand skinflint, the master usurer of the time, Jean V, duke of Brittany, refused to publish the edict in his states, but, underhandedly, notified all those of his subjects who dealt with Gilles. No one now dared to buy the Marshal's domains for fear of incurring the wrath of the king, so Jean V remained the sole purchaser and fixed the prices. You may judge how liberal his prices were.

"That explains Gilles's hatred of his family who had solicited these letters patent of the king, and why, as long as he lived, he had nothing to do with his wife, nor with his daughter whom he consigned to a dungeon at Pouzauges.

"Now to return to the question which I put a while ago,

how and with what motives Gilles quitted the court. I
think the facts which I have outlined will partially explain.

"It is evident that for quite a while, long before the
Marshal retired to his estates, Charles had been assailed
by the complaints of Gilles's wife and other relatives. Moreover, the courtiers must have execrated the young man on
account of his riches and luxuries; and the king, the same
king who abandoned Jeanne d'Arc when he considered that
she could no longer be useful to him, found an occasion to
avenge himself on Gilles for the favours Gilles had done
him. When the king needed money to finance his debaucheries or to raise troops he had not considered the Marshal
lavish. Now that the Marshal was ruined the king censured
him for his prodigality, held him at arm's length, and spared
him no reproach and no menace.

"We may be sure Gilles had no reason to regret leaving
this court, and another thing is to be taken into consideration.
He was doubtless sick and tired of the nomadic existence of
a soldier. He was doubtless impatient to get back to a pacific
atmosphere among books. Moreover, he seems to have been
completely dominated by the passion for alchemy, for which
he was ready to abandon all else. For it is worth noting
that this science, which threw him into demonomania when
he hoped to stave off inevitable ruin with it, he had loved
for its own sake when he was rich. It was in fact toward
the year 1426, when his coffers bulged with gold, that he
attempted the 'great work' for the first time.

"We shall find him, then, bent over his retorts in the
château de Tiffauges. That is the point to which I have
brought my history, and now I am about to begin on the
series of crimes of magic and sadism."

"But all this," said Des Hermies, "does not explain how,
from a man of piety, he was suddenly changed into a Satanist, from a placid scholar into a violator of little children,
a 'ripper' of boys and girls."

"I have already told you that there are no documents

to bind together the two parts of this life so strangely divided, but in what I have been narrating you can pick out some of the threads of the duality. To be precise, this man, as I have just had you observe, was a true mystic. He witnessed the most extraordinary events which history has ever shown. Association with Jeanne d'Arc certainly stimulated his desires for the divine. Now from lofty Mysticism to base Satanism there is but one step. In the Beyond all things touch. He carried his zeal for prayer into the territory of blasphemy. He was guided and controlled by that troop of sacrilegious priests, transmuters of metals, and evokers of demons, by whom he was surrounded at Tiffauges."

"You think, then, that the Maid of Orleans was really responsible for his career of evil?"

"To a certain point. Consider. She roused an impetuous soul, ready for anything, as well for orgies of saintliness as for ecstasies of crime.

"There was no transition between the two phases of his being. The moment Jeanne was dead he fell into the hands of sorcerers who were the most learned of scoundrels and the most unscrupulous of scholars. These men who frequented the château de Tiffauges were fervent Latinists, marvellous conversationalists, possessors of forgotten arcana, guardians of world-old secrets. Gilles was evidently more fitted to live with them than with men like Dunois and La Hire. These magicians, whom all the biographers agree to represent—wrongly, I think—as vulgar parasites and base knaves, were, as I view them, the patricians of intellect of the fifteenth century. Not having found places in the Church, where they would certainly have accepted no position beneath that of cardinal or pope, they could, in those troubled times of ignorance, but take refuge in the patronage of a great lord like Gilles. And Gilles was, indeed, the only one at that epoch who was intelligent enough and educated enough to understand them.

"To sum up: natural mysticism on one hand, and, on the other, daily association with savants obsessed by Satanism.

The sword of Damocles hanging over his head, to be conjured away by the will of the Devil, perhaps. An ardent, a mad curiosity concerning the forbidden sciences. All this explains why, little by little, as the bonds uniting him to the world of alchemists and sorcerers grow stronger, he throws himself into the occult and is swept on by it into the most unthinkable crimes.

"Then as to being a 'ripper' of children—and he didn't immediately become one, no, Gilles did not violate and trucidate little boys until after he became convinced of the vanity of alchemy—why, he does not differ greatly from the other barons of his times.

"He exceeds them in the magnitude of his debauches, in opulence of murders, and that's all. It's a fact. Read Michelet. You will see that the princes of this epoch were redoubtable butchers. There was a sire de Giac who poisoned his wife, put her astride of his horse and rode at breakneck speed for five leagues, until she died. There was another, whose name I have forgotten, who collared his father, dragged him barefoot through the snow, and calmly thrust him into a subterranean prison and left him there until he died. And how many others! I have tried, without success, to find whether in battles and forays the Marshal committed any serious misdeeds. I have discovered nothing, except that he had a pronounced taste for the gibbet; for he liked to string up all the renegade French whom he surprised in the ranks of the English or in the cities which were not very much devoted to the king.

"We shall find his taste for this kind of torture manifesting itself later on in the château de Tiffauges.

"Now, in conclusion, add to all these factors a formidable pride, a pride which incites him to say, during his trial, 'So potent was the star under which I was born that I have done what no one in the world has done nor ever can do.'

"And assuredly, the Marquis de Sade is only a timid bourgeois, a mediocre fantasist, beside him!"

"Since it is difficult to be a saint," said Des Hermies,

"there is nothing for it but to be a Satanist. One of the two extremes. 'Execration of impotence, hatred of the mediocre,' that, perhaps, is one of the more indulgent definitions of Diabolism."

"Perhaps. One can take pride in going as far in crime as a saint in virtue. And that expresses Gilles de Rais exactly."

"All the same, it's a mean subject to handle."

"It certainly is, but happily the documents are abundant. Satan was terrible to the Middle Ages——"

"And to the modern."

"What do you mean?"

That Satanism has come down in a straight, unbroken line from that age to this."

"Oh, no; you don't believe that at this very hour the devil is being evoked and the black mass celebrated?"

"Yes."

"You are sure?"

"Perfectly."

"You amaze me. But, man! do you know that to witness such things would aid me signally in my work? No joking, you believe in a contemporary Satanistic manifestation? You have proofs?"

"Yes, and of them we shall speak later, for today I am very busy. Tomorrow evening, when we dine with Carhaix. Don't forget. I'll come by for you. Meanwhile think over the phrase which you applied a moment ago to the magicians: 'If they had entered the Church they would not have consented to be anything but cardinals and popes,' and then just think what kind of a clergy we have nowadays. The explanation of Satanism is there, in great part, anyway, for without sacrilegious priests there is no mature Satanism."

"But what do these priests want?"

"Everything!" exclaimed Des Hermies.

"Hmmm. Like Gilles de Rais, who asked the demon for 'knowledge, power, riches,' all that humanity covets, to be deeded to him by a title signed with his own blood."

CHAPTER V

"Come right in and get warm. Ah, messieurs, you must not do that any more," said Mme. Carhaix, seeing Durtal draw from his pocket some bottles wrapped in paper, while Des Hermies placed on the table some little packages tied with twine. "You mustn't spend your money on us."

"Oh, but you see we enjoy doing it, Mme. Carhaix. And your husband?"

"He is in the tower. Since morning he has been going from one tantrum into another."

"My, the cold is terrible today," said Durtal, "and I should think it would be no fun up there."

"Oh, he isn't grumbling for himself but for his bells. Take off your things."

They took off their overcoats and came up close to the stove.

"It isn't what you would call hot in here," said Mme. Carhaix, "but to thaw this place you would have to keep a fire going night and day."

"Why don't you get a portable stove?"

"Oh, heavens! that would asphyxiate us."

"It wouldn't be very comfortable at any rate," said Des Hermies, "for there is no chimney. You might get some joints of pipe and run them out of the window, the way you have fixed this tubing. But, speaking of that kind of apparatus, Durtal, doesn't it seem to you that those hideous galvanized iron contraptions perfectly typify our utilitarian epoch?

"Just think, the engineer, offended by any object that

hasn't a sinister or ignoble form, reveals himself entire in this invention. He tells us, 'You want heat. You shall have heat—and nothing else.' Anything agreeable to the eye is out of the question. No more snapping, crackling wood fire, no more gentle, pervasive warmth. The useful without the fantastic. Ah, the beautiful jets of flame darting out from a red cave of coals and spurting up over a roaring log."

"But there are lots of stoves where you can see the fire," objected madame.

"Yes, and then it's worse yet. Fire behind a grated window of mica. Flame in prison. Depressing! Ah, those fine fires of faggots and dry vine stocks out in the country. They smell good and they cast a golden glow over everything. Modern life has set that in order. The luxury of the poorest of peasants is impossible in Paris except for people who have copious incomes."

The bell-ringer entered. Every hair of his bristling moustache was beaded with a globule of snow. With his knitted bonnet, his sheepskin coat, his fur mittens and goloshes, he resembled a Samoyed, fresh from the pole.

"I won't shake hands," he said, "for I am covered with grease and oil. What weather! Just think, I've been scouring the bells ever since early this morning. I'm worried about them."

"Why?"

"Why! You know very well that frost contracts the metal and sometimes cracks or breaks it. Some of these bitterly cold winters we have lost a good many, because bells suffer worse than we do in bad weather.—Wife, is there any hot water in the other room, so I can wash up?"

"Can't we help you set the table?" Des Hermies proposed.

But the good woman refused. "No, no, sit down. Dinner is ready."

"Mighty appetizing," said Durtal, inhaling the odour of a peppery *pot-au-feu,* perfumed with a symphony of vegetables, of which the keynote was celery.

"Everybody sit down," said Carhaix, reappearing with a clean blouse on, his face shining of soap and water.

They sat down. The glowing stove purred. Durtal felt the sudden relaxation of a chilly soul dipped into a warm bath: at Carhaix's one was so far from Paris, so remote from the epoch. . . .

The lodge was poor, but cosy, comfortable, cordial. The very table, set country style, the polished glasses, the covered dish of sweet butter, the cider pitcher, the somewhat battered lamp casting reflections of tarnished silver on the great cloth, contributed to the atmosphere of home.

"Next time I come I must stop at the English store and buy a jar of that reliable orange marmalade," said Durtal to himself, for by common consent with Des Hermies he never dined with the bell-ringer without furnishing a share of the provisions. Carhaix set out a *pot-au-feu* and a simple salad and poured his cider. Not to be an expense to him, Des Hermies and Durtal brought wine, coffee, liquor, desserts, and managed so that their contributions would pay for the soup and the beef which would have lasted for several days if the Carhaixes had eaten alone.

"This time I did it!" said Mme. Carhaix triumphantly, serving to each in turn a mahogany-colour bouillon whose iridescent surface was looped with rings of topaz.

It was succulent and unctuous, robust and yet delicate, flavoured as it was with the broth of a whole flock of boiled chickens. The diners were silent now, their noses in their plates, their faces brightened by steam from the savoury soup. soup, two selected dishes, a salad, and a dessert.

"Now is the time to repeat the chestnut dear to Flaubert, 'You can't dine like this in a restaurant,'" said Durtal.

"Let's not malign the restaurants," said Des Hermies. "They afford a very special delight to the person who has the instinct of the inspector. I had an opportunity to gratify this instinct just the other night. I was returning from a call on a patient, and I dropped into one of these establishments where for the sum of three francs you are entitled to soup, two selected dishes, a salad, and a dessert.

"The restaurant, where I go as often as once a month, has an unvarying clientele, hostile highbrows, officers in mufti, members of Parliament, bureaucrats.

"While laboriously gnawing my way through a redoubtable sole with sauce au gratin, I examined the habitués seated all around me and I found them singularly altered since my last visit. They had become bony or bloated; their eyes were either hollow, with violet rings around them, or puffy, with crimson pouches beneath; the fat people had become yellow and the thin ones were turning green.

"More deadly than the forgotten venefices of the days of the Avignon papacy, the terrible preparations served in this place were slowly poisoning its customers.

"It was interested, as you may believe. I made myself the subject of a course of toxicological research, and, studying my food as it went down, I identified the frightful ingredients masking the mixtures of tannin and powdered carbon with which the fish was embalmed; and I penetrated the disguise of the marinated meats, painted with sauces the colour of sewage; and I diagnosed the wine as being coloured with fuscin, perfumed with furfurol, and enforced with molasses and plaster.

"I have promised myself to return every month to register the slow but sure progress of these people toward the tomb."

"Oh!" cried Mme. Carhaix.

"And you will claim," said Durtal, "that you aren't Satanic?"

"See, Carhaix, he's at it already. He won't even give us time to get our breath, but must be dogging us about Satanism. It's true I promised him I'd try and get you to tell us something about it tonight. Yes," continued Des Hermies, in response to Carhaix's look of astonishment, "yesterday, Durtal, who is engaged, as you know, in writing a history of Gilles de Rais, declared that he possessed all the information there was about Diabolism in the Middle Ages. I asked him if he had any material on the Satanism of the present day. He asked me what I was talking about, and wouldn't believe that these practices are being carried on right now."

"But they are," replied Carhaix, becoming grave. "It is only too true."

"Before we go any further, there is one question I'd like to put to Des Hermies," said Durtal. "Can you, honestly, without joking, without letting that saturnine smile play around the corner of your mouth, tell me, in perfectly good faith, whether you do or do not believe in Catholicism?"

"He!" exclaimed the bell-ringer. "Why, he's worse than an unbeliever, he's a heresiarch."

"The fast is, if I were certain of anything, I would be inclined toward Manicheism," said Des Hermies. "It's one of the oldest and it is *the* simplest of religions, and it best explains the abominable mess everything is in at the present time.

"The Principle of Good and the Principle of Evil, the God of Light and the God of Darkness, two rivals, are fighting for our souls. That's at least clear. Right now it is evident that the Evil God has the upper hand and is reigning over the world as master. Now—and on this point, Carhaix, who is distressed by these theories, can't reprehend me—I am for the under dog. That's a generous and perfectly proper idea."

"But Manicheism is impossible!" cried the bell-ringer. "Two infinities cannot exist together."

"But nothing can exist if you get to reasoning. The moment you argue the Catholic dogma everything goes to pieces. The proof that two infinities can coexist is that this idea passes beyond reason and enters the category of those things referred to in Ecclesiasticus: 'Inquire not into things higher than thou, for many things have shown themselves to be above the sense of men.'

"Manicheism, you see, must have had some good in it, because it was bathed in blood. At the end of the twelfth century thousands of Albigenses were roasted for practising this doctrine. Of course, I can't say that the Manicheans didn't abuse their cult, mostly made up of devil worship, because we know very well they did.

"On this point I am not with them," he went on slowly, after a silence. He was waiting till Mme. Carhaix, who had got up to remove the plates, should go out of the room to fetch the beef.

"While we are alone," he said, seeing her disappear through the stairway door, "I can tell you what they did. An excellent man named Psellus has revealed to us, in a book entitled *De operatione Dæmonum,* the fact that they tasted of the two excrements at the beginning of their ceremonial, and that they mixed human semen with the host."

"Horrible!" exclaimed Carhaix.

"Oh, as they took both kinds of communion, they did better than that," returned Des Hermies. "They cut children's throats and mixed the blood with ashes, and this paste, dissolved in liquid, constituted the Eucharistic wine."

"You bring us right back to Satanism," said Durtal.

"Why, yes, as you see, I haven't strayed off your subject."

"I am sure Monsieur Des Hermies has been saying something awful," murmured Mme. Carhaix as she came in, bearing a platter on which was a piece of beef smothered in vegetables.

"Oh, Madame," protested Des Hermies.

They burst out laughing and Carhaix cut up the meat, while his wife poured the cider and Durtal uncorked the bottle of anchovies.

"I am afraid it's cooked too much," said the woman, who was a great deal more interested in the beef than in other-world adventures, and she added the famous maxim of housekeepers, "When the broth is good the beef won't cut."

The men protested that it wasn't stringy a bit, it was cooked just right.

"Have an anchovy and a little butter with your meat, Monsieur Durtal."

"Wife, let's have some of the red cabbage that you preserved," said Carhaix, whose pale face was lighted up while his great canine eyes were becoming suspiciously moist. Visibly he was jubilant. He was at table with friends, in his tower, safe from the cold. "But, empty your glasses. You are not drinking," he said, holding up the cider pot.

"Let's see, Des Hermies, you were claiming yesterday that Satanism has pursued an uninterrupted course since the Middle Ages," said Durtal, wishing to get back to the subject which haunted him.

"Yes, and the documents are irrefutable. I'll put you into a position to prove them whenever you wish.

"At the end of the fifteenth century, that is to say at the time of Gilles de Rais—to go no further back—Satanism had assumed the proportions that you know. In the sixteenth it was worse yet. No need to remind you, I think, of the demoniac pactions of Catherine de Medici and of the Valois, of the trial of the monk Jean de Vaulx, of the investigations of the Sprengers and the Lancres and those learned inquisitors who had thousands of necromancers and sorcerers roasted alive. All that is known, too well known. One case is not too well known for me to cite here: that of the priest Benedictus who cohabited with the she-devil Armellina and consecrated the hosts holding them upside down. Here are the diabolical threads which bind that century to this. In the seventeenth century, in which the sorcery trials continue, and in which the 'possessed' of Loudun appear, the black religion flourishes, but already it has been driven under cover.

"I will cite you an example, one among many, if you like.

"A certain abbé Guibourg made a specialty of these abominations. On a table serving as tabernacle a woman lay down, naked or with her skirts lifted up over her head, and with her arms outstretched. She held the altar lights during the whole office.

"Guibourg thus celebrated masses on the abdomen of Mme. de Montespan, of Mme. d'Argenson, of Mme. de

Saint-Pont. As a matter of fact these masses were very frequent under the Grand Monarch. Numbers of women went to them as in our times women flock to have their fortunes told with cards.

"The ritual of these ceremonies was sufficiently atrocious. Generally a child was kidnapped and burnt in a furnace out in the country somewhere, the ashes were saved and mixed with the blood of another child whose throat had been cut, and of this mixture a paste was made resembling that of the Manicheans of which I was speaking. Abbé Guibourg officiated, consecrated the host, cut it into little pieces and mixed it with this mixture of blood and ashes. That was the material of the Sacrament."

"What a horrible priest!" cried Mme. Carhaix, indignant.

"Yes, he celebrated another kind of mass, too, that abbé did. It was called—hang it—it's unpleasant to say——"

"Say it, Monsieur des Hermies. When people have as great a hatred for that sort of thing as we here, they need not blink any fact. It isn't that kind of thing which is going to take me away from my prayers."

"Nor me," added her husband.

"Well, this sacrifice was called the Spermatic Mass."

"Oh!"

"Guibourg, wearing the alb, the stole, and the maniple, celebrated this mass with the sole object of making pastes to conjure with. The archives of the Bastille inform us that he acted thus at the request of a lady named Des Oeillettes:

"This woman, who was indisposed, gave some of her blood; the man who accompanied her stood patiently beside the bed where the scene took place, and Guibourg gathered up some of his semen into the chalice, then added powdered blood and some flour, and after sacrilegious ceremonies the Des Oeillettes woman departed bearing her paste."

"My heavenly Saviour!" sighed the bell-ringer's wife, "what a lot of filth."

"But," said Durtal, "in the Middle Ages the mass was celebrated in a different fashion. The altar then was the naked buttocks of a woman; in the seventeenth century it was the abdomen, and now?"

"Nowadays a woman is hardly ever used for an altar, but let us not anticipate. In the eighteenth century we shall again find abbés—among how many other monsters—who defile holy objects. One Canon Duer occupied himself specially with black magic and the evocation of the devil. He was finally executed as a sorcerer in the year of grace 1718. There was another who believed in the Incarnation of the Holy Ghost as the Paraclete, and who, in Lombary, which he stirred up to a feverish pitch of excitement, ordained twelve apostles and twelve apostolines to preach his gospel. This man, abbé Beccarelli, like all the other priests of his ilk, abused both sexes, and he said mass without confessing himself of his lecheries. As his cult grew he began to celebrate travestied offices in which he distributed to his congregation aphrodisiac pills presenting this peculiarity, that after having swallowed them the men believed themselves changed into women and the women into men.

"The recipe for these hippomanes is lost," continued Des Hermies with almost a sad smile. "To make a long story short, Beccarelli met with a very miserable end. He was prosecuted for sacrilege and sentenced, in 1708, to row in the galleys for seven years."

"These frightful stories seem to have taken away your appetite," said Mme. Carhaix. "Come, Monsieur des Hermies, a little more salad?"

"No, thanks. But now we've come to the cheese, I think it's time to open the wine," and he uncapped one of the bottles which Durtal had brought.

"It's a light Chinon wine, but not too weak. I discovered it in a little shop down by the quay," said Durtal.

"I see," he went on after a silence, "that the tradition of unspeakable crimes has been maintained by worthy successors of Gilles de Rais. I see that in all centuries there have been fallen priests who have dared commit sins against the Holy Ghost. But at the present time it all seems incredible.

Surely nobody is cutting children's throats as in the days of Bluebeard and of abbé Guibourg."

"You mean that nobody is brought to justice for doing it. They don't assassinate now, but they kill designated victims by methods unknown to official science—ah, if the confessionals could speak!" cried the bell-ringer.

"But tell me, what class of people are these modern covenanters with the Devil?"

"Prelates, abbesses, mission superiors, confessors of communities; and in Rome, the centre of present-day magic, they're the very highest dignitaries," answered Des Hermies. "As for the laymen, they are recruited from the wealthy class. That explains why these scandals are hushed up if the police chance to discover them.

Then, let us assume that the sacrifices to the Devil are not preceded by preliminary murders. Perhaps in some cases they aren't. The worshippers probably content themselves with bleeding a fœtus which had been aborted as soon as it became matured to the point necessary. Bloodletting is supererogatory anyway, and serves merely to whet the appetite. The main business is to consecrate the host and put it to an infamous use. The rest of the procedure varies. There is at present no regular ritual for the black mass."

"Well, then, is a priest absolutely essential to the celebration of these offices?"

"Certainly. Only a priest can operate the mystery of Transsubstantiation. I know there are certain occultists who claim to have been consecrated by the Lord, as Saint Paul was, and who think they can consummate a veritable sacrifice just like a real priest. Absurd! But even in default of real masses with ordained celebrants, the people possessed by the mania of sacrilege do none the less realize the sacred stupration of which they dream.

"Listen to this. In 1855 there existed at Paris an association composed of women, for the most part. These women took communion several times a day and retained the sacred

wafer in their mouths to be spat out later and trodden underfoot or soiled by disgusting contacts."

"You are sure of it?"

"Perfectly. These facts were revealed by a religious
journal, *Les annales de la sainteté,* and the archbishop of
Paris could not deny them. I add that in 1874 women
were likewise enrolled at Paris to practise this odious commerce. They were paid so much for every wafer they
brought in. That explains why they presented themselves
at the sacred table of different churches every day."

"And that is not the half of it! Look," said Carhaix, in
his turn, rising and taking from his bookshelf a blue
brochurette. "Here is a review, *La voix de la septaine,* dated
1843. It informs us that for twenty-five years, at Agen,
a Satanistic association regularly celebrated black masses, and
committed murder, and polluted three thousand three hundred and twenty hosts! And Monsignor the Bishop of
Agen, who was a good and ardent prelate, never dared deny
the monstrosities committed in his diocese!"

"Yes, we can say it among ourselves," Des Hermies returned, "in the nineteenth century the number of foul-
minded abbés has been legion. Unhappily, though the documents are certain, they are difficult to verify, for no ecclesiastic boasts of such misdeeds. The celebrants of Deicidal
masses dissemble and declare themselves devoted to Christ.
They even affirm that they defend Him by exorcising the
possessed.

"That's a good one. The 'possessed' are made so or kept
so by the priests themselves, who are thus assured of subjects and accomplices, especially in the convents. All kinds
of murderous and sadistic follies can be covered with the
antique and pious mantle of exorcism."

"Let us be just," said Carhaix. "The Satanist would not
be complete if he were not an abominable hypocrite."

"Hypocrisy and pride are perhaps the most characteristic
vices of the perverse priest," suggested Durtal.

"But in the long run," Des Hermies went on, "in spite

of the most adroit precautions, everything comes out. Up to now I have spoken only of local Satanistic associations, but there are others, more extensive, which ravage the old world and the new, for Diabolism is quite up to date in one respect. It is highly centralized and very capably administered. There are committees, subcommittees, a sort of curia, which rules America and Europe, like the curia of a pope.

"The biggest of these societies founded as long ago as 1855 is the society of the Re-Theurgistes Optimates. Beneath an apparent unity it is divided into two camps, one aspiring to destroy the universe and reign over the ruins, the other thinking simply of imposing upon the world a demoniac cult of which it shall be high priest.

"This society has its seat in America. It was formerly directed by one Longfellow, an adventurer, born in Scotland, who entitled himself grand priest of the New Evocative Magism. For a long time it has had branches in France, Italy, Germany, Russia, Austria, even Turkey.

"It is at the present moment moribund, or perhaps quite dead, but another has just been created. The object of this one is to elect an antipope who will be the exterminating Antichrist. And those are only two of them. How many others are there, more or less important numerically, more or less secret, which, by common accord, at ten o'clock the morning of the Feast of the Holy Sacrament, celebrate black masses at Paris, Rome, Bruges, Constantinople, Nantes, Lyons, and in Scotland—where sorcerers swarm!

"Then, outside of these universal associations and local assemblies, isolated cases abound, on which little light can be shed, and that with great difficulty. Some years ago there died, in a state of penitence, a certain comte de Lautree, who presented several churches with statues which he had bewitched so as to satanize the faithful. At Bruges a priest of my acquaintance contaminates the holy ciboria and uses them to prepare spells and conjurements. Finally one may, among all these, cite a clear case of possession. It is the case of Cantiamille, who in 1865 turned not only the city of Auxerre, but the whole diocese of Sens, upside down.

"This Cantianille, placed in a convent of Mont-Saint-Sulpice, was violated, when she was barely fifteen years old, by a priest who dedicated her to the Devil. This priest himself had been corrupted, in early childhood, by an ecclesiastic belonging to a sect of possessed which was created the very day Louis XVI was guillotined.

"What happened in this convent, where many nuns, evidently mad with hysteria, were associated in erotic devilry and sacrilegious rages with Cantianille, reads for all the world like the procedure in the trials of wizards of long ago, the histories of Gaufrédy and Madeleine Palud, of Urbain Grandier and Madeleine Bavent, or the Jesuit Girard and La Cadière, histories, by the way, in which much might be said about hystero-epilepsy on one hand and about Diabolism on the other. At any rate, Cantianille, after being sent away from the convent, was exorcised by a certain priest of the diocese, abbé Thorey, who seems to have been contaminated by his patient. Soon at Auxerre there were such scandalous scenes, such frenzied outbursts of Diabolism, that the bishop had to intervene. Cantianille was driven out of the country, abbé Thorey was disciplined, and the affair went to Rome.

"The curious thing about it is that the bishop, terrified by what he had seen, requested to be dismissed, and retired to Fontainebleau, where he died, still in terror, two years later."

"My friends," said Carhaix, consulting his watch, "it is a quarter to eight. I must be going up into the tower to sound the angelus. Don't wait for me. Have your coffee. I shall rejoin you in ten minutes."

He put on his Greenland costume, lighted a lantern, and opened the door. A stream of glacial air poured in. White molecules whirled in the blackness.

"The wind is driving the snow in through the loopholes along the stair," said the woman. "I am always afraid that Louis will take cold in his chest this kind of weather. Oh,

well, Monsieur des Hermies, here is the coffee. I appoint
you to the task of serving it. At this hour of day my poor
old limbs won't hold me up any longer. I must go lie
down."

"The fact is," sighed Des Hermies, when they had wished
her good night, "the fact is that mama Cahaix is rapidly
getting old. I have vainly tried to brace her up with tonics.
They do no good. She has worn herself out. She has
climbed too many stairs in her life, poor woman!"

"All the same, it's very curious, what you have told me,"
said Durtal. "To sum up, the most important thing about
Satanism is the black mass."

"That and the witchcraft and incubacy and succubacy
which I will tell you about; or rather, I will get another
more expert than I in these matters to tell you about them.
Sacrilegious mass, spells, and succubacy. There you have
the real quintessence of Satanism."

"And these hosts consecrated in blasphemous offices, what
use is made of them when they are not simply destroyed?"

"But I already told you. They are used to consummate
infamous acts. Listen," and Des Hermies took from the
bell-ringers bookshelf the fifth volume of the *Mystik* of
Görres. "Here is the flower of them all:

" 'These priests, in their baseness, often go so
far as to celebrate the mass with great hosts which
then they cut through the middle and afterwards
glue to a parchment, similarly cloven, and use
abominably to satisfy their passions.' "

"Holy sodomy, in other words?"

"Exactly."

At this moment the bell, set in motion in the tower,
boomed out. The chamber in which Durtal and Des
Hermies were sitting trembled and a droning filled the air.
It seemed that waves of sound came out of the walls, un-
rolling in a spiral from the very rock, and that one was
transported, in a dream, into the inside of one of these shells
which, when held up to the ear, simulate the roar of rolling

billows. Des Hermies, accustomed to the mighty resonance of the bells at short range, thought only of the coffee, which he had put on the stove to keep hot.

Then the booming of the bell came more slowly. The humming departed from the air. The window panes, the glass of the bookcase, the tumblers on the table, ceased to rattle and gave off only a tenuous tinkling.

A step was heard on the stair. Carhaix entered, covered with snow.

"Cristi, boys, it blows!" He shook himself, threw his heavy outer garments on a chair, and extinguished his lantern. "There were blinding clouds of snow whirling in between the sounding-shutters. I can hardly see. Dog's weather. The lady has gone to bed? Good. But you haven't drunk your coffee?" he asked as he saw Durtal filling the glasses.

Carhaix went up to the stove and poked the fire, then dried his eyes, which the bitter cold had filled with tears, and drank a great draught of coffee.

"Now. That hits the spot. How far had you got with your lecture, Des Hermies?"

"I finished the rapid exposé of Satanism, but I haven't yet spoken of the genuine monster, the only real master that exists at the present time, that defrocked abbé——"

"Oh!" exclaimed Carhaix. "Take care. The mere name of that man brings disaster."

"Bah! Canon Docre—to utter his ineffable name—can do nothing to us. I confess I cannot understand why he should inspire any terror. But never mind. I should like for Durtal, before we hunt up the canon, to see your friend Gévingey, who seems to be best and most intimately acquainted with him. A conversation with Gévingey would considerably amplify my contributions to the study of Satanism, especially as regards venefices and succubacy. Let's see. Would you mind if we invited him here to dine?"

Carhaix scratched his head, then emptied the ashes of his pipe on his thumbnail.

"Well, you see, the fact is, we have had a slight disagreement."

"What about?"

"Oh, nothing very serious. I interrupted his experiments here one day. But pour yourself some liqueur, Monsieur Durtal, and you, Des Hermies, why, you aren't drinking at all," and while, lighting their cigarettes, both sipped a few drops of almost proof cognac, Carhaix resumed, "Gévingey, who, though an astrologer, is a good Christian and an honest man—whom, indeed, I should be glad to see again—wished to consult my bells.

"That surprises you, but it's so. Bells formerly played quite an important part in the forbidden science. The art of predicting the future with their sounds is one of the least known and most disused branches of the occult. Gévingey had dug up some documents, and wished to verify them in the tower."

"Why, what did he do?"

"How do I know? He stood under the bell, at the risk of breaking his bones—a man of his age on the scaffolding there! He was halfway into the bell, the bell like a great hat, you see, coming clear down over his hips. And he soliloquized aloud and listened to the repercussions of his voice making the bronze vibrate.

"He spoke to me also of the interpretation of dreams about bells. According to him, whoever, in his sleep, sees bells swinging, is menaced by an accident; if the bell chimes, it is presage of slander; if it falls, ataxia is certain; if it breaks, it is assurance of afflictions and miseries. Finally he added, I believe, that if the night birds fly around a bell by moonlight one may be sure that sacrilegious robbery will be committed in the church, or that the curate's life is in danger.

"Be all that as it may, this business of touching the bells, getting up into them—and you know they're consecrated—of attributing to them the gift of prophecy, of involving them in the interpretation of dream—an art formally for-

bidden in Leviticus—displeased me, and I demanded, somewhat rudely, that he desist."

"But you did not quarrel?"

"No, and I confess I regret having been so hasty."

"Well then, I will arrange it. I shall go see him—
agreed?" said Des Hermies.

"By all means."

"With that we must run along and give you a chance to
get to bed, seeing that you have to be up at dawn."

"Oh, at half-past five for the six o'clock angelus, and
then, if I want to, I can go back to bed, for I don't have to
ring again till a quarter to eight, and then all I have to
do is sound a couple of times for the curate's mass. As you
can see, I have a pretty easy thing of it."

"Mmmm!" exclaimed Durtal, "if I had to get up so
early!"

"It's all a matter of habit. But before you go won't you
have another little drink? No? Really? Well, good
night!"

He lighted his lantern, and in single file, shivering, they
descended the glacial, pitch-dark, winding stair.

CHAPTER VI

Next morning Durtal woke later than usual. Before he opened his eyes there was a sudden flash of light in his brain, and troops of demon worshippers, like the societies of which Des Hermies had spoken, went defiling past him, dancing a saraband. "A swarm of lady acrobats hanging head downward from trapezes and praying with joined feet!" he said, yawning. He looked at the window. The panes were flowered with crystal fleurs de lys and frost ferns. Then he quickly drew his arms back under the covers and snuggled up luxuriously.

"A fine day to stay at home and work," he said. "I will get up and light a fire. Come now, a little courage—" and—instead of tossing the covers aside he drew them up around his chin.

"Ah, I know that you are not pleased to see me taking a morning off," he said, addressing his cat, which was hunched up on the counterpane at his feet, gazing at him fixedly, its eyes very black.

This beast, though affectionate and fond of being caressed, was crabbed and set in its ways. It would tolerate no whims, no departures from the regular course of things. It understood that there was a fixed hour for rising and for going to bed, and when it was displeased it allowed a shade of annoyance to pass into its eyes, the sense of which its master could not mistake.

If he returned before eleven at night, the cat was waiting for him in the vestibule, scratching the wood of the door, miaouing, even before Durtal was in the hall; then it rolled its languorous green-golden eyes at him, rubbed against his trouser leg, stood up on its hind feet like a tiny rearing horse and affectionately wagged its head at him as he approached. If eleven o'clock had passed it did not run along in front of him, but would only, very grudgingly, rise when he came up, and then it would arch its back and suffer no caresses. When he came later yet, it would not budge, and would complain and groan if he took the liberty of stroking its head or scratching its throat.

This morning it had no patience with Durtal's laziness. It squatted on its hunkers, and swelled up, then it approached stealthily and sat down two steps away from its master's face, staring at him with an atrociously false eye, signifying that the time had come for him to abdicate and leave the warm place for a cold cat.

Amused by its manœuvres, Durtal did not move, but returned its stare. The cat was enormous, common, and yet bizarre with its rusty coat yellowish like old coke ashes and grey as the fuzz on a new broom, with little white tufts like the fleece which flies up from the burnt-out faggot. It was a genuine gutter cat, long-legged, with a wild-beast head. It was regularly striped with waving lines of ebony, its paws were encircled by black bracelets and its eyes lengthened by two great zigzags of ink.

"In spite of your kill-joy character and your single track mind you testy, old bachelor, you are a very nice cat," said Durtal, in an insinuating, wheedling tone. "Then too, for many years now, I have told you what one tells no man. You are the drain pipe of my soul, you inattentive and indulgent confessor. Never shocked, you vaguely approve the mental misdeeds which I confess to you. You let me relieve myself and you don't charge me anything for the service. Frankly, that is what you are here for. I spoil you with care and attentions because you are the spiritual vent of solitude and celibacy, but that doesn't prevent you, with your spiteful way of looking at me, from being insufferable at times, as you are today, for instance!"

The cat continued to stare at him, its ears sticking straight up as if they would catch the sense of his words from the inflections of his voice. It understood, doubtless, that Durtal was not disposed to jump out of bed, for it went back to its old place, but now turned its back full on him.

"Oh come," said Durtal, discouraged, looking at his watch, "I've simply got to get up and go to work on Gilles de Rais," and with a bound he sprang into his trousers. The cat, rising suddenly, galloped across the counterpane and rolled itself up into the warm covers, without waiting an instant longer.

"How cold it is!" and Durtal slipped on a knit jacket and went into the other room to start a fire. "I shall freeze!" he murmured.

Fortunately his apartment was easy to heat. It consisted simply of a hall, a tiny sitting-room, a minute bedroom, and a large enough bathroom. It was on the fifth floor, facing a sufficiently airy court. Rent, eight hundred francs.

It was furnished without luxury. The little sitting-room Durtal had converted into a study, hiding the walls behind black wood bookcases crammed with books. In front of the window were a great table, a leather armchair, and a few straight chairs. He had removed the glass from the mantelpiece, and in the panel, just over the mantelshelf, which was covered with an old fabric, he had nailed an antique painting on wood, representing a hermit kneeling beside a cardinal's hat and purple cloak, beneath a hut of boughs. The colours of the landscape background had faded, the blues to grey, the whites to russet, the greens to black, and time had darkened the shadows to a burnt-onion hue. Along the edges of the picture, almost against the black oak frame, a continuous narrative unfolded in unintelligible episodes, intruding one upon the other, portraying Lilliputian figures, in houses of dwarfs. Here the Saint, whose name Durtal had sought in vain, crossed a curly, wooden sea in a sailboat; there he marched through a village as big as a fingernail; then he disappeared into the shadows of the painting and was discovered higher up in a grotto in the Orient, surrounded by dromedaries and bales of merchandise; again he was lost from sight, and after another game of hide-and-seek he emerged, smaller than ever, quite alone, with a staff in his hand and a knapsack on his back, mounting toward a strange, unfinished cathedral.

It was a picture by an unknown painter, an old Dutchman, who had perhaps visited certain of the Italian masters, for he had appropriated colours and processes peculiar to them.

The bedroom contained a big bed, a chest of drawers waist-high, and some easy chairs. On the mantel were an antique clock and copper candlesticks. On the wall there was a fine photograph of a Botticelli in the Berlin museum, representing a plump and penitent Virgin who was like a housewife in tears. She was surrounded by gentleman-, lady-, and little-boy-angels. The languishing young men held spliced wax tapers that were like bits of rope; the coquettish hoydens had flowers stuck in their long hair; and the mischievous cherub-pages looked rapturously at the infant Jesus, who stood beside the Virgin and held out his hands in benediction.

Then there was a print of Breughel, engraved by Cock, "The wise and the foolish virgins": a little panel, cut in the middle by a corkscrew cloud which was flanked at each side by angels with their sleeves rolled up and their cheeks puffed out, sounding the trumpet, while in the middle of the cloud another angel, bizarre and sacerdotal, with his navel indicated beneath his languorously flowing robe, unrolled a banderole on which was written the verse of the Gospel, *"Ecce sponsus venit, exite obviam ei."*

Beneath the cloud, at one side, sat the wise virgins, good Flemings, with their lighted lamps, and sang canticles as they turned the spinning wheel. At the other side were the foolish virgins with their empty lamps. Four joyous gossips were holding hands and dancing in a ring on the greensward, while the fifth played the bagpipe and beat time with her foot. Above the cloud the five wise virgins, slender and

ethereal now, naked and charming, brandished flaming
tapers and mounted toward a Gothic church where Christ
stood to welcome them; while on the other side the foolish
virgins, imperfectly draped, beat vainly on a closed door with
their dead torches.

The blessed naïveté of the Primitives, the homely touches
in the scenes of earth and of heaven! Durtal loved this
old engraving. He saw in it a union of the art of an Ostade
purified and that of a Thierry Bouts.

Waiting for his grate, in which the charcoal was crackling
and peeling and running like frying grease, to become red,
he sat down in front of his desk and ran over his notes.

"Let's see," he said to himself, rolling a cigarette, "we
had come to the time when that excellent Gilles de Rais begins the quest of the 'great work.' It is easy to figure what
knowledge he possessed about the method of transmuting
metals into gold.

"Alchemy was already highly developed a century before
he was born. The writings of Albertus Magnus, Arnaud
de Villeneuve, and Raymond Lully were in the hands of the
hermetics. The manuscripts of Nicolas Flamel circulated,
and there is no doubt that Gilles had acquired them, for he
was an avid collector of the rare. Let us add that at that
epoch the edict of Charles interdicting spagyric labours under
pain of prison and hanging, and the bull, *Spondent pariter
quas non exhibent,* which Pope John XXII fulminated
against the alchemists, were still in vigour. These treatises
were, then, forbidden, and in consequence desirable. It is
certain that Gilles had long studied them, but from that to
understanding them is a far cry.

"For they were written in an impossible jargon of alle-
gories, twisted and obscure metaphors, incoherent symbols,
ambiguous parables, enigmas, and ciphers. And here is an
example." He took from one of the shelves of the library
a manuscript which was none other than the Asch-
Mezareph, the book of the Jew Abraham and of Nicolas
Flamel, restored, translated, and annotated by Eliphas Levi.

This manuscript had been lent him by Des Hermies, who had discovered it one day among some old papers.

"In this is what claims to be the recipe for the philosopher's stone, for the grand quintessential and tinctural essence. The figures are not precisely clear," he said to himself, as he ran his eye over the pen drawings, retouched in colour, representing, under the title of *"The chemical coitus,"* various bottles and flasks each containing a liquid and imprisoning an allegorical creature. A green lion, with a crescent moon over him, hung head downward. Doves were trying to fly out through the neck of the bottle or to peck a way through the bottom. The liquid was black and undulated with waves of carmine and gold, or white and granulated with dots of ink, which sometimes took the shape of a frog or a star. Sometimes the liquid was milky and troubled, sometimes flames rose from it as if there were a film of alcohol over the surface.

Eliphas Levi explained the symbolism of these bottled volatiles as fully as he cared to, but abstained from giving the famous recipe for the grand magisterium. He was keeping up the pleasantry of his other books, in which, beginning with an air of solemnity, he affirmed his intention of unveiling the old arcana, and, when the time came to fulfil his promise, begged the question, alleging the excuse that he would perish if he betrayed such burning secrets. The same excuse, which had done duty through the ages, served in masking the perfect ignorance of the cheap occultists of the present day.

"As a matter of fact, the 'great work' is simple," said Durtal to himself, folding up the manuscript of Nicolas Flamel. "The hermetic philosophers discovered—and modern science, after long evading the issue, no longer denies—that the metals are compounds, and that their components are identical. They vary from each other according to the different proportions of their elements. With the aid of an agent which will displace these proportions one may transmute mercury, for example, into silver, and lead into gold.

"And this agent is the philosopher's stone: mercury—not the vulgar mercury, which to the alchemists was but an aborted metallic sperm—but the philosophers' mercury, called also the green lion, the serpent, the milk of the Virgin, the pontic water.

"Only the recipe for this mercury, or stone of the sages, has ever been revealed—and it is this that the philosophers of the Middle Ages, the Renaissance, all centuries, including our own, have sought so frantically.

"And in what has it not been sought?" said Durtal, thumbing his notes. "In arsenic, in ordinary mercury, tin, salts of vitriol, saltpetre and nitre; in the juices of spurge, poppy, and purslane; in the bellies of starved toads; in human urine, in the menstrual fluid and the milk of women."

Now Gilles de Rais must have been completely baffled. Alone at Tiffauges, without the aid of initiates, he was incapable of making fruitful experiments. At that time Paris was the centre of the hermetic science in France. The alchemists gathered under the vaults of Notre Dame and studied the hieroglyphics which Nicolas Flamel, before he died, had written on the walls of the charnal Des Innocents and on the portal of Saint Jacques de la Boucherie, describing cabalistically the preparation of the famous stone.

The Marshal could not go to Paris because the English soldiers barred the roads. There was only one thing to do. He wrote to the most celebrated of the southern transmuters, and had them brought to Tiffauges at great expense.

"From documents which we posses we can see his supervising the construction of the athanor, or alchemists' furnace, buying pelicans, crucibles, and retorts. He turned one of the wings of his château into a laboratory and shut himself up in it with Antonio di Palermo, François Lombard, and 'Jean Petit, goldsmith of Paris,' all of whom busied themselves night and day with the concoction of the 'great work.' "

They were completely unsuccessful. At the end of their resources, these hermetists disappeared, and there ensued at

Tiffauges an incredible coming-and-going of adepts and their helpers. They arrived from all parts of Brittany, Poitou, and Maine, alone or escorted by promoters and sorcerers. Gilles de Sillé and Roger de Bricqueville, cousins and friends of the Marshal, scurried about the country, beating up the game and driving it in to Gilles de Rais, while a priest of his chapel, Eustache Blanchet, went to Italy where workers in metals were legion.

While waiting, Gilles de Rais, not to be discouraged, continued his experiments, all of which missed fire. He finally came to believe that the magicians were right after all, and that no discovery was possible without the aid of Satan.

And one night, with a sorcerer newly arrived from Poitiers, Jean de la Rivière, he betakes himself to a forest in the vicinity of the château de Tiffauges. With his servitors Henriet and Poitou, he remains on the verge of the wood into which the sorcerer penetrates. The night is heavy and there is no moon. Gilles becomes nervous, scrutinizing the shadows, listening to the muted sounds of the nocturnal landscape; his companions, terrified, huddle close together, trembling and whispering at the slightest stirring of the air. Suddenly a cry of anguish is raised. They hesitate, then they advance, groping in the darkness. In a sudden flare of light they perceive de la Rivière trembling and deathly pale, clutching the handle of his lantern convulsively. In a low voice he recounts how the Devil has risen in the form of a leopard and rushed past without looking at the evocator, without saying a word.

The next day the sorcerer vanished, but another arrived. This was a bungler named Du Mesnil. He required Gilles to sign with blood a deed binding him to give the Devil all the Devil asked of him "except his life and soul," but, although to aid the conjurements Gilles consented to have the Office of the Damned sung in his chapel on All Saints' Day, Satan did not appear.

The Marshal was beginning to doubt the powers of his

magicians, when the outcome of a new endeavor convinced him that frequently the Devil does appear.

An evocator whose name has been lost held a séance with Gilles and de Sillé in a chamber at Tiffauges.

On the ground he traces a great circle and commands his two companions to step inside it. Sillé refuses. Gripped by a terror which he cannot explain, he begins to tremble all over. He goes to the window, opens it, and stands ready for flight, murmuring exorcisms under his breath. Gilles, bolder, stands in the middle of the circle, but at the first conjurations he too trembles and tries to make the sign of the cross. The sorcerer orders him not to budge. At one moment he feels something seize him by the neck. Panic-stricken, he vacillates, supplicating Our Lady to save him. The evocator, furious, throws him out of the circle. Gilles precipitates himself through the door, de Sillé jumps out of the window, they meet below and stand aghast. Howls are heard in the chamber where the magician is operating. There is "a sound as of sword strokes raining on a wooden billet," then groans, cries of distress, the appeals of a man being assassinated.

They stand rooted to the spot. When the clamours ceases they venture to open the door and find the sorcerer lying in pools of blood, his forehead caved in, his body horribly mangled.

They carry him out. Gilles, smitten with remorse, gives the man his own bed, bandages him, and has him confessed. For several days the sorcerer hovers between life and death but finally recovers and flees from the castle.

Gilles was despairing of obtaining from the Devil the recipe for the sovereign magisterium, when Eustache Blanchet's return from Italy was announced. Eustache brought the master of Florentine magic, the irresistible evoker of demons and larvæ, Francesco Prelati.

This man struck awe into Gilles. Barely twenty-three years old, he was one of the wittiest, the most erudite, and the most polished men of the time. What had he done before he came to install himself at Tiffauges, there to begin, with Gilles, the most frightful series of sins against the Holy Ghost that has ever been known? His testimony in the criminal trial of Gilles does not furnish us any very detailed information on his own score. He was born in the diocese of Lucca, at Pistoia, and had been ordained a priest by the Bishop of Arezzo. Some time after his entrance into the priesthood, he had become the pupil of a thaumaturge of Florence, Jean de Fontenelle, and had signed a pact with a demon named Barron. From that moment onward, this insinuating and persuasive, learned and charming abbé, must have given himself over to the most abominable of sacrileges and the most murderous practices of black magic.

At any rate Gilles came completely under the influence of this man. The extinguished furnaces were relighted, and that Stone of the Sages, which Prelati had seen, flexible, frail, red and smelling of calcinated marine salt, they sought together furiously, invoking Hell.

Their incantations were all in vain. Gilles, disconsolate, redoubled them, but they finally produced a dreadful result and Prelati narrowly escaped with his life.

One afternoon Eustache Blanchet, in a gallery of the château, perceives the Marshal weeping bitterly. Plaints of supplication are heard through the door of a chamber in which Prelati has been evoking the Devil.

"The Demon is in there beating my poor Francis. I implore you, go in!" cries Gilles, but Blanchet, frightened, refuses. Then Gilles makes up his mind, in spite of his fear. He is advancing to force the door, when it opens and Prelati staggers out and falls, bleeding, into his arms. Prelati is able, with the support of his friends, to gain the chamber of the Marshal, where he is put to bed, but he has sustained so merciless a thrashing that he goes into delirium and his fever keeps mounting. Gilles, in despair, stays beside him, cares for him, has him confessed, and weeps for joy when Prelati is out of danger.

"The fate of the unknown sorcerer and of Prelati, both getting dangerously wounded in an empty room, under identical circumstances—I tell you, it's a remarkable coincidence," said Durtal to himself.

"And the documents which relate these facts are authentic. They are, indeed, excerpts from the procedure in Gilles's trial. The confessions of the accused and the depositions of the witnesses agree, and it is impossible to think that Gilles and Prelati lied, for in confessing these Satanic evocations they condemned themselves, by their own words, to be burned alive.

"If in addition they had declared that the Evil One had appeared to them, that they had been visited by succubi; if they had affirmed that they had heard voices, smelled odours, even touched a body; we might conclude that they had had hallucinations similar to those of certain Bicêtre subjects, but as it was there could have been no misfunctioning of the senses, no morbid visions, because the wounds, the marks of the blows, the material fact, visible and tangible, are present for testimony.

"Imagine how thoroughly convinced of the reality of the Devil a mystic like Gilles de Rais must have been after witnessing such scenes!

"In spite of his discomfitures, he could not doubt—and Prelati, half-killed, must have doubted even less—that if Satan pleased, they should finally find this powder which would load them with riches and even render them almost immortal—for at that epoch the philosopher's stone passed not only for an agent in the transmutation of base metals, such as tin, lead, copper, into noble metals like silver and gold, but also for a panacea curing all ailments and prolonging life, without infirmities, beyond the limits formerly assigned to the patriarchs.

"Singular science," ruminated Durtal, raising the fender of his fireplace and warming his feet, "in spite of the railleries of this time, which, in the matter of discoveries but exhumes lost things, the hermetic philosophy was not wholly vain.

"The master of contemporary science, Dumas, recognizes, under the name of isomery, the theories of the alchemists, and Berthelot declares, 'No one can affirm *a priori* that the fabrication of bodies reputed to be simple is impossible.' Then there have been verified and certified achievements. Besides Nicolas Flamel, who really seems to have succeeded in the 'great work,' the chemist Van Helmont, in the eighteenth century, received from an unknown man a quarter of a grain of philosopher's stone and with it transformed eight ounces of mercury into gold.

"At the same epoch, Helvetius, who combated the dogma of the spagyrics, received from another unknown a powder of projection with which he converted an ingot of lead into gold. Helvetius was not precisely a charlatan, neither was Spinoza, who verified the experiment, a credulous simpleton.

"And what is to be thought of that mysterious man Alexander Sethon who, under the name of the Cosmopolite, went all over Europe, operating before princes, in public, transforming all metals into gold? This alchemist, who seems to have had a sincere disdain for riches, as he never kept the gold which he created, but lived in poverty and prayer, was imprisoned by Christian II, Elector of Saxony, and endured martyrdom like a saint. He suffered himself to be beaten with rods and pierced with pointed stakes, and he refused to give up a secret which he claimed, like Nicolas Flamel, to have received from God.

"And to think that these researches are being carried on at the present time! Only, most of the hermetics now deny medical and divine virtues to the famous stone. They think simply that the grand magisterium is a ferment, which, thrown into metals in fusion, produces a molecular transformation similar to that which organic matter undergoes when fermented with the aid of a leaven.

"Des Hermies, who is well acquainted with the underworld of science, maintains that more than forty alchemic furnaces are now alight in France, and that in Hanover and Bavaria the adepts are more numerous yet.

"Have they rediscovered the incomparable secret of antiquity? In spite of certain affirmations, it is hardly probable. Nobody need manufacture artificially a metal whose origins are so unaccountable that a deposit is likely to be found anywhere. For instance, in a law suit which took place at Paris in the month of November, 1886, between M. Popp, constructor of pneumatic city clocks, and financiers who had been backing him, certain engineers and chemists of the School of Mines declared that gold could be extracted from common silex, so that the very walls sheltering us might be placers, and the mansards might be loaded with nuggets!

"At any rate," he continued, smiling, "these sciences are not propitious."

He was thinking of an old man who had installed an alchemic laboratory on the fifth floor of a house in the rue Saint Jacques. This man, named Auguste Redoutez, went every afternoon to the Bibliothèque Nationale and pored over the works of Nicolas Flamel. Morning and evening he pursued the quest of the "great work" in front of his furnace.

The 16th of March the year before, he came out of the Bibliothèque with a man who had been sitting at the same table with him, and as they walked along together Redoutez declared that he was finally in possession of the famous secret. Arriving in his laboratory, he threw pieces of iron into a retort, made a projection, and obtained crystals the colour of blood. The other examined the salts and made a flippant remark. The alchemist, furious, threw himself upon him, struck him with a hammer, and had to be overpowered and carried in a strait-jacket to Saint Anne, pending investigation.

"In the sixteenth century, in Luxemburg, initiates were roasted in iron cages. The following century, in Germany, they were clothed in rags and hanged on gilded gibbets.

Now that they are tolerated and left in peace they go mad. Decidedly, fate is against them," Durtal concluded.

He rose and went to answer a ring at the door. He came back with a letter which the concierge had brought. He opened it.

"Why, what is this?" he exclaimed. His astonishment grew as he read:

"Monsieur,

"I am neither an adventuress nor a seeker of adventures, nor am I a society woman grown weary of drawing-room conversation. Even less am I moved by the vulgar curiosity to find out whether an author is the same in the flesh as he is in his books. Indeed I am none of the things which you may think I am, from my writing to you this way. The fact is that I have just finished reading your last book,"

"She has taken her time," murmured Durtal, "it appeared a year ago."

"melancholy as an imprisoned soul vainly beating its wings against the bars of its cage."

"Oh, hell! What a compliment. Anyway, it rings false, like all of them."

"And now, Monsieur, though I am convinced that it is always folly and madness to try to realize a desire, will you permit that a sister in lassitude meet you some evening in a place which you shall designate, after which we shall return, each of us, into our own interior, the interior of persons destined to fall because they are out of line with their 'fellows'? Adieu, Monsieur, be assured that I consider you a somebody in a century of nobodies.

"Not knowing whether this note will elicit a reply, I abstain from making myself known. This evening a maid will call upon your concierge and ask him if there is a letter for Mme. Maubel."

"Hmm!" said Durtal, folding up the letter. "I know her. She must be one of these withered dames who are always trying to cash outlawed kiss-tickets and soul-warrants in the lottery of love. Forty-five years old at least. Her clientele is composed of boys, who are always satisfied if they don't have to pay, and men of letters, who are yet more easily satisfied—for the ugliness of authors' mistresses is proverbial. Unless this is simply a practical joke. But who would be playing one on me—I don't know anybody—and why?"

In any case, he would simply not reply.

But in spite of himself he reopened the letter.

"Well now, what do I risk? If this woman wants to sell me an over-ripe heart, there is nothing forcing me to purchase it. I don't commit myself to anything by going to an assignation. But where shall I meet her? Here? No! Once she gets into my apartment complications arise, for it is much more difficult to throw a woman out of your house than simply to walk off and leave her at a street corner. Suppose I designated the corner of the rue de Sèvres and the rue de la Chaise, under the wall of the Abbaye-au-Bois. It is solitary, and then, too, it is only a minute's walk from here. Or no, I will begin vaguely, naming no meeting-place at all. I shall solve that problem later, when I get her reply."

He wrote a letter in which he spoke of his own spiritual lassitude and declared that no good could come of an interview, for he no longer sought happiness on earth.

"I will add that I am in poor health. That is always a good one, and it excuses a man from 'being a man' if necessary," he said to himself, rolling a cigarette.

"Well, that's done, and she won't get much encouragement out of it. Oh, wait. I omitted something. To keep from giving her a hold on me I shall do well to let her know that a serious and sustained liaison with me is impossible 'for family reasons.' And that's enough for one time."

He folded the letter and scrawled the address.

Then he held the sealed envelope in his hand and reflected.

"Of course I am a fool to answer her. Who knows what situations a thing like this is going to lead to? I am well aware that whoever she be, a woman is an incubator of sorrow and annoyance. If she is good she is probably stupid, or perhaps she is an invalid, or perhaps she is so disastrously fecund that she gets pregnant if you look at her. If she is bad, one may expect to be dragged through every disgusting kind of degradation. Oh, whatever you do, you're in for it."

He regurgitated the memories of his youthful amours. Deception. Disenchantment. How pitilessly base a woman is while she is young!

". . . To be thinking of things like that now at my age! As if I had any need of a woman now!"

But in spite of all, his pseudonymous correspondent interested him.

"Who knows? Perhaps she is good-looking, or at least not very ill-looking. It doesn't cost me anything to find out."

He re-read her letter. No misspelling. The handwriting not commercial. Her ideas about his book were mediocre enough, but who would expect her to be a critic? "Discreet scent of heliotrope," he added, sniffing the envelope.

"Oh, well, let's have our little fling."

And as he went out to get some breakfast he left his reply with the concierge.

CHAPTER VII

"If this continues I shall lose my mind," murmured Durtal as he sat in front of his table reperusing the letters which he had been receiving from that woman for the last week. She was an indefatigable letter-writer, and since she had begun her advances he had not had time to answer one letter before another arrived.

"My!" he said, "let's try and see just where we do stand. After that ungracious answer to her first note she immediately sends me this:

" 'Monsieur,

" 'This is a farewell. If I were weak enough to write you any more letters they would become as tedious as the life I lead. Anyway, have I not had the best part of you, in that hesitant letter of yours which shook me out of my lethargy for an instant? Like yourself, monsieur, I know, alas! that nothing happens, and that our only certain joys are those we dream of. So, in spite of my feverish desire to know you, I fear that you were right in saying that a meeting would be for both of us the source of regrets to which we ought not voluntarily expose ourselves. . . .'

"Then what bears witness to the perfect futility of this exordium is the way the missive ends:

" 'If you should take the fancy to write me, you can safely address your letters "Mme. Maubel, rue Littré, general delivery." I shall be passing the rue Littré post-office Monday. If you wish to let matters remain just where they are—and thus cause me a great deal of pain—will you not tell me so, frankly?'

"Whereupon I was simple-minded enough to compose an epistle as ambiguous as the first, concealing my furtive advances under an apparent reluctance, thus letting her know that I was securely hooked. As her third note proves:

" 'Never accuse yourself, monsieur—I repress a tenderer name which rises to my lips—of being unable to give me consolation. Weary, disabused, as we are, and done with it all, let us sometimes permit our souls to speak to each other—low, very low—as I have spoken to you this night, for henceforth my thought is going to follow you wherever you are.'

"Four pages of the same tune," he said, turning the leaves, "but this is better:

" 'Tonight, my unknown friend, one word only. I have passed a horrible day, my nerves in revolt and crying out against the petty sufferings they are subjected to every minute. A slamming door, a harsh or squeaky voice floating up to me out of the street. . . . Yet there are whole hours when I am so far from being sensitive that if the house were burning I should not move. Am I about to send you a page of comic lamentations? Ah, when one has not the gift of rendering one's grief superbly and transforming it into literary or musical passages which weep magnificently, the best thing is to keep still about it.

" 'I bid you a silent goodnight. As on the first day, I am harassed by the conflict of the desire to see you and the dread of touching a dream lest it perish. Ah, yes, you spoke truly. Miserable, miserable wretches that we are, our timorous souls are so afraid of any reality that they dare not think a sympathy which has taken possession of them capable of surviving an interview with the person who gave it birth. Yet, in spite of this fine casuistry, I simply must confess to you—no, no, nothing. Guess if you can, and forgive me for this banal letter. Or rather, read between the lines, and perhaps you will find there a little bit of my heart and a great deal of what I leave unsaid.

"'A foolish letter with "I" written all over it. Who would suspect that while I wrote it my sole thought was of You?'"

"So far, so good. This woman at least piqued my curiosity. And what peculiar ink," he thought. It was myrtle green, very thin, very pale. With his finger-nail he detached some of the fine dust of rice powder, perfumed with heliotrope, clinging to the seal of the letters.

"She must be blonde," he went on, examining the tint of the powder, "for it isn't the 'Rachel' shade that brunettes use. Now up to that point everything had been going nicely, but then and there I spoiled it. Moved by I know not what folly, I wrote her a yet more roundabout letter, which, however, was very pressing. In attempting to fan her flame I kindled myself—for a spectre—and at once I received this:

"'What shall I do? I neither wish to see you, nor can I consent to annihilate my overwhelming desire to meet you. Last night, in spite of me, your name, which was burning me, sprang from my lips. My husband, one of your admirers, it seems, appeared to be somewhat humiliated by the preoccupation which, indeed, was absorbing me and causing unbearable shivers to run all through me. A common friend of yours and mine—for why should I not tell you that you know me, if to have met socially is to "know" anyone?—one of your friends, then, came up and said that frankly he was very much taken with you. I was in a state of such utter lack of self-control that I don't know what I should have done had it not been for the unwitting assistance which somebody gave me by pronouncing the name of a grotesque person of whom I can never think without laughing. Adieu. You are right. I tell myself that I will never write you again, and I go and do it anyway.

" 'Your own—as I cannot be in reality without wounding us both.'

"Then when I wrote a burning reply, this was brought by a maid on a dead run:

" 'Ah, if I were not afraid, afraid!—and you know you are just as much afraid as I am—how I should fly to you! No, you cannot hear the thousand conversations with which my soul fatigues yours. . . . Oh, in my miserable existence there are hours when madness seizes me. Judge for yourself. The whole night I spent appealing to you furiously. I wept with exasperation. This morning my husband came into the room. My eyes were bloodshot. I began to laugh crazily, and when I could speak I said to him, "What would you think of a person who, questioned as to his profession, replied, 'I am a chamber succubus'?" "Ah, my dear, you are ill," said he. "Worse than you think," said I.

" 'But if I come to see you, what could we talk about, in the state you yourself are in?' Your letter has completely unbalanced me. You arraign your malady with a certain brutality which makes my body rejoice but alienates my soul a little. Ah, what if our dreams could really come true!

" 'Ah, say a word, just one word, from out your own heart. Don't be afraid that even one of your letters can possibly fall into other hands than mine.'

"So, so, so. This is getting to be no laughing matter," concluded Durtal, folding up the letter. "The woman is married to a man who knows me, it seems. What a situation! Let's see, now. Whom have I ever visited?" He tried vainly to remember. No woman he had ever met at an evening party would address such declarations to him. And that common friend. "But I have no friends, except Des Hermies. I'd better try and find out whom he has been seeing recently. But as a physician he meets scores of people! And then, how can I explain to him? Tell him the story? He will burst into a roar and disillusion me before I have got halfway through the narrative."

And Durtal became irritated, for within him a really incomprehensible phenomenon was taking place. He was burning for this unknown woman. He was positively obsessed by her. He who had renounced all carnal relations years ago, who, when the barns of his senses were opened, contented himself with driving the disgusting herd of sin to the commercial shambles to be summarily knocked in the head by the butcher girls of love, he, he! was getting himself to believe—in the teeth of all experience, in the teeth of good judgment—that with a woman as passionate as this one seemed to be, he would experience superhuman sensations and novel abandon.

And he imagined her as he would have her, blonde, firm of flesh, lithe, feline, melancholy, capable of frenzies; and the picture of her brought on such a tension of nerves that his teeth rattled.

For a week, in the solitude in which he lived, he had dreamed of her and had become thoroughly aroused and incapable of doing any work, even of reading, for the image of this woman interposed itself between him and the page.

He tried suggesting to himself ignoble visions. He would imagine this creature in moments of corporal distress and thus calm his desires with unappetizing hallucinations; but the procedure which had formerly been very effective when he desired a woman and could not have her now failed utterly. He somehow could not imagine his unknown in quest of bismuth or of linen. He could not see her otherwise than rebellious, melancholy, dizzy with desire, kindling him with her eyes, inflaming him with her pale hands.

And his sensual resurrection was incredible—an aberrated Dog Star flaming in a physical November, at a spiritual All Hallows. Tranquil, dried up, safe from crises, without veritable desires, almost impotent, or rather completely forgetful of sex for months at a time, he was suddenly roused—and for an unreality!—by the mystery of mad letters.

"Enough!" he cried, smiting the table a jarring blow.

He clapped on his hat and went out, slamming the door behind him.

"I know how to make my imagination behave!" and he rushed over to the Latin Quarter to see a prostitute he knew. "I have been a good boy too long," he murmured as he hurried down the street. "One can't stay on the straight and narrow path for ever."

He found the woman at home and had a miserable time. She was a buxom brunette with festive eyes and the teeth of a wolf. An expert, she could, in a few seconds, drain one's marrow, granulate the lungs, and demolish the loins.

She chid him for having been away so long, then cajoled him and kissed him. He felt pathetic, listless, out of breath, out of place, for he had no genuine desires. He finally flung himself on a couch and, enervated to the point of crying, he went through the back-breaking motions mechanically, like a dredge.

Never had he so execrated the flesh, never had he felt such repugnance and lassitude, as when he issued from that room. He strolled haphazard down the rue Soufflot, and the image of the unknown obsessed him, more irritating, more tenacious.

"I begin to understand the superstition of the succubus. I must try some bromo-exorcism. Tonight I will swallow a gram of bromide of potassium. That will make my senses be good."

But he realized that the trouble was not primarily physical, that really it was only the consequence of an extraordinary state of mind. His love for that which departed from the formula, for that projection *out of the world* which had recently cheered him in art, had deviated and sought expression in a woman. She embodied his need to soar upward from the terrestrial humdrum.

"It is those precious unworldly studies, those cloister thoughts picturing ecclesiastical and demoniac scenes, which have prepared me for the present folly," he said to himself. His unsuspected, and hitherto unexpressed, mysticism, which had determined his choice of subject for his last work was now sending him out, in disorder, to seek new pains and pleasures.

As he walked along he recapitulated what he knew of the woman. She was married, blonde, in easy circumstances because she had her own sleeping quarters and a maid. She lived in the neighbourhood, because she went to the rue Littré post-office for her mail. Her name, supposing she had prefixed her own initial to the name of Maubel, was Henriette, Hortense, Honorine, Hubertine, or Hélène. What else? She must frequent the society of artists, because she had met him, and for years he had not been in a bourgeois drawing-room. She was some kind of a morbid Catholic, because that word succubus was unknown to the profane. That was all. Then there was her husband, who, gullible as he might be, must nevertheless suspect their liaison, since, by her own confession, she dissembled her obsession very badly.

"This is what I get for letting myself be carried away. For I, too, wrote at first to amuse myself with aphrodisiac statements. Then I ended by becoming completely hysterical. We have taken turns fanning smouldering ashes which now are blazing. It is too bad that we have both become inflamed at the same time—for her case must be the same as mine, to judge from the passionate letters she writes. What shall I do? Keep on tantalizing myself for a chimera? No! I'll bring matters to a head, see her, and if she is good-looking, sleep with her. I shall have peace, anyway."

He looked about him. Without knowing how he had

got there he found himself in the Jardin des Plantes. He oriented himself, remembered that there was a café on the side facing the quay, and went to find it.

He tried to control himself and write a letter at once ardent and firm, but the pen shook in his fingers. He wrote at a gallop, confessed that he regretted not having consented, at the outset, to the meeting she proposed, and, attempting to check himself, declared, "We must see each other. Think of the harm we are doing ourselves, teasing each other at a distance. Think of the remedy we have at hand, my poor darling, I implore you."

He must indicate a place of meeting. He hesitated. "Let me think," he said to himself. "I don't want her to alight at my place. Too dangerous. Then the best thing to do would be to offer her a glass of port and a biscuit and conduct her to Lavenue's, which is a hotel as well as a café. I will reserve a room. That will be less disgusting than an assignation house. Very well, then, let us put in place of the rue de la Chaise the waiting-room of the Gare Montparnasse. Sometimes it is quite empty. Well, that's done." He gummed the envelope and felt a kind of relief. "Ah! I was forgetting. Garçon! The Bottin de Paris."

He searched for the name Maubel, thinking that by some chance it might be her own. Of course it was hardly probable, but she seemed so imprudent that with her anything was to be expected. He might very easily have met a Mme. Maubel and forgotten her. He found a Maubé and a Maubec, but no Maubel. "Of course, that proves nothing," he said, closing the directory. He went out and threw his letter into the box. "The joker in this is the husband. But hell, I am not likely to take his wife away from him very long."

He had an idea of going home, but he realized that he would do no work, that alone he would relapse into daydream. "If I went up to Des Hermies's place. Yes, today was his consultation day, it's an idea."

He quickened his pace, came to the rue Madame, and rang at an entresol. The housekeeper opened the door.

"Ah, Monsieur Durtal, he is out, but he will be in soon. Will you wait?"

"But you are sure he is coming back?"

"Why, yes. He ought to be here now," she said, stirring the fire.

As soon as she had retired Durtal sat down, then, becoming bored, he went over and began browsing among the books which covered the wall as in his own place.

"Des Hermies certainly has some curious items," he murmured, opening a very old book. Here's a treatise written centuries ago to suit my case exactly. *Manuale exorcismorum.* Well, I'll be damned! It's a Plantin. And what does this manual have to recommend in the treatment of the possessed?

"Hmmm. Contains some quaint counter-spells. Here are some for energumens, for the bewitched; here are some against love-philtres and against the plague; against spells cast on comestibles; some, even, to keep butter and milk sweet. That isn't odd. The Devil entered into everything in the good old days. And what can this be?" In his hand he held two little volumes with crimson edges, bound in fawn-coloured calf. He opened them and looked at the title, *The anatomy of the mass,* by Pierre du Moulin, dated, Geneva, 1624. "Might prove interesting." He went to warm his feet, and hastily skimmed through one of the volumes. "Why!" he said, "it's mighty good."

On the page which he was reading was a discussion of the priesthood. The author affirmed that none might exercise the functions of the priesthood if he was not sound in body, or if any of his members had been amputated, and asking apropos of this, if a castrated man could be ordained a priest, he answered his own question, "No, unless he carries upon him, reduced to powder, the parts which are wanting." He added, however, that Cardinal Tolet did not admit this interpretation, which nevertheless had been universally adopted.

Durtal, amused, read on. Now du Moulin was debating with himself the point whether it was necessary to interdict abbés ravaged by lechery. And in answer he cited himself the melancholy glose of Canon Maximianus, who, in his Distinction 81, sighs, "It is commonly said that none ought to be deposed from his charge for fornication, in view of the fact that few can be found exempt from this vice."

"Why! You here?" said Des Hermies, entering. "What are you reading? *The anatomy of the mass?* Oh, it's a poor thing, for Protestants. I am just about distracted. Oh, my friend, what brutes those people are," and like a man with a great weight on his chest he unburdened himself.

"Yes, I have just come from a consultation with those whom the journals characterize as "princes of science.' For a quarter of an hour I have had to listen to the most contradictory opinions. On one point, however, all agreed: that my patient was a dead man. Finally they compromised and decided that the poor wretch's torture should be needlessly prolonged by a course of moxas. I timidly remarked that it would be simpler to send for a confessor, and then assuage the sufferings of the dying man with repeated injections of morphine. If you had seen their faces! They came as near as anything to denouncing me as a tout for the priests.

"And such is contemporary science. Everybody discovers a new or forgotten disease, and trumpets a forgotten or a new remedy, and nobody knows a thing! And then, too, what good does it do one not to be hopelessly ignorant since there is so much sophistication going on in pharmacy that no physician can be sure of having his prescriptions filled to the letter? One example among many: at present, sirup of white poppy, the diacodia of the old Codex, does not exist. It is manufactured with laudanum and sirup of sugar, as if they were the same thing!

"We have got so we no longer dose substances but prescribe ready-made remedies and use those surprising specifics which fill up the fourth pages of the journals. It's a compromise medicine, a democratic medicine, one cure for all cases. It's scandalous, it's silly.

"No, there is no use in talking. The old therapeutics based on experience was better than this. At least it knew that remedies ingested in pill, powder, or bolus form were treacherous, so it prescribed them only in the liquid state. Now, too, every physician specializes. The oculists see only the eyes, and, to cure them, quite calmly poison the body. With their pilocarpine they have ruined the health of how many people for ever! Others treat cutaneous affections. They drive an eczema inward on an old man who as soon as he is 'cured' becomes childish or dangerous. There is no more solidarity. Allegiance to one party means hostility to all others. Its a mess. Now my honourable conferères are stumbling around, taking a fancy to medicaments which they don't even know how to use. Take antipyrine, for example. It is one of the very few really active products that the chemists have found in a long time. Well, where is the doctor who knows that, applied in a compress with iodide and cold Bondonneau spring water, antipyrine combats the supposedly incurable ailment, cancer? And if that seems incredible, it is true, nevertheless."

"Honestly," said Durtal, "you believe that the old-time doctors came nearer healing?"

"Yes, because, miraculously, they know the effects of certain invariable remedies prepared without fraud. Of course it is self-evident that when old Paré eulogized 'sack medicine' and ordered his patients to carry pulverized medicaments in a little sack whose form varied according to the organ to be healed, assuming the form of a cap for the head, of a bagpipe for the stomach, of an ox tongue for the spleen, he probably did not obtain very signal results. His claim to have cured gastralgia by appositions of powder of red rose, coral and mastic, wormwood and mint, aniseed and nutmeg, is certainly not to be borne out, but he also had other systems, and often he cured, because he possessed the science of simples, which is now lost.

"The present-day physicians shrug their shoulders when the name of Ambrose Paré is mentioned. They used to pooh-pooh the idea of the alchemists that gold had medicinal virtue. Their fine scorn does not now prevent them from using alternate doses of the salts and of the filings of this metal. They use concentrated arseniate of gold against anemia, muriate against syphilis, cyanide against amenorrhea and scrofula, and chloride of sodium and gold against old ulcers. No, I assure you, it is disgusting to be a physician, for in spite of the fact that I am a doctor of science and have extensive hospital experience I am quite inferior to humble country herborists, solitaries, who know a great deal more than I about what is useful to know—and I admit it."

"And homeopathy?"

"It has some good things about it and some bad ones. It also palliates without curing. It sometimes represses maladies, but for grave and acute cases it is impotent, just like this Mattei system, which, however, is useful as an intermediary to stave off a crisis. With its blood- and lymph-purifying products, its antiscrofoloso, its angiotico, its anti-canceroso, it sometimes modifies morbid states in which other methods are of no avail. For instance, it permits a patient whose kidneys have been demoralized by iodide of potassium to gain time and recuperate so that he can safely begin to drink iodide again!

"I add that terrific shooting pains, which rebel even against chloroform and morphine, often yield to an application of 'green electricity.' You ask me, perhaps, of what ingredients this liquid electricity is made. I answer that I know absolutely nothing about it. Mattei claims that he has been able to fix in his globules and liquors the electrical properties of certain plants, but he has never given out his recipe, hence he can tell whatever stories suit him. What is curious, anyway, is that this system, thought out by a Roman count, a Catholic, has its most important following and propaganda among Protestant pastors, whose original asininity becomes abysmal in the unbelievable homilies which accompany their essays on healing. Indeed, considered seriously, these systems are a lot of wind. The truth is that in the art of healing we grope along at hazard. Nevertheless, with a little experience and a great deal of nerve we can manage so as not too shockingly to depopulate the cities. Enough of that, old man, and now where have you been keeping yourself?"

"Just what I was going to ask you. You haven't been to see me for over a week."

"Well, just now everybody in the world is ill and I am racing around all the time. By the way, I've been attending Chantelouve, who has a pretty serious attack of gout. He complains of your absence, and his wife, whom I should not have taken for an admirer of your books, of your last novel especially, speaks to me unceasingly of them and you. For a person customarily so reserved, she seems to me to have become quite enthusiastic about you, does Mme. Chantelouve. Why, what's the matter?" he exclaimed, seeing how red Durtal had become.

"Oh, nothing, but I've got to be going. Good night."

"Why, aren't you feeling well?"

"Oh, it's nothing, I assure you."

"Oh, well," said Des Hermies, knowing better than to insist. "Look at this," and took him into the kitchen and showed him a superb leg of mutton hanging beside the window. "I hung it up in a draft so as to get some of the crass freshness out of it. We'll eat it when we have the astrologer Gévingey to dine with us at Carhaix's. As I am the only person alive who knows how to boil a *gigot à l'Anglaise*, I am going to be the cook, so I shan't come by for you. You will find me in the tower, disguised as a scullery maid."

Once outside, Durtal took a long breath. Well, well,

his unknown was Chantelouve's wife. Impossible! She had never paid the slightest attention to him. She was silent and cold. Impossible! And yet, why had she spoken that way to Des Hermies? But surely if she had wanted to see him she would have come to his apartment, since they were acquaintances. She would not have started this correspondence under a pseudonym——

"H. de Maubel!" he said suddenly, "why, Mme. Chantelouve's name is Hyacinthe, a boy's name which suits her very well. She lives in the rue Babneux not vary far from the rue Littré post-office. She is a blonde, she has a maid, she is a fervent Catholic. She's the one."

And he experienced, almost simultaneously, two absolutely distinct sensations.

Of disappointment, first, for his unknown pleased him better. Mme. Chantelouve would never realize the ideal he had fashioned for himself, the tantalizing features, the agile, wild animal body, the melancholy and ardent bearing, which he had dreamed. Indeed, the mere fact of knowing the unknown rendered her less desirable, more vulgar. Accessibility killed the chimera.

At the same time he experienced a lively relief. He might have been dealing with a hideous old crone, and Hyacinthe, as he immediately began to call her, was desirable. Thirty-three at most, not pretty, but peculiar; blonde, slight and supple, with no hips, she seemed thin because she was small-boned. The face, mediocre, spoiled by too big a nose, but the lips incandescent, the teeth superb, her complexion ever so faint a rose in the slightly bluish milk white of rice water a little troubled.

Then her real charm, the really deceptive enigma of her, was in her eyes; ash-grey eyes which seemed uncertain, myopic, and which conveyed an expression of resigned boredom. At certain moments the pupils glowed like a gem of grey water and sparks of silver twinkled to the surface. By turns they were dolent, forsaken, languorous, and haughty. He remembered that those eyes had often brought his heart into his throat!

In spite of circumstantial evidence, he reflected that those impassioned letters did not correspond in any way to this woman in the flesh. Never was woman more controlled, more adept in the lies of good breeding. He remembered the Chantelouve at-homes. She seemed attentive, made no contribution to the conversation, played the hostess smiling, without animation. It was a kind of case of dual personality. In one visible phase a society woman, prudent and reserved, in another concealed phase a wild romantic, mad with passion, hysterical of body, nymphomaniac of soul. It hardly seemed probable.

"No," he said, "I am on the wrong track. It's merely by chance that Mme. Chantelouve spoke of my books to Des Hermies, and I mustn't jump to the conclusion that she is smitten with me and that she has been writing me these hot letters. It isn't she, but who on earth is it?"

He continued to revolve the question, without coming any nearer a solution. Again he called before his eyes the image of this woman, and admitted that she was really potently seductive, with a fresh, girlish body, flexible, and without a lot of repugnant flesh—and mysterious, with her concentrated air, her plaintive eyes, and even her coldness, real or feigned.

He summarized all that he really knew about her: simply that she was a widow when she married Chantelouve, that she had no children, that her first husband, a manufacturer of chasubles, had, for unknown reasons, committed suicide. That was all. On the other hand, too, too much was known about Chantelouve!

Author of a history of Poland and the cabinets of the north; of a history of Boniface VIII and his times; a life of the blessed Jeanne de Valois, founder of the Annonciade; a biography of the Venerable Mother Anne de Xaintonge, teacher of the Company of Saint Ursula; and other books of the same kind, published by Lecoffre, Palmé, Poussielgue, in the inevitable shagreen or sheep bindings stamped with dendriform patterns: Chantelouve was preparing his candidacy

for the Académie des Inscriptions et Belles-Lettres, and
hoped for the support of the party of the Ducs. That was
why he received influential hypocrites, provincial Tartufes,
and priests every week. He doubtless had to drive himself
to do this, because in spite of his slinking slyness he was
jovial and enjoyed a joke. On the other hand, he aspired to
figure in the literature that counts at Paris, and he expended
a good deal of ingenuity inveigling men of letters to his house
on another evening every week, to make them his aides, or
at least keep them from openly attacking him, so soon as his
candidacy—an entirely clerical affair—should be announced.
It was probably to attract and placate his adversaries that he
had contrived these baroque gatherings to which, out of curiosity as a matter of fact, the most utterly different kinds
of people came.

He had other motives. It was said that he had no
scruples about exploiting his social acquaintances. Durtal
had even noticed that at each of the dinners given by Chantelouve a well-dressed stranger was present, and the rumour
went about that this guest was a wealthy provincial to whom
men of letters were exhibited like a wax-work collection, and
from whom, before or afterward, important sums were borrowed.

"It is undeniable that the Chantelouves have no income
and that they live in style. Catholic publishing houses and
magazines pay even worse than the secular, so in spite of
his established reputation in the clerical world, Chantelouve
cannot possibly maintain such a standard of living on his
royalties.

"There simply is no telling what these people are up to.
That this woman's home life is unhappy, and that she does
not love the sneaky sacristan to whom she is married, is
quite possible, but what is her real rôle in that household?
Is she accessory to Chantelouve's pecuniary dodges? If that
is the case I don't see why she should pick on me. If she is
in connivance with her husband, she certainly ought to have
sense enough to seek an influential or wealthy lover, and she

is perfectly aware that I fulfil neither the one nor the other condition. Chantelouve knows very well that I am incapable of paying for her gowns and thus contributing to the upkeep of their establishment. I make about three thousand livres, and I can hardly contrive to keep myself going.

"So that is not her game. I don't know that I want to have anything to do with their kind of people," he concluded, somewhat chilled by these reflections. "But I am a big fool. What I know about them proves that my unknown beloved is not Chantelouve's wife, and, all things considered, I am glad she isn't."

CHAPTER VIII

Next day his ferment had subsided. The unknown never left him, but she kept her distance. Her less certain features were effaced in mist, her fascination became feebler, and she no longer was his sole preoccupation.

The idea, suddenly formed on a word of Des Hermies, that the unknown must be Chantelouve's wife, had, in fashion, checked his fever. If it was she—and his contrary conclusions of the evening before seemed hardly valid when he took up one by one the arguments by which he had arrived at them—then her reasons for wanting him were obscure, dangerous, and he was on his guard, no longer letting himself go in complete self-abandon.

And yet, there was another phenomenon taking place within him. He had never paid any especial attention to Hyacinthe Chantelouve, he had never been in love with her. She interested him by the mystery of her person and her life, but outside her drawing-room he had never given her a thought. Now ruminating about her he began almost to desire her.

Suddenly she benefited by the face of the unknown, for when Durtal evoked her she came confused to his sight, her physiognomy mingled with that which he had visualized when the first letters came.

Though the sneaking scoundrelism of her husband displeased him, he did not think her the less attractive, but his desires were no longer beyond control. In spite of the distrust which she aroused, she might be an interesting mistress, making up for her barefaced vices by her good grace, but she was no longer the non-existent, the chimera raised in a moment of uncertainty.

On the other hand, if his conjectures were false, if it was not Mme. Chantelouve who had written the letters, then the other, the unknown, lost a little of her subtlety by the mere fact that she could be incarnated in a creature whom he knew. Still remote, she became less so; then her beauty deteriorated, because, in turn, she took on certain features of Mme. Chantelouve, and if the latter had profited, the former, on the contrary, lost by the confusion which Durtal had established.

In one as in the other case, whether she were Mme. Chantelouve or not, he felt appeased, calmed. At heart he did not know, when he revolved the adventure, whether he preferred his chimera, even diminished, or this Hyacinthe, who at least, in her reality, was not a disenchanting frump, wrinkled with age. He profited by the respite to get back to work, but he had presumed too much upon his powers. When he tried to begin his chapter on the crimes of Gilles de Rais he discovered that he was incapable of sewing two sentences together. He wandered in pursuit of the Marshal and caught up with him, but the prose in which he wished to embody the man remained listless and lifeless, and he could think only patchily.

He threw down his pen and sank into an armchair. In revery he was transported to Tiffauges, where Satan, who had refused so obstinately to show himself, now became incarnate in the unwitting Marshal, to wallow him, vociferating, in the joys of murder.

"For this, basically, is what Satanism is," said Durtal to himself. "The external semblance of the Demon is a minor matter. He has no need of exhibiting himself in human or bestial form to attest his presence. For him to prove himself, it is enough that he choose a domicile in souls which he ulcerates and incites to inexplicable crimes. Then, he can hold his victims by that hope which he breathes into them, that instead of living in them as he does, and as they don't often know, he will obey evocations, appear to them, and deal out, duly, legally, the advantages he concedes in exchange for certain forfeits. Our very willingness to make a pact with him must be able often to produce his infusion into us.

"All the modern theories of the followers of Maudsley and Lombroso do not, in fact, render the singular abuses of the Marshal comprehensible. Nothing could be more just than to class him as a monomaniac, for he was one, if by the word monomaniac we designate every man who is dominated by a fixed idea. But so is every one of us, more or less, from the business man, all whose thoughts converge on the one idea of gain, to the artist absorbed in bringing his masterpiece into the world. But why was the Marshal a monomaniac, how did he become one? That is what all the Lombrosos in the world can't tell you. Encephalic lesions, adherence of the *pia mater* to the cerebrum, mean absolutely nothing in this question. For they are simple resultants, effects derived from a cause which ought to be explained, and which no materialist can explain. It is easy to declare that a disturbance of the cerebral lobes produces assassins and demonomaniacs. The famous alienists of our time claim that analysis of the brain of an insane woman disclosed a lesion or a deterioration of the grey matter. And suppose it did! It would still be a question whether, in the case of a woman possessed with demonomania, the lesion produced the demonomania, or the demonomania produced the lesion. . . . Admitting that there was a lesion! The spiritual Comprachicos have never resorted to cerebral surgery. They don't amputate the lobes—supposed to be reliably identified —after carefully trepanning. They simply act upon the pupil by inculcating ignoble ideas in him, developing his bad instincts, pushing him little by little into the paths of vice; and if this gymnastic of persuasion deteriorates the cerebral tissues in the subject, that proves precisely that the lesion is only the derivative and not the cause of the psychological state.

"And then, and then, these doctrines which consist nowadays in confounding the criminal with the insane, the demonomaniac with the mad, have absolutely no foundation. Nine years ago a lad of fourteen, Felix Lemaître, assassinated a little boy whom he did not know. He just wanted to see the child suffer, just wanted to hear him cry. Felix slashed the little fellow's stomach with a knife, turned the blade round and round in the warm flesh, then slowly sawed his victim's head off. Felix manifested no remorse, and in the ensuing investigation proved himself to be intelligent and atrocious. Dr. Legrand Du Saule and other specialists kept him under vigilant surveillance for months, and could not discover the slightest pathological symptom. And he had had fairly good rearing and certainly had not been corrupted by others.

"His behaviour was like that of the conscious or unconscious demonomaniacs who do evil for evil's sake. They are no more mad than the rapt monk in his cell, than the man who does good for good's sake. Anybody but a medical theorist can see that the desire for good and the desire for evil simply form the two opposing poles of the soul. In the fifteenth century these extremes were represented by Jeanne d'Arc and the Marshal de Rais. Now there is no more reason for attributing madness to Gilles than there is for attributing it to Jeanne d'Arc, whose admirable excesses certainly have no connection with vesania and delirium.

"All the same, some frightful nights must have been passed in that fortress," said Durtal. He was thinking of the château de Tiffauges, which he had visited a year ago, believing that it would aid him in his work to live in the country where Gilles had lived and to dig among the ruins.

He had established himself in the little hamlet which stretches along the base of the abandoned donjon. He learned what a living thing the legend of Bluebeard was in this isolated part of La Vendée on the border of Brittany.

"He was a young man who came to a bad end," said the young women. More fearful, their grandmothers crossed themselves as they went along the foot of the wall in the evening. The memory of the disembowelled children persisted. The Marshal, known only by his surname, still had power to terrify.

Durtal had gone every day from the inn where he lodged to the château, towering over the valleys of the Crume and of the Sèvre, facing hills excoriated with blocks of granite and overgrown with formidable oaks, whose roots, protruding out of the ground, resembled monstrous nests of frightened snakes.

One might have believed oneself transported into the real Brittany. There was the same melancholy, heavy sky, the same sun, which seemed older than in other parts of the world and which but feebly gilded the sorrowful, age-old forests and the mossy sandstone. There were the same endless stretches of broken, rocky soil, pitted with ponds of rusty water, dotted with scattered clumps of gorse and fruze copse, and sprinkled with pink harebells and nameless yellow prairie flowers.

One felt that this iron-grey sky; this starving soil, empurpled only here and there by the bleeding flower of the buckwheat; that these roads, bordered with stones placed one on top of the other, without cement or plaster; that these paths, bordered with impenetrable hedges; that these grudging plants; these inhospitable fields; these crippled beggars, eaten with vermin, plastered with filth; that even the flocks, undersized and wasted, the dumpy little cows, the black sheep whose blue eyes had the cold, pale gleam that is in the eyes of the Slav or of the tribade; had perpetuated their primordial state, preserving an identical landscape through all the centuries.

Except for an incongruous factory chimney further away on the bank of the Sèvre, the countryside of Tiffauges remained in perfect harmony with the immense château, erect among its ruins. Within the close, still to be traced by the ruins of the towers, was a whole plain, now converted into a miserable truck garden. Cabbages, in long bluish lines, impoverished carrots, consumptive navews, spread over this enormous circle where iron mail had clanked in the tournament and where processionals had slowly devolved, in the smoke of incense, to the chanting of psalms.

A thatched hut had been built in a corner. The peasant inhabitants, returned to a state of savagery, no longer understood the meaning of words, and could be roused out of their apathy only by the display of a silver coin. Seizing the coin, they would hand over the keys.

For hours one could browse around at ease among the ruins, and smoke and daydream. Unfortunately, certain parts were inaccessible. The donjon was still shut off, on the Tiffauges side, by a vast moat, at the bottom of which mighty trees were growing. One would have had to pass over the tops of the trees, growing to the very verge of the wall, to gain a porch on the other side, for there was now no drawbridge.

But quite accessible was another part which overhung the Sèvre. There the wings of the castle, overgrown with ivy and white-crested viburnum, were intact. Spongy, dry as pumice stone, silvered with lichen and gilded with moss, the towers rose entire, though from their crenelated collarettes whole blocks were blown away on windy nights.

Within, room succeeded glacial room, cut into the granite, surmounted with vaulted roofs, and as close as the hold of a ship. Then by spiral stairways one descended into similar chambers, joined by cellar passageways into the walls of which were dug deep niches and lairs of unknown utility.

Beneath, those corridors, so narrow that two persons could not walk along them abreast, descended at a gentle slope, and bifurcated so that there was a labyrinth of lanes, leading to veritable cells, on the walls of which the nitre scintillated in the light of the lantern like steel mica or twinkling grains of sugar. In the cells above, in the dungeons beneath, one stumbled over rifts of hard earth, in the centre or in a corner of which yawned now the mouth of an unsealed oubliette, now a well.

Finally, at the summit of one of the towers, that at the left as one entered, there was a roofed gallery running parallel to a circular foothold cut from the rock. There, without doubt, the men-at-arms had been stationed to fire on their assailants through wide loopholes opening overhead and underfoot. In this gallery the voice, even the lowest, followed the curving walls and could be heard all around the circuit.

Briefly, the exterior of the castle revealed a fortified place built to stand long sieges, and the dismantled interior made one think of a prison in which flesh, mildewed by the moisture, must rot in a few months. Out in the open air again, one felt a sensation of well-being, of relief, which one lost on traversing the ruins of the isolated chapel and penetrating, by a cellar door, to the crypt below.

This chapel, low, squat, its vaulted roof upheld by massive columns on whose capitals lozenges and bishop's croziers were carved, dated from the eleventh century. The altar stone survived intact. Brackish daylight, which seemed to have been filtered through layers of horn, came in at the openings, hardly lighting the shadowed, begrimed walls and the earth floor, which too was pierced by the entrance to an oubliette or by a well shaft.

In the evening after dinner he had often climbed up on the embankment and followed the cracked walls of the ruins. On bright nights one part of the castle was thrown back into shadow, and the other, by contrast, stood forth, washed in silver and blue, as if rubbed with mercurial lusters, above the Sèvre, along whose surface streaks of moonlight darted like the backs of fishes. The silence was overpowering. After nine o'clock not a dog, not a soul. He would return to the poor chamber of the inn, where an old woman, in black, wearing the cornet head-dress her ancestors wore in the sixteenth century, waited with a candle to bar the door as soon as he returned.

"All this," said Durtal to himself, "is the skeleton of a dead keep. To reanimate it we must revisualize the opulent flesh which once covered these bones of sandstone. Documents give us every detail. This carcass was magnificently clad, and if we are to see Gilles in his own environment, we must remember all the sumptuosity of fifteenth century furnishing.

"We must reclothe these walls with wainscots of Irish wood or with high warp tapestries of gold and thread of Arras, so much sought after in that epoch. Then this hard, black soil must be repaved with green and yellow bricks or black and white flagstones. The vault must be starred with gold and sown with crossbows on a field *azur,* and the Marshal's cross, *sable* on shield *or,* must be set shining there."

Of themselves the furnishings returned, each to its own place. Here and there were high-backed signorial chairs, thrones, and stools. Against the walls were sideboards on whose carved panels were bas-reliefs representing the Annunciation and the Adoration of the Magi. On top of the sideboards, beneath lace canopies, stood the painted and gilded statues of Saint Anne, Saint Marguerite, and Saint Catherine, so often reproduced by the wood-carvers of the Middle Ages. There were linen-chests, bound in iron, studded with great nails, and covered with sowskin leather. Then there were coffers fastened by great metal clasps and overlaid with leather or fabric on which fair faced angels, cut from illuminated missal-backgrounds, had been mounted. There were great beds reached by carpeted steps. There were tasselled pillows and counterpanes heavily perfumed, and canopies and curtains embroidered with armories or sprinkled with stars.

So one must reconstruct the decorations of the other rooms, in which nothing was standing but the walls and the high, basket-funneled fireplaces, whose spacious hearths, wanting andirons, were still charred from the old fires. One could easily imagine the dining-rooms and those terrible repasts which Gilles deplored in his trial at Nantes. Gilles admitted with tears that he had ordered his diet so as to kindle the fury of his senses, and these reprobate menus can be easily reproduced. When he was at table with Eustache Blanchet, Prelati, Gilles de Sillé, all his trusted companions, in the great room, the plates and the ewers filled with water of medlar, rose, and melilote for washing the hands, were placed on credences. Gilles ate beef-, salmon-, and bream-pies; levert- and squab-tarts; roast heron, stork, crane, peacock, bustard, and swan; venison in verjuice; Nantes lampreys; salads of briony, hops, beard of judas, mallow; vehement dishes seasoned with marjoram and mace, coriander and sage, peony and rosemary, basil and hyssop, grain of paradise and ginger; perfumed, acidulous dishes, giving one a violent thirst; heavy pastries; tarts of elder-flower and rape; rice with milk of hazelnuts sprinkled with cinnamon; stuffy dishes necessitating copious drafts of beer and fermented mulberry juice, of dry wine, or wine aged to tannic bitterness, of heady hypocras charged with cinnamon, with almonds, and with musk, of raging liquors clouded with golden particles—mad drinks which spurred the guests in this womanless castle to frenzies of lechery and made them, at the end of the meal, writhe in monstrous dreams.

"Remain the costumes to be restored," said Durtal to himself, and he imagined Gilles and his friends, not in their damaskeened field harness, but in their indoor costumes, their robes of peace. He visualized them in harmony with the luxury of their surroundings. They wore glittering vestments, pleated jackets, bellying out in a little flounced skirt at the waist. The legs were encased in dark skin-tight hose. On their heads were the artichoke chaperon hats like that of Charles VII in his portrait in the Louvre. The torso was enveloped in silver-threaded damask, which was crusted with jewelleries and bordered with marten.

He thought of the costume of the women of the time, robes of precious tentered stuffs, with tight sleeves, great collars thrown back over the shoulders, cramping bodices, long trains lined with fur. And as he thus dressed an imaginary manikin, hanging ropes of heavy stones, purplish

or milky crystals, cloudy uncut gems, over the slashed corsage, a woman slipped in, filled the robe, swelled the bodice,
and thrust her head under the two-horned steeple-headdress.
From behind the pendent lace smiled the composite features
of the unknown and of Mme. Chantelouve. Delighted, he
gazed at the apparition without ever perceiving whom he
had evoked, when his cat, jumping into his lap, distracted his
thoughts and brought him back to his room.

"Well, well, she won't let me alone," and in spite of himself he began to laugh at the thought of the unknown following him even to the château de Tiffauges. "It's foolish to
let my thoughts wander this way," he said, drawing himself
up, "but daydream is the only good thing in life. Everything else is vulgar and empty.

"No doubt about it, that was a singular epoch, the Middle
Epoch of ignorance and darkness, the history professors and
Ages," he went on, lighting a cigarette. "For some it's all
white and for others utterly black. No intermediate shade.
atheists reiterate. Dolorous and exquisite epoch, say the
artists and the religious savants.

"What is certain is that the immutable classes, the nobility, the clergy, the bourgeoisie, the people, had loftier
souls at that time. You can prove it: society has done
nothing but deteriorate in the four centuries separating us
from the Middle Ages.

"True, a baron then was usually a formidable brute. He
was a drunken and lecherous bandit, a sanguinary and
boisterous tyrant, but he was a child in mind and spirit.
The Church bullied him, and to deliver the Holy Sepulchre
he sacrificed his wealth, abandoned home, wife, and children,
and accepted unconscionable fatigues, extraordinary sufferings, unheard-of dangers.

By pious heroism he redeemed the baseness of his morals.
The race has since become moderate. It has reduced, sometimes even done away with, its instincts of carnage and
rape, but it has replaced them by the monomania of business,
the passion for lucre. It has done worse. It has sunk to

such a state of abjectness as to be attracted by the doings of the lowest of the low. The aristocracy disguises itself as a mountebank, puts on tights and spangles, gives public trapeze performances, jumps through hoops, and does weight-lifting stunts in the trampled tan-bark ring!

"The clergy, then a good example—if we except a few convents ravaged by frenzied Satanism and lechery—launched itself into superhuman transports and attained God. Saints swarmed, miracles multiplied, and while still omnipotent the Church was gentle with the humble, it consoled the afflicted, defended the little ones, and mourned or rejoiced with the people of low estate. Today it hates the poor, and mysticism dies in a clergy which checks ardent thoughts and preaches sobriety of mind, continence of postulation, common sense in prayer, bourgeoisie of the soul! Yet here and there, buried in cloisters far from these lukewarm priests, there perhaps still are real saints who weep, monks who pray, to the point of dying of sorrow and prayer, for each of us. And they—with the demoniacs—are the sole connecting link between that age and this.

"The smug, sententious side of the bourgeoisie already existed in the time of Charles VII. But cupidity was repressed by the confessor, and the tradesman, just like the labourer, was maintained by the corporations, which denounced overcharging and fraud, saw that decried merchandise was destroyed, and fixed a fair price and a high standard of excellence for commodities. Trades and professions were handed down from father to son. The corporations assured work and pay. People were not, as now, subject to the fluctuations of the market and the merciless capitalistic exploitation. Great fortunes did not exist and everybody had enough to live on. Sure of the future, unhurried, they created marvels of art, whose secret remains for ever lost.

"All the artisans who passed the three degrees of apprentice, journeyman, and master, developed subtlety and became veritable artists. They ennobled the simplest of iron work, the commonest faience, the most ordinary chests and coffers.

Those corporations, putting themselves under the patronage of Saints—whose images, frequently besought, figured on their banners—preserved through the centuries the honest existence of the humble and notably raised the spiritual level of the people whom they protected.

"All that is decisively at an end. The bourgeoise has taken the place forfeited by a wastrel nobility which now subsists only to set ignoble fashions and whose sole contribution to our 'civilization' is the establishment of gluttonous dining clubs, so-called gymnastic societies, and pari-mutuel associations. Today the business man has but these aims, to exploit the working man, manufacture shoddy, lie about the quality of merchandise, and give short weight.

"As for the people, they have been relieved of the indispensable fear of hell, and notified, at the same time, that they are not to expect to be recompensed, after death, for their sufferings here. So they scamp their ill-paid work and take to drink. From time to time, when they have ingurgitated too violent liquids, they revolt, and then they must be slaughtered, for once let loose they would act as a crazed stampeded herd.

"Good God, what a mess! And to think that the nineteenth century takes on airs and adulates itself. There is one word in the mouths of all. Progress. Progress of whom? Progress of what? For this miserable century hasn't invented anything great.

"It has constructed nothing and destroyed everything. At the present hour it glorifies itself in this electricity which it thinks it discovered. But electricity was known and used in remotest antiquity, and if the ancients could not explain its nature nor even its essence, the moderns are just as incapable of identifying that force which conveys the spark and carries the voice—acutely nasalized—along the wire. This century thinks it discovered the terrible science of hypnotism, which the priests and Brahmins in Egypt and India knew and practised to the utmost. No, the only thing this century has invented is the sophistication of products. Therein it is passed master. It has even gone so far as to adulterate excrement. Yes, in 1888 the two houses of parliament had to pass a law destined to suppress the falsification of fertilizer. Now that's the limit."

The doorbell rang. He opened the door and nearly fell over backward.

Mme. Chantelouve was before him.

Stupefied, he bowed, while Mme. Chantelouve, without a word, went straight into the study. There she turned around, and Durtal, who had followed, found himself face to face with her.

"Won't you please sit down?" He advanced an armchair and hastened to push back, with his foot, the edge of the carpet turned up by the cat. He asked her to excuse the disorder. She made a vague gesture and remained standing.

In a calm but very low voice she said, "It is I who wrote you those mad letters. I have come to drive away this bad fever and get it over with in a quite frank way. As you yourself wrote, no liaison between us is possible. Let us forget what has happened. And before I go, tell me that you bear me no grudge."

He cried out at this. He would not have it so. He had not been beside himself when he wrote her those ardent pages, he was in perfectly good faith, he loved her——

"You love me! Why, you didn't even know that those letters were from me. You loved an unknown, a chimera. Well, admitting that you are telling the truth, the chimera does not exist now, for here I am."

"You are mistaken. I knew perfectly that it was Mme. Chantelouve hiding behind the pseudonym of Mme. Maubel." And he half-explained to her, without, of course, letting her know of his doubts, how he had lifted her mask.

"Ah!" She reflected, blinking her troubled eyes. "At any rate," she said, again facing him squarely, "you could not have recognized me in the first letters, to which you re-

sponded with cries of passion. Those cries were not addressed to me."

He contested this observation, and became entangled in
the dates and happenings and in the sequence of the notes.
She at length lost the thread of his remarks. The situation
was so ridiculous that both were silent. Then she sat down
and burst out laughing.

Her strident, shrill laugh, revealing magnificent, but
short and pointed teeth, in a mocking mouth, vexed him.

"She has been playing with me," he said to himself, and
dissatisfied with the turn the conversation had taken, and
furious at seeing this woman so calm, so different from her
burning letters, he asked, in a tone of irritation, "Am I to
know why you laugh?"

"Pardon me. It's a trick my nerves play on me, sometimes in public places. But never mind. Let us be reasonable and talk things over. You tell me you love me——"

"And I mean it."

"Well, admitting that I too am not indifferent, where is
this going to lead us? Oh, you know so well, you poor dear,
that you refused, right at first, the meeting which I asked in
a moment of madness—and you gave well-thought-out reasons for refusing."

"But I refused because I did not know then that you
were the women in the case! I have told you that it was
several days later that Des Hermies unwittingly revealed
your identity to me. Did I hesitate as soon as I knew?
No! I immediately implored you to come."

"That may be, but you admit that I'm right when I claim
that you wrote your first letters to another and not me."

She was pensive for a moment. Durtal began to be pro-
digiously bored by this discussion. He thought it more
prudent not to answer, and was seeking a change of subject
that would put an end to the deadlock.

She herself got him out of his difficulty. "Let us not
discuss it any more," she said, smiling, "we shall not get any-

where. You see, this is the situation: I am married to a very nice man who loves me and whose only crime is that he represents the rather insipid happiness which one has right at hand. I started this correspondence with you, so I am to blame, and believe me, on his account I suffer. You have work to do, beautiful books to write. You don't need to have a crazy woman come walking into your life. So, you see, the best thing is for us to remain friends, but true friends, and go no further."

"And it is the woman who wrote me such vivid letters, who now speaks to me of reason, good sense, and God knows what!"

"But be frank, now. You don't love me."

"I don't?"

He took her hands, gently. She made no resistance, but looking at him squarely she said, "Listen. If you had loved me you would have come to see me; and yet for months you haven't tried to find out whether I was alive or dead."

"But you understand that I could not hope to be welcomed by you on the terms we now are on, and too, in your parlour there are guests, your husband—I have never had you even a little bit to myself at your home."

He pressed her hands more tightly and came closer to her. She regarded him with her smoky eyes, in which he now saw that dolent, almost dolorous expression which had captivated him. He completely lost control of himself before this voluptuous and plaintive face, but with a firm gesture she freed her hands.

"Enough. Sit down, now, and let's talk of something else. Do you know your apartment is charming? Which saint is that?" she asked, examining the picture, over the mantel, of the monk on his knees beside a cardinal's hat and cloak.

"I do not know."

"I will find out for you. I have the lives of all the saints at home. It ought to be easy to find out about a cardinal who renounced the purple to go live in a hut. Wait. I think Saint Peter Damian did, but I am not sure. I have such a poor memory. Help me think."

"But I don't know who he is!"

She came closer to him and put her hand on his shoulder. "Are you angry at me?"

"I should say I am! When I desire you frantically, when I've been dreaming for a whole week about this meeting, you come here and tell me that all is over between us, that you do not love me——"

She became demure. "But if I did not love you, would I have come to you? Understand, then, that reality kills a dream; that it is better for us not to expose ourselves to fearful regrets. We are not children, you see. No! Let me go. Do not squeeze me like that!" Very pale, she struggled in his embrace. "I swear to you that I will go away and that you shall never see me again if you do not let me loose." Her voice became hard. She was almost hissing her words. He let go of her. "Sit down there behind the table. Do that for me." And tapping the floor with her heel, she said, in a tone of melancholy, "Then it is impossible to be friends, only friends, with a man. But it would be very nice to come and see you without having evil thoughts to fear, wouldn't it?" She was silent. Then she added, "Yes, just to see each other—and if we did not have any sublime things to say to each other, it is also very nice to sit and say nothing!"

Then she said, "My time is up. I must go home."

"And leave me with no hope?" he exclaimed, kissing her gloved hands.

She did not answer, but gently shook her head, then, as he looked pleadingly at her, she said, "Listen. If you will promise to make no demands on me and to be good, I will come here night after next at nine o'clock."

He promised whatever she wished. And as he raised his head from her hands and as his lips brushed lightly over her breast, which seemed to tighten, she disengaged her hands, caught his nervously, and, clenching her teeth, offered her neck to his lips. Then she fled.

"Oof!" he said, closing the door after her. He was at the same time satisfied and vexed.

Satisfied, because he found her enigmatic, changeful, charming. Now that he was alone he recalled her to memory. He remembered her tight black dress, her fur cloak, the warm collar of which had caressed him as he was covering her neck with kisses. He remembered that she wore no jewellery, except sparkling blue sapphire eardrops. He remembered the wayward blonde hair escaping from under the dark green otter hat. Holding his hands to his nostrils he sniffed again the sweet and distant odour, cinnamon lost among stronger perfumes, which he had caught from the contact of her long, fawn-coloured suède gloves, and he saw again her moist, rodent teeth, her thin, bitten lips, and her troubled eyes, of a grey and opaque lustre which could suddenly be transfigured with radiance. "Oh, night after next it will be great to kiss all that!"

Vexed also, both with himself and with her. He reproached himself with having been brusque and reserved. He ought to have shown himself more expansive and less restrained. But it was her fault, for she had abashed him! The incongruity between the woman who cried with voluptuous suffering in her letters and the woman he had seen, so thoroughly mistress of herself in her coquetries, was truly too much!

"However you look at them, these women are astonishing creatures," he thought. "Here is one who accomplishes the most difficult thing you can imagine: coming to a man's room after having written him excessive letters. I, I act like a goose. I stand there ill at ease. She, in a second, has the self-assurance of a person in her own home, or visiting in a drawing-room. No awkwardness, pretty gestures, a few words, and eyes which supply everything! She isn't very agreeable," he thought, reminded of the curt tone she had used when disengaging herself, "and yet she has her tender spots," he continued dreamily, remembering not so much her words as certain inflections of her voice and a certain bewildered look in her eyes. "I must go about it prudently that night," he concluded, addressing his cat, which, never having seen a woman before, had fled at the arrival of Mme. Chantelouve and taken refuge under the bed, but had now advanced almost grovelling, to sniff the chair where she had sat.

"Come to think of it, she is an old hand, Mme. Hyacinthe! She would not have a meeting in a café nor in the street. She scented from afar the assignation house or the hotel. And though, from the mere fact of my not inviting her here, she could not doubt that I did not want to introduce her to my lodging, she came here deliberately. Then, this first denial, come to think of it, is only a fine farce. If she were not seeking a liaison she would not have visited me. No, she wanted me to beg her to do what she wanted to do. Like all women, she wanted me to offer her what she desired. I have been rolled. Her arrival has knocked the props out from under my whole method. But what does it matter? She is no less desirable," he concluded, happy to get rid of disagreeable reflections and plunge back into the delirious vision which he retained of her. "That night won't be exactly dreary," he thought, seeing again her eyes, imagining them in surrender, deceptive and plaintive, as he would disrobe her and make a body white and slender, warm and supple, emerge from her tight skirt. "She has no children. That is an earnest promise that her flesh is quite firm, even at thirty!"

A whole draft of youth intoxicated him. Durtal, astonished, took a look at himself in the mirror. His tired eyes brightened, his face seemed more youthful, less worn. "Lucky I had just shaved," he said to himself. But gradually, as he mused, he saw in this mirror, which he was so little in the habit of consulting, his features droop and his eyes lose their sparkle. His stature, which had seemed to increase in this spiritual upheaval, diminished again. Sadness returned to his thoughtful mien. "I haven't what you would call the physique of a lady's man," he concluded. "What does she see in me? for she could very easily find someone else with whom to be unfaithful to her husband. Enough of these rambling thoughts. Let's cease to think them. To sum up the situation: I love her with my head and not my heart. That's the important thing. Under such conditions, whatever happens, a love affair is brief, and I am almost certain to get out of it without committing any follies."

CHAPTER IX

The next morning he woke, thinking of her, just as he had been doing when he went to sleep. He tried to rationalize the episode and revolved his conjectures over and over. Once again he put himself this question: "Why, when I went to her house, did she not let me see that I pleased her? Never a look, never a word to encourage me. Why this correspondence, when it was so easy to insist on having me to dine, so simple to prepare an occasion which would bring us together, either at her home or elsewhere?" And he answered himself, "It would have been usual and not at all diverting. She is perhaps skilled in these matters. She knows that the unknown frightens a man's reason away, that the unembodied puts the soul in ferment, and she wished to give me a fever before trying an attack—to call her advances by their right name.

"It must be admitted that if my conjectures are correct she is strangely astute. At heart she is, perhaps, quite simply a crazy romantic or a comedian. It amuses her to manufacture little adventures, to throw tantalizing obstacles in the way of the realization of a vulgar desire. And Chantelouve? He is probably aware of his wife's goings on, which perhaps facilitate his career. Otherwise, how could she arrange to come here at nine o'clock at night, instead of the morning or afternoon on pretence of going shopping?"

To this new question there could be no answer, and little by little he ceased to interrogate himself on the point. He began to be obsessed by the real woman as he had been by the imaginary creature. The latter had completely vanished. He did not even remember her physiognomy now. Mme.

Chantelouve, just as she was in reality, without borrowing the other's features, had complete possession of him and fired his brain and senses to white heat. He began to desire her madly and to wish furiously for tomorrow night. And if she did not come? He felt cold in the small of his back at the idea that she might be unable to get away from home or that she might wilfully stay away.

"High time it was over and done with," he said, for this Saint Vitus' dance went on not without certain diminution of force, which disturbed him. In fact he feared, after the febrile agitation of his nights, to reveal himself as a sorry paladin when the time came. "But why bother?" he rejoined, as he started toward Carhaix's, where he was to dine with the astrologer Gèvingey and Des Hermies.

"I shall be rid of my obsession awhile," he murmured, groping along in the darkness of the tower.

Des Hermies, hearing him come up the stair, opened the door, casting a shaft of light into the spiral. Durtal, reaching the landing, saw his friend in shirt sleeves and enveloped in an apron.

"I am, as you see, in the heat of composition," and upon a stew-pan boiling on the stove Des Hermies cast that brief and sure look which a mechanic gives his machine, then he consulted, as if it were a manometer, his watch, hanging to a nail. "Look," he said, raising the pot lid.

Durtal bent over and through a cloud of vapour he saw a coiled napkin rising and falling with the little billows. "Where is the leg of mutton?"

"It, my friend, is sewn into that cloth so tightly that the air cannot enter. It is cooking in this pretty, singing sauce, into which I have thrown a handful of hay, some pods of garlic and slices of carrot and onion, some grated nutmeg, and laurel and thyme. You will have many compliments to make me if Gèvingey doesn't keep us waiting too long, because a *gigot à l'Anglaise* won't stand being cooked to shreds."

Carhaix's wife looked in.

"Come in," she said. "My husband is here."

Durtal found him dusting the books. They shook hands. Durtal, at random, looked over some of the dusted books lying on the table.

"Are these," he asked, "technical works about metals and bell-founding or are they about the liturgy of bells?"

"They are not about founding, though there is sometimes reference to the founders, the 'sainterers' as they were called in the good old days. You will discover here and there some details about alloys of red copper and fine tin. You will even find, I believe, that the art of the 'sainterer' has been in decline for three centuries, probably due to the fact that the faithful no longer melt down their ornaments of precious metals, thus modifying the alloy. Or is it because the founders no longer invoke Saint Anthony the Eremite when the bronze is boiling in the furnace? I do not know. It is true, at any rate, that bells are now made in carload lots. Their voices are without personality. They are all the same. They're like docile and indifferent hired girls when formerly they were like those aged servants who became part of the family whose joys and griefs they have shared. But what difference does that make to the clergy and the congregation? At present these auxiliaries devoted to the cult do not represent any symbol. And that explains the whole difficulty.

"You asked me, a few second. ago, whether these books treated of bells from the liturgical point of view. Yes, most of them give tabulated explanations of the significance of the various component parts. The interpretations are simple and offer little variety."

"What are a few of them?"

"I can sum them all up for you in a very few words. According to the *Rational* of Guillaume Durand, the hardness of the metal signifies the force of the preacher. The percussion of the clapper on the sides expresses the idea that the preacher must first scourge himself to correct himself of his own vices before reproaching the vices of others. The wooden frame represents the cross of Christ, and the cord, which formerly served to set the bell swinging, allegorizes the science of the Scriptures which flows from the mystery of the Cross itself.

"The most ancient liturgists expound practically the same symbols. Jean Beleth, who lived in 1200, declares also that the bell is the image of the preacher, but adds that its motion to and fro, when it is set swinging, teaches that the preacher must by turns elevate his language and bring it down within reach of the crowd. For Hugo of Saint Victor the clapper is the tongue of the officiating priest, which strikes the two sides of the vase and announces thus, at the same time, the truth of the two Testaments. Finally, if we consult Fortunatus Amalarius, perhaps the most ancient of the liturgists, we find simply that the body of the bell denotes the mouth of the preacher and the hammer his tongue."

"But," said Durtal, somewhat disappointed, "it isn't—what shall I say?—very profound."

The door opened.

"Why, how are you!" said Carhaix, shaking hands with Gèvingey, and then introducing him to Durtal.

While the bell-ringer's wife finished setting the table, Durtal examined the newcomer. He was a little man, wearing a soft black felt hat and wrapped up like an omnibus conductor in a cape with a military collar of blue cloth.

His head was like an egg with the hollow downward. The skull, waxed as if with siccatif, seemed to have grown up out of the hair, which was hard and like filaments of dried coconut and hung down over his neck. The nose was bony, and the nostrils opened like two hatchways, over a toothless mouth which was hidden by a moustache grizzled like the goatee springing from the short chin. At first glance one would have taken him for an art-worker, a wood engraver or a glider of saints' images, but on looking at him more closely, observing the eyes, round and grey, set close to the nose, almost crossed, and studying his solemn voice and obsequious manners, one asked oneself from what quite special kind of sacristy the man had issued.

He took off his things and appeared in a black frock coat of square, boxlike cut. A fine gold chain, passed about his neck, lost itself in the bulging pocket of an old vest. Durtal gasped when Gèvingey, as soon as he had seated himself, complacently put his hands on exhibition, resting them on his knees. Enormous, freckled with blotches of orange, and terminating in milk-white nails cut to the quick, the fingers were covered with huge rings, the sets of which formed a phalanx.

Seeing Durtal's gaze fixed on his fingers, he smiled. "You examine my valuables, monsieur. They are of three metals, gold, platinum, and silver. This ring bears a scorpion, the sign under which I was born. That with its two accoupled triangles, one pointing downward and the other upward, reproduces the image of the macrocosm, the seal of Solomon, the grand pantacle. As for the little one you see here," he went on, showing a lady's ring set with a tiny sapphire between two roses, "that is a present from a person whose horoscope I was good enough to cast."

"Ah!" said Durtal, somewhat surprised at the man's self-satisfaction.

"Dinner is ready," said the bell-ringer's wife.

Des Hermies, doffing his apron, appeared in his tight cheviot garments. He was not so pale as usual, his cheeks being red from the heat of the stove. He set the chairs around.

Carhaix served the broth, and everyone was silent, taking spoonfuls of the cooler broth at the edge of the bowl. Then madame brought Des Hermies the famous leg of mutton to cut. It was a magnificent red, and large drops flowed beneath the knife. Everybody ecstasized when tasting this robust meat, aromatic with a purée of turnips sweetened with caper sauce.

Des Hermies bowed under a storm of compliments. Carhaix filled the glasses, and, somewhat confused in the presence of Gèvingey, paid the astrologer effusive attention to hake him forget their former ill-feeling. Des Hermies assisted in this good work, and wishing also to be useful to Durtal, brought the conversation around to the subject of horoscopes.

Then Gèvingey mounted the rostrum. In a tone of satisfaction he spoke of his vast labours, of the six months a horoscope required, of the surprise of laymen when he declared that such work was not paid for by the price he asked, five hundred francs.

"But you see I cannot give my science for nothing," he said. "And now people doubt astrology, which was revered in antiquity. Also in the Middle Ages, when it was almost sacred. For instance, messieurs, look at the portal of Notre Dame. The three doors which archeologists—not initiated into the symbolism of Christianity and the occult—designate by the names of the door of Judgment, the door of the Virgin, and the door of Saint Marcel or Saint Anne, really represent Mysticism, Astrology, and Alchemy, the three great sciences of the Middle Ages. Today you find people who say, 'Are you quite sure that the stars have an influence on the destiny of man?' But, messieurs, without entering here into details reserved for the adept, in what way is this spiritual influence stranger than that corporal influence which certain planets, the moon, for example, exercise on the organs of men and women?

"You are a physician, Monsieur Des Hermies, and you are not unaware that the doctors Gillespin, Jackson, and Balfour, of Jamaica, have established the influence of the constellations on human health in the West Indies. At every change of the moon the number of sick people augments. The acute crises of fever coincide with the phases of our satellite. Finally, there are *lunatics*. Go out in the country and ascertain at what periods madness becomes epidemic. But does this serve to convince the incredulous?" he asked sorrowfully, contemplating his rings.

"It seems to me, on the contrary, that astrology is picking

up," said Durtal. "There are now two astrologers casting horoscopes in the next column to the secret remedies on the fourth page of the newspapers."

"And it's a shame! Those people don't even know the first thing about the science. They are simply tricksters who hope thus to pick up some money. What's the use of speaking of them when they *don't even exist!* Really it must be admitted that only in England and America is there anybody who knows how to establish the genethliac theme and construct a horoscope."

"I am very much afraid," said Des Hermides, "that not only these so-called astrologers, but also all the mages, theosophists, occultists, and cabalists of the present day, know absolutely nothing—those with whom I am acquainted are indubitably, incontestably, ignorant imbeciles. And that is the pure truth, messieurs. These people are, for the most part, down-and-out journalists or broken spendthrifts seeking to exploit the taste of a public weary of positivism. They plagiarize Eliphas Levi, steal from Fabre d'Olivet, and write treatises of which they themselves are incapable of making head or tail. It's a real pity, when you come to think of it."

"The more so as they discredit sciences which certainly contain verities omitted in their jumble," said Durtal.

"Then another lamentable thing," said Des Hermies, "is that in addition to the dupes and simpletons, these little sects harbour some frightful charlatans and windbags."

"Péladan, among others. Who does not know that shoddy mage, commercialized to his fingertips?" cried Durtal.

"Oh, yes, that fellow——"

"Briefly, messieurs," resumed Gèvingey, "all these people are incapable of obtaining in practise any effect whatever. The only man in this century who, without being either a saint or a diabolist, has penetrated the mysteries, is William Crookes." And as Durtal, who appeared to doubt the apparitions sworn to by this Englishman, declared that no theory could explain them, Gèvingey perorated, "Permit me, messieurs. We have the choice between two diverse, and I venture to say, very clear-cut doctrines. Either the apparition is formed by the fluid disengaged by the medium in trance to combine with the fluid of the persons present; or else there are in the air immaterial beings, elementals as they are called, which manifest themselves under very nearly determinable conditions; or else, and this is the theory of pure spiritism, the phenomena are produced by souls evoked from the dead."

"I know it," Durtal said, "and that horrifies me. I know also the Hindu dogma of the migrations of souls after death. These disembodied souls stray until they are reincarnated or until they attain, from avatar to avatar, to complete purity. Well, I think it's quite enough to live once. I'd prefer nothingness, a hole in the ground, to all those metamorphoses. It's more consoling to me. As for the evocation of the dead, the mere thought that the butcher on the corner can force the soul of Hugo, Balzac, Baudelaire, to converse with him, would put me beside myself, if I believed it. Ah, no. Materialism, abject as it is, is less vile than that."

"Spiritism," said Carhaix, "is only a new name for the ancient necromancy condemned and cursed by the Church."

Gèvingey looked at his rings, then emptied his glass.

"In any case," he returned, "you will admit that these theories can be upheld, especially that of the elementals, which, setting Satanism aside, seems the most veridic, and certainly is the most clear. Space is peopled by microbes. Is it more surprising that space should also be crammed with spirits and larvæ? Water and vinegar are alive with animalcules. The microscope shows them to us. Now why should not the air, inaccessible to the sight and to the instruments of man, swarm, like the other elements, with beings more or less corporeal, embryos more or less mature?"

"That is probably why cats suddenly look upward and

gaze curiously into space at something that is passing and that we can't see," said the bell-ringer's wife.

"No, thanks," said Gèvingey to Des Hermies, who was offering him another helping of egg-and-dandelion salad.

"My friends," said the bell-ringer, "you forget only one doctrine, that of the Church, which attributes all these inexplicable phenomena to Satan. Catholicism has known them for a long time. It did not need to wait for the first manifestations of the spirits—which were produced, I believe, in 1847, in the United States, through the Fox family—before decreeing that spirit rapping came from the Devil. You will find in Saint Augustine the proof, for he had to send a priest to put an end to noises and overturning of objects and furniture, in the diocese of Hippo, analogous to those which Spiritism points out. At the time of Theodoric also, Saint Cæsaræus ridded a house of lemurs haunting it. You see, there are only the City of God and the City of the Devil. Now, since God is above these cheap manipulations, the occultists and spiritists satanize more or less, whether they wish to or not."

"Nevertheless, Spiritism has accomplished one important thing. It has violated the threshold of the unknown, broken the doors of the sanctuary. It has brought about in the extranatural a revolution similar to that which was effected in the terrestrial order in France in 1789. It has democratized evocation and opened a whole new vista. Only, it has lacked initiates to lead it, and, proceeding at random without science, it has agitated good and bad spirits together. In Spiritism you will find a jumble of everything. It is the hash of mystery, if I may be permitted the expression."

"The saddest thing about it," said Des Hermies, laughing, "is that at a séance one never sees a thing! I know that experiments have been successful, but those which I have witnessed—well, the experimenters seemed to take a long shot and miss."

"That is not surprising," said the astrologer, spreading some firm candied orange jelly on a piece of bread, "the first

law to observe in magism and Spiritism is to send away the
unbelievers, because very often their fluid is antagonistic to
that of the clairvoyant or the medium."

"Then how can there be any assurance of the reality of
the phenomena?" thought Durtal.

Carhaix rose. "I shall be back in ten minutes." He put
on his greatcoat, and soon the sound of his steps was lost in
the tower.

"True," murmured Durtal, consulting his watch. "It's a
quarter to eight."

There was a moment of silence in the room. As all refused to have any more dessert, Mme. Carhaix took up the
tablecloth and spread an oilcloth in its place.

The astrologer played with his rings, turning them about;
Durtal was rolling a pellet of crumbled bread between his
fingers; Des Hermies, leaning over to one side, pulled from
his patch pocket his embossed Japanese pouch and made a
cigarette.

Then when the bell-ringer's wife had bidden them good
night and retired to her room, Des Hermies got the kettle
and the coffee pot.

"Want any help?" Durtal proposed.

"You can get the little glasses and uncork the liqueur
bottles, if you will."

As he opened the cupboard, Durtal swayed, dizzy from
the strokes of the bells which shook the walls and filled
the room with clamour.

"If there are spirits in this room, they must be getting
knocked to pieces," he said, setting the liqueur glasses on the
table.

"Bells drive phantoms and spectres away," Gèvingey answered, doctorally, filling his pipe.

"Here," said Des Hermies, "will you pour hot water
slowly into the filter? I've got to feed the stove. It's
getting chilly here. My feet are freezing.

Carhaix returned, blowing out his lantern.

"The bell was in good voice, this clear, dry night," and he took off his mountaineer cap and his overcoat.

"What do you think of him?" Des Hermies asked Durtal in a very low voice, and pointed at the astrologer, now lost in a cloud of pipe smoke.

"In repose he looks like an old owl, and when he speaks he makes me think of a melancholy and discursive schoolmaster."

"Only one," said Des Hermies to Carhaix, who was holding a lump of sugar over Des Hermies's coffee cup.

"I hear, monsieur, that you are occupied with a history of Gilles de Rais," said Gèvingey to Durtal.

"Yes, for the time being I am up to my eyes in Satanism with that man."

"And," said Des Hermies, "we were just going to appeal to your extensive knowledge. You only can enlighten my friend on one of the most obscure questions of Diabolism."

"Which one?"

"That of incubacy and succubacy."

Gévingey did not answer at once. "That is a much graver question than Spiritism," he said at last, "and grave in a different way. But monsieur already knows something about it?"

"Only that opinions differ. Del Rio and Bodin, for instance, consider the incubi as masculine demons which couple with women and the succubi as demons who consummate the carnal act with men.

"According to their theories the incubi take the semen lost by men in dream and make use of it. So that two questions arise: first, can a child be born of such a union? The possibility of this kind of procreation has been upheld by the Church doctors, who affirm, even, that children of such commerce are heavier than others and can drain three nurses without taking on flesh. The second question is whether the demon who copulates with the mother or the man whose semen has been taken is the father of the child.

To which Saint Thomas answers, with more or less subtle arguments, that the real father is not the incubus but the man."

"For Sinistrari d'Ameno," observed Durtal, "the incubi and succubi are not precisely demons, but animal spirits, intermediate between the demon and the angel, a sort of satyr or faun, such as were revered in the time of paganism, a sort of imp, such as were exorcised in the Middle Ages. Sinistrari adds that they do not need to pollute a sleeping man, since they possess genitals and are endowed with prolificacy."

"Well, there is nothing further," said Gévingey. "Görres, so learned, so precise, in his *Mystik* passes rapidly over this question, even neglects it, and the Church, you know, is completely silent, for the Church does not like to treat this subject and views askance the priest who does occupy himself with it."

"I beg your pardon," said Carhaix, always ready to defend the Church. "The Church has never hesitated to declare itself on this detestable subject. The existence of succubi and incubi is certified by Saint Augustine, Saint Thomas, Saint Bonaventure, Denys le Chartreux, Pope Innocent VIII, and how many others! The question is resolutely settled for every Catholic. It also figures in the lives of some of the saints, if I am not mistaken. Yes, in the legend of Saint Hippolyte, Jacques de Voragine tells how a priest, tempted by a naked succubus, cast his stole at its head and it suddenly became the corpse of some dead woman whom the Devil had animated to seduce him."

"Yes," said Gévingey, whose eyes twinkled. "The Church recognizes succubacy, I grant. But let me speak, and you will see that my observations are not uncalled for.

"You know very well, messieurs," addressing Des Hermies and Durtal, "what the books teach, but within a hundred years everything has changed, and if the facts I am are unknown to the many members of the clergy, and you will not find them cited in any book whatever.

"At present it is less frequently demons than bodies raised from the dead which fill the indispensable rôle of incubus and succubus. In other words, formerly the living being subject to succubacy was known to be possessed. Now that vampirism, by the evocation of the dead, is joined to demonism, the victim is worse than possessed. The Church did not know what to do. Either it must keep silent or reveal the possibility of the evocation of the dead, already forbidden by Moses, and this admission was dangerous, for it popularized the knowledge of acts that are easier to produce now than formerly, since without knowing it Spiritism has traced the way.

"So the Church has kept silent. And Rome is not unaware of the frightful advance incubacy has made in the cloisters in our days."

"That proves that continence is hard to bear in solitude," said Des Hermies.

"It merely proves that the soul is feeble and that people have forgotten how to pray," said Carhaix.

"However that may be, messieurs, to instruct you completely in this matter, I must divide the creatures smitten with incubacy or succubacy into two classes. The first is composed of persons who have directly and voluntarily given themselves over to the demoniac action of the spirits. These persons are quite rare and they all die by suicide or some other form of violent death. The second is composed of persons on whom the visitation of spirits has been imposed by a spell. These are very numerous, especially in the convents dominated by the demoniac societies. Ordinarily these victims end in madness. The psychopathic hospitals are crowded with them. The doctors and the majority of the priests do not know the cause of their madness, but the cases are curable. A thaumaturge of my acquaintance has saved a good many of the bewitched who without his aid would be howling under hydrotherapeutic douches. There are certain fumigations, certain exsufflations, certain commandments written on a sheet of virgin parchment thrice blessed and worn like an amulet which almost always succeed in delivering the patient."

"I want to ask you," said Des Hermies, "does a woman receive the visit of the incubus while she is asleep or while she is awake?"

"A distinction must be made. If the woman is not the victim of a spell, if she voluntarily consorts with the impure spirit, she is always awake when the carnal act takes place. If, on the other hand, the woman is the victim of sorcery, the sin is committed either while she is asleep or while she is awake, but in the latter case she is in a cataleptic state which prevents her from defending herself. The most powerful of present-day exorcists, the man who has gone most thoroughly into this matter, one Johannès, Doctor of Theology, told me that he had saved nuns who had been ridden without respite for two, three, even four days by incubi!"

"I know that priest," remarked Des Hermies.

"And the act is consummated in the same manner as the normal human act?"

"Yes and no. Here the dirtiness of the details makes me hesitate," said Gévingey, becoming slightly red. "What I can tell you is more than strange. Know, then, that the organ of the incubus is bifurcated and at the same time penetrates both vases. Formerly it extended, and while one branch of the fork acted in the licit channels, the other at the same time reached up to the lower part of the face. You may imagine, gentlemen, how life must be shortened by operations which are multiplied through all the senses."

"And you are sure that these are facts?"

"Absolutely."

"But come now, you have proofs?"

Gévingey was silent, then, "The subject is so grave and I have gone so far that I had better go the rest of the way.

I am not mad nor the victim of hallucination. Well, messieurs, I slept one time in the room of the most redoubtable master Satanism now can claim."

"Canon Docre," Des Hermies interposed.

"Yes, and my sleep was fitful. It was broad daylight. I swear to you that the succubus came, irritant and palpable and most tenacious. Happily, I remembered the formula of deliverance, which kept me——

"So I ran that very day to Doctor Johannès, of whom I have spoken. He immediately and forever, I hope, liberated me from the spell."

"If I did not fear to be indiscreet, I would ask you what kind of thing this succubus was, whose attack you repulsed."

"Why, it was like any naked woman," said the astrologer hesitantly.

"Curious, now, if it had demanded its little gifts, its little gloves—" said Durtal, biting his lips.

"And do you know what has become of the terrible Docre?" Des Hermies inquired.

"No, thank God. They say he is in the south, somewhere around Nîmes, where he formerly resided."

"But what does this abbé do?" inquired Durtal.

"What does he do? He evokes the Devil, and he feeds white mice on the hosts which he consecrates. His frenzy for sacrilege is such that he had the image of Christ tattooed on his heels so that he could always step on the Saviour!"

"Well," murmured Carhaix, whose militant moustache bristled while his great eyes flamed, "if that abominable priest were here, I swear to you that I would respect his feet, but that I would throw him downstairs head first."

"And the black mass?" inquired Des Hermies.

"He celebrates it with foul men and women. He is openly accused of having influenced people to make wills in his favor and of causing inexplicable death. Unfortunately, there are no laws to repress sacrilege, and how can you prosecute a man who sends maladies from a distance and kills slowly in such a way that at the autopsy no traces of poison appear?"

"The modern Gilles de Rais!" exclaimed Durtal.

"Yes, less savage, less frank, more hypocritically cruel. He does not cut throats. He probably limits himself to 'sendings' or to causing suicide by suggestion," said Des Hermies, "for he is, I believe, a master hypnotist."

"Could he insinuate into a victim the idea to drink, regularly, in graduated doses, a toxin which he would designate, and which would simulate the phases of a malady?" asked Durtal.

"Nothing simpler. 'Open window burglars' that the physicians of the present day are, they recognize perfectly the ability of a more skilful man to pull off such jobs. The experiments of Beaunis, Liégois, Liébaut, and Bernheim are conclusive: you can even get a person assassinated by another to whom you suggest, without his knowledge, the will to the crime."

"I was thinking of something, myself," said Carhaix, who had been reflecting and not listening to this discussion of hypnotism. "Of the Inquisition. It certainly had its reason for being. It is the only agent that could deal with this fallen priest whom the Church has swept out."

"And remember," said Des Hermies, with his crooked smile playing around the corner of his mouth, "that the ferocity of the Inquisition has been greatly exaggerated. No doubt the benevolent Bodin speaks of driving long needles between the nails and the flesh of the sorcerers' fingers. 'An excellent gehenna,' says he. He eulogizes equally the torture by fire, which he characterizes as 'an exquisite death.' But he wishes only to turn the magicians away from their detestable practises and save their souls. Then Del Rio declares that 'the question' must not be applied to demoniacs after they have eaten, for fear they will vomit. He worried about their stomachs, this worthy man. Wasn't it also he who decreed that the torture must not be repeated twice in the same day, so as to give fear and pain a chance to calm down? Admit that the good Jesuit was not devoid of delicacy!"

"Docre," Gévingey went on, not paying any attention to the words of Des Hermies, "is the only individual who has rediscovered the ancient secrets and who obtains results in practise. He is rather more powerful, I would have you believe, than all those fools and quacks of whom we have been speaking. And they know the terrible canon, for he has sent many of them serious attacks of ophthalmia which the oculists cannot cure. So they tremble when the name Docre is pronounced in their presence."

"But how did a priest fall so low?"

"I can't say. If you wish ampler information about him," said Gévingey, addressing Des Hermies, "question your friend Chantelouve."

"Chantelouve!" cried Durtal.

"Yes, he and his wife used to be quite intimate with Canon Docre, but I hope for their sakes that they have long since ceased to have dealings with the monster."

Durtal listened no more. Mme. Chantelouve knew Canon Docre! Ah, was she Satanic, too? No, she certainly did not act like a possessed. "Surely this astrologer is cracked," he thought. She! And he called her image before him, and thought that tomorrow night she would probably give herself to him. Ah, those strange eyes of hers, those dark clouds suddenly cloven by radiant light!

She came now and took complete possession of him, as before he had ascended to the tower. "But if I didn't love you would I have come to you?" That sentence which she had spoken, with a caressing inflection of the voice, he heard again, and again he saw her mocking and tender face.

"Ah, you are dreaming," said Des Hermies, tapping him on the shoulder. "We have to go. It's striking ten."

When they were in the street they said good night to Gévingey, who lived on the other side of the river. Then they walked along a little way.

"Well," said Des Hermies, "are you interested in my astrologer?"

"He is slightly mad, isn't he?"

"Slightly? Humph."

"Well, his stories are incredible."

"Everything is incredible," said Des Hermies placidly,

turning up the collar of his overcoat. "However, I will admit that Gévingey astounds me when he asserts that he was visited by a succubus. His good faith is not to be doubted, for I know him to be a man who means what he says, though he is vain and doctorial. I know, too, that at La Salpêtière such occurrences are not rare. Women smitten with hystero-epilepsy see phantoms beside them in broad daylight and mate with them in a cataleptic state, and every night couch with visions that must be exactly like the fluid creatures of incubacy. But these women are hystero-epileptics, and Gévingey isn't, for I am his physician. Then, what can be believed and what can be proved? The materialists have taken the trouble to revise the accounts of the sorcery trials of old. They have found in the possession-cases of the Ursulines of Loudun and the nuns of Poitiers, in the history, even, of the convulsionists of Saint Médard, the symptoms of major hysteria, the same contractions of the whole system, the same muscular dissolutions, the same lethargies, even, finally, the famous arc of the circle. And what does this demonstrate, that these demonomaniacs were hystero-epileptics? Certainly. The observations of Dr. Richet, expert in such matters, are conclusive, but wherein do they invalidate possession? From the fact that the patients of la Salpêtrière are not possessed, though they are hysterical, does it follow that others, smitten with the same malady as they, are not possessed? It would have to be demonstrated also that all demonopathics are hysterical, and that is false, for there are women of sound mind and perfectly good sense who are demonopathic without knowing it. And admitting that the last point is controvertible, there remains this un-answerable question: is a woman possessed because she is hysterical, or is she hysterical because she is possessed? Only the Church can answer. Science cannot.

"No, come to think it over, the effrontery of the positivists is appalling. They decree that Satanism does not exist. They lay everything at the account of major hysteria, and they don't even know what this frightful malady is and what are its causes. No doubt Charcot determines very well the phases of the attack, notes the nonsensical and passional attitudes, the contortionistic movements; he discovers hysterogenic zones and can, by skilfully manipulating the ovaries, arrest or accelerate the crises, but as for foreseeing them and learning the sources and the motives and curing them, that's another thing. Science goes all to pieces on the question of this inexplicable, stupefying malady, which, consequently, is subject to the most diversified interpretations, not one of which can be declared exact. For the soul enters into this, the soul in conflict with the body, the soul overthrown in the demoralization of the nerves. You see, old man, all this is as dark as a bottle of ink. Mystery is everywhere and reason cannot see its way."

"Mmmm," said Durtal, who was now in front of his door. "Since anything can be maintained and nothing is certain, succubacy has it. Basically it is more literary—and cleaner—than positivism."

CHAPTER X

The day was long and hard to kill. Waking at dawn, full of thoughts of Mme. Chantelouve, he could not stay in one place, and kept inventing excuses for going out. He had no cakes, bonbons, and exotic liqueurs, and one must not be without all the little essentials when expecting a visit from a woman. He went by the longest route to the avenue de l'Opéra to buy fine essences of cedar and of that alkermes which makes the person tasting it think he is in an Oriental pharmaceutic laboratory. "The idea is," he said, "not so much to treat Hyacinthe as to astound her by giving her a sip of an unknown elixir."

He came back laden with packages, then went out again, and in the street was assailed by an immense ennui. After an interminable tour of the quays he finally tumbled into a beer hall. He fell on a bench and opened a newspaper.

What was he thinking as he sat, not reading but just looking at the police news? Nothing, not even of her. From having revolved the same matter over and over again and again his mind had reached a deadlock and refused to function. Durtal merely found himself very tired, very drowsy, as one in a warm bath after a night of travel.

"I must go home pretty soon," he said when he could collect himself a little, "for père Rateau certainly has not cleaned house in the thorough fashion which I commanded, and of course I don't want the furniture to be covered with dust. Six o'clock. Suppose I dine, after a fashion, in some not too unreliable place."

He remembered a nearby restaurant where he had eaten before without a great deal of dread. He chewed his way laboriously through an extremely dead fish, then through a piece of meat, flabby and cold; then he found a very few lentils, stiff with insecticide, beneath a great deal of sauce; finally he savoured some ancient prunes, whose juice smelt of mould and was at the same time aquatic and sepulchral.

Back in his apartment, he lighted fires in his bedroom and in his study, then he inspected everything. He was not mistaken. The concierge had upset the place with the same brutality, the same haste, as customarily. However, he must have tried to wash the windows, because the glass was streaked with finger marks.

Durtal effaced the imprints with a damp cloth, smoothed out the folds in the carpet, drew the curtains, and put the bookcases in order after dusting them with a napkin. Everywhere he found grains of tobacco, trodden cigarette ashes, pencil sharpenings, pen points eaten with rust. He also found cocoons of cat fur and crumpled bits of rough draft manuscript which had been whirled into all corners by the furious sweeping.

He finally could not help asking himself why he had so long tolerated the fuzzy filth which obscured and incrusted his household. While he dusted, his indignation against Rateau increased mightily. "Look at that," he said, perceiving his wax candles grown as yellow as tallow ones. He changed them. "That's better." He arranged his desk into studied disarray. Notebooks, and books with paper-cutters in them for book-marks, he laid in careful disorder. "Symbol of work," he said, smiling, as he placed an old folio, open, on a chair. Then he passed into his bedroom. With a wet sponge he freshened up the marble of the dresser, then he smoothed the bed cover, straightened his photographs and engravings, and went into the bathroom. Here he paused, disheartened. In a bamboo rack over the wash-bowl there was a chaos of phials. Resolutely he grabbed the perfume bottles, scoured the bottoms and necks with emery, rubbed the labels with gum elastic and bread crumbs, then he soaped

the tub, dipped the combs and brushes in an ammoniac solution, got his vapourizer to working and sprayed the room
with Persian lilac, washed the linoleum, and scoured the
seat and the pipes. Seized with a mania for cleanliness, he
polished, scrubbed, scraped, moistened, and dried, with great
sweeping strokes of the arm. He was no longer vexed at
the concierge; he was even sorry the old villain had not left
him more to do.

Then he shaved, touched up his moustache, and proceeded
to make an elaborate toilet, asking himself, as he dressed,
whether he had better wear button shoes or slippers. He
decided that shoes were less familiar and more dignified but
resolved to wear a flowing tie and a blouse, thinking that
this artistic negligée would please a woman.

"All ready," he said, after a last stroke of the brush. He
made the turn of the other rooms, poked the fires, and fed
the cat, which was running about in alarm, sniffing all the
cleaned objects and doubtless thinking that those he rubbed
against every day without paying any attention to them had
been replaced by new ones.

"Oh, the 'little essentials' I am forgetting!" Durtal put
the teakettle on the hob and placed cups, teapot, sugar bowl,
cakes, bonbons, and tiny liqueur glasses on an old lacquered
"waiter" so as to have everything on hand when it was time
to serve.

"Now I'm through. I've given the place a thorough
cleaning. Let her come," he said to himself, realigning some
books whose backs stuck out further than the others on the
shelves. "Everything in good shape. Except the chimney of
the lamp. Where it bulges, there are caramel specks and
blobs of soot, but I can't get the thing out; I don't want to
burn my fingers; and anyway, with the shade lowered a bit
she won't notice.

"Well, how shall I proceed when she does come?" he asked
himself, sinking into an armchair. "She enters. Good. I
take her hands. I kiss them. Then I bring her into this
room. I have her sit down beside the fire, in this chair. I

station myself, facing her, on this stool. Advancing a little, touching her knees, I can seize her. I make her bend over. I am supporting her whole weight. I bring her lips to mine and I am saved!

"——Or rather lost. For then the bother begins. I can't bear to think of getting her into the bedroom. Undressing and going to bed! That part is appalling unless you know each other very well. And when you are just becoming acquainted! The nice way is to have a cosy little supper for two. The wine has an ungodly kick to it. She immediately passes out, and when she comes to she is lying in bed under a shower of kisses. As we can't do it that way we shall have to avoid mutual embarrassment by making a show of passion. If I speed up the tempo and pretend to be in a frenzy perhaps we shall not have time to think about the miserable details. So I must possess her here, in this very spot, and she must think I have lost my head when she succumbs.

"It's hard to arrange in this room, because there isn't any divan. The best way would be to throw her down on the carpet. She can put her hands over her eyes, as they always do. I shall take good care to turn down the lamp before she rises.

"Well, I had better prepare a cushion for her head." He found one and slid it under the chair. "And I had better not wear suspenders, for they often cause ridiculous delays." He took them off and put on a belt. "But then there is that damned question of the skirts! I admire the novelists who can get a virgin unharnessed from her corsets and deflowered in the winking of an eye—as if it were possible! How annoying to have to fight one's way through all those starched entanglements! I do hope Mme. Chantelouve will be considerate and avoid those ridiculous difficulties as much as possible—for her own sake."

He consulted his watch. "Half-past eight. I mustn't expect her for nearly an hour, because, like all women, she will come late. What kind of an excuse will she make to Chantelouve, to get away tonight? Well, that is none of my business. Hmmm. This water heater beside the fire looks like the invitation to the toilet, but no, the tea things handy banish any gross idea."

And if Hyacinthe did not come?

"She will come," he said to himself, suddenly moved. "What motive would she have for staying away? She knows that she cannot inflame me more than I am inflamed." Then, jumping fom phase to phase of the same old question, "This will turn out badly, of course," he decided. "Once I am satisfied, disenchantment is inevitable. Oh, well, so much the better, for with this romance going on I cannot work."

"Miserable me! relapsing—only in mind, alas!—to the age of twenty. I am waiting for a woman. I who have scorned the doings of lovers for years and years. I look at my watch every five minutes, and I listen, in spite of myself, thinking it is her step I hear on the stair.

"No, there is no getting around it. The little blue flower, the perennial of the soul, is difficult to extirpate, and it keeps growing up again. It does not show itself for twenty years, and then all of a sudden, you know not why nor how, it sprouts, and then forth comes a burst of blossoms. My God! I am getting foolish."

He jumped from his chair. There was a gentle ring. "Not nine o'clock yet. It isn't she," he murmured, opening the door.

He squeezed her hands and thanked her for being so punctual.

She said she was not feeling well. "I came only because I didn't want to keep you waiting in vain."

His heart sank.

"I have a fearful headache," she said, passing her gloved hands over her forehead.

He took her furs and motioned her to the armchair. Prepared to follow his plan of attack, he sat down on the stool, but she refused the armchair and took a seat beside the table. Rising, he bent over her and caught hold of her fingers.

"Your hand is burning," she said.

"Yes, a bit of fever, because I get so little sleep. If you knew how much I have thought about you! Now I have you here, all to myself," and he spoke of that persistent odour of cinnamon, faint, distant, expiring amid the less definite odours which her gloves exhaled, "well," and he sniffed her fingers, "you will leave some of yourself here when you go away."

She rose, sighing. "I see you have a cat. What is his name?"

"Mouche."

She called to the cat, which fled precipitately.

"Mouche! Mouche!" Durtal called, but Mouche took refuge under the bed and refused to come out. "You see he is rather bashful. He has never seen a woman."

"Oh, would you try to make me think you have never received a woman here?"

He swore that he never had, that she was the first. . . .

"And you were not really anxious that this—first—should come?"

He blushed. "Why do you say that?"

She made a vague gesture. "I want to tease you," she said, sitting down in the armchair. "To tell you the truth, I do not know why I like to ask you such presumptuous questions."

He had sat down in front of her. So now, at last, the scene was set as he wished and he must begin the attack. His knee touched hers.

"You know," he said, "that you cannot presume here. You have claims on——"

"No, I haven't and I want none."

"Why?"

"Because. . . . Listen," and her voice became grave and firm. "The more I reflect, the more inclined I am to ask

you, for heaven's sake, not to destroy our dream. And then.
. . . Do you want me to be frank, so frank that I shall doubtless seem a monster of selfishness? Well, personally, I do
not wish to spoil the—the—what shall I say?—the extreme
happiness our relation gives me. I know I explain badly
and confusedly, but this is the way it is: I possess you when
and how I please, just as, for a long time, I have possessed
Byron, Baudelaire, Gérard de Nerval, those I love———"

"You mean. . . . ?"

"That I have only to desire them, to desire you, before I
go to sleep. . . ."

"And?"

"And you would be inferior to my chimera, to the Durtal
I adore, whose caresses make my nights delirious!"

He looked at her in stupefaction. She had that dolent,
troubled look in her eyes. She even seemed not to see him,
but to be looking into space. He hesitated. . . . In a sudden
flash of thought he saw the scenes of incubacy of which
Gévingey had spoken. "We shall untangle all this later,"
he thought within himself, "meanwhile—" He took her
gently by the arms, drew her to him and abruptly kissed her
mouth.

She rebounded as if she had had an electric shock. She
struggled to rise. He strained her to him and embraced her
furiously, then with a strange gurgling cry she threw her
head back and caught his leg between both of hers.

He emitted a howl of rage, for he felt her haunches move.
He understood now—or thought he understood! She wanted
a miserly pleasure, a sort of solitary vice. . . .

He pushed her away. She remained there, quite pale,
choking, her eyes closed, her hands outstretched like those of
a frightened child. Then Durtal's wrath vanished. With a
little cry he came up to her and caught her again, but she
struggled, crying, "No! I beseech you, let me go."

He held her crushed against his body and attempted to
make her yield.

"I implore you, let me go."

Her accent was so despairing that he relinquished her. Then he debated with himself whether to throw her brutally on the floor and violate her. But her bewildered eyes frightened him.

She was panting and her arms hung limp at her sides as she leaned, very pale, against the bookcase.

"Ah!" he said, marching up and down, knocking into the furniture, "I must really love you, if in spite of your supplications and refusals——'

She joined her hands to keep him away.

"Good God!" he said, exasperated, "what are you made of?"

She came to herself, and, offended, she said to him, "Monsieur, I too suffer. Spare me," and pell-mell she spoke of her husband, of her confessor, and became so incoherent that Durtal was frightened. She was silent, then in a singing voice she said, "Tell me, you will come to my house tomorrow night, won't you?"

"But I suffer too!"

She seemed not to hear him. In her smoky eyes, far, far back, there seemed to be a twinkle of feeble light. She murmured, in the cadence of a canticle, "Tell me, dear, you will come tomorrow night, won't you?"

"Yes," he said at last.

Then she readjusted herself and without saying a word quitted the room. In silence he accompanied her to the entrance. She opened the door, turned around, took his hand and very lightly brushed it with her lips.

He stood there stupidly, not knowing what to make of her behaviour.

"What does she mean?" he exclaimed, returning to the room, putting the furniture back in place and smoothing the disordered carpet. "Heavens, I wish I could as easily restore order to my brain. Let me think, if I can. What is she after? Because, of course, she has something in view. She does not want our relation to culminate in the act itself. Does she really fear disillusion, as she claims? Is she really thinking how grotesque the amorous somersaults are? Or is she, as I believe, a melancholy and terrible player-around-the-edges, thinking only of herself? Well, her obscene selfishness is one of those complicated sins that have to be shriven by the very highest confessor. She's a plain teaser!

"I don't know. Incubacy enters into this. She admits—so placidly!—that in dream she cohabits at will with dead or living beings. Is she Satanizing, and is this some of the work of Canon Docre? He's a friend of hers.

"So many riddles impossible to solve. What is the meaning of this unexpected invitation for tomorrow night? Does she wish to yield nowhere except in her own home? Does she feel more at ease there, or does she think the propinquity of her husband will render the sin more piquant? Does she loathe Chantelouve, and is this a meditated vengeance, or does she count on the fear of danger to spur our senses?

"After all, I think it is probably a final coquetry, an appetizer before the repast. And women are so funny anyway! She probably thinks these delays and subterfuges are necessary to differentiate her from a cocotte. Or perhaps there is a physical necessity for stalling me off another day."

He sought other reasons but could find none.

"Deep down in my heart," he said, vexed in spite of himself by this rebuff, "I know I have been an imbecile. I ought to have acted the cave man and paid no attention to her supplications and lies. I ought to have taken violent possession of her lips and breast. Then it would be finished, whereas now I must begin at the beginning again, and God damn her! I have other things to do.

"Who knows whether she isn't laughing at me this very moment? Perhaps she wanted me to be more violent and bold—but no, her soul-sick voice was not feigned, her poor eyes did not simulate bewilderment, and then what would she have meant by that *respectful* kiss—for there was an impalpable shade of respect and gratitude in that kiss which she planted on my hand!"

She was too much for him. "Meanwhile, in this hurly-burly I have forgotten my refreshments. Suppose I take off my shoes, now that I am alone, for my feet are swollen from parading up and down the room. Suppose I do better yet and go to bed, for I am incapable of working or reading," and he drew back the covers.

"Decidedly, nothing happens the way one foresees it, yet my plan of attack wasn't badly thought out," he said, crawling in. With a sigh he blew out the lamp, and the cat, reassured, passed over him, lighter than a breath, and curled up without a sound.

CHAPTER XI

Contrary to his expectations, he slept all night, with clenched fists, and woke next morning quite calm, even gay. The scene of the night before, which ought to have exacerbated his senses, produced exactly the opposite effect. The truth is that Durtal was not of those who are attracted by difficulties. He always made one hardy effort to surmount them, then when that failed he would withdraw, with no desire to renew the combat. If Mme. Chantelouve thought to entice him by delays, she had miscalculated. This morning, already, he was weary of the comedy.

His reflections began to be slightly tinged with bitterness. He was angry at the woman for having wished to keep him in suspense, and he was angry at himself for having permitted her to make a fool of him. Then certain expressions, the impertinence of which had not struck him at first, chilled him now. "Her nervous trick of laughing, which sometimes caught her in public places," then her declaration that she did not need his permission, nor even his person, in order to possess him, seemed to him unbecoming, to say the least, and uncalled for, as he had not run after her nor indeed made any advances to her at all.

"I will fix you," he said, "when I get some hold over you."

But in the calm awakening of this morning the spell of the woman had relaxed. Resolutely he thought, "Keep two dates with her. This one tonight at her house. It won't count, because nothing can be done. For I intend neither to allow myself to be assaulted nor to attempt an assault. I certainly have no desire to be caught by Chantelouve *in flagrante delicto,* and probably get into a shooting scrape and be haled into police court. Have her here once. If she does not yield then, why, the matter is closed. She can go and tickle somebody else."

And he made a hearty breakfast, and sat down to his writing table and ran over the scattered notes for his book.

"I had got," he said, glancing at his last chapter, "to where the alchemic experiments and diabolic evocations have proved unavailing. Prelati, Blanchet, all the sorcerers and sorcerers' helpers whom the Marshal has about him, admit that to bring Satan to him Gilles must make over his soul and body to the Devil or commit crimes.

"Gilles refuses to alienate his existence and sell his soul, but he contemplates murder without any horror. This man, so brave on the battlefield, so courageous when he accompanied Jeanne d'Arc, trembles before the Devil and is afraid when he thinks of eternity and of Christ. The same is true of his accomplices. He has made them swear on the Testament to keep the secret of the confounding turpitudes which the château conceals, and he can be sure that not one will violate the oath, for, in the Middle Ages, the most reckless of freebooters would not commit the inexpiable sin of deceiving God.

"At the same time that his alchemists abandon their unfruitful furnaces, Gilles begins a course of systematic gluttony, and his flesh, set on fire by the essences of inordinate potations and spiced dishes, seethes in tumultuous eruption.

"Now, there are no women in the château. Gilles appears to have despised the sex ever since leaving the court. After experience of the ribalds of the camps and frequentation, with Xaintrailles and La Hire, of the prostitutes of Charles VII, it seems that a dislike for the feminine form came over him. Like others whose ideal of concupiscence is deteriorated and deviated, he certainly comes to be disgusted by the delicacy of the grain of the skin of women and by that odour of femininity which all sodomists abhor.

"He depraves the choir boys who are under his authority. He chose them in the first place, these little psaltry ministrants, for their beauty, and 'beautiful as angels' they are. They are the only ones he loves, the only ones he spares in his murderous transports.

"But soon infantile pollution seems to him an insipid delicacy. The law of Satanism which demands that the elect of Evil, once started, must go the whole way, is once more fulfilled. Gilles's soul must become thoroughly cankered, a red tabernacle, that in it the Very Low may dwell at ease.

"The litanies of lust arise in an atmosphere that is like the wind over a slaughter house. The first victim is a very small boy whose name we do not know. Gilles disembowels him, and, cutting off the hands and tearing out the eyes and heart, carries these members into Prelati's chamber. The two men offer them, with passionate objurgations, to the Devil, who holds his peace. Gilles, confounded, flees. Prelati rolls up the poor remains in linen and, trembling, goes out at night to bury them in consecrated ground beside a chapel dedicated to Saint Vincent.

"Gilles preserves the blood of this child to write formulas of evocation and conjurements. It manures a horrible crop. Not long afterward the Marshal reaps the most abundant harvest of crimes that has ever been sown.

"From 1432 to 1440, that is to say during the eight years between the Marshal's retreat and his death, the inhabitants of Anjou, Poitu, and Brittany walk the highways wringing their hands. All the children disappear. Shepherd boys are abducted from the fields. Little girls coming out of school, little boys who have gone to play ball in the lanes or at the edge of the wood, return no more.

"In the course of an investigation ordered by the duke of Brittany, the scribes of Jean Touscheronde, duke's commissioner in these matters, compile interminable lists of lost children.

"Lost, at la Rochebernart, the child of the woman

Péronne, 'a child who did go to school and who did apply himself to his book with exceeding diligence.'

"Lost, at Saint Etienne de Montluc, the son of Guillaume Brice, 'and this was a poor man and sought alms.'

"Lost, at Mâchecoul, the son of Georget le Barbier, 'who was seen, a certain day, knocking apples from a tree behind the hôtel Rondeau, and who since hath not been seen.'

"Lost, at Thonaye, the child of Mathelin Thouars, 'and he had been heard to cry and lament and the said child was about twelve years of age.'

"At Mâchecoul, again, the day of Pentecost, mother and father Sergent leave their eight-year-old boy at home, and when they return from the fields 'they did not find the said child of eight years of age, wherefore they marvelled and were exceeding grieved.'

"At Chantelou, it is Pierre Badieu, mercer of the parish, who says that a year or thereabouts ago, he saw, in the domain de Rais, 'two little children of the age of nine who were brothers and the children of Robin Pavot of the aforesaid place, and since that time neither have they been seen neither doth any know what hath become of them.'

"At Nantes, it is Jeanne Darel who deposes that 'on the day of the feast of the Holy Father, her true child named Olivier did stray from her, being of the age of seven and eight years, and since the day of the feast of the Holy Father neither did she see him nor hear tidings.'

"And the account of the investigation goes on, revealing hundreds of names, describing the grief of the mothers who interrogate passersby on the highway, and telling of the keening of the families from whose very homes children have been spirited away when the elders went to the fields to hoe or to sow the hemp. These phrases, like a desolate refrain, recur again and again, at the end of every deposition: 'They were seen complaining dolorously,' 'Exceedingly they did lament.' Wherever the bloodthirsty Gilles dwells the women weep.

"At first the frantic people tell themselves that evil

fairies and malicious genii are dispersing the generation, but little by little terrible suspicions are aroused. As soon as the Marshal quits a place, as he goes from the château de Tiffauges to the château de Champtocé, and from there to the castle of La Suze or to Nantes, he leaves behind him a wake of tears. He traverses a countryside and in the morning children are missing. Trembling, the peasant realizes also that wherever Prelati, Roger de Bricqueville, Gilles de Sillé, any of the Marshal's intimates, have shown themselves, little boys have disappeared. Finally, the peasant learns to look with horror upon an old woman, Perrine Martin, who wanders around, clad in grey, her face covered —as is that of Gilles de Sillé—with a black stamin. She accosts children, and her speech is so seductive, her face, when she raises her veil, so benign, that all follow her to the edge of a wood, where men carry them off, gagged, in sacks. And the frightened people call this purveyor of flesh, this ogress, 'La Meffraye,' from the name of a bird of prey.

"These emissaries spread out, covering all the villages and hamlets, tracking the children down at the orders of the Chief Huntsman, the sire de Bricqueville. Not content with these beaters, Gilles takes to standing at a window of the château, and when young mendicants, attracted by the renown of his bounty, ask an alms, he runs an appraising eye over them, has any who excite his lust brought in and thrown into an underground prison and kept there until, being in appetite, he is pleased to order a carnal supper.

"How many children did he disembowel after deflowering them? He himself did not know, so many were the rapes he had consummated and the murders he had committed. The texts of the times enumerate between seven and eight hundred, but the estimate is inaccurate and seems overconservative. Entire regions were devastated. The hamlet of Tiffauges had no more young men. La Suze was without male posterity. At Champtocé the whole foundation room of a tower was filled with corpses. A witness cited in the inquest, Guillaume Hylairet, declared also, "that one hight

Du Jardin hath heard say that there was found in the said castle a wine pipe full of dead little children.'

"Even today traces of these assassinations linger. Two years ago at Tiffauges a physician discovered an oublitte and brought forth piles of skulls and bones.

"Gilles confessed to frightful holocausts, and his friends confirmed the atrocious details.

"At dusk, when their senses are phosphorescent, enkindled by inflammatory spiced beverages and by 'high' venison, Gilles and his friends retire to a distant chamber of the château. The little boys are brought from their cellar prisons to this room. They are disrobed and gagged. The Marshal fondles them and forces them. Then he hacks them to pieces with a dagger, taking great pleasure in slowly dismembering them. At other times he slashes the boy's chest and drinks the breath from the lungs; sometimes he opens the stomach also, smells it, enlarges the incision with his hands, and seats himself in it. Then while he macerates the warm entrails in mud, he turns half around and looks over his shoulder to contemplate the supreme convulsions, the last spasms. He himself says afterwards, 'I was happier in the enjoyment of tortures, tears, fright, and blood, than in any other pleasure.'

"Then he becomes weary of these fecal joys. An unpublished passage in his trial proceedings informs us that 'The said sire heated himself with little boys, sometimes also with little girls, with whom he had congress in the belly, saying that he had more pleasure and less pain than acting in nature.' After which, he slowly saws their throats, cuts them to pieces, and the corpses, the linen and the clothing, are put in the fireplace, where a smudge fire of logs and leaves is burning, and the ashes are thrown into the latrine, or scattered to the winds from the top of a tower, or buried in the moats and mounds.

"Soon his furies become aggravated. Until now he has appeased the rage of his senses with living or moribund beings. He wearies of stuprating palpitant flesh and becomes a lover of the dead. A passionate artist, he kisses, with cries of enthusiasm, the well-made limbs of his victims. He establishes sepulchral beauty contests, and whichever of the truncated heads receives the prize he raises by the hair and passionately kisses the cold lips.

"Vampirism satisfies him for months. He polutes dead children, appeasing the fever of his desires in the blood smeared chill of the tomb. He even goes so far—one day when his supply of children is exhausted—as to disembowel a pregnant woman and sport with the fœtus. After these excesses he falls into horrible states of coma, similar to those heavy lethargies which overpowered Sergeant Bertrand after his violations of the grave. But if that leaden sleep is one of the known phases of ordinary vampirism, if Gilles de Rais was merely a sexual pervert, we must admit that he distinguished himself from the most delirious sadists, the most exquisite virtuosi in pain and murder, by a detail which seems extrahuman, it is so horrible.

"As these terrifying atrocities, these monstrous outrages, no longer suffice him, he corrodes them with the essence of a rare sin. It is no longer the resolute, sagacious cruelty of the wild beast playing with the body of a victim. His ferocity does not remain merely carnal; it becomes spiritual. He wishes to make the child suffer both in body and soul. By a thoroughly Satanic cheat he deceives gratitude, dupes affection, and desecrates love. At a leap he passes the bounds of human infamy and lands plump in the darkest depth of Evil.

"He contrives this: One of the unfortunate children is brought into his chamber, and hanged, by Bricqueville, Prelati, and de Sillé, to a hook fixed into the wall. Just at the moment when the child is suffocating, Gilles orders him to be taken down and the rope untied. With some precaution, he takes the child on his knees, revives him, caresses him, rocks him, dries his tears, and pointing to the accomplices, says, 'These men are bad, but you see they obey me. Do not be afraid. I will save your life and take you back to your mother,' and while the little one, wild with joy, kisses him and at that moment loves him, Gilles gently makes an incision in the back of the neck, rendering the child 'languishing,' to follow Gilles's own expression, and when the head, not quite detached, bows, Gilles kneads the body, turns it about, and violates it, bellowing.

"After these abominable pastimes he may well believe that the art of the charnalist has beneath his fingers expressed its last drop of pus, and in a vaunting cry he says to his troop of parasites, "There is no man on earth who dare do as I have done.'

"But if in Love and Well-doing the infinite is approachable for certain souls, the out-of-the-world possibilities of Evil are limited. In his excesses of stupration and murder the Marshal cannot go beyond a fixed point. In vain he may dream of unique violations, of more ingenious slow tortures, but human imagination has a limit and he has already reached it—even passed it, with diabolic aid. Insatiable he seethes—there is nothing material in which to express his ideal. He can verify that axiom of demonographers, that the Evil One dupes all persons who give themselves, or are willing to give themselves, to him.

"As he can descend no further, he tries returning on the way by which he has come, but now remorse overtakes him, overwhelms him, and wrenches him without respite. His nights are nights of expiation. Besieged by phantoms, he howls like a wounded beast. He is found rushing along the solitary corridors of the château. He weeps, throws himself on his knees, swears to God that he will do penance. He promises to found pious institutions. He does establish, at Mâchecoul, a boys' academy in honour of the Holy Innocents. He speaks of shutting himself up in a cloister, of going to Jerusalem, begging his bread on the way.

"But in this fickle and aberrated mind ideas superpose themselves on each other, then pass away, and those which disappear leave their shadow on those which follow. Abruptly, even while weeping with distress, he precipitates himself into new debauches and, raving with delirium, hurls himself upon the child brought to him, gouges out the eyes, runs his finger around the bloody, milky socket, then he seizes a spiked club and crushes the skull. And while the gurgling blood runs over him, he stands, smeared with spattered brains, and grinds his teeth and laughs. Like a hunted beast he flees into the wood, while his henchmen remove the crimson stains from the ground and dispose prudently of the corpse and the reeking garments.

"He wanders in the forests surrounding Tiffauges, dark, impenetrable forests like those which Brittany still can show at Carnoet. He sobs as he walks along. He attempts to thrust aside the phantoms which accost him. Then he looks about him and beholds obscenity in the shapes of the aged trees. It seems that nature perverts itself before him, that his very presence depraves it. For the first time he understands the motionless lubricity of trees. He discovers priapi in the branches.

"Here a tree appears to him as a living being, standing on its root-tressed head, its limbs waving in the air and spread wide apart, subdivided and resubdivided into haunches, which again are divided and re-subdivided. Here between two limbs another branch is jammed, in a stationary fornication which is reproduced in diminished scale from bough to twig to the top of the tree. There it seems the trunk is a phallus which mounts and disappears into a skirt of leaves or which, on the contrary, issues from a green clout and plunges into the glossy belly of the earth.

"Frightful images rise before him. He sees the skin of little boys, the lucid white skin, vellum-like, in the pale, smooth bark of the slender beeches. He recognizes the pachydermatous skin of the beggar boys in the dark and wrinkled envelope of the old oaks. Beside the bifurcations of the branches there are yawning holes, puckered orifices in the bark, simulating emunctoria, or the protruding anus of a beast. In the joints of the branches there are other visions, elbows, armpits furred with grey lichens. Even in the trunks there are incisions which spread out into great lips beneath tufts of brown, velvety moss.

"Everywhere obscene forms rise from the ground and spring, disordered, into a firmament which satanizes. The clouds swell into breasts, divide into buttocks, bulge as if with fecundity, scattering a train of spawn through space. They accord with the sombre bulging of the foliage, in which now there are only images of giant or dwarf hips, feminine triangles, great V's, mouths of Sodom, glowing cicatrices, humid vents. This landscape of abomination changes. Gilles now sees on the trunks frightful cancers and horrible wens. He observes exostoses and ulcers, membranous sores, tubercular chancres, atrocious caries. It is an arboreal lazaret, a venereal clinic.

"And there, at a detour of the forest aisle, stands a mottled red beech.

"Amid the sanguinary falling leaves he feels that he has been spattered by a shower of blood. He goes into a rage. He conceives the delusion that beneath the bark lives a wood nymph, and he would feel with his hands the palpitant flesh of the goddess, he would trucidate the Dryad, violate her in a place unknown to the follies of men.

"He is jealous of the woodman who can murder, can massacre, the trees, and he raves. Tensely he listens and hears in the soughing wind a response to his cries of desire. Overwhelmed, he resumes his walk, weeping, until he arrives at the château and sinks to his bed exhausted, an inert mass.

"The phantoms take more definite shape, now that he sleeps. The lubric enlacements of the branches, dilated crevices and cleft mosses, the coupling of the diverse beings of the wood, disappear; the tears of the leaves whipped by the wind are dried; the white abscesses of the clouds are resorbed into the grey of the sky; and—in an awful silence—the incubi and succubi pass.

"The corpses of his victims, reduced to ashes and scattered, return to the larva state and attack his lower parts. He writhes, with the blood bursting his veins. He rebounds in a somersault, then he crawls to the crucifix, like a wolf, on all fours, and howling, strains his lips to the feet of the Christ.

"A sudden reaction overwhelms him. He trembles before the image whose convulsed face looks down on him. He adjures Christ to have pity, supplicates Him to spare a sinner, and sobs and weeps, and when, incapable of further effort, he whimpers, he hears, terrified, in his own voice, the lamentations of the children crying for their mothers and pleading for mercy."

.   .   .   .

And Durtal, coming slowly out of the vision he had conjured up, closed his notebook and remarked, "Rather petty, my own spiritual conflict regarding a woman whose sin—like my own, to be sure—is commonplace and bourgeois."

CHAPTER XII

"Easy to find an excuse for this visit, though it will seem strange to Chantelouve, whom I have neglected for months," said Durtal on his way toward the rue Bagneux. "Supposing he is home this evening—and he probably isn't, because surely Hyacinthe will have seen to that—I can tell him that I have learned of his illness through Des Hermies and that I have come to see how he is getting along."

He paused on the stoop of the building in which Chantelouve lived. At each side and over the door were these antique lamps with reflectors, surmounted by a sort of casque of sheet iron painted green. There was an old iron balustrade, very wide, and the steps, with wooden sides, were paved with red tile. About this house there was a sepulchral and also clerical odour, yet there was also something homelike—though a little too imposing—about it such as is not to be found in the cardboard houses they build nowadays. You could see at a glance that it did not harbour the apartment house promiscuities: decent, respectable couples with kept women for neighbours. The house pleased him, and he considered Hyacinthe the more desirable for her substantial environment.

He rang at a first-floor apartment. A maid led him through a long hall into a sitting-room. He noticed, at a glance, that nothing had changed since his last visit. It was the same vast, high-ceilinged room with windows reaching to heaven. There was the huge fireplace; on the mantel-piece the same reproduction, reduced, in bronze, of Fremiet's Jeanne d'Arc, between the two globe lamps of Japanese porcelain. He recognized the grand piano, the table loaded with albums, the divan, the chairs in the style of Louis XV with tapestried covers. In front of every window there were imitation Chinese vases, mounted on tripods of imitation ebony and containing sickly palms. On the walls were religious pictures, without expression, and a portrait of Chantelouve in his youth, three-quarter length, his hand resting on a pile of his works. An ancient Russian icon in nielloed silver and one of these Christs in carved wood, executed in the seventeenth century by Bogard de Nancy, in an antique frame of gilded wood backed with velvet, were the only things that slightly relieved the banality of the decoration. The rest of the furniture looked like that of a bourgeois household fixed up for Lent, or for a charity dance or for a visit from the priest. A great fire blazed on the hearth. The room was lighted by a very high lamp with a wide shade of pink lace——

"Stinks of the sacristy!" Durtal was saying to himself at the moment the door opened.

Mme. Chantelouve entered, the lines of her figure advantageously displayed by a wrapper of white swanskin, which gave off a fragrance of frangipane. She pressed Durtal's hand and sat down facing him, and he perceived under the wrap her indigo silk stockings in little patent leather bootines with straps across the insteps.

They talked about the weather. She complained of the way the winter hung on, and declared that although the furnace seemed to be working all right she was always shivering, was always frozen to death. She told him to feel her hands, which indeed were cold, then she seemed worried about his health.

"You look pale," she said.

"You might at least say that I *am* pale," he replied.

She did not answer immediately, then, "Yesterday I saw how much you desire me," she said. "But why, why, want to go so far?"

He made a gesture, indicating vague annoyance.

"How funny you are!" she went on. "I was re-reading one of your books today, and I noticed this phrase, 'The only women you can continue to love are those you lose.' Now admit that you were right when you wrote that."

"It all depends. I wasn't in love then."

She shrugged her shoulders. "Well," she said, "I must tell my husband you are here."

Durtal remained silent, wondering what rôle Chantelouve actually played in this triangle.

Chantelouve returned with his wife. He was in his dressing-gown and had a pen in his mouth. He took it out and put it on the table, and after assuring Durtal that his health was completely restored, he complained of overwhelming labours. "I have had to quit giving dinners and receptions," he said, "I can't even go visiting. I am in harness every day at my desk."

And when Durtal asked him the nature of these labours, he confessed to a whole series of unsigned volumes on the lives of the saints, to be turned out by the gross by a Tours firm for exportation.

"Yes," said his wife, laughing, "and these are *sadly neglected* saints whose biographies he is preparing."

And as Durtal looked at him inquiringly, Chantelouve, also laughing, said, "It was their persons that were *sadly neglected*. The subjects are chosen for me, and it does seem as if the publisher enjoyed making me eulogize frowziness. I have to describe Blessed Saints most of whom were deplorably unkempt: Labre, who was so lousy and ill-smelling as to disgust the beasts in the stables; Saint Cunegonde who 'through humility' neglected her body; Saint Oportune who never used water and who washed her bed only with her tears; Saint Silvia who never removed the grime from her face; Saint Radegonde who never changed her hair shirt and who slept on a cinder pile; and how many others, around whose heads I must draw a golden halo!"

"There are worse than those," said Durtal. "Read the

life of Marie Alacoque. You will see that she, to mortify herself, licked up with her tongue the dejections of one sick person and sucked an abscess from the toe of another."

"I know, but I must admit that I am less touched than revolted by these tales."

"I prefer Saint Lucius the martyr," said Mme. Chantelouve. "His body was so transparent that he could see through his chest the vileness of his heart. His kind of 'vileness' at least we can stand. But I must admit that this utter disregard of cleanliness makes me suspicious of the monasteries and renders your beloved Middle Ages odious to me."

"Pardon me, my dear," said her husband, "you are greatly mistaken. The Middle Ages were not, as you believe, an epoch of uncleanliness. People frequented the baths assiduously. At Paris, for example, where these establishments were numerous, the 'stove-keepers' went about the city announcing that the water was hot. It is not until the Renaissance that uncleanliness becomes rife in France. When you think that that delicious Reine Margot kept her body macerated with perfumes but as grimy as the inside of a stovepipe! and that Henri Quatre plumed himself on having 'reeking feet and a fine armpit.'"

"My dear, for heaven's sake," said madame, "spare us the details."

While Chantelouve was speaking, Durtal was watching him. He was small and rotund, with a bay window which his arms would not have gone around. He had rubicund cheeks, long hair very much pomaded, trailing in the back and drawn up in crescents along his temples. He had pink cotton in his ears. He was smooth shaven and looked like a pious but convivial notary. But his quick, calculating eye belied his jovial and sugary mien. One divined in his look the cool, unscrupulous man of affairs, capable, for all his honeyed ways, of doing one a bad turn.

"He must be aching to throw me into the street," said

Durtal to himself, "because he certainly knows all about his wife's goings-on."

But if Chantelouve wished to be rid of his guest he did not show it. With his legs crossed and his hands folded one over the other, in the attitude of a priest, he appeared to be mightly interested in Durtal's work. Inclining a little, listening as if in a theatre, he said, "Yes, I know the material on the subject. I read a book some time ago about Gilles de Rais which seemed to me well handled. It was by abbé Bossard."

"It is the most complete and reliable of the biographies of the Marshal."

"But," Chantelouve went on, "there is one point which I never have been able to understand. I have never been able to explain to myself why the name Bluebeard should have been attached to the Marshal, whose history certainly has no relation to the tale of the good Perrault."

"As a matter of fact the real Bluebeard was not Gilles de Rais, but probably a Breton king, Comor, a fragment of whose castle, dating from the sixth century, is still standing, on the confines of the forest of Carnoet. The legend is simple. The king asked Guerock, count of Vannes, for the hand of his daughter, Triphine. Guerock refused, because he had heard that the king maintained himself in a constant state of widowerhood by cutting his wives' throats. Finally Saint Gildas promised Guerock to return his daughter to him safe and sound when he should reclaim her, and the union was celebrated.

"Some months later Triphine learned that Comor did indeed kill his consorts as soon as they became pregnant. She was big with child, so she fled, but her husband pursued her and cut her throat. The weeping father commanded Saint Gildas to keep his promise, and the Saint resuscitated Triphine.

"As you see, this legend comes much nearer than the history of our Bluebeard to the told tale arranged by the ingenious Perrault. Now, why and how the name Blue-beard passed from King Comor to the Marshal de Rais, I cannot tell. You know what pranks oral tradition can play."

"But with your Gilles de Rais you must have to plunge into Satanism right up to the hilt," said Chantelouve after a silence.

"Yes, and it would really be more interesting if these scenes were not so remote. What would have a timely appeal would be a study of the Diabolism of the present day."

"No doubt," said Chantelouve, pleasantly.

"For," Durtal went on, looking at him intently, "un-heard-of things are going on right now. I have heard tell of sacrilegious priests, of a certain canon who has revived the sabbats of the Middle Ages."

Chantelouve did not betray himself by so much as a flicker of the eyelids. Calmly he uncrossed his legs and looking up at the ceiling he said, "Alas, certain scabby wethers succeed in stealing into the fold, but they are so rare as hardly to be worth thinking about." And he deftly changed the subject by speaking of a book he had just read about the Fronde.

Durtal, somewhat embarrassed, said nothing. He understood that Chantelouve refused to speak of his relations with Canon Docre.

"My dear," said Mme. Chantelouve, addressing her husband, "you have forgotten to turn up your lamp wick. It is smoking. I can smell it from here, even through the closed door."

She was most evidently conveying him a dismissal. Chantelouve rose and, with a vaguely malicious smile, excused himself as being obliged to continue his work. He shook hands with Durtal, begged him not to stay away so long in future, and gathering up the skirts of his dressing-gown he left the room.

She followed him with her eyes, then rose, in her turn,

ran to the door, assured herself with a glance that it was closed, then returned to Durtal, who was leaning against the mantel. Without a word she took his head between her hands, pressed her lips to his mouth and opened it.

He grunted furiously.

She looked at him with indolent and filmy eyes, and he saw sparks of silver dart to their surface. He held her in his arms. She was swooning but vigilantly listening. Gently she disengaged herself, sighing, while he, embarrassed, sat down at a little distance from her, clenching and unclenching his hands.

They spoke of banal things: she boasting of her maid, who would go through fire for her, he responding only by gestures of approbation and surprise.

Then suddenly she passed her hands over her forehead. "Ah!" she said, "I suffer cruelly when I think that he is there working. No, it would cost me too much remorse. What I say is foolish, but if he were a different man, a man who went out more and made conquests, it would not be so bad."

He was irritated by the inconsequentiality of her plaints. Finally, feeling completely safe, he came closer to her and said, "You spoke of remorse, but whether we embark or whether we stand on the bank, isn't our guilt exactly the same?"

"Yes, I know. My confessor talks to me like that—only more severely—but I think you are both wrong."

He could not help laughing, and he said to himself, "Remorse is perhaps the condiment which keeps passion from being too unappetizing to the blasé." Then aloud he jestingly, "Speaking of confessors, if I were a casuist it seems to me I would try to invent new sins. I am not a casuist, and yet, having looked about a bit, I believe I *have* found a new sin."

"You?" she said, laughing in turn. "Can I commit it?"

He scrutinized her features. She had the expression of a greedy child.

"You alone can answer that. Now I must admit that the sin is not absolutely new, for it fits into the known category of lust. But it has been neglected since pagan days, and was never well defined in any case."

"Do not keep me in suspense. What is this sin?"

"It isn't easy to explain. Nevertheless I will try. Lust, I believe, can be classified into: ordinary sin, sin against nature, bestiality, and let us add *demoniality* and sacrilege. Well, there is, in addition to these, what I shall call Pygmalionism, which embraces at the same time cerebral onanism and incest.

"Imagine an artist falling in love with his child, his creation: with an Hérodiade, a Judith, a Helen, a Jeanne d'Arc, whom he has either described or painted, and evoking her, and finally possessing her in dream.

"Well, this love is worse than normal incest. In the latter sin the guilty one commits only a half-offence, because his daughter is not born solely of his substance, but also of the flesh of another. Thus, logically, in incest there is a quasi-natural side, almost licit, because part of another person has entered into the engendering of the *corpus delicti;* while in Pygmalionism the father violates the child of his soul, of that which alone is purely and really his, which alone he can impregnate without the aid of another. The offence is, then, entire and complete. Now, is there not also disdain of nature, of the work of God, since the subject of the sin is no longer—as even in bestiality—a palpable and living creature, but an unreal being created by a projection of the desecrated talent, a being almost celestial, since, by genius, by artistry, it often becomes immortal?

"Let us go further, if you wish. Suppose that an artist depicts a saint and becomes enamoured of her. Thus we have complications of crime against nature and of sacrilege. An enormity!"

"Which, perhaps, is exquisite!"

He was taken aback by the word she had used. She rose, opened the door, and called her husband.

"Dear," she said, "Durtal has discovered a new sin!"

"Surely not," said Chantelouve, his figure framed in the doorway. "The book of sins is an edition *ne varietur*. New sins cannot be invented, but old ones may be kept from falling into oblivion. Well, what is this sin of his?"

Durtal explained the theory.

"But it is simply a refined expression of succubacy. The consort is not one's work become animate, but a succubus which by night takes that form."

"Admit, at any rate, that this cerebral hermaphrodism, self-fecundation, is a distinguished vice at least—being the privilege of the artist—a vice reserved for the elect, inaccessible to the mob."

"If you like exclusive obscenity—" laughed Chantelouve. "But I must get back to the lives of the saints; the atmosphere is fresher and more benign. So excuse me, Durtal. I leave it to my wife to continue this Marivaux conversation about Satanism with you."

He said it in the simplest, most debonair fashion to be imagined, but with just the slightest trace of irony.

Which Durtal perceived. "It must be quite late," he thought, when the door closed after Chantelouve. He consulted his watch. Nearly eleven. He rose to take leave.

"When shall I see you?" he murmured, very low.

"Your apartment tomorrow night at nine."

He looked at her with beseeching eyes. She understood, but wished to tease him. She kissed him maternally on the forehead, then consulted his eyes again. The expression of supplication must have remained unchanged, for she responded to their imploration by a long kiss which closed them, then came down to his lips, drinking their dolorous emotion.

Then she rang and told her maid to light Durtal through the hall. He descended, satisfied that she had engaged herself to yield tomorrow night.

CHAPTER XIII

He began again, as on the other evening, to clean house and establish a methodical disorder. He slipped a cushion under the false disarray of the armchair, then he made roaring fires to have the rooms good and warm when she came.

But he was without impatience. That silent promise which he had obtained, that Mme. Chantelouve would not leave him panting this night, moderated him. Now that his uncertainty was at an end, he no longer vibrated with the almost painful acuity which hitherto her malignant delays had provoked. He soothed himself by poking the fire. His mind was still full of her, but plethoric, content. When his thoughts stirred at all it was, at the very most, to revolve the question, "How shall I go about it, when the time comes, so as not to be ridiculous?" This question, which had so harassed him the other night, left him troubled but inert. He did not try to solve it, but decided to leave everything to chance, since the best planned strategy was almost always abortive.

Then he revolted against himself, accused himself of stagnation, and walked up and down to shake himself out of a torpor which might have been attributed to the hot fire. Well, well, was it because he had had to wait so long that his desires had left him, or at least quit bothering him—no, they had not, why, he was yearning now for the moment when he might crush that woman! He thought he had the explanation of his lack of enthusiasm in the stage fright inseparable from any beginning. "It will not be really exquisite tonight until after the newness wears off and the grotesque with it. After I know her I shall be able to consort with her again without feeling solicitous about her and conscious of myself. I wish we were on that happy basis now."

The cat, sitting on the table, cocked up its ears, gazed at the door with its black eyes, and fled. The bell rang and Durtal went to let her in.

Her costume pleased him. He took off her furs. Her skirt was of a plum colour so dark that it was almost black, the material thick and supple, outlining her figure, squeezing her arms, making an hourglass of her waist, accentuating the curve of her hips and the bulge of her corset.

"You are charming," he said, kissing her wrists, and he was pleased to find that his lips had accelerated her pulse. She did not speak, could hardly breathe. She was agitated and very pale.

He sat down facing her. She looked at him with her mysterious, half sleepy eyes. He felt that he was falling in love all over again. He forgot his reasonings and his fears, and took acute pleasure in penetrating the mystery of these eyes and studying the vague smile of this dolorous mouth.

He enlaced her fingers in his, and for the first time, in a low voice, he called her Hyacinthe.

She listened, her breast heaving, her hands in a fever. Then in a supplicating voice, "I implore you," she said, "let us have none of that. Only desire is good. Oh, I am rational, I mean what I say. I thought it all out on the way here. I left him very sad tonight. If you knew how I feel —I went to church today and was afraid and hid myself when I saw my confessor——"

These plaints he had heard before, and he said to himself, "You may sing whatever tune you want to, but you shall dance tonight." Aloud he answered in monosyllables as he continued to take possession of her.

He rose, thinking she would do the same, or that if she remained seated he could better reach her lips by bending over her.

"Your lips, your lips—the kiss you gave me last night—" he murmured, as his face came close to hers. She put up her lips and stood, and they embraced, but as his hands went seeking she recoiled.

"Think how ridiculous it all is," she said in a low voice, "to undress, put on night clothes—and that silly scene, getting into bed!"

He avoided declaring, but attempted, by an embrace which bent her over backward, to make her understand that she could spare herself those embarrassments. Tacitly, in his own turn, feeling her body stiffen under his fingers, he understood that she absolutely would not give herself in the room here, in front of the fire.

"Oh well," she said, disengaging herself, "if you will have it!"

He made way to allow her to go into the other room, and seeing that she desired to be alone he drew the portière.

Sitting before the fire he reflected. Perhaps he ought to have pulled down the bed covers, and not left her the task, but without doubt the action would have been too direct, too obvious a hint. Ah! and that water heater! He took it and, keeping away from the bedroom door, went to the bathroom, placed the heater on the toilet table, and then, swiftly, he set out the rice powder box, the perfumes, the combs, and, returning into his study, he listened.

She was making as little noise as possible, walking on tiptoe as if in the presence of the dead. She blew out the candles, doubtless wishing no more light than the rosy glow of the hearth.

He felt positively annihilated. The irritating impression of the lips and eyes of Hyacinthe was far from him now. She was nothing but a woman, like any other, undressing in a man's room. Memories of similar scenes overwhelmed him. He remembered girls who like her had crept about on the carpet so as not to be heard, and who had stopped short, ashamed, for a whole second, if they bumped against the water pitcher. And then, what good was this going to

do him? Now that she was yielding he no longer desired
her! Disillusion had come even before possession, not
waiting, as usual, till afterward. He was distressed to the
point of tears.

The frightened cat glided under the curtain, ran from
one room to the other, and finally came back to his master
and jumped onto his knees. Caressing him, Durtal said to
himself, "Decidedly, she was right when she refused. It
will be grotesque, atrocious. I was wrong to insist, but
no, it's her fault, too. She must have wanted to do this or
she wouldn't have come. What a fool to think she could
aggravate passion by delay. She is fearfully clumsy. A
moment ago when I was embracing her and really was
aroused, it would perhaps have been delicious, but now! And
what do I look like? A young bridegroom waiting—or a
green country boy. Oh God, how stupid! Well," he said,
straining his ears and hearing no sound from the other room,
"she's in bed. I must go in.

"I suppose it took her all this time to unharness herself
from her corset. She was a fool to wear one," he concluded,
when, drawing the curtain, he stepped into the other room.

Mme. Chantelouve was buried under the thick coverlet,
her mouth half-open and her eyes closed; but he saw that
she was peering at him through the fringe of her blonde
eyelashes. He sat down on the edge of the bed. She
huddled up, drawing the cover over her chin.

"Cold, dear?"

"No," and she opened wide her eyes, which flashed
sparks.

He undressed, casting a rapid glance at Hyacinthe's face.
It was hidden in the darkness, but was sometimes revealed
by a flare of the red hot fire, as a stick, half consumed and
smouldering, would suddenly burst into flame. Swiftly he
slipped between the covers. He clasped a corpse; a body so
cold that it froze him, but the woman's lips were burning
as she silently gnawed his features. He lay stupefied in the
grip of this body wound around his own, supple as the . . .

and hard! He could not move; he could not speak for the shower of kisses traveling over his face. Finally, he succeeded in disengaging himself, and, with his free arm he sought her; then suddenly, while she devoured his lips he felt a nervous inhibition, and, naturally, without profit, he withdrew.

"I detest you!" she exclaimed.

"Why?"

"I detest you!"

He wanted to cry out, "And I you!" He was exasperated, and would have given all he owned to get her to dress and go home.

The fire was burning low, unflickering. Appeased, now, he sat up and looked into the darkness. He would have liked to get up and find another nightshirt, because the one he had on was tearing and getting in his way. But Hyacinthe was lying on top of it—then he reflected that the bed was deranged and the thought affected him, because he liked to be snug in winter, and knowing himself incapable of respreading the covers, he foresaw a cold night.

Once more, he was enlaced; the gripe of the woman's on his own was renewed; rational, this time, he attended to her and crushed her with mighty caresses. In a changed voice, lower, more guttural, she uttered ignoble things and silly cries which gave him pain—My dear!—oh, hon!—oh I can't stand it!"—aroused nevertheless, he took this body which creaked as it writhed, and he experienced the extraordinary sensation of a spasmodic burning within a swaddle of ice-packs.

He finally jumped over her, out of bed, and lighted the candles. On the dresser the cat sat motionless, considering Durtal and Mme. Chantelouve alternately. Durtal saw an inexpressible mockery in those black eyes and, irritated, chased the beast away.

He put some more wood on the fire, dressed, and started to leave the room. Hyacinthe called him gently, in her usual voice. He approached the bed. She threw her arms around his neck and hung there, kissing him hungrily. Then sinking back and putting her arms under the cover, she said, "The deed is done. Now will you love me any better?"

He did not have the heart to answer. Ah yes, his disillusion was complete. The satiety following justified his lack of appetite preceding. She revolted him, horrified him. Was it possible to have so desired a woman, only to come to —that? He had idealized her in his transports, he had dreamed in her eyes—he knew not what! He had wished to exalt himself with her, to rise higher than the delirious ravenings of the senses, to soar out of the world into joys supernal and unexplored. And his dream had been shattered. He remained fettered to earth. Was there no means of escaping out of one's self, out of earthly limitations, and attaining an upper ether where the soul, ravished, would glory in its giddy flight?

Ah, the lesson was hard and decisive. For having one time hoped so much, what regrets, what a tumble! Decidedly, Reality does not pardon him who despises her; she avenges herself by shattering the dream and trampling it and casting the fragments into a cesspool.

"Don't be vexed, dear, because it is taking me so long," said Mme. Chantelouve behind the curtain.

He thought crudely, "I wish you would get to hell out of here," and aloud he asked politely if she had need of his services.

"She was so mysterious, so enticing," he resumed to himself. "Her eyes, remote, deep as space, and reflecting cemeteries and festivals at the same time. And she has shown herself up for all she is, within an hour. I have seen a new Hyacinthe, talking like a silly little milliner in heat. All the nastinesses of women unite in her to exasperate me."

After a thoughtful silence he concluded, "I must be young indeed to have lost my head the way I did."

As if echoing his thought, Mme. Chantelouve, coming out through the portière, laughed nervously and said, "A woman of my age doing a mad thing like that!" She looked at him, and though he forced a smile she understood.

"You will sleep tonight," she said, sadly, alluding to Durtal's former complaints of sleeplessness on her account.

He begged her to sit down and warm herself, but she said she was not cold.

"Why, in spite of the warmth of the room you were cold as ice!"

"Oh, I am always that way. Winter and summer my flesh is chilly."

He thought that in August this frigid body might be agreeable, but now!

He offered her some bonbons, which she refused, then she said she would take a sip of the alkermes, which he poured into a tiny silver goblet. She took just a drop, and amicably they discussed the taste of this preparation, in which she recognized an aroma of clove, tempered by flower of cinnamon moistened with distillate of rose water.

Then he became silent.

"My poor dear," she said, "how I should love him if he were more confiding and not always on his guard."

He asked her to explain herself.

"Why, I mean that you can't forget yourself and simply let yourself be loved. Alas, you were reasoning all the time——"

"I was not!"

She kissed him tenderly. "You see I love you, anyway." And he was surprised to see how sad and moved she looked, and he observed a sort of frightened gratitude in her eyes.

"She is easily satisfied," he said to himself.

"What are you thinking about?"

"You!"

She sighed. Then, "What time is it?"

"Half past ten."

"I must go. He is waiting for me. No, don't say anything——"

She passed her hands over her cheeks. He seized her

gently by the waist and kissed her, holding her thus enlaced until they were at the door.

"You will come again soon, won't you?"

"Yes. . . . Yes."

He returned to the fireside.

"Oof! it's done," he thought, in a whirl of confused emotions. His vanity was satisfied, his selfesteem was no longer bleeding, he had attained his ends and possessed this woman. Moreover, her spell over him had lost its force. He was regaining his entire liberty of mind, but who could tell what trouble this liaison had yet in store for him? Then, in spite of everything, he softened.

After all, what could he reproach her with? She loved as well as she could. She was, indeed, ardent and plaintive. Even this dualism of a mistress who was a low cocotte in bed and a fine lady when dressed—or no, too intelligent to be called a fine lady—was a delectable pimento. Her carnal appetites were excessive and bizarre. What, then, was the matter with him?

And at last he quite justly accused himself. It was his own fault if everything was spoiled. He lacked appetite. He was not really tormented except by a cerebral erethism. He was used up in body, filed away in soul, inept at love, weary of tendernesses even before he received them and disgusted when he had. His heart was dead and could not be revived. And his mania for thinking, thinking! previsualizing an incident so vividly that actual enactment was an anticlimax—but probably would not be if his mind would leave him alone and not be always jeering at his efforts. For a man in his state of spiritual impoverishment all, save art, was but a recreation more or less boring, a diversion more or less vain. "Ah, poor woman, I am afraid she is going to get pretty sick of me. If only she would consent to come no more! But no, she doesn't deserve to be treated in that fashion," and, seized by pity, he swore to himself that the next time she visited him he would caress her and try to persuade her that the disillusion which he had so ill concealed did not exist.

He tried to spread up the bed, get the tousled blankets together, and plump the pillows, then he lay down.

He put out his lamp. In the darkness his distress increased. With death in his heart he said to himself, "Yes, I was right in declaring that the only women you can continue to love are those you lose.

"To learn, three years later, when the woman is inaccessible, chaste and married, dead, perhaps, or out of France— to learn that she loved you, though you had not dared believe it while she was near you, ah, that's the dream! These real and intangible loves, these loves made up of melancholy and distant regrets, are the only ones that count. Because there is no flesh in them, no earthly leaven.

"To love at a distance and without hope; never to possess; to dream chastely of pale charms and impossible kisses extinguished on the waxen brow of death: ah, that is something like it. A delicious straying away from the world, and never the return. As only the unreal is not ignoble and empty, existence must be admitted to be abominable. Yes, imagination is the only good thing which heaven vouchsafes to the skeptic and pessimist, alarmed by the eternal abjectness of life."

CHAPTER XIV

From this scene he had learned an alarming lesson: that the flesh domineers the soul and refuses to admit any schism. The flesh decisively does not intend that one shall get along without it and indulge in out-of-the-world pleasures which it can partake only on condition that it keep quiet. For the first time, reviewing these turpitudes, he really understood the meaning of that now obsolete word *chastity,* and he savoured it in all its pristine freshness. Just as a man who has drunk too deeply the night before thinks, the morning after, of drinking nothing but mineral water in future, so he dreamed, today, of pure affection far from a bed.

He was still ruminating these thoughts when Des Hermies entered.

They spoke of amorous misadventures. Astonished at once by Durtal's languor and the ascetic tone of his remarks, Des Hermies exclaimed, "Ah, we had a gay old time last night?"

With the most decisive bad grace Durtal shook his head.

"Then," replied Des Hermies, "you are superior and inhuman. To love without hope, immaculately, would be perfect if it did not induct such brainstorms. There is no excuse for chastity, unless one has a pious end in view, or unless the senses are failing, and if they are one had best see a doctor, who will solve the question more or less unsatisfactorily. To tell the truth, everything on earth culminates in the act you reprove. The heart, which is supposed to be the noble part of man, has the same form as the penis, which is the so-called ignoble part of man. There's symbolism in that similarity, because every love which is of the heart soon extends to the organ resembling it. The human imagination, the moment it tries to create artificially animated beings, involuntarily reproduces in them the movements of animals propagating. Look at the machines, the action of the piston and the cylinder; Romeos of steel and Juliets of cast iron. Nor do the loftier expressions of the human intellect get away from the advance and withdrawal copied by the machines. One must bow to nature's law if one is neither impotent nor a saint. Now you are neither the one nor the other, I think, but if, from inconceivable motives, you desire to live in temporary continence, follow the prescription of an occultist of the sixteenth century, the Neapolitan Piperno. He affirms that whoever eats vervain cannot approach a woman for seven days. Buy a jar, and let's try it."

Durtal laughed. "There is perhaps a middle course: never consummate the carnal act with her you love, and, to keep yourself quiet, frequent those you do not love. Thus, in a certain measure, you would conjure away possible disgust."

"No, one would never get it out of one's head that with the woman of whom one was enamoured one would experience carnal delights absolutely different from those which one feels with the others, so your method also would end badly. And too, the women who would not be indifferent to one, have not charity and discretion enough to admire the wisdom of this selfishness, for of course that's what it is, But what say, now, to putting on your shoes? It's almost six o'clock and Mama Carhaix's beef can't wait."

It had already been taken out of the pot and couched on a platter amid vegetables when they arrived. Carhaix, sprawling in an armchair, was reading his breviary.

"What's going on in the world?" he asked, closing his book.

"Nothing. Politics doesn't interest us, and General

Boulanger's American tricks of publicity weary you as much as they do us, I suppose. The other newspaper stories are just a little more shocking or dull than usual.—Look out, you'll burn your mouth," as Durtal was preparing to take a spoonful of soup.

"In fact," said Durtal, grimacing, "this marrowy soup, so artistically golden, is like liquid fire. But speaking of the news, what do you mean by saying there is nothing of pressing importance? And the trial of that astonishing abbè Boudes going on before the Assizes of Aveyron! After trying to poison his curate through the sacramental wine, and committing such other crimes as abortion, rape, flagrant misconduct, forgery, qualified theft and usury, he ended by appropriating the money put in the coin boxes for the souls in purgatory, and pawning the ciborium, chalice, all the holy vessels. That case is worth following."

Carhaix raised his eyes to heaven.

"If he is not sent to jail, there will be one more priest for Paris," said Des Hermies.

"How's that?"

"Why, all the ecclesiastics who get in bad in the provinces, or who have a serious falling out with the bishop, are sent here where they will be less in view, lost in the crowd, as it were. They form a part of that corporation known as 'scratch priests.' "

"What are they?"

"Priests loosely attached to a parish. You know that in addition to a curate, ministrants, vicars, and regular clergy, there are in every church adjunct priests, supply priests. Those are the ones I am talking about. They do the heavy work, celebrate the morning masses when everybody is asleep and the late masses when everybody is doing. It is they who get up at night to take the sacrament to the poor, and who sit up with the corpses of the devout rich and catch cold standing under the dripping church porches at funerals, and get sunstroke or pneumonia in the cemetery. They do all the dirty work. For a five or ten franc fee they act as substitutes for colleagues who have good livings and are tired of service. They are men under a cloud for the most part. Churches take them on, ready to fire them at a moment's notice, and keep strict watch over them while waiting for them to be interdicted or to have their *celebret* taken away. I simply mean that the provincial parishes excavate on the city the priests who for one reason or another have ceased to please."

"But what do the curates and other titulary abbés *do,* if they unload their duties onto the backs of others?"

"They do the elegant, easy work, which requires no effort, no charity. They shrive society women who come to confession in their most stunning gowns; they teach proper little prigs the catechism, and preach, and play the linelight rôles in the gala ceremonials which are got up to pander to the tastes of the faithful. At Paris, not counting the scratch priests, the clergy is divided thus: Man-of-the-world priests in easy circumstances: these are placed at la Madeleine and Saint Roch where the congregations are wealthy. They are wined and dined, they pass their lives in drawing-rooms, and comfort only elegant souls. Other priests who are good desk clerks, for the most part, but who have neither the education nor the fortune necessary to participate in the inconsequentialities of the idle rich. They live more in seclusion and visit only among the middle class. They console themselves for their unfashionableness by playing cards with each other and uttering crude commonplaces at the table."

"Now, Des Hermies," said Carhaix, "you are going too far. I claim to know the clerical world myself, and there are, even in Paris, honest men who do their duty. They are covered with opprobrium and spat on. Every Tom, Dick, and Harry accuses them of the foulest vices. But after all, it must be said that the abbé Boudes and the Canon Docres are exceptions, thank God! and outside of Paris there are veritable saints, especially among the country clergy."

"It's a fact that Satanic priests are relatively rare, and

the lecheries of the clergy and the knaveries of the episcopate are evidently exaggerated by an ignoble press. But that isn't what I have against them. If only they were gamblers and libertines! But they're lukewarm, mediocre, lazy, imbeciles. That is their sin against the Holy Ghost, the only sin which the All Merciful does not pardon."

"They are of their time," said Durtal. "You wouldn't expect to find the soul of the Middle Ages inculcated by the milk-and-water seminaries."

"Then," Carhaix observed, "our friend forgets that there are impeccable monastic orders, the Carthusians, for instance."

"Yes, and the Trappists and the Franciscans. But they are cloistered orders which live in shelter from an infamous century. Take, on the other hand, the order of Saint Dominic, which exists for the fashionable world. That is the order which produces jewelled dudes like Monsabre and Didon. Enough said."

"They are the hussars of religion, the jaunty lancers, the spick and span and primped-up Zouaves, while the good Capuchins are the humble poilus of the soul," said Durtal.

"If only they loved bells," sighed Carhaix, shaking his head. "Well, pass the Coulommiers," he said to his wife, who was taking up the salad bowl and the plates.

In silence they ate this Brie-type cheese. Des Hermies filled the glasses.

"Tell me," Durtal asked Des Hermies, "do you know whether a woman who receives visits from the incubi necessarily has a cold body? In other words, is a cold body a presumable symptom of incubacy, as of old the inability to shed tears served the Inquisition as proof positive to convict witches?"

"Yes, I can answer you. Formerly women smitten with incubacy had frigid flesh even in the month of August. The books of the specialists bear witness. But now the majority of the creatures who voluntarily or involuntarily summon or receive the amorous larvæ have, on the contrary, a skin that is burning and dry to the touch. This transformation is not yet general, but tends to become so. I remember very well that Dr. Johannès, he of whom Gévingey told you, was often obliged, at the moment when he attempted to deliver the patient, to bring the body back to normal temperature with lotions of dilute hydriodate of potassium."

"Ah!" said Durtal, who was thinking of Mme. Chantelouve.

"You don't know what has become of Dr. Johannès?" asked Carhaix.

"He is living very much in retirement at Lyons. He continues, I believe, to cure venefices, and he preaches the blessed coming of the Paraclete."

"For heaven's sake, who is this doctor?" asked Durtal.

"He is a very intelligent and learned priest. He was superior of a community, and he directed, here in Paris, the only review which ever was really mystical. He was a theologian much consulted, a recognized master of divine jurisprudence; then he had distressing quarrels with the papal Curia at Rome and with the Cardinal-Archbishop of Paris. His exorcisms and his battles against the incubi, especially in the female convents, ruined him.

"Ah, I remember the last time I saw him, as if it were yesterday. I met him in the rue Grenelle coming out of the Archbishop's house, the day he quitted the Church, after a scene which he told me all about. Again I can see that priest walking with me along the deserted boulevard des Invalides. He was pale, and his defeated but impressive voice trembled. He had been summoned and commanded to explain his actions in the case of an epileptic woman whom he claimed to have cured with the aid of a relic, the seamless robe of Christ preserved at Argenteuil. The Cardinal, assisted by two grand vicars, listened to him, standing.

"When he had likewise furnished the information which they demanded about his cures of witch spells, Cardinal Guibert said, 'You had best go to La Trappe.'

"And I remember word for word his reply, 'If I have

violated the laws of the Church, I am ready to undergo the penalty of my fault. If you think me culpable, pass a canonical judgment and I will execute it, I swear on my sacerdotal honour; but I wish a formal sentence, for, in law, nobody is bound to condemn himself: *"Nemo se tradere tenetur,"* says the Corpus Juris Canonici.'

"There was a copy of his review on the table. The Cardinal pointed to a page and asked, 'Did you write that?'

" 'Yes, Eminence.'

" 'Infamous doctrines!' and he went from his office into the next room, crying, 'Out of my sight!'

"Then Johannès advanced as far as the threshold of the other room, and falling on his knees, he said, 'Eminence, I had no intention of offending. If I have done so, I beg forgiveness.'

"The Cardinal cried more loudly, 'Out of my sight before I call for assistance!'

"Johannès rose and left.

" 'All my old ties are broken,' he said, as he parted from me. He was so sad that I had not the heart to question him further."

There was a silence. Carhaix went up to his tower to ring a peal. His wife removed the dessert dishes and the cloth. Des Hermies prepared the coffee. Durtal, pensive, rolled his cigarette.

Carhaix, when he returned, as if enveloped in a fog of sounds, exclaimed, "A while ago, Des Hermies, you were speaking of the Franciscans. Do you know that that order, to live up to its professions of poverty, was supposed not to possess even a bell? True, this rule has been relaxed somewhat. It was too severe! Now they have a bell, but only one."

"Just like most other abbeys, then."

"No, because all communities have at least three, in honour of the holy and triple Hypostasis."

"Do you mean to say that the number of bells a monastery or church can have is limited by rule?"

"Formerly it was. There was a pious hierarchy of ringing: the bells of a convent could not sound when the bells of a church pealed. They were the vassals, and, respectful and submissive as became their rank, they were silent when the Suzerain spoke to the multitudes. These principles of procedure, consecrated, in 1590, by a canon of the Council of Toulouse and confirmed by two decrees of the Congress of Rites, are no longer followed. The rulings of San Carlo Borromeo, who decreed that a church should have from five to seven bells, a boy's academy three, and a parochial school two, are abolished. Today churches have more or fewer bells as they are more or less rich. . . . Oh, well, why worry? Where are the little glasses?"

His wife brought them, shook hands with the guests, and retired.

Then while Carhaix was pouring the cognac, Des Hermies said in a low voice, "I did not want to speak before her, because these matters distress and frighten her, but I received a singular visit this morning from Gévingey, who is running over to Lyons to see Dr. Johannès. He claims to have been bewitched by Canon Docre, who, it seems, is making a flying visit to Paris. What have been their relations? I don't know. Anyway, Gévingey is in a deplorable state."

"Just what seems to be the matter with him?" asked Durtal.

"I positively do not know. I made a careful auscultation and examined him thoroughly. He complains of needles pricking him around the heart. I observed nervous trouble and nothing else. What I am most worried about is a state of enfeeblement inexplicable in a man who is neither cancerous nor diabetical."

"Ah," said Carhaix, "I suppose people are not bewitched now with wax images and needles, with the 'Manei' or the 'Dagyde' as it was called in the good old days."

"No, those practises are now out of date and almost everywhere fallen into disuse. Gévingey who took me completely into his confidence this morning, told me what extraordinary recipes the frightful canon uses. These are, it seems, the unrevealed secrets of modern magic."

"Ah, that's what interests me," exclaimed Durtal.

"Of course I limit myself to repeating what was told me," resumed Des Hermies, lighting his cigarette. "Well, Docre keeps white mice in cages, and he takes them along when he travels. He feeds them on consecrated hosts and on pastes impregnated with poisons skilfully dosed. When these unhappy beasts are saturated, he takes them, holds them over a chalice, and with a very sharp instrument he pricks them here and there. The blood flows into the vase and he uses it, in a way which I shall explain in a moment, to strike his enemies with death. Formerly he operated on chickens and guinea pigs, but he used the grease, not the blood, of these animals, become thus execrated and venomous tabernacles.

"Formerly he also used a recipe discovered by the Satanic society of the Re-Theurgistes-Optimates, of which I have spoken before, and he prepared a hash composed of flour, meat, Eucharist bread, mercury, animal semen, human blood, acetate of morphine and aspic oil.

"Latterly, and according to Gévingey this abomination is more perilous yet, he stuffs fishes with communion bread and with toxins skilfully graduated. These toxins are chosen from those which produce madness or lockjaw when absorbed through the pores. Then, when these fishes are thoroughly permeated with the substances sealed by sacrilege, Docre takes them out of the water, lets them rot, distills them, and expresses from them an essential oil one drop of which will produce madness. This drop, it appears, is applied externally, by touching the hair, as in Balzac's *Thirteen*."

"Hmmm," said Durtal, "I am afraid that a drop of this oil long ago fell on the scalp of poor old Gévingey."

"What is interesting about this story is not the outlandishness of these diabolical pharmacopœia so much as the psychology of the persons who invent and manipulate them. Think. This is happening at the present day, and it is the priests who have invented philtres unknown to the sorcerers of the Middle Ages."

"The priests, no! A priest. And what a priest!" remarked Carhaix.

"Gévingey is very precise. He affirms that others use them. Bewitchment by veniniferous blood of mice took place in 1879 at Châlons-sur-Marne in a demoniac circle—to which the canon belonged, it is true. In 1883, in Savoy, the oil of which I have spoken was prepared in a group of defrocked abbés. As you see, Docre is not the only one who practises this abominable science. It is known in the convents; some laymen, even, have an inkling of it."

"But now, admitting that these preparations are real and that they are active, you have not explained how one can poison a man with them either from a distance or near at hand."

"Yes, that's another matter. One has a choice of two methods to reach the enemy one is aiming at. The first and least used is this: the magician employs a voyant, a woman who is known in that world as 'a flying spirit'; she is a somnambulist, who, put into a hypnotic state, can betake herself, in spirit, wherever one wishes her to go. It is then possible to have her transmit the magic poisons to a person whom one designates, hundreds of leagues away. Those who are stricken in this manner have seen no one, and they go mad or die without suspecting the venefice. But these voyants are not only rare, they are also unreliable, because other persons can likewise fix them in a cataleptic state and extract confessions from them. So you see why persons like Docre have recourse to the second method, which is surer. It consists in evoking, just as in Spiritism, the soul of a dead person and sending it to strike the victim with the prepared spell. The result is the same but the vehicle is different. There," concluded Des Hermies, "reported with painstaking exactness, are the confidences which our friend Gévingey made me this morning."

"And Dr. Johannès cures people poisoned in this manner?" asked Carhaix.

"Yes, Dr. Johannès—to my knowledge—has made inexplicable cures."

"But with what?"

"Gévingey tells me, in this connection, that the doctor celebrates a sacrifice to the glory of Melchisedek. I haven't the faintest idea what this sacrifice is, but Gévingey will perhaps enlighten us if he returns cured."

"In spite of all, I should not be displeased, once in my life to get a good look at Canon Docre," said Durtal.

"Not I! He is the incarnation of the Accursed on earth!" cried Carhaix, assisting his friends to put on their overcoats.

He lighted his lantern, and while they were descending the stair, as Durtal complained of the cold, Des Hermies burst into a laugh.

"If your family had known the magical secrets of the plants, you would not shiver this way," he said. It was learned in the sixteenth century that a child might be immune to heat or cold all his life if his hands were rubbed with juice of absinth before the twelfth month of his life had passed. That, you see, is a tempting prescription, less dangerous than those which Canon Docre abuses."

Once below, after Carhaix had closed the door of his tower, they hastened their steps, for the north wind swept the square.

"After all," said Des Hermies, "Satanism aside—and yet Satanism also is a phase of religion—admit that, for two miscreants of our sort, we hold singularly pious conversations. I hope they will be counted in our favour up above."

"No merit on our part," replied Durtal, "for what else is there to talk about? Conversations which do not treat of religion or art are so base and vain."

CHAPTER XV

The memory of these frightful magisteria kept racing through his head next day, and, while smoking cigarettes beside the fire, Durtal thought of Docre and Johannès fighting across Gévingey's back, smiting and parrying with incantations and exorcisms.

"In the Christian symbolism," he said to himself, "the fish is one of the representations of Christ. Doubtless the Canon thinks to aggravate his sacrileges by feeding fishes on genuine hosts. His is the reverse of the system of the mediæval witches who chose a vile beast dedicated to the Devil to submit the body of the Saviour to the processes of digestion. How real is the pretended power which the deicide chemists are alleged to wield? What faith can we put in the tales of evoked larvæ killing a designated person to order with corrosive oil and blood virus? None, unless one is extremely credulous, and even a bit mad.

"And yet, come to think of it, we find today, unexplained and surviving under other names, the mysteries which were so long reckoned the product of mediæval imagination and superstition. At the charity hospital Dr. Louis transfers maladies from one hypnotized person to another. Wherein is that less miraculous than evocation of demons, than spells cast by magicians or pastors? A larva, a flying spirit, is not, indeed, more extraordinary than a microbe coming from afar and poisoning one without one's knowledge, and the atmosphere can certainly convey spirits as well as bacilli. Certainly the ether carries, untransformed, emanations, effluences, electricity, for instance, or the fluids of a magnet which sends to a distant subject an order to traverse all

Paris to rejoin it. Science has no call to contest these phenomena. On the other hand, Dr. Brown-Sequard rejuve-
nates infirm old men and revitalizes the impotent with dis-
tillations from the parts of rabbits and cavies. Were not the
elixirs of life and the love philtres which the witches sold
to the senile and impotent composed of similar or analogous
substances? Human semen entered almost always, in the
Middle Ages, into the compounding of these mixtures. Now,
hasn't Dr. Brown-Sequard, after repeated experiments, recently demonstrated the virtues of semen taken from one
man and instilled into another?

"Finally, the apparitions, doppelgänger, bilocations—to
speak thus of the spirits—that terrified antiquity, have not
ceased to manifest themselves. It would be difficult to prove
that the experiments carried on for three years by Dr.
Crookes in the presence of witnesses were cheats. If he has
been able to photograph visible and tangible spectres, we
must recognize the veracity of the mediæval thaumaturges.
Incredible, of course—and wasn't hypnotism, possession of
one soul by another which could dedicate it to crime—incredible only ten years ago?

"We are groping in shadow, that is sure. But Des
Hermies hit the bull's-eye when he remarked, 'It is less important to know whether the modern pharmaceutic sacrileges are potent, than to study the motives of the Satanists
and fallen priests who prepare them.'

"Ah, if there were some way of getting acquainted with
Canon Docre, of insinuating oneself into his confidence, perhaps one would attain clear insight into these questions. I
learned long ago that there are no people interesting to know
except saints, scoundrels, and cranks. They are the only
persons whose conversation amounts to anything. Persons
of good sense are necessarily dull, because they revolve over
and over again the tedious topics of everyday life. They are
the crowd, more or less intelligent, but they are the crowd,
and they give me a pain. Yes, but who will put me in
touch with this monstrous priest?" and, as he poked the fire,

Durtal said to himself, "Chantelouve, if he would, but he won't. There remains his wife, who used to be well acquainted with Docre. I must interrogate her and find out whether she still corresponds with him and sees him."

The entrance of Mme. Chantelouve into his reflections saddened him. He took out his watch and murmured, "What a bore. She will come again, and again I shall have to—if only there were any possibility of convincing her of the futility of the carnal somersaults! In any case, she can't be very well pleased, because, to her frantic letter soliciting a meeting, I responded three days later by a brief, dry note, inviting her to come here this evening. It certainly was lacking in lyricism, too much so, perhaps."

He rose and went into his bedroom to make sure that the fire was burning brightly, then he returned and sat down, without even arranging his room as he had the other times. Now that he no longer cared for this woman, gallantry and self-consciousness had fled. He awaited her without impatience, his slippers on his feet.

"To tell the truth, I have had nothing pleasant from Hyacinthe except that kiss we exchanged when her husband was only a few feet away. I certainly shall not again find her lips a-flame and fragrant. Here her kiss is insipid."

Mme. Chantelouve rang earlier than usual.

"Well," she said, sitting down. "You wrote me a nice letter."

"How's that?"

"Confess frankly that you are through with me."

He denied this, but she shook her head.

"Well," he said, "what have you to reproach me with? Having written you only a short note? But there was someone here, I was busy and I didn't have time to assemble pretty speeches. Not having set a date sooner? I told you our relation necessitates precautions, and we can't see each other very often. I think I gave you clearly to understand my motives——"

"I am so stupid that I probably did not understand them. You spoke to me of 'family reasons,' I believe."

"Yes."

"Rather vague."

"Well, I couldn't go into detail and tell you that——"

He stopped, asking himself whether the time had come to break decisively with her, but he remembered that he wanted her aid in getting information about Docre.

"That what? Tell me."

He shook his head, hesitating, not to tell her a lie, but to insult and humiliate her.

"Well," he went on, "since you force me to do it, I will confess, at whatever cost, that I have had a mistress for several years—I add that our relations are now purely amical——"

"Very well," she interrupted, "your family reasons are sufficient."

"And then," he pursued, in a lower tone, "if you wish to know all, well—I have a child by her."

"A child! Oh, you poor dear." She rose. "Then there is nothing for me to do but withdraw."

But he seized her hands, and, at the same time satisfied with the success of his deception and ashamed of his brutality, he begged her to stay awhile. She refused. Then he drew her to him, kissed her hair, and cajoled her. Her troubled eyes looked deep into his.

"Ah, then!" she said. "No, let me undress."

"Not for the world!"

"Yes!"

"Oh, the scene of the other night beginning all over again," he murmured, sinking, overwhelmed, into a chair. He felt borne down, burdened by an unspeakable weariness.

He undressed beside the fire and warmed himself while waiting for her to get to bed. When they were in bed she enveloped him with her supple, cold limbs.

"Now is it true that I am to come here no more?"

He did not answer, but understood that she had no intention of going away and that he had to do with a person of the staying kind.

"Tell me."

He buried his head in her breast to keep from having to answer.

"Tell me in my lips."

He beset her furiously, to make her keep silent, then he lay disabused, weary, happy that it was over. When they lay down again she put her arm about his neck and ran her tongue around in his mouth like an auger, but he paid little heed to caresses and remained feeble and pathetic. Then she bent over, reached him, and he groaned.

"Ah!" she exclaimed suddenly, rising, "at last I have heard you cry!"

He lay, broken in body and spirit, incapable of thinking two thoughts in sequence. His brain seemed to whir, undone, in his skull.

He collected himself, however, rose and went into the other room to dress and let her do the same.

Through the drawn portière separating the two rooms he saw a little pinhole of light which came from the wax candle placed on the mantel opposite the curtain. Hyacinthe, going back and forth, would momentarily intercept this light, then it would flash out again.

"Ah," she said, "my poor darling, you have a child."

"The shot struck home," said he to himself, and aloud, "Yes, a little girl."

"How old?"

"She will soon be six," and he described her as flaxen-haired, lively, but in very frail health, requiring multiple precautions and constant care.

"You must have very sad evenings," said Mme. Chantelouve, in a voice of emotion, from behind the curtain.

"Oh yes! If I were to die tomorrow, what would become of those two unfortunates?"

His imagination took wing. He began himself to believe

the mother and her. His voice trembled. Tears very nearly came to his eyes.

"He is unhappy, my darling is," she said, raising the curtain and returning, clothed, into the room. "And that is why he looks so sad, even when he smiles!"

He looked at her. Surely at that moment her affection was not feigned. She really clung to him. Why, oh, why, had she had to have those rages of lust? If it had not been for those they could probably have been good comrades, sin moderately together, and love each other better than if they wallowed in the sty of the senses. But no, such a relation was impossible with her, he concluded, seeing those sulphurous eyes, that ravenous, despoiling mouth.

She had sat down in front of his writing table and was playing with a penholder. "Were you working when I came in? Where are you in your history of Gilles de Rais?"

"I am getting along, but I am hampered. To make a good study of the Satanism of the Middle Ages one ought to get really into the environment, or at least fabricate a similar environment, by becoming acquainted with the practitioners of Satanism all about us—for the psychology is the same, though the operations differ." And looking her straight in the eye, thinking the story of the child had softened her, he hazarded all on a cast, "Ah! if your husband would give me the information he has about Canon Docre!"

She stood motionless, but her eyes clouded over. She did not answer.

"True," he said, "Chantelouve, suspecting our liaison——"

She interrupted him. "My husband has no concern with the relations which may exist between you and me. He evidently suffers when I go out, as tonight, for he knows where I am going; but I admit no right of control either on his part or mine. He is free, and I am free, to go wherever we please. I must keep house for him, watch out for his interests, take care of him, love him like a devoted companion, and that I do, with all my heart. As to being responsible for my acts, they're none of his business, no more his than anybody else's."

She spoke in a crisp, incisive tone.

"The devil;" said Durtal. "You certainly reduce the importance of the rôle of husband."

"I know that my ideas are not the ideas of the world I live in, and they appear not to be yours. In my first marriage they were a source of trouble and disaster—but I have an iron will and I bend the people who love me. In addition, I despise deceit, so when a few years after marriage I became smitten on a man I quite frankly told my husband and confessed my fault."

"Dare I ask you in what spirit he received this confidence?"

"He was so grieved that in one night his hair turned white. He could not bear what he called—wrongly, I think —my treason, and he killed himself."

"Ah!" said Durtal, dumbfounded by the placid and resolute air of this woman, "but suppose he had strangled you first?"

She shrugged her shoulders and picket a cat hair off her skirt.

"The result," he resumed after a silence, "being that you are now almost free, that your second husband tolerates——"

"Let us not discuss my second husband. He is an excellent man who deserves a better wife. I have absolutely no reason to speak of Chantelouve otherwise than with praise, and then—oh, let's talk of something else, for I have had sufficient botheration on this subject from my confessor, who interdicts me from the Holy Table."

He contemplated her, and saw yet another Hyacinthe, a hard, pertinacious woman whom he had not known. Not a sign nor an accent of emotion, nothing, while she was describing the suicide of her first husband—she did not even seem to imagine that she had a crime on her conscience. She remained pitiless, and yet, a moment ago, when she was commiserating him because of his fictitious parenthood, he had thought she was trembling. "After all, perhaps she is acting a part—like myself."

He remained awed by the turn the conversation had taken. He sought, mentally, a way of getting back to the subject from which Hyacinthe had diverted him, of the Satanism of Canon Docre.

"Well, let us think of that no more," she said, coming very near. She smiled, and was once more the Hyacinthe he knew.

"But if on my account you can no longer take communion——"

She interrupted him. "Would you be sorry if I did not love you?" and she kissed his eyes. He squeezed her politely in his arms, but he felt her trembling, and from motives of prudence he got away.

"Is he so inexorable, your confessor?"

"He is an incorruptible man, of the old school. I chose him expressly."

"If I were a woman it seems to me I should take, on the contrary, a confessor who was pliable and caressible and who would not violently pillory my dainty little sins. I would have him indulgent, oiling the hinges of confession, enticing forth with beguiling gestures the misdeeds that hung back. It is true there would be risk of seducing a confessor who perhaps would be defenceless——"

"And that would be incest, because the priest is a spiritual father, and it would also be sacrilege, because the priest is consecrated.—Oh," speaking to herself, "I was mad, mad —" suddenly carried away.

He observed her; sparks glinted in the myopic eyes of this extraordinary woman. Evidently he had just stumbled, unwittingly, onto a guilty secret of hers.

"Well," and he smiled, "do you still commit infidelities to me with a false me?"

"I do not understand."

"Do you receive, at night, the visit of the incubus which resembles me?"

"No. Since I have been able to possess you in the flesh I have no need to evoke your image."

"What a downright Satanist you are!"

"Maybe. I have been so constantly associated with priests."

"You're a great one," he said, bowing. "Now listen to me, and do me a great favour. You know Canon Docre?"

"I should say!"

"Well, what in the world is this man, about whom I hear so much?"

"From whom?"

"Gévingey and Des Hermies."

"Ah, you consult the astrologer! Yes, he met the Canon in my own house, but I didn't know that Docre was acquainted with Des Hermies, who didn't attend our receptions in those days."

"Des Hermies has never seen Docre. He knows him, as I do, only by hearsay, from Gévingey. Now, briefly, how much truth is there in the stories of the sacrileges of which this priest is accused?"

"I don't know. Docre is a gentleman, learned and well bred. He was even the confessor of royalty, and he would certainly have become a bishop if he had not quitted the priesthood. I have heard a great deal of evil spoken about him, but, especially in the clerical world, people are so fond of saying all sorts of things."

"But you knew him personally."

"Yes, I even had him for a confessor."

"Then it isn't possible that you don't know what to make of him?"

"Very possible, indeed presumable. Look here, you have been beating around the bush a long time. Exactly what do you want to know?"

"Everything you care to tell me. Is he young or old, handsome or ugly, rich or poor?"

"He is forty years old, very fastidious of his person, and he spends a lot of money."

"Do you believe that he indulges in sorcery, that he celebrates the black mass?"

"It is quite possible."

"Pardon me for dunning you, for extorting information from you as if with forceps—suppose I were to ask you a really personal question—this faculty of incubacy. . . .?"

"Why, certainly I got it from him. I hope you are satisfied."

"Yes and no. Thanks for your kindness in telling me—I know I am abusing your good nature—but one more question. Do you know of any way whereby I may see Canon Docre in person?"

"He is at Nîmes."

"Pardon me. For the moment, he is in Paris."

"Ah, you know that! Well, if I knew of a way, I would not tell you, be sure. It would not be good for you to get to seeing too much of this priest."

"You admit, then, that he is dangerous?"

"I do not admit nor deny. I tell you simply that you have nothing to do with him."

"Yes I have. I want to get material for my book from him."

"Get it from somebody else. Besides," she said, putting on her hat in front of the glass, "my husband got a bad scare and broke with that man and refuses to receive him."

"That is no reason why——"

"What do you mean?"

"Oh, nothing." He repressed the remark: "Why you should not see him."

She did not insist. She was poking her hair under her veil. "Heavens! what a fright I look!"

He took her hands and kissed them. "When shall I see you again?"

"I thought I wasn't to come here any more."

"Oh, now, you know I love you as a good friend. Tell me, when will you come again?"

"Tomorrow night, unless it is inconvenient for you."

"Not at all."

"Then, *au revoir.*"

Their lips met.

"And above all, don't think about Canon Docre," she said, turning and shaking her finger at him threateningly as she went out.

"Devil take you and your reticence," he said to himself, closing the door after her."

CHAPTER XVI

"When I think," said Durtal to himself the next morning, "that in bed, at the moment when the most pertinacious will succumbs, I held firm and refused to yield to the instances of Hyacinthe wishing to establish a footing here, and that after the carnal decline, at that instant when annihilated man recovers—alas!—his reason, I supplicated her, myself, to continue her visits, why, I simply cannot understand myself. Deep down, I have not got over my firm resolution of breaking with her, but I could not dismiss her like a cocotte. And," to justify his inconsistency, "I hoped to get some information about the canon. Oh, on that subject I am not through with her. She's got to make up her mind to speak out and quit answering me by monosyllables and guarded phrases as she did yesterday.

"Indeed, what can she have been up to with that abbé who was her confessor and who, by her own admission, launched her into incubacy? She has been his mistress, that is certain. And how many other of these priests she has gone around with have been her lovers also? For she confessed, in a cry, that those are the men she loves. Ah, if one went about much in the clerical world one would doubtless learn remarkable things concerning her and her husband. It is strange, all the same that Chantelouve, who plays a singular rôle in that household, has acquired a deplorable reputation, and she hasn't. Never have I heard anybody speak of her dodges—but, oh, what a fool I am! 'It isn't strange. Her husband doesn't confine himself to religious and polite circles. He hobnobs with men of letters, and in consequence exposes himself to every sort of slander, while she, if she takes a lover, chooses him out of a pious society in which not one of us would ever be received. And then, abbés are discreet. But how explain her infatuation with me? By the simple fact that she is surfeited of priests and a layman serves as a change of diet.

"Just the same, she is quite singular, and the more I see her the less I understand her. There are in her three distinct beings.

"First the woman seated or standing up, whom I knew in her drawing-room, reserved, almost haughty, who becomes a good companion in private, affectionate and even tender.

"Then the woman in bed, completely changed in voice and bearing, a harlot spitting mud, losing all shame.

"Third and last, the pitiless vixen, the thorough Satanist, whom I perceived yesterday.

"What is the binding-alloy that amalgamates all these beings of hers? I can't say. Hypocrisy, no doubt. No. I don't think so, for she is often of a disconcerting frankness —in moments, it is true, of forgetfulness and unguardedness. Seriously, what is the use of trying to understand the character of this pious harlot? And to be candid with myself, what I wish ideally will never be realized; she does not ask me to take her to swell places, does not force me to dine with her, exacts no revenue: she isn't trying to compromise and blackmail me. I shan't find a better—but, oh, Lord! I now prefer to find no one at all. It suits me perfectly to entrust my carnal business to mercenary agents. For my twenty francs I shall receive more considerate treatment. There is no getting around it, only professionals know how to cook up a delicious sensual dish.

"Odd," he said to himself after a reflective silence, "but, all proportions duly observed, Gilles de Rais divides himself like her, into three different persons.

"First, the brave and honest fighting man.

"Then the refined and artistic criminal.

"Finally the repentant sinner, the mystic.

"He is a mass of contradictions and excesses. Viewing his life as a whole one finds each of his vices compensated by a contradictory virtue, but there is no key characteristic which reconciles them.

"He is of an overweening arrogance, but when contrition takes possession of him, he falls on his knees in front of the people of low estate, and has the tears, the humility of a saint.

"His ferocity passes the limits of the human scale, and yet he is generous and sincerely devoted to his friends, whom he cares for like a brother when the Demon has mauled them.

"Impetuous in his desires, and nevertheless patient; brave in battle, a coward confronting eternity; he is despotic and violent, yet he is putty in the hands of his flatterers. He is now in the clouds, now in the abyss, never on the trodden plain, the lowlands of the soul. His confessions do not throw any light on his invariable tendency to extremes. When asked who suggested to him the idea of such crimes, he answers, 'No one. The thought came to me only from myself, from my reveries, my daily pleasures, my taste for debauchery.' And he arraigns his indolence and constantly asserts that delicate repasts and strong drink have helped uncage the wild animal in him.

"Unresponsive to mediocre passions, he is carried away alternately by good as well as evil, and he bounds from spiritual pole to spiritual pole. He dies at the age of thirty-six, but he has completely exhausted the possibilities of joy and grief. He has adored death, loved as a vampire, kissed inimitable expressions of suffering and terror, and has, himself, been racked by implacable remorse, insatiable fear. He has nothing more to try, nothing more to learn, here below.

"Let's see," said Durtal, running over his notes. "I left him at the moment when the expiation begins. As I had written in one of my preceding chapters, the inhabitants of the region dominated by the châteaux of the Marshal know now who the inconceivable monster is who carries children off and cuts their throats. But no one dare speak. When, at a turn in the road, the tall figure of the butcher is seen approaching, all flee, huddle behind the hedges, or shut themselves up in the cottages.

"And Gilles passes, haughty and sombre, in the solitude of villages where no one dares venture abroad. Impunity seems assured him, for what peasant would be mad enough to attack a master who could have him gibbeted at a word?

"Again, if the humble give up the idea of bringing Gilles de Rais to justice, his peers have no intention of combating him for the benefit of peasants whom they disdain, and his liege, the duke of Brittany, Jean V, burdens him with favours and blandishments in order to extort his lands from him at a low price.

"A single power can rise and, above feudal complicities, above earthly interest, avenge the oppressed and the weak. The Church. And it is the Church in fact, in the person of Jean de Malestroit, which rises up before the monster and fells him.

"Jean de Malestroit, Bishop of Nantes, belongs to an illustrious line. He is a near kinsman of Jean V, and his incomparable piety, his infallible Christian wisdom, and his enthusiastic charity, make him venerated, even by the duke.

"The wailing of Gilles's decimated flock reaches his ears. In silence he begins an investigation and, setting spies upon the Marshal, waits only for an opportune moment to begin the combat. And Gilles suddenly commits an inexplicable crime which permits the Bishop to march forthwith upon him and smite him.

"To recuperate his shattered fortune, Gilles has sold his signorie of Saint Etienne de Mer Morte to a subject of Jean V, Guillaume le Ferron, who delegates his brother, Jean le Ferron, to take possession of the domain.

"Some days later the Marshal gathers the two hundred men of his military household and at their head marches on Saint Etienne. There, the day of Pentecost, when the as-

sembled people are hearing mass, he precipitates himself,
sword in hand, into the church, sweeps aside the faithful,
throwing them into tumult, and, before the dumbfounded
priest, threatens to cleave Jean le Ferron, who is praying.
The ceremony is broken off, the congregation take flight.
Gilles drags le Ferron, pleading for mercy, to the château,
orders that the drawbridge be let down, and by force occu-
pies the place, while his prisoner is carried away to Tiffauges and thrown into an underground dungeon.

"Gilles has, at one and the same time, violated the un-
written law of Brittany forbidding any baron to raise troops
without the consent of the duke, and committed double sacrilege in profaning a chapel and seizing Jean le Ferron, who
is a tonsured clerk of the Church.

"The Bishop learns of this outrage and prevails upon the
reluctant Jean V to march against the rebel. Then, while
one army advances on Saint Etienne, which Gilles aban-
dons to take refuge with his little band in the fortified manor
of Mâchecoul, another army lays siege to Tiffauges.

"During this time the priest hastens his redoubled investigations. He delegates commissioners and procurators in all
the villages where children have disappeared. He himself
quits his palace at Nantes, travels about the countryside,
and takes the depositions of the bereft. The people at last
speak, and on their knees beseech the Bishop to protect them.
Enraged by the atrocities which they reveal, he swears that
justice shall be done.

"It takes a month to hear all the reports. By letters-
patent Jean de Malestroit establishes publicly the 'infamatio'
of Gilles, then, when all the forms of canonic procedure
have been gone through with, he launches the mandate of
arrest.

"In this writ of warrant, given at Nantes the 13th day
of September in the year of Our Lord 1440, the Bishop
notes all the crimes imputed to the Marshal, then, in an
energetic style, he commands his diocese to march against

the assassin and dislodge him. 'Thus we do enjoin you, each and all, individually, by these presents, that ye cite immediately and peremptorily, without counting any man upon his neighbor, without discharging the burden any man upon his neighbour, that ye cite before us or before the Official of our cathedral church, for Monday of the feast of Exaltation of the Holy Cross, the 19th of September, Gilles, noble baron de Rais, subject to our puissance and to our jurisdiction; and we do ourselves cite him by these presents to appear before our bar to answer for the crimes which weigh upon him. Execute these orders, and do each of you cause them to be executed.'

"And the next day the captain-at-arms, Jean Labbé, acting in the name of the duke, and Robin Guillaumet, notary, acting in the name of the Bishop, present themselves, escorted by a small troop, before the château of Mâchecoul.

"What sudden change of heart does the Marshal now experience? Too feeble to hold his own in the open field, he can nevertheless defend himself behind the sheltering ramparts—yet he surrenders.

"Roger de Bricqueville and Gilles de Sillé, his trusted councillors, have taken flight. He remains alone with Prelati, who also attempts, in vain, to escape. He, like Gilles, is loaded with chains. Robin Guillaumet searches the fortress from top to bottom. He discovers bloody clothes, imperfectly calcinated ashes which Prelati has not had time to throw into the latrines. Amid universal maledictions and cries of horror Gilles and his servitors are conducted to Nîmes and incarcerated in the château de la Tour Neuve.

"Now this part is not very clear," said Durtal to himself. "Remembering what a daredevil the Marshal had been, how can we reconcile ourselves to the idea that he could give himself up to certain death and torture without striking a blow?

"'Was he softened, weakened by his nights of debauchery, terrified by the audacity of his own sacrileges, ravaged and torn by remorse? Was he tired of living as he did, and did he give himself up, as so many murderers do, because he was irresistibly attracted to punishment? Nobody knows. Did he think himself above the law because of his lofty rank? Or did he hope to disarm the duke by playing upon his venality, offering him a ransom of manors and farm land?

"One answer is as plausible as another. He may also have known how hesitant Jean V had been, for fear of rousing the wrath of the nobility of his duchy, about yielding to the objurgations of the Bishop and raising troops for the pursuit and arrest.

"Well, there is no document which answers these questions. An author can take some liberties here and set down his own conjectures. But that curious trial is going to give me some trouble.

"As soon as Gilles and his accomplices are incarcerated, two tribunals are organized, one ecclesiastical to judge the crimes coming under the jurisdiction of the Church, the other civil to judge those on which the state must pass.

"To tell the truth, the civil tribunal, which is present at the ecclesiastical hearings, effaces itself completely. As a matter of form it makes a brief cross-examination—but it pronounces the sentence of death, which the Church cannot permit itself to utter, according to the old adage, *'Ecclesia abhorret a sanguine.'*

"The ecclesiastical trial lasts five weeks, the civil, forty-eight hours. It seems that, to hide behind the robes of the Bishop, the duke of Brittany has voluntarily subordinated the rôle of civil justice, which ordinarily stands up for its rights against the encroachments of the ecclesiastical court.

"Jean de Malestroit presides over the hearings. He chooses for assistants the Bishops of Mans, of Saint Brieuc, and of Saint Lô, then in addition he surrounds himself with a troop of jurists who work in relays in the interminable sessions of the trial. Some of the more important are Guillaume de Montigné, advocate of the secular court; Jean

Blanchet, bachelor of laws; Guillaume Groyguet and Robert de la Rivière, licentiates *in utroque jure,* and Hervé Lévi, senescal of Quimper. Pierre de l'Hospital, chancellor of Brittany, who is to preside over the civil hearings after the canonic judgment, assists Jean de Malestroit.

"The public prosecutor is Guillaume Chapeiron, curate of Saint Nicolas, an eloquent and subtile man. Adjunct to him, to relieve him of the fatigue of the readings, are Geoffroy Pipraire, dean of Sainte Marie, and Jacques de Pentcoetdic, Official of the Church of Nantes.

"In connection with the episcopal jurisdiction, the Church has called in the assistance of the extraordinary tribunal of the Inquisition, for the repression of the crime of heresy, then comprehending perjury, blasphemy, sacrilege, all the crimes of magic.

"It sits at the side of Jean de Malestroit in the redoubtable and learned person of Jean Blouyn of the order of Saint Dominic, delegated by the Grand Inquisitor of France, Guillaume Merici, to the functions of Vice Inquisitor of the city and diocese of Nantes.

"The tribunal constituted, the trial opens the first thing in the morning, because judges and witnesses, in accordance with the custom of the times, must proceed fasting to the giving and hearing of evidence. The testimony of the parents of the victims is heard, and Robin Guillaumet, acting sergeant-at-arms, the man who arrested the Marshal at Mâchecoul, reads the citation bidding Gilles de Rais appear. He is brought in and declares disdainfully that he does not recognize the competence of the Tribunal, but, as canonic procedure demands, the Prosecutor at once 'in order that by this means the correction of sorcery be not prevented,' petitions for and obtains from the tribunal a ruling that this objection be quashed as being null in law and 'frivolous.' He begins to read to the accused the counts on which he is to be tried. Gilles cries out that the Prosecutor is a liar and a traitor. Then Guillaume Chapeiron extends his hand toward the crucifix, swears that he is telling the truth, and challenges the Marshal to take the same oath. But this man, who has recoiled from no sacrilege, is troubled. He refuses to perjure himself before God, and the session ends with Gilles still vociferating outrageous denunciations of the Prosecutor.

"The preliminaries completed, a few days later, the public hearings begin. The act of indictment is read aloud to the accused, in front of an audience who shudder when Chapeiron indefatigably enumerates the crimes one by one, and formally accuses the Marshal of having practised sorcery and magic, of having polluted and slain little children, of having violated the immunities of Holy Church at Saint Etienne de Mer Morte.

"Then after a silence he resumes his discourse, and making no account of the murders, but dwelling only on the crimes of which the punishment, foreseen by canonic law, can be fixed by the Church, he demands that Gilles be smitten with double excommunication, first as an evoker of demons, a heretic, apostate and renegade, second as a sodomist and perpetrator of sacrilege.

"Gilles, who has listened to this incisive and scathing indictment, completely loses control of himself. He insults the judges, calls them simonists and ribalds, and refuses to answer the questions put to him. The Prosecutor and advocates are unmoved; they invite him to present his defence.

"Again he denounces them, insults them, but when called upon to refute them he remains silent.

"The Bishop and Vice Inquisitor declare him in contempt and pronounce against him the sentence of excommunication, which is soon made public. They decide in addition that the hearing shall be continued next day—·—"

A ring of the doorbell interrupted Durtal's perusal of his notes. Des Hermies entered.

"I have just seen Carhaix. He is ill," he said.

"That so? What seems to be the matter?"

"Nothing very serious. A slight attack of bronchitis. He'll be up in a few days if he will consent to keep quiet."

"I must go see him tomorrow," said Durtal.

"And what are you doing?" enquired Des Hermies. "Working hard?"

"Why, yes. I am digging into the trial of the noble baron de Rais. It will be as tedious to read as to write!"

"And you don't know yet when you will finish your volume?"

"No," answered Durtal, stretching. "As a matter of fact I wish it might never be finished. What will become of me when it is? I'll have to look around for another subject, and, when I find one, do all the drudgery of planning and then getting the introductory chapter written—the mean part of any literary work is getting started. I shall pass mortal hours doing nothing. Really, when I think it over, literature has only one excuse for existing; it saves the person who makes it from the disgustingness of life."

"And, charitably, it lessens the distress of us few who still love art."

"Few indeed!"

"And the number keeps diminishing. The new generation no longer interests itself in anything except gambling and jockeys."

"Yes, you're quite right. The men can't spare from gambling the time to read, so it is only the society women who buy books and pass judgment on them. It is to The Lady, as Schopenhauer called her, to the little goose, as I should characterize her, that we are indebted for these shoals of lukewarm and mucilaginous novels which nowadays get puffed."

"You think, then, that we are in for a pretty literature. Naturally you can't please women by enunciating vigorous ideas in a crisp style."

"But," Durtal went on, after a silence, "it is perhaps best that the case should be as it is. The rare artists who remain have no business to be thinking about the public. The artist lives and works far from the drawing-room, far from the clamour of the little fellows who fix up the custom-made literature. The only legitimate source of vexation to an author is to see his work, when printed, exposed to the contaminating curiosity of the crowd."

"That is," said Des Hermies, "a veritable prostitution. To advertise a thing for sale is to accept the degrading familiarities of the first comer."

"But our impenitent pride—and also our need of the miserable sous—make it impossible for us to keep our manuscripts sheltered from the asses. Art ought to be—like one's beloved—out of reach, out of the world. Art and prayer are the only decent ejaculations of the soul. So when one of my books appears, I let go of it with horror. I get as far as possible from the environment in which it may be supposed to circulate. I care very little about a book of mine until years afterward, when it has disappeared from all the shop windows and is out of print. Briefly, I am in no hurry to finish the history of Gilles de Rais, which, unfortunately, is getting finished in spite of me. I don't give a damn how it is received."

"Are you doing anything this evening?"

"No. Why?"

"Shall we dine together?"

"Certainly."

And while Durtal was putting on his shoes, Des Hermies remarked, "To me the striking thing about the so-called literary world of this epoch is its cheap hypocrisy. What a lot of laziness, for instance, that word dilettante has served to cover."

"Yes, it's a great old alibi. But it is confounding to see that the critic who today decrees himself the title of dilettante accepts it as a term of praise and does not even suspect that he is slapping himself. The whole thing can be resolved into syllogism:

"The dilettante has no personal temperament, since he objects to nothing and likes everything.   ·

"Whoever has no personal temperament has no talent."

"Then," rejoined Des Hermies, putting on his hat, "an author who boasts of being a dilettante, confesses by that very thing that he is no author?"

"Exactly."

CHAPTER XVII

Toward the end of the afternoon Durtal quit work and went up to the towers of Saint Sulpice.

He found Carhaix in bed in a chamber connecting with the one in which they were in the habit of dining. These rooms were very similar, with their walls or unpapered stone, and with their vaulted ceilings, only, the bedroom was darker. The window opened its half-wheel not on the place Saint Sulpice but on the rear of the church, whose roof prevented any light from getting in. This cell was furnished with an iron bed, whose springs shrieked, with two cane chairs, and with a table that had a shabby covering of green baize. On the bare wall was a crucifix of no value, with a dry palm over it. That was all. Carhaix was sitting up in bed reading, with books and papers piled all around him. His eyes were more watery and his face paler than usual. His beard, which had not been shaved for several days, grew in grey clumps on his hollow cheeks, but his poor features were radiant with an affectionate, affable smile.

To Durtal's questions he replied, "It is nothing. Des Hermies gives me permission to get up tomorrow. But what a frightful medicine!" and he showed Durtal a potion of which he had to take a teaspoonful every hour.

"What is it he's making you take?"

But the bell-ringer did not know. Doubtless to spare him the expense, Des Hermies himself always brought the bottle.

"Isn't it tiresome lying in bed?"

"I should say! I am obliged to entrust my bells to an assistant who is no good. Ah, if you heard him ring! It makes me shudder, it sets my teeth on edge."

"Now you mustn't work yourself up," said his wife. "In two days you will be able to ring your bells yourself."

But he went on complaining. "You two don't understand. My bells are used to being well treated. They're like domestic animals, those instruments, and they obey only their master. Now they won't harmonize, they jangle. I can hardly recognize their voices."

"What are you reading?" asked Durtal, wishing to change a subject which he judged to be dangerous.

"Books about bells! Ah, Monsieur Durtal, I have some inscriptions here of truly rare beauty. Listen," and he opened a worm-bored book, "listen to this motto printed in raised letters on the bronze robe of the great bell of Schaffhausen, 'I call the living, I mourn the dead, I break the thunder.' And this other which figured on an old bell in the belfry of Ghent, 'My name is Roland. When I toll, there is a fire; when I peal, there is a tempest in Flanders.'"

"Yes," Durtal agreed, "there is a certain vigour about that one."

"Ah," said Carhaix, seeming not to have heard the other's remark, "it's ridiculous. Now the rich have their names and titles inscribed on the bells which they give to the churches, but they have so many qualities and titles that there is no room for a motto. Truly, humility is a forgotten virtue in our day."

"If that were the only forgotten virtue!" sighed Durtal.

"Ah!" replied Carhaix, not to be turned from his favourite subject, "and if this were the only abuse! But bells now rust from inactivity. The metal is no longer hammer-hardened and is not vibrant. Formerly these magnificent auxiliaries of the ritual sang without cease. The canonical hours were sounded, Matins and Laudes before daybreak, Prime at dawn, Tierce at nine o'clock, Sexte at noon, Nones at three, and then Vespers and Compline. Now we announce the curate's mass, ring three angeluses, morning, noon, and evening, occasionally a Salute, and on certain days launch a few peals for prescribed ceremonies. And that's all. It's only in the convents where the bells do not sleep, for these, at least, the night offices are kept up."

"You mustn't talk about that," said his wife, straightening the pillows at his back. "If you keep working yourself up, you will never get well."

"Quite right," he said, resigned, "but what would you have? I shall still be a man with a grievance, whom nothing can pacify," and he smiled at his wife who was bringing him a spoonful of the potion to swallow.

The doorbell rang. Mme. Carhaix went to answer it and a hilarious and red-faced priest entered, crying in a great voice, "It's Jacob's ladder, that stairway! I climbed and climbed and climbed, and I'm all out of breath," and he sank, puffing, into an armchair.

"Well, my friend," he said at last, coming into the bedroom, "I learned from the beadle that you were ill, and I came to see how you were getting on."

Durtal examined him. An irrepressible gaiety exuded from this sanguine, smooth-shaven face, blue from the razor. Carhaix introduced them. They exchanged a look, of distrust on the priest's side, of coldness on Durtal's.

Durtal felt embarrassed and in the way, while the honest pair were effusively and with excessive humility thanking the abbé for coming up to see them. It was evident that for this pair, who were not ignorant of the sacrileges and scandalous self-indulgences of the clergy, an ecclesiastic was a man elect, a man so superior that as soon as he arrived nobody else counted.

Durtal took his leave, and as he went downstairs he thought, "That jubilant priest sickens me. Indeed, a gay priest, physician, or man of letters must have an infamous soul, because they are the ones who see clearly into human misery and console it, or heal it, or depict it. If after that they can act the clown—they are unspeakable! Though I'll admit that thoughtless persons deplore the sadness of the

novel of observation and its resemblance to the life it represents. These people would have it jovial, smart, highly coloured, aiding them, in their base selfishness, to forget the
hag-ridden existences of their brothers.

"Truly, Carhaix and his wife are peculiar. They bow
under the paternal despotism of the priests—and there are
moments when that same despotism must be no joke—and
revere them and adore them. But then these two are simple believers, with humble, unsmirched souls. I don't know
the priest who was there, but he is rotund and rubicund, he
shakes in his fat and seems bursting with joy. Despite the
example of Saint Francis of Assisi, who was gay—spoiling
him for me—I have difficulty in persuading myself that this
abbé is an elevated being. It's all right to say that the best
thing for him is to be mediocre; to ask how, if he were otherwise, he would make his flock understand him; and add that
if he really had superior gifts he would be hated by his colleagues and persecuted by his bishop."

While conversing thus disjointedly with himself Durtal
had reached the base of the tower. He stopped under the
porch. "I intended to stay longer up there," thought he.
"It's only half-past five. I must kill at least half an hour
before dinner."

The weather was almost mild. The clouds had been
swept away. He lighted a cigarette and strolled about the
square, musing. Looking up he hunted for the bell-ringer's
window and recognized it. Of the windows which opened
over the portico it alone had a curtain.

"What an abominable construction," he thought, contemplating the church. "Think. That cube flanked by
two towers presumes to invite comparison with the façade of
Notre Dame. What a jumble," he continued, examining
the details. "From the foundation to the first story are
Ionic columns with volutes, then from the base of the tower
to the summit are Corinthian columns with acanthus leaves.
What significance can this salmagundi of pagan orders have

on a Christian church? And as a rebuke to the over-orna-mented bell tower there stands the other tower unfinished, looking like an abandoned grain elevator, but the less hide-ous of the two, at that.

"And it took five or six architects to erect this indigent heap of stones. Yet Servandoni and Oppenord and their ilk were the real major prophets, the ....zekiels of building. Their work is the work of seers looking beyond the eighteenth cen-tury to the day of transportation by steam. For Saint Sulpice is not a church, it's a railway station!

"And the interior of the edifice is not more religious nor artistic than the exterior. The only thing in it that pleases me is good Carhaix's aërial cave." Then he looked about him. "This square is very ugly, but how provincial and homelike it is! Surely nothing could equal the hideousness of that seminary, which exhales the rancid, frozen odour of a hospital. The fountain with its polygonal basins, its sauce-pan urns, its lion-headed spouts, its niches with prelates in them, is no masterpiece. Neither is the city hall, whose ad-ministrative style is a cinder in the eye. But on this square, as in the neighbouring streets, Servandoni, Garancière, and Ferrou, one respires an atmosphere compounded of benign silence and mild humidity. You think of a clothes-press that hasn't been open for years, and, somehow, of incense. This square is in perfect harmony with the houses in the decayed streets around here, with the shops where religious parapher-nalia are sold, the image and ciborium factories, the Catholic bookstores with books whose covers are the colour of apple seeds, macadam, nutmeg, bluing.

"Yes, it's dilapidated and quiet."

The square was then almost deserted. A few women were going up the church steps, met by mendicants who mur-mured paternosters as they rattled their tin cups. An ec-clesiastic, carrying under his arm a book bound in black cloth, saluted white-eyed women. A few dogs were running about. Children were chasing each other or jumping rope.

The enormous chocolate-coloured la Villette omnibus and the little honey-yellow bus of the Auteuil line went past, almost empty. Hackmen were standing beside their hacks on the sidewalk, or in a group around a comfort station, talking. There were no crowds, no noise, and the great trees gave the square the appearance of the silent mall of a little town.

"Well," said Durtal, considering the church again, "I really must go up to the top of the tower some clear day." Then he shook his head. "What for? A bird's-eye view of Paris would have been interesting in the Middle Ages, but now! I should see, as from a hill top, other heights, a network of grey streets, the whiter arteries of the boulevards, the green plaques of gardens and squares, and, away in the distance, files of houses like lines of dominoes stood up on end, the black dots being windows.

"And then the edifices emerging from this jumble of roofs, Notre Dame, la Sainte Chapelle, Saint Severin, Saint Etienne du Mont, the Tour Saint Jacques, are put out of countenance by the deplorable mass of newer edifices. And I am not at all eager to contemplate that specimen of the art of the maker of toilet articles which l'Opera is, nor that bridge arch, l'arc de la Triomphe, nor that hollow chandelier, the Tour Eiffel! It's enough to see them separately, from the ground, as you turn a street corner. Well, I must go and dine, for I have an engagement with Hyacinthe and I must be back before eight."

He went to a neighbouring wine shop where the dining-room, depopulated at six o'clock, permitted one to ruminate in tranquillity, while eating fairly sanitary food and drinking not too dangerously coloured wines. He was thinking of Mme. Chantelouve, but more of Docre. The mystery of this priest haunted him. What could be going on in the soul of a man who had had the figure of Christ tattooed on his heels the better to trample Him?

What hate the act revealed! Did Docre hate God for

not having given him the blessed ecstasies of a saint, or more humanly for not having raised him to the highest ecclesiastical dignities? Evidently the spite of this priest was inordinate and his pride unlimited. He seemed not displeased to be an object of terror and loathing, for thus he was somebody. Then, for a thorough-paced scoundrel, as this man seemed to be, what delight to make his enemies languish in slow torment by casting spells on them with perfect impunity.

"And sacrilege carries one out of oneself in furious transports, in voluptuous delirium, which nothing can equal. Since the Middle Ages it has been the coward's crime, for human justice does not prosecute it, and one can commit it with impunity, but it is the most extreme of excesses for a believer, and Docre believes in Christ, or he wouldn't hate Him so.

"A monster! And what ignoble relations he must have had with Chantelouve's wife! Now, how shall I make her speak up? She gave me quite clearly to understand, the other day, that she refused to explain herself on this topic. Meanwhile, as I have not intention of submitting to her young girl follies tonight, I will tell her that I am not feeling well, and that absolute rest and quiet are necessary."

He did so, an hour later when she came in.

She proposed a cup of tea, and when he refused, she embraced him and nursed him like a baby. Then withdrawing a little, "You work too hard. You need some relaxation. Come now, to pass the time you might court me a little, because up to now I have done it all. No? That idea does not amuse him. Let us try something else. Shall we play hide-and-seek with the cat? He shrugs his shoulders. Well, since there is nothing to change your grouchy expression, let us talk. What has become of your friend Des Hermies?"

"Nothing in particular."

"And his experiments with Mattei medicine?"

"I don't know whether he continues to prosecute them or not."

"Well, I see that the conversational possibilities of that topic are exhausted. You know your replies are not very encouraging, dear."

"But," he said, "everybody sometimes gets so he doesn't answer questions at great length. I even know a young woman who becomes excessively laconic when interrogated on a certain subject."

"Of a canon, for instance."

"Precisely."

She crossed her legs, very coolly. "That young woman undoubtedly had reasons for keeping still. But perhaps that young woman is really eager to oblige the person who cross-examines her; perhaps, since she last saw him, she has gone to a great deal of trouble to satisfy his curiosity."

"Look here, Hyacinthe darling, explain yourself," he said, squeezing her hands, an expression of joy on his face.

"If I have made your mouth water so as not to have a grouchy face in front of my eyes, I have succeeded remarkably."

He kept still, wondering whether she was making fun of him or whether she really was ready to tell him what he wanted to know.

"Listen," she said. "I hold firmly by my decision of the other night. I will not permit you to become acquainted with Canon Docre. But at a settled time I can arrange, without your forming any relations with him, to have you be present at the ceremony you most desire to know about."

"The Black Mass?"

"Yes. Within a week Docre will have left Paris. If once, in my company, you see him, you will never see him afterward. Keep your evenings free all this week. When the time comes I will notify you. But you may thank me, dear, because to be useful to you I am disobeying the commands of my confessor, whom I dare not see now, so I am damning myself."

He kissed her, then, "Seriously, that man is really a monster?"

"I fear so. In any case I would not wish anybody the misfortune of having him for an enemy."

"I should say not, if he poisons people by magic, as he seems to have done Gévingey."

"And he probably has. I should not like to be in the astrologer's shoes."

"You believe in Docre's potency, then. Tell me, how does he operate, with the blood of mice, with broths, or with oil?"

"So you know about that! He does employ these substances. In fact, he is one of the very few persons who know how to manage them without poisoning themselves. It's as dangerous as working with explosives. Frequently, though, when attacking defenceless persons, he uses simpler recipes. He distils extracts of poison and adds sulphuric acid to fester the wound, then he dips in this compound the point of a lancet with which he has his victim-pricked by a flying spirit or a larva. It is ordinary, well-known magic, that of Rosicrucians and tyros."

Durtal burst out laughing. "But, my dear, to hear you, one would think death could be sent to a distance like a letter."

"Well, isn't cholera transmitted by letters? Ask the sanitary corps. Don't they disinfect all mail in the time of epidemics?"

"I don't contradict that, but the case is not the same."

"It is too, because it is the question of transmission, invisibility, distance, which astonishes you."

"What astonishes me more than that is to hear of the Rosicrucians actively satanizing. I confess that I had never considered them as anything more than harmless suckers and funereal fakes."

"But all societies are composed of suckers and the wily leaders who exploit them. That's the case of the Rosicrucians. Yes, their leaders privately attempt crime. One does not need to be erudite or intelligent to practise the ritual of spells. At any rate, and I affirm this, there is among them a former man of letters whom I know. He lives with a married woman, and they pass the time, he and she, trying to kill the husband by scorcery."

"Well, it has its advantages over divorce, that system has."

She pouted. "I shan't say another word. I think you are making fun of me. You don't believe in anything——"

"Indeed. I was not laughing at you. I haven't very precise ideas on this subject. I admit that at first blush all this seems improbable, to say the least. But when I think that all the efforts of modern science do but confirm the discoveries of the magic of other days, I keep my mouth shut. It is true," he went on after a silence,—"to cite only one fact—that people can no longer laugh at the stories of women being changed into cats in the Middle Ages. Recently there was brought to M. Charcot a little girl who suddenly got down on her hands and knees and ran and jumped around, scratching and spitting and arching her back. So that metamorphosis is possible. No, one cannot too often repeat it, the truth is that we know nothing and have no right to deny anything. But to return to your Rosicrucians. Using purely chemical formulæ, they get along without sacrilege?"

"That is as much as to say that their venefices— supposing they know how to prepare them well enough to accomplish their purpose, though I doubt that—are easy to defeat. Yet I don't mean to say that this group, one member of which is an ordained priest, does not make use of contaminated Eucharists at need."

"Another nice priest! But since you are so well informed, do you know how spells are conjured away?"

"Yes and no. I know that when the poisons are sealed by sacrilege, when the operation is performed by a master, Docre or one of the princes of magic at Rome, it is not at all easy—nor healthy—to attempt to apply an antidote. Though I have heard of a certain abbé at Lyons who, practically alone, is succeeding right now in these difficult cures."

"Dr. Johannès!"

"You know him!"

"No. But Gévingey, who has gone to seek his medical aid, has told me of him."

"Well, I don't know how he goes about it, but I know that spells which are not complicated with sacrilege are usually evaded by the law of return. The blow is sent back to him who struck it. There are, at the present time, two churches, one in Belgium, the other in France, where, when one prays before a statue of the Virgin, the spell which has been cast on one flies off and goes and strikes one's adversary."

"Rats!"

"One of these churches is at Tougres, eighteen kilometres from Liége, and the name of it is Notre Dame de Retour. The other is the church of l'Epine, 'the thorn,' a little village near Châlons. This church was built long ago to conjure away the spells produced with the aid of the thorns which grew in that country and served to pierce images cut in the shape of hearts."

"Near Châlons," said Durtal, digging in his memory, "it does seem to me now that Des Hermies, speaking of bewitchment by the blood of white mice, pointed out that village as the habitation of certain diabolic circles."

"Yes, that country in all times has been a hotbed of Satanism."

"You are mighty well up on these matters. Is it Docre who transmitted this knowledge to you?"

"Yes, I owe him the little I am able to pass on to you. He took a fancy to me and even wanted to make me his pupil. I refused, and am glad now I did, for I am much more wary than I was then of being constantly in a state of mortal sin."

"Have you ever attended the Black Mass?"

"Yes. And I warn you in advance that you will regret having seen such terrible things. It is a memory that persists and horrifies, even—especially—when one does not personally take part in the offices."

He looked at her. She was pale, and her filmed eyes blinked rapidly.

"It's your own wish," she continued. "You will have no complaint if the spectacle terrifies you or wrings your heart."

He was almost dumbfounded to see how sad she was and with what difficulty she spoke.

"Really. This Docre, where did he come from, what did he do formerly, how did he happen to become a master Satanist?"

"I don't know very much about him. I know he was a supply priest in Paris, then confessor of a queen in exile. There were terrible stories about him, which, thanks to his influential patronage, were hushed up under the Empire. He was interned at La Trappe, then driven out of the priesthood, excommunicated by Rome. I learned in addition that he had several times been accused of poisoning, but had always been acquitted because the tribunals had never been able to get any evidence. Today he lives I don't know how, but at ease, and he travels a good deal with a woman who serves as voyant. To all the world he is a scoundrel, but he is learned and perverse, and then he is so charming."

"Oh," he said, "how changed your eyes and voice are! Admit that you are in love with him."

"No, not now. But why should I not tell you that we were mad about each other at one time?"

"And now?"

"It is over. I swear it is. We have remained friends and nothing more."

"But then you often went to see him. What kind of a place did he have? At least it was curious and heterodoxically arranged?"

"No, it was quite ordinary, but very comfortable and clean. He had a chemical laboratory and an immense library. The only curious book he showed me was an office of the Black Mass on parchment. There were admirable illuminations, and the binding was made of the tanned skin of a child who had died unbaptized. Stamped into the cover, in the shape of a fleuron, was a great host consecrated in a Black Mass."

"What did the manuscript say?"

"I did not read it."

They were silent. Then she took his hands.

"Now you are yourself again. I knew I should cure you of your bad humour. Admit that I am awfully good-natured not to have got angry at you."

"Got angry? What about?"

"Because it is not very flattering to a woman to be able to entertain a man only by telling him about another one."

"Oh, no, it isn't that way at all," he said, kissing her eyes tenderly.

"Let me go now," she said, very low, "this enervates me, and I must get home. It's late."

She sighed and fled, leaving him amazed and wondering in what weird activities the life of that woman had been passed.

CHAPTER XVIII

The day after that on which he had spewed such furious vituperation over the Tribunal, Gilles de Rais appeared again before his judges. He presented himself with bowed head and clasped hands. He had once more jumped from one extreme to the other. A few hours had sufficed to break the spirit of the energumen, who now declared that he recognized the authority of the magistrates and begged forgiveness for having insulted them.

They affirmed that for the love of Our Lord they forgot his imprecations, and, at his prayer, the Bishop and the Inquisitor revoked the sentence of excommunication which they had passed on him the day before.

This hearing was, in addition, taken up with the arraignment of Prelati and his accomplices. Then, authorized by the ecclesiastical text which says that a confession cannot be regarded as sufficient if it is *"dubia, vaga, generalis illativa, jocosa,"* the Prosecutor asserted that to certify the sincerity of his confessions Gilles must be subjected to the "canonic question," that is, to torture.

The Marshal besought the Bishop to wait until the next day, and claiming the right of confessing immediately to such judges as the Tribunal were pleased to designate, he swore that he would thereafter repeat his confession before the public and the court.

Jean de Malestroit granted this request, and the Bishop of Saint Brieuc and Pierre de l'Hospital were appointed to hear Gilles in his cell. When he had finished the recital of his debauches and murders they ordered Prelati to be brought to them.

At sight of him Gilles burst into tears and when, after the interrogatory, preparations were made to conduct the Italian back to his dungeon, Gilles embraced him, saying, "Farewell, Francis my friend, we shall never see each other again in this world. I pray God to give you good patience and I hope in Him that we may meet again in great joy in Paradise. Pray God for me and I shall pray for you."

And Gilles was left alone to meditate on his crimes which he was to confess publicly at the hearing next day. That day was the impressive day of the trial. The room in which the Tribunal sat was crammed, and there were multitudes sitting on the stairs, standing in the corridors, filling the neighbouring courts, blocking the streets and lanes. From twenty miles around the peasants were come to see the memorable beast whose very name, before his capture, had served to close the doors those evenings when in universal trembling the women dared not weep aloud.

This meeting of the Tribunal was to be conducted with the most minute observance of all the forms. All the assize judges, who in a long hearing generally had their places filled by proxies, were present.

The courtroom, massive, obscure, upheld by heavy Roman pillars, had been rejuvenated. The wall, ogival, threw to cathedral height the arches of its vaulted ceiling, which were joined together, like the sides of an abbatial mitre, in a point. The room was lighted by sickly daylight which was filtered through small panes between heavy leads. The azure of the ceiling was darkened to navy blue, and the golden stars, at that height, were as the heads of steel pins. In the shadows of the vaults appeared the ermine of the ducal arms, dimly seen in escutcheons which were like great dice with black dots.

Suddenly the trumpets blared, the room was lighted up, and the Bishops entered. Their mitres of cloth of gold flamed like the lightning. About their necks were brilliant collars with orphreys crusted, as were the robes, with carbuncles. In silent processional the Bishops advanced, weighted down by their rigid copes, which fell in a flare from their shoulders and were like golden bells split in the back. In their hands they carried the crozier from which hung the maniple, a sort of green veil.

At each step they glowed like coals blown upon. Themselves were sufficient to light the room, as they reanimated with their jewels the pale sun of a rainy October day and scattered a new lustre to all parts of the room, over the mute audience.

Outshone by the shimmer of the orphreys and the stones, the costumes of the other judges appeared darker and discordant. The black vestments of secular justice, the white and black robe of Jeon Blouyn, the silk symars, the red woollen mantles, the scarlet chaperons lined with fur, seemed faded and common.

The Bishops seated themselves in the front row, surrounding Jean de Malestroit, who from a raised seat dominated the court.

Under the escort of the men-at-arms Gilles entered. He was broken and haggard and had aged twenty years in one night. His eyes burned behind seared lids. His cheeks shook. Upon injunction he began the recital of his crimes.

In a laboured voice, choked by tears, he recounted his abductions of children, his hideous tactics, his infernal stimulations, his impetuous murders, his implacable violations. Obsessed by the vision of his victims, he described their agonies drawn out or hastened, their cries, the rattle in their throats. He confessed to having wallowed in the elastic warmth of their intestines. He confessed that he had ripped out their hearts through wounds enlarged and opening like ripe fruit. And with the eyes of a somnambulist he looked down at his fingers and shook them as if blood were dripping from them.

The thunder-struck audience kept a mournful silence which was lacerated suddenly by a few short cries, and the attendants, at a run, carried out fainting women, mad with horror.

He seemed to see nothing, to hear nothing. He continued to tell off the frightful rosary of his crimes. Then his voice became raucous. He was coming to the sepulchral violations, and now to the torture of the little children whom he had cajoled in order to cut their throats as he kissed them.

He divulged every detail. The account was so formidable, so atrocious, that beneath their golden caps the bishops blanched. These priests, tempered in the fires of confessional, these judges who in that time of demonomania and murder had never heard more terrifying confessions, these prelates whom no depravity had ever astonished, made the sign of the Cross, and Jean de Malestroit rose and for very shame veiled the face of the Christ.

Then all lowered their heads, and without a word they listened. The Marshal, bathed in sweat, his face downcast, looked now at the crucifix whose invisible head and bristling crown of thorns gave their shapes to the veil.

He finished his narrative and broke down completely. Till now he had stood erect, speaking as if in a daze, recounting to himself, aloud, the memory of his ineradicable crimes. But at the end of the story his forces abandoned him. He fell on his knees and, shaken by terrific sobs, he cried, "O God, O my Redeemer, I beseech mercy and pardon!" Then the ferocious and haughty baron, the first of his caste no doubt, humiliated himself. He turned toward the people and said, weeping, "Ye, the parents of those whom I have so cruelly put to death, give, ah give me, the succour of your pious prayers!"

Then in its white splendour the soul of the Middle Ages burst forth radiant.

Jean de Malestroit left his seat and raised the accused, who was beating the flagstones with his despairing forehead. The judge in de Malestroit disappeared, the priest alone remained. He embraced the sinner who was repenting and lamenting his fault.

A shudder overran the audience when Jean de Malestroit, with Gilles's head on his breast, said to him, "Pray that the just and rightful wrath of the Most High be averted, weep that your tears may wash out the blood lust from your being!"

And with one accord everybody in the room knelt down and prayed for the assassin. When the orisons were hushed there was an instant of wild terror and commotion. Driven beyond human limits of horror and pity, the crowd tossed and surged. The judges of the Tribunal, silent, enervated, reconquered themselves.

With a gesture, brushing away his tears, the Prosecutor arrested the proceedings. He said that the crimes were "clear and apparent," that the proofs were manifest, that the court would now "in its conscience and soul" chastise the culprit, and he demanded that the day of passing judgment be fixed. The Tribunal designated the day after the next.

And that day the Official of the church of Nantes, Jacques de Pentcoetdic, read in succession the two sentences. The first, passed by the Bishop and the Inquisitor for the acts coming under their common jurisdiction, began thus:

"The Holy Name of Christ invoked, we, Jean, Bishop of Nantes, and Brother Jean Blouyn, bachelor in our Holy Scriptures, of the order of the preaching friars of Nantes, and delegate of the Inquisitor of heresies for the city and diocese of Nantes, in session of the Tribunal and having before our eyes God alone——"

And after enumerating the crimes it concluded:

"We pronounce, decide, and declare, that thou, Gilles de Rais, cited unto our Tribunal, art heinously guilty of heresy, apostasy, and evocation of demons; that for these crimes thou hast incurred the sentence of excommunication and all other penalties determined by the law."

The second judgment, rendered by the Bishop alone, on the crimes of sodomy, sacrilege, and violation of the immunities of the Church, which more particularly concerned his authority, ended in the same conclusions and in the pronunciation, in almost identical form, of the same penalty.

Gilles listened with bowed head to the reading of these judgments. When it was over the Bishop and the Inquisitor said to him, "Will you, now that you detest your errors, your evocations, and your crimes, be reincorporated into the Church our Mother?"

And upon the ardent prayers of the Marshal they relieved him of all excommunication and admitted him to participate in the sacraments. The justice of God was satisfied, the crime was recognized, punished, but effaced by contrition and penitence. Only human justice remained.

The Bishop and the Inquisitor remanded the culprit to the secular court, which, holding against him the abductions and the murders, pronounced the penalty of death and attainder. Prelati and the other accomplices were at the same time condemned to be hanged and burned alive.

"Cry to God mercy," said Pierre de l'Hospital, who presided over the civil hearings, "and dispose yourself to die in good state with a great repentance for having committed such crimes."

The recommendation was unnecessary. Gilles now faced death without fear. He hoped, humbly, avidly, in the mercy of the Saviour. He cried out fervently for the terrestrial expiation, the stake, to redeem him from the eternal flames after his death.

Far from his châteaux, in his dungeon, alone, he had opened himself and viewed the cloaca which had so long been fed by the residual waters escaped from the abattoirs of Tiffauges and Mâchecoul. He had sobbed in despair of ever draining this stagnant pool. And thunder-smitten by grace, in a cry of horror and joy, he had suddenly seen his soul overflow and sweep away the dank fen before a torrential current of prayer and ecstasy. The butcher of Sodom had destroyed himself, the companion of Jeanne d'Arc had reappeared, the mystic whose soul poured out to God, in bursts of adoration, in floods of tears.

Then he thought of his friends and wished that they also might die in a state of grace. He asked the Bishop of Nantes that they might be executed not before nor after him, but at the same time. He carried his point that he was the most guilty and that he must instruct them in saving their souls and assist them at the moment when they should mount the scaffold. Jean de Malestroit granted the supplication.

"What is curious," said Durtal, interrupting his writing to light a cigarette, "is that——"

A gentle ring. Mme. Chantelouve entered.

She declared that she could stay only two minutes. She had a carriage waiting below. "Tonight," said said, "I will call for you at nine. First write me a letter in practically these terms," and she handed him a paper. He unfolded it and read this declaration:

> "I certify that all that I have said and written about the Black Mass, about the priest who celebrated it, about the place where I claimed to have witnessed it, about the persons alleged to have been there, is pure invention. I affirm that I imagined all these incidents, that, in consequence, all that I have narrated is false."

"Docre's?" he asked, studying the handwriting, minute, pointed, twisted, aggressive.

"Yes, and he wants this declaration, not dated, to be made in the form of a letter from you to a person consulting you on the subject."

"Your canon distrusts me."

"Of course. You write books."

"It doesn't please me infinitely to sign that," murmured Durtal. "What if I refuse?"

"You will not go to the Black Mass."

His curiosity overcame his reluctance. He wrote and signed the letter and Mme. Chantelouve put it in her card-case.

"And in what street is the ceremony to take place?"

"In the rue Olivier de Serres."

"Where is that?"

"Near the rue de Vaugirard, away up."

"Is that where Docre lives?"

"No, we are going to a private house which belongs to a lady he knows. Now, if you'll be so good, put off your cross-examination to some other time, because I am in an awful hurry. At nine o'clock. Don't forget. Be all ready."

He had hardly time to kiss her and she was gone.

"Well," said he, "I already had data on incubacy and poisoning by spells. There remained only the Black Mass, to make me thoroughly acquainted with Satanism as it is practised in our day. And I am to see it! I'll be damned if I thought there were such undercurrents in Paris. And how circumstances hang together and lead to each other! I had to occupy myself with Gilles de Rais and the diabolism of the Middle Ages to get contemporary diabolism revealed to me." And he thought of Docre again. "What a sharper that priest is! Among the occultists who maunder today in the universal decomposition of ideas he is the only one who interests me.

"The others, the mages, the theosophists, the cabalists, the spiritists, the hermetics, the Rosicrucians, remind me, when they are not mere thieves, of children playing and scuffling in a cellar. And if one descend lower yet, into the hole-in-the-wall places of the pythonesses, clairvoyants, and mediums, what does one find except agencies of prostitution and gambling? All these pretended peddlers of the future are extremely nasty; that's the only thing in the occult of which one can be sure."

Des Hermies interrupted the course of these reflections by ringing and walking in. He came to announce that Gévingey had returned and that they were all to dine at Carhaix's the night after next.

"Is Carhaix's bronchitis cured?"

"Yes, completely."

Preoccupied with the idea of the Black Mass, Durtal could not keep silent. He let out the fact that he was to witness the ceremony—and, confronted by Des Hermies's stare of stupefaction, he added that he had promised secrecy and that he could not, for the present, tell him more.

"You're the lucky one!" said Des Hermies. "Is it too much to ask you the name of the abbé who is to officiate?"

"Not at all. Canon Docre."

"Ah!" and the other was silent. He was evidently trying to divine by what manipulations his friend had been able to get in touch with the renegade.

"Some time ago you told me," Durtal said, "that in the Middle Ages the Black Mass was said on the naked buttocks of a woman, that in the seventeenth century it was celebrated on the abdomen, and now?"

"I believe that it takes place before an altar as in church. Indeed it was sometimes celebrated thus at the end of the fifteenth century in Biscay. It is true that the Devil then officiated in person. Clothed in rent and soiled episcopal habits, he gave communion with round pieces of shoe leather for hosts, saying, 'This is my body.' And he gave these disgusting wafers to the faithful to eat after they had kissed his left hand and his breech. I hope that you will not be obliged to render such base homage to your canon."

Durtal laughed. "No, I don't think he requires a pretend like that. But look here, aren't you of the decided opinion that the creatures who so piously, infamously, follow these offices are a bit mad?"

"Mad? Why? The cult of the Demon is no more insane than that of God. One is rotten and the other resplendent, that is all. By your reckoning all people who worship any god whatever would de demented. No. The affiliates of Satanism are mystics of a vile order, but they are mystics. Now, it is highly probable that their exaltations into the extra-terrestrial of Evil coincide with the rages of their frenzied senses, for lechery is the wet nurse of Demonism. Medicine classes, rightly or wrongly, the hunger for ordure in the unknown categories of neurosis, and well it may, for nobody knows anything about neuroses except that everybody has them. It is quite certain that in this, more than in any previous century, the nerves quiver at the least shock. For instance, recall the newspaper accounts of executions of criminals. We learn that the executioner goes about his work timidly, that he is on the point of fainting, that he has nervous prostration when he decapitates a man. Then compare this nervous wreck with the invincible torturers of the olden time. They would thrust your arm into a sleeve of moistened parchment which when set on fire would draw up and in a leisurely fashion reduce your flesh to dust. Or they would drive wedges into your thighs and split the bones. They would crush your thumbs in the thumbscrew. Or they would singe all the hair off your epidermis with a poker, or roll up the skin from your abdomen and leave you with a kind of apron. They would drag you at the cart's tail, give you the strappado, roast you, drench you with ignited alcohol, and through it all preserve an impassive countenance and tranquil nerves not to be shaken by any cry or plaint. Only, as these exercises were somewhat fatiguing, the torturers, after the operation, were ravenously hungry and required a deal of drink. They were sanguinaries of a mental stability not to be shaken, while now! But to return to your companions in sacrilege. This evening, if they are not maniacs, you will find them —doubt it not—repulsive lechers. Observe them closely. I am sure that to them the invocation of Beelzebub is a prelibation of carnality. Don't be afraid, because, Lord! in this group there won't be any to make you imitate the martyr of whom Jacques de Voragine speaks in his history of Saint Paul the Eremite. You know that legend?"

"No."

"Well, to refresh your soul I will tell you. This martyr, who was very young, was stretched out, his hands and feet bound, on a bed, then a superb specimen of femininity was brought in, who tried to force him. As he was burning and was about to sin, he bit off his tongue and spat it in the face of the woman, "and thus pain drove out temptation," says the good de Voragine."

"My heroism would not carry me so far as that, I confess. But must you go so soon?"

"Yes, I have a pressing engagement."

"What a queer age," said Durtal, conducting him to the door. "It is just at the moment when positivism is at its zenith that mysticism rises again and the follies of the occult begin."

"Oh, but it's always been that way. The tail ends of all centuries are alike. They're always periods of vacillation and uncertainty. When materialism is rotten-ripe magic takes root. This phenomenon reappears every hundred years. Not to go further back, look at the decline of the last century. Alongside of the rationalists and atheists you find Saint-Germain, Cagliostro, Saint-Martin, Gabalis, Cazotte, the Rosicrucian societies, the infernal circles, as now. With that, good-bye and good luck."

"Yes," said Durtal, closing the door, "but Cagliostro and his ilk had a certain audacity, and perhaps a little knowledge, while the mages of our time—what inept fakes!"

CHAPTER XIX

In a fiacre they went up the rue de Vaugirard. Mme. Chantelouve was as in a shell and spoke not a word. Durtal looked closely at her when, as they passed a street lamp, a shaft of light played over her veil a moment, then winked out. She seemed agitated and nervous beneath her reserve. He took her hand. She did not withdraw it. He could feel the chill of it through her glove, and her blonde hair tonight seemed disordered, dry, and not so fine as usual.

"Nearly there?"

But in a low voice full of anguish she said, "Do not speak."

Bored by this taciturn, almost hostile tête-à-tête, he began to examine the route through the windows of the cab. The street stretched out interminable, already deserted, so badly paved that at every step the cab springs creaked. The lamp-posts were beginning to be further and further apart. The cab was approaching the ramparts.

"Singular itinerary," he murmured, troubled by the woman's cold, inscrutable reserve.

Abruptly the vehicle turned up a dark street, swung around, and stopped.

Hyacinthe got out. Waiting for the cabman to give him his change, Durtal inspected the lay of the land. They were in a sort of blind alley. Low houses, in which there was not a sign of life, bordered a lane that had no sidewalk. The pavement was like billows. Turning around, when the cab drove away, he found himself confronted by a long high wall above which dry leaves rustled in the shadows. A little door with a square grating in it was cut into the thick unlighted wall, which was seamed with fissures. Suddenly, further away, a ray of light shot out of a show window, and, doubtless attracted by the sound of the cab wheels, a man wearing the black apron of a wineshop keeper lounged through the shop door and spat on the threshold.

"This is the place," said Mme. Chantelouve.

She rang. The grating opened. She raised her veil. A shaft of lantern light struck her full in the face, the door opened noiselessly, and they penetrated into a garden.

"Good evening, madame."

"Good evening, Marie. In the chapel?"

"Yes. Does madame wish me to guide her?"

"No, thanks."

The woman with the lantern scrutinized Durtal. He perceived, beneath a hood, wisps of grey hair falling in disorder over a wrinkled old face, but she did not give him time to examine her and returned to a tent beside the wall serving her as a lodge.

He followed Hyacinthe, who traversed the dark lanes, between rows of palms, to the entrance of a building. She opened the doors as if she were quite at home, and her heels clicked resolutely on the flagstones.

"Be careful," she said, going through a vestibule. "There are three steps."

They came out into a court and stopped before an old house. She rang. A little man advanced, hiding his features, and greeted her in an affected, sing-song voice. She passed, saluting him, and Durtal brushed a fly-blown face, the eyes liquid, gummy, the cheeks plastered with cosmetics, the lips painted.

"I have stumbled into a lair of sodomists.—You didn't tell me that I was to be thrown into such company," he said to Hyacinthe, overtaking her at the turning of a corridor lighted by a lamp.

"Did you expect to meet saints here?"

She shrugged her shoulders and opened a door. They

were in a chapel with a low ceiling crossed by beams gaudily painted with coal-tar pigment. The windows were hidden by great curtains. The walls were cracked and dingy. Durtal recoiled after a few steps. Gusts of humid, mouldy air and of that indescribable new-stove acridity poured out of the registers to mingle with an irritating odour of alkali, resin, and burnt herbs. He was choking, his temples throbbing.

He advanced groping, attempting to accustom his eyes to the half-darkness. The chapel was vaguely lighted by sanctuary lamps suspended from chandeliers of gilded bronze with pink glass pendants. Hyacinthe made him a sign to sit down, then she went over to a group of people sitting on divans in a dark corner. Rather vexed at being left here, away from the centre of activity, Durtal noticed that there were many women and few men present, but his efforts to discover their features were unavailing. As here and there a lamp swayed, he occasionally caught sight of a Junonian brunette, then of a smooth-shaven, melancholy man. He observed that the women were not chattering to each other. Their conversation seemed awed and grave. Not a laugh, not a raised voice, was heard, but an irresolute, furtive whispering, unaccompanied by gesture.

"Hmm," he said to himself. "It doesn't look as if Satan made his faithful happy."

A choir boy, clad in red, advanced to the end of the chapel and lighted a stand of candles. Then the altar became visible. It was an ordinary church altar on a tabernacle above which stood an infamous, derisive Christ. The head had been raised and the neck lengthened, and wrinkles, painted in the cheeks, transformed the grieving face to a bestial one twisted into a mean laugh. He was naked, and where the loincloth should have been, there was a viril member projecting from a bush of horsehair. In front of the tabernacle the chalice, covered with a pall, was placed. The choir boy folded the altar cloth, wiggled his haunches, stood tiptoe on one foot and flipped his arms as if to fly away like a cherub, on pretext of reaching up to light the black tapers whose odour of coal tar and pitch was now added to the pestilential smell of the stuffy room.

Durtal recognized beneath the red robe the "fairy" who had guarded the chapel entrance, and he understood the rôle reserved for this man, whose sacrilegious nastiness was substituted for the purity of childhood acceptable to the Church.

Then another choir boy, more hideous yet, exhibited himself. Hollow chested, racked by coughs, withered, made up with white grease paint and vivid carmine, he hobbled about humming. He approached the tripods flanking the altar, stirred the smouldering incense pots and threw in leaves and chunks of resin.

Durtal was beginning to feel uncomfortable when Hyacinthe rejoined him. She excused herself for having left him by himself so long, invited him to change his place, and conducted him to a seat far in the rear, behind all the rows of chairs.

"This is a real chapel, isn't it?" he asked.

"Yes. This house, this church, the garden that we crossed, are the remains of an old Ursuline convent. For a long time this chapel was used to store hay. The house belonged to a livery-stable keeper, who sold it to that woman," and she pointed out a stout brunette of whom Durtal before had caught a fleeting glimpse.

"Is she married?"

"No. She is a former nun who was debauched long ago by Docre."

"Ah. And those gentlemen who seem to be hiding in the darkest places?"

"They are Satanists. There is one of them who was a professor in the School of Medicine. In his home he has an oratorium where he prays to a statue of Venus Astarte mounted on an altar."

"No!"

"I mean it. He is getting old, and his demoniac orisons increase tenfold his forces, which he is using up with creatures of that sort," and with a gesture she indicated the choir boys.

"You guarantee the truth of this story?"

"You will find it narrated at great length in a religious journal. *Les annales de la sainteté.* And though his identity was made pretty patent in the article, the man did not dare prosecute the editors.—What's the matter with you?" she asked, looking at him closely.

"I'm strangling. The odour from those incense burners is unbearable."

"You will get used to it in a few seconds."

"But what do they burn that smells like that?"

"Asphalt from the street, leaves of henbane, datura, dried nightshade, and myrrh. These are perfumes delightful to Satan, our master." She spoke in that changed, guttural voice which had been hers at times when in bed with him. He looked her squarely in the face. She was pale, the lips pressed tight, the pluvious eyes blinking rapidly.

"Here he comes!" she murmured suddenly, while women in front of them scurried about or knelt in front of the chairs.

Preceded by the two choir boys the canon entered, wearing a scarlet bonnet from which two buffalo horns of red cloth protruded. Durtal examined him as he marched toward the altar. He was tall, but not well built, his bulging chest being out of proportion to the rest of his body. His peeled forehead made one continuous line with his straight nose. The lips and cheeks bristled with that kind of hard, clumpy beard which old priests have who have always shaved themselves. The features were round and insinuating, the eyes, like apple pips, close together, phosphorescent. As a whole his face was evil and sly, but energetic, and the hard, fixed eyes were not the furtive, shifty orbs that Durtal had imagined.

The canon solemnly knelt before the altar, then mounted the steps and began to say mass. Durtal saw then that he had nothing on beneath his sacrificial habit. His black socks and his flesh bulging over the garters, attached high up on his legs, were plainly visible. The chasuble had the shape of an ordinary chasuble but was of the dark red colour of dried blood, and in the middle, in a triangle around which was an embroidered border of colchicum, savin, sorrel, and spurge, was the figure of a black billy-goat presenting his horns.

Docre made the genuflexions, the full- or half-length inclinations specified by the ritual. The kneeling choir boys sang the Latin responses in a crystalline voice which trilled on the ultimate syllables of the words.

"But it's a simple low mass," said Durtal to Mme. Chantelouve.

She shook her head. Indeed, at that moment the choir boys passed behind the altar and one of them brought back copper chafing-dishes, the other, censers, which they distributed to the congregation. All the women enveloped themselves in the smoke. Some held their heads right over the chafing-dishes and inhaled deeply, then, fainting, unlaced themselves, heaving raucous sighs.

The sacrifice ceased. The priest descended the steps backward, knelt on the last one, and in a sharp, tripidant voice cried:

"Master of Slanders, Dispenser of the benefits of crime, Administrator of sumptuous sins and great vices, Satan, thee we adore, reasonable God, just God!

"Superadmirable legate of false trances, thou receivest our beseeching tears; thou savest the honour of families by aborting wombs impregnated in the forgetfulness of the good orgasm; thou dost suggest to the mother the hastening of untimely birth, and thine obstetrics spares the still-born children the anguish of maturity, the contamination of original sin.

"Mainstay of the despairing Poor, Cordial of the Vanquished, it is thou who endowest them with hypocrisy, ingratitude, and stiff-neckedness, that they may defend themselves against the children of God, the Rich.

"Suzerain of Resentment, Accountant of Humiliations, Treasurer of old Hatreds, thou alone dost fertilize the brain of man whom injustice has crushed; thou breathest into him the idea of meditated vengeance, sure misdeeds; thou incitest him to murder; thou givest him the abundant joy of accomplished reprisals and permittest him to taste the intoxicating draught of the tears of which he is the cause.

"Hope of Virility, Anguish of the Empty Womb, thou dost not demand the bootless offering of chaste loins, thou dost not sing the praises of Lenten follies; thou alone receivest the carnal supplications and petitions of poor and avaricious families. Thou determinest the mother to sell her daughter, to give her son; thou aidest sterile and reprobate loves; Guardian of strident Neuroses, Leaden Tower of Hysteria, bloody Vase of Rape!

"Master, thy faithful servants, on their knees, implore thee and supplicate thee to satisfy them when they wish the torture of all those who love them and aid them; they supplicate thee to assure them the joy of delectable misdeeds unknown to justice, spells whose unknown origin baffles the reason of man; they ask, finally, glory, riches, power, of thee, King of the Disinherited, Son who art to overthrow the inexorable Father!"

Then Docre rose, and erect, with arms outstretched, vociferated in a ringing voice of hate:

"And thou, thou whom, in my quality of priest, I force, whether thou wilt or no, to descend into this host, to incarnate thyself in this bread, Jesus, Artisan of Hoaxes, Bandit of Homage, Robber of Affection, hear! Since the day when thou didst issue from the complaisant bowels of a Virgin, thou hast failed all thine engagements, belied all thy promises. Centuries have wept, awaiting thee, fugitive

God, mute God! Thou wast to redeem man and thou hast not, thou wast to appear in thy glory, and thou sleepest. Go, lie, say to the wretch who appeals to thee, 'Hope, be patient, suffer; the hospital of souls will receive thee; the angels will assist thee; Heaven opens to thee.' Impostor! thou knowest well that the angels, disgusted at thine inertness, abandon thee! Thou wast to be the Interpreter of our plaints, the Chamberlain of our tears; thou wast to convey them to the Father and thou hast not done so, for this intercession would disturb thine eternal sleep of happy satiety.

"Thou hast forgotten the poverty thou didst preach, enamoured vassal of Banks! Thou hast seen the weak crushed beneath the press of profit; thou hast heard the death rattle of the timid, paralyzed by famine, of women disembowelled for a bit of bread, and thou hast caused the Chancery of thy Simoniacs, thy commercial representatives, thy Popes, to answer by dilatory excuses and evasive promises, sacristy Shyster, huckster God!

"Master, whose inconceivable ferocity engenders life and inflicts it on the innocent whom thou darest damn—in the name of *what* original sin?—whom thou darest punish—by the virtue of *what* covenants?—we would have thee confess thine impudent cheats, thine inexpiable crimes! We would drive deeper the nails into thy hands, press down the crown of thorns upon thy brow, bring blood and water from the dry wounds of thy sides.

"And that we can and will do by violating the quietude of thy body, Profaner of ample vices, Abstractor of stupid purities, cursed Nazarene, do-nothing King, coward God!"

"Amen!" trilled the soprano voices of the choir boys.

Durtal listened in amazement to this torrent of blasphemies and insults. The foulness of the priest stupefied him. A silence succeeded the litany. The chapel was foggy with the smoke of the censers. The women, hitherto taciturn, flustered now, as, remounting the altar, the canon turned toward them and blessed them with his left hand in a sweeping gesture. And suddenly the choir boys tinkled the prayer bells.

It was a signal. The women fell to the carpet and writhed. One of them seemed to be worked by a spring. She threw herself prone and waved her legs in the air. Another, suddenly struck by a hideous strabism, clucked, then becoming tongue-tied stood with her mouth open, the tongue turned back, the tip cleaving to the palate. Another, inflated, livid, her pupils dilated, lolled her head back over her shoulders, then jerked it brusquely erect and belaboured herself, tearing her breast with her nails. Another, sprawling on her back, undid her skirts, drew forth a rag, enormous, meteorized; then her face twisted into a horrible grimace, and her tongue, which she could not control, stuck out, bitten at the edges, harrowed by red teeth, from a bloody mouth.

Suddenly Durtal rose, and now he heard and saw Docre distinctly.

Docre contemplated the Christ surmounting the tabernacle, and with arms spread wide apart he spewed forth frightful insults, and, at the end of his forces, muttered the billingsgate of a drunken cabman. One of the choir boys knelt before him with his back toward the altar. A shudder ran around the priest's spine. In a solemn but jerky voice he said, *"Hoc est enim corpus meum,"* then, instead of kneeling, after the consecration, before the precious Body, he faced the congregation, and appeared tumefied, haggard, dripping with sweat. He staggered between the two choir boys, who, raising the chasuble, displayed his naked belly. Docre made a few passes and the host sailed, tainted and soiled, over the steps.

Durtal felt himself shudder. A whirlwind of hysteria shook the room. While the choir boys sprinkled holy water on the pontiff's nakedness, women rushed upon the Eucharist and, grovelling in front of the altar, clawed from the bread humid particles and drank and ate divine ordure.

Another woman, curled up over a crucifix, emitted a rend-

ing laugh, then cried to Docre, "Father, father!" A crone
tore her hair, leapt, whirled around and around as on a pivot
and fell over beside a young girl who, huddled to the wall,
was writhing in convulsions, frothing at the mouth, weeping,
and spitting out frightful blasphemies. And Durtal, terrified, saw through the fog the red horns of Docre, who,
seated now, frothing with rage, was chewing up sacramental
wafers, taking them out of his mouth, wiping himself with
them, and distributing them to the women, who ground
them underfoot, howling, or fell over each other struggling
to get hold of them and violate them.

The place was simply a madhouse, a monstrous pande-
monium of prostitutes and maniacs. Now, while the choir
boys gave themselves to the men, and while the woman who
owned the chapel, mounted the altar caught hold of the
phallus of the Christ with one hand and with the other held
a chalice between "His" naked legs, a little girl, who hitherto had not budged, suddenly bent over forward and howled,
howled like a dog. Overcome with disgust, nearly asphyxi-
ated, Durtal wanted to flee. He looked for Hyacinthe. She
was no longer at his side. He finally caught sight of her
close to the canon and, stepping over the writhing bodies on
the floor, he went to her. With quivering nostrils she was
inhaling the effluvia of the perfumes and of the couples.

"The sabbatic odour!" she said to him between clenched
teeth, in a strangled voice.

"Here, let's get out of this!"

She seemed to wake, hesitated a moment, then without
answering she followed him. He elbowed his way through
the crowd, jostling women whose protruding teeth were
ready to bite. He pushed Mme. Chantelouve to the door,
crossed the court, traversed the vestibule, and, finding the
portress' lodge empty, he drew the cord and found himself
in the street.

There he stopped and drew the fresh air deep into his
lungs. Hyacinthe, motionless, dizzy, huddled to the wall
away from him.

He looked at her. "Confess that you would like to go in there again."

"No." she said with an effort. "These scenes shatter me. I am in a daze. I must have a glass of water."

And she went up the street, leaning on him, straight to the wine shop, which was open. It was an ignoble lair, a little room with tables and wooden benches, a zinc counter, cheap bar fixtures, and blue-stained wooden pitchers; in the ceiling a U-shaped gas bracket. Two pick-and shovel labourers were playing cards. They turned around and laughed. The proprietor took the excessively short-stemmed pipe from his mouth and spat into the sawdust. He seemed not at all surprised to see this fashionably gowned woman in his dive. Durtal, who was watching him, thought he surprised an understanding look exchanged by the proprietor and the woman.

The proprietor lighted a candle and mumbled into Durtal's ear, "Monsieur, you can't drink here with these people watching. I'll take you to a room where you can be alone."

"Hmmm," said Durtal to Hyacinthe, who was penetrating the mysteries of a spiral staircase, "A lot of fuss for a glass of water!"

But she had already entered a musty room. The paper was peeling from the walls, which were nearly covered with pictures torn out of illustrated weeklies and tacked up with hairpins. The floor was all in pieces. There were a wooden bed without any curtains, a chamber pot with a piece broken out of the side, a wash bowl and two chairs.

The man brought a decanter of gin, a large one of water, some sugar, and glasses, then went downstairs.

Her eyes were sombre, mad. She enlaced Durtal.

"No!" he shouted, furious at having fallen into this trap. "I've had enough of that. It's late. Your husband is waiting for you. It's time for you to go back to him——"

She did not even hear him.

"I want you," she said, and she took him treacherously and obliged him to desire her. She disrobed, threw her skirts on the floor, opened wide the abominable couch, and raising her chemise in the back she rubbed her spine up and down over the coarse grain of the sheets. A look of swooning ecstasy was in her eyes and a smile of joy on her lips.

She seized him, and, with ghoulish fury, dragged him into obscenities of whose existence he had never dreamed. Suddenly, when he was able to escape, he shuddered, for he prceived that the bed was strewn with fragments of hosts.

"Oh, you fill me with horror! Dress, and let's get out of here."

While, with a faraway look in her eyes, she was silently putting on her clothes, he sat down on a chair. The fetidness of the room nauseated him. Then, too—he was not absolutely convinced of Transubstantiation—he did not believe very firmly that the Saviour resided in that soiled bread—but—In spite of himself, the sacrilege he had involuntarily participated in saddened him.

"Suppose it were true," he said to himself, "that the Presence were real, as Hyacinthe and that miserable priest attest— No, decidedly, I have had enough. I am through. The occasion is timely for me to break with this creature whom from our very first interview I have only tolerated, and I'm going to seize the opportunity."

Below, in the dive, he had to face the knowing smiles of the labourers. He paid, and without waiting for his change, he fled. They reached the rue de Vaugirard and he hailed a cab.

As they were whirled along they sat lost in their thoughts, not looking at each other.

"Soon?" asked Mme. Chantelouve, in an almost timid tone when he left her at her door.

"No," he answered. "We have nothing in common. You wish everything and I wish nothing. Better break. We might drag out our relation, but it would finally terminate in recrimination and bitterness. Oh, and then—after what happened this evening, no! Understand me? No!"

And he gave the cabman his address and huddled himself into the furthest corner of the fiacre.

CHAPTER XX

"He doesn't lead a humdrum life, that canon!" said Des Hermies, when Durtal had related to him the details of the Black Mass. "It's a veritable seraglio of hystero-epileptics and erotomaniacs that he has formed for himself. But his vices lack warmth. Certainly, in the matter of contumelious blasphemies, of sacrilegious atrocities, and sensual excitation, this priest may seem to have exceeded the limits, to be almost unique. But the bloody and investuous side of the old sabbats is wanting. Docre is, we must admit, greatly inferior to Gilles de Rais. His works are incomplete, insipid; weak, if I may say so."

"I like that. You know it isn't easy to procure children whom one may disembowel with impunity. The parents would raise a row and the police would interfere."

"Yes, and it is to difficulties of this sort that we must evidently attribute the bloodless celebration of the Black Mass. But I am thinking just now of the women you described, the ones that put their heads over the chafing-dishes to drink in the smoke of the burning resin. They employ the procedure of the Aissaouas, who hold their heads over the braseros whenever the catalepsy necessary to their orgies is slow in coming. As for the other phenomena you cite, they are known in the hospitals, and except as symptoms of the demoniac effluence they teach us nothing new. Now another thing. Not a word of this to Carhaix, because he would be quite capable of closing his door in your face if he knew you had been present at an office in honour of Satan."

They went downstairs from Durtal's apartment and walked along toward the tower of Saint Sulpice.

"I didn't bring anything to eat, because you said you would look after that," said Durtal, "but this morning I sent Mme. Carhaix—in lieu of desserts and wine—some real Dutch gingerbread, and a couple of rather surprising liqueurs, an elixir of life which we shall take, by way of appetizer, before the repast, and a flask of crême de céléri. I have discovered an honest distiller."

"Impossible!"

"You shall see. This elixir of life is manufactured from Socotra aloes, little cardamom, saffron, myrrh, and a heap of other aromatics. It's inhumanly bitter, but it's exquisite."

"I am anxious to taste it. The least we can do is fête Gévingey a little on his deliverance."

"Have you seen him?"

"Yes. He's looking fine. We'll make him tell us about his cure."

"I keep wondering what he lives on."

"On what his astrological skill brings him."

"Then there are rich people who have their horoscopes cast?"

"We must hope so. To tell you the truth, I think Gévingey is not in very easy circumstances. Under the Empire he was astrologer to the Empress, who was very superstitious and had faith—as did Napoleon, for that matter—in predictions and fortune telling, but since the fall of the Empire I think Gévingey's situation has changed a good deal for the worse. Nevertheless he passes for being the only man in France who has preserved the secrets of Cornelius Agrippa, Cremona, Ruggieri, Gauric, Sinibald the Swordsman, and Tritemius."

While discoursing they had climbed the stair and arrived at the bell-ringer's door.

The astrologer was already there and the table was set.

All grimaced a bit as they tasted the black and active liqueur which Durtal poured.

Joyous to have all her family about her, Mama Carhaix brought the rich soup. She filled the plates.

When a dish of vegetables was passed and Durtal chose a leek, Des Hermies said, laughing, "Look out! Porta, a thaumaturge of the late sixteenth century, informs us that this plant, long considered an emblem of virility, perturbs the quietude of the most chaste."

"Don't listen to him," said the bell-ringer's wife. "And you, Monsieur Gévingey, some carrots?"

Durtal looked at the astrologer. His head still looked like a sugar-loaf, his hair was the same faded, dirty brown of hydroquinine or ipecac powders, his bird eyes had the same startled look, his enormous hands were covered with the same phalanx of rings, he had the same obsequious and imposing manner, and sacerdotal tone, but he was freshened up considerably, the wrinkles had gone out of his skin, and his eyes were brighter, since his visit to Lyons.

Durtal congratulated him on the happy result of the treatment.

"It was high time, monsieur, I was putting myself under the care of Dr. Johannès, for I was nearly gone. Not possessing a shred of the gift of voyance and knowing no extralucid cataleptic who could inform me of the clandestine preparations of Canon Docre, I could not possibly defend myself by using the laws of countersign and of the shock in return."

"But," said Des Hermies, "admitting that you could, through the intermediation of a flying spirit, have been aware of the operations of the priest, how could you have parried them?"

"The law of countersigns consists, when you know in advance the day and hour of the attack, in going away from home, thus throwing the spell off the track and neutralizing it, or in saying an hour beforehand, 'Here I am. Strike!'

The last method is calculated to scatter the fluids to the wind and paralyze the powers of the assailant. In magic, any act known and made public is lost. As for the shock in return, one must also know beforehand of the attempt if one is to cast back the spells on the person sending them before one is struck by them.

"I was certain to perish. A day had passed since I was bewitched. Two days more and I should have been ready for the cemetery."

"How's that?"

"Every individual struck by magic has three days in which to take measures. That time past, the ill is incurable. So when Docre announced to me that he condemned me to death by his own authority and when, two hours later, on returning home, I felt desperately ill, I lost no time packing my grip and starting for Lyons."

"And there?" asked Durtal.

"There I saw Dr. Johannès. I told him of Docre's threat and of my illness. He said to me simply. 'That priest can dress the most virulent poisons in the most frightful sacrileges. The fight will be bitter, but I shall conquer,' and he immediately called in a woman who lives in his house, a voyant.

"He hypnotized her and she, at his injunction, explained the nature of the sorcery of which I was the victim. She reconstructed the scene. She literally saw me being poisoned by food and drink mixed with menstrual fluid that had been reinforced with macerated sacramental wafers and drugs skilfully dosed. That sort of spell is so terrible that aside from Dr. Johannès no thaumaturge in France dare try to cure it.

"So the doctor finally said to me, 'Your cure can be obtained only through an invincible power. We must lose no time. We must at once scarifice to the glory of Melchisedek.'

"He raised an altar, composed of a table and a wooden tabernacle. It was shaped like a little house surmounted by a cross and encircled, under the pediment, by the dial-like figure of the tetragram. He brought the silver chalice, the unleavened bread and the wine. He donned his sacerdotal habits, put on his finger the ring which has received the supreme benedictions, then he began to read from a special missal the prayers of the sacrifice.

"Almost at once the voyant cried, 'Here are the spirits evoked for the spell. These are they which have carried the venefice, obedient to the command of the master of black magic, Canon Docre!'

"I was sitting beside the altar. Dr. Johannès placed his left hand on my head and raising toward heaven his right he besought the Archangel Michael to assist him, and adjured the glorious legions of the invincible seraphim to dominate, to enchain, the spirits of Evil.

"I was already feeling greatly relieved. The sensation of internal gnawing which tortured me in Paris was diminishing. Dr. Johannès continued to recite his orisons, then when the moment came for the deprecatory prayer, he took my hand, laid it on the altar, and three times chanted:

"'May the projects and the designs of the worker of iniquity, who has made enchantment against you, be brought to naught; may any influence obtained by Satanic means, any attack directed against you, be null and void of effect; may all the maledictions of your enemy be transformed into benedictions from the highest summits of the eternal hills; may his fluids of death be transmuted into ferments of life; finally, may the Archangels of Judgment and Chastisement decide the fate of the miserable priest who has put his trust in the works of Darkness and Evil.'

"'You,' he said to me, 'are delivered. Heaven has cured you. May your heart therefore repay the living God and Jesus Christ, through the glorious Mary, with the most ardent devotion.'

"He offered me unleavened bread and wine. I was saved. You who are a physician, Monsieur Des Hermies, can bear witness that human science was impotent to aid me—and now look at me!"

"Yes," Des Hermies replied, "without discussing the means, I certify the cure, and, I admit, it is not the first time that to my knowledge similar results have been obtained.—No thanks," to Mme. Carhaix, who was inviting him to take another helping from a plate of sausages with horseradish in creamed peas. "But," said Durtal, "permit me to ask you several questions. Certain details interest me. What were the sacerdotal ornaments of Dr. Johannès?"

"His costume was a long robe of vermilion cashmere caught up at the waist by a red and white sash. Above this robe he had a white mantle of the same stuff, cut, over the chest, in the form of a cross upside down."

"Cross upside down?"

"Yes, this cross, reversed like the figure of the Hanged Man in the old-fashioned Tarot card deck, signifies that the priest Melchisedek must die in the Old Man—that is, man affected by original sin—and live again the Christ, to be powerful with the power of the Incarnate Word which died for us."

Carhaix seemed ill at ease. His fanatical and suspicious Catholicism refused to countenance any save the prescribed ceremonies. He made no further contribution to the conversation, and in significant silence filled the glasses, seasoned the salad, and passed the plates.

"What sort of a ring was that you spoke of?"

"It is a symbolic ring of pure gold. It has the image of a serpent, whose head, in relief, set with a ruby, is connected by a fine chain with a tiny circlet which fastens the jaws of the reptile."

"What I should like awfully to know is the origin and the aim of this sacrifice. What has Melchisedek to do with your affair?"

"Ah," said the astrologer, "Melchisedek is one of the most mysterious of all the figures in the Holy Bible. He was king of Salem, sacrificer to the Most High God. He blessed Abraham and Abraham gave him tithes of the spoil of the vanquished kings of Sodom and Gomorrah. That is the story in Genesis 14:18-20. But Saint Paul cites him also, in Hebrews 7, and in the third verse of that chapter says that Melchisedek, 'without father, without mother, without descent, having neither beginning of day, nor end of life, but made like unto the Son of God, abideth, a priest continually.' In Hebrews 5:6 Paul, quoting Psalm 110:4, says Jesus is called 'a priest forever after the order of Melchisedek.'

"All this, you see, is obscure enough. Some exegetes recognize in him the prophetic figure of the Saviour, others, that of Saint Joseph, and all admit that the sacrifice of Melchisedek offering to Abraham the blood and wine of which he had first made oblation to the Lord prefigures, to follow the expression of Isidore of Damietta, the archetype of the divine mysteries, otherwise known as the holy mass."

"Very well," said Des Hermies, "but all that Scripture does not explain the alexipharmacal virtues which Dr. Johannès attributes to the sacrifice."

"You are asking more than I can answer. Only Dr. Johannès could tell you. This much I can say. Theology teaches us that the mass, as it is celebrated, is the re-enaction of the Sacrifice of Calvary, but the sacrifice to the glory of Melchisedek is not that. It is, in some sort, the future mass, the glorious office which will be known during the earthly reign of the divine Paraclete. This sacrifice is offered to God by man regenerated, redeemed by the infusion of the Love of the Holy Ghost. Now, the hominal being whose heart has thus been purified and sanctified is invincible, and the enchantments of hell cannot prevail against him if he makes use of this sacrifice to dissipate the Spirits of Evil. That explains to you the potency of Dr. Johannès, whose heart unites, in this ceremony, with the divine heart of Jesus."

"Your exposition is not very clear," Carhaix mildly objected.

"Then it must be supposed that Johannès is a man amended ahead of time, an apostle animated by the Holy Ghost?"

"And so he is," said the astrologer, firmly assured.

"Will you please pass the gingerbread?" Carhaix requested.

"Here's the way to fix it," said Durtal. "First cut a slice very thin, then take a slice of ordinary bread, equally thin, butter them and put them together. Now tell me if this sandwich hasn't the exquisite taste of fresh walnuts."

"Well," said Des Hermies, pursuing his cross-examination, "aside from that, what has Dr. Johannès been doing in this long time since I last saw him?"

"He leads what ought to be a peaceful life. He lives with friends who revere and adore him. With them he rests from the tribulations of all sorts—save one—that he has been subjected to. He would be perfectly happy if he did not have to repulse the attacks launched at him almost daily by the tonsured magicians of Rome."

"Why do they attack him?"

"A thorough explanation would take a long time. Johannès is commissioned by Heaven to break up the venomous practises of Satanism and to preach the coming of the glorified Christ and the divine Paraclete. Now the diabolical Curia which holds the Vatican in its clutches has every reason of self-interest for putting out of the way a man whose prayers fetter their conjurements and neutralize their spells."

"Ah!" exclaimed Durtal, "and would it be too much to ask you how this former priest foresees and checks these astonishing assaults?"

"No indeed. The doctor can tell by the flight and cry of certain birds. Falcons and male sparrow-hawks are his sentinels. If they fly toward him or away from him, to East or West, whether they emit a single cry or many; these are omens, letting him know the hour of the combat so that he can be on guard. Thus he told me one day, the sparrow-hawks are easily influenced by the spirits, and he uses them as the hypnotist makes use of somnambulism, as the spiritist makes use of tables and slates."

"They are the telegraph wires for magic despatches."

"Yes. And of course you know that the method is not new. Indeed, its origin is lost in the darkness of the ages. Ornithomancy is world-old. One finds traces of it in the Holy Bible, and the Zohar asserts that one may receive numerous notifications if one knows how to observe the flight and distinguish the cries of birds."

"But," said Durtal, "why is the sparrow-hawk chosen in preference to other birds?"

"Well, it has always been, since remotest antiquity, the harbinger of charms. In Egypt the god with the head of a hawk was the one who possessed the science of the hieroglyphics. Formerly in that country the hierogrammatists swallowed the heart and blood of the hawk to prepare themselves for the magic rites. Even today African chiefs put a hawk feather in their hair, and this bird is sacred in India."

"How does your friend go about it," asked Mme. Carhaix, "raising and housing birds of prey?—because that is what they are."

"He does not raise them nor house them. They nest in the high bluffs along the Saône, near Lyons. They come and see him in time of need."

Durtal, looking around this cozy dining-room and recalling the extraordinary conversations which had been held here, was thinking, "How far we are from the language and the ideas of modern times.—All that takes us back to the Middle Ages," he said, finishing his thought aloud.

"Happily!" exclaimed Carhaix, who was rising to go and ring his bells.

"Yes," said Des Hermies, "and what is mighty strange in this day of crass materialism is the idea of battles fought in space, over the cities, between a priest of Lyons and prelates of Rome."

"And between this priest and the Rosicrusians and Canon Docre."

Durtal remembered that Mme. Chantelouve had assured him that the chiefs of the Rosicrucians were making frantic efforts to establish connections with the devil and prepare spells.

"You think that the Rosicrucians are satanizing?"

"They would like to, but they don't know how. They are limited to reproducing, mechanically, the few fluidic and veniniferous operations revealed to them by the three brahmins who visited Paris a few years ago."

"I am thankful, myself," said Mme. Carhaix, as she took leave of the company, "that I am not mixed up in any of this frightful business, and that I can pray and live in peace."

Then while Des Hermies, as usual, prepared the coffee and Durtal brought the liqueur glasses, Gévingey filled his pipe, and when the sound of the bells died away—dispersed and as if absorbed by the pores of the wall—he blew out a great cloud of smoke and said, "I passed some delightful days with the family with whom Dr. Johannès is living. After the shocks which I had received, it was a privilege without equal to complete my convalescence in that sweet atmosphere of Christian Love. And, too, Johannès is of all men I have ever met the most learned in the occult sciences. No one, except his antithesis, the abominable Docre, has penetrated so far into the arcana of Satanism. One may even say that in France these two are the only ones who have crossed the terrestrial threshold and obtained, each in his field, sure results. But in addition to the charm of his conversation and the scope of his knowledge—for even on the subject in which I excel, that of astrology, he surprised me—Johannès delighted me with the beauty of his vision of the future transformation of peoples. He is really, I swear, the prophet whose earthly mission of suffering and glory has been authorized by the Most High."

"I don't doubt it," said Durtal, smiling, "but his theory

of the Paraclete is, if I am not mistaken, the very ancient heresy of Montanus which the Church has formally condemned."

"All depends on the manner in which the coming of the Paraclete is conceived," interjected the bell-ringer, returning at that moment. "It is also the orthodox doctrine of Saint Irenæus, Saint Justin, Scotus Erigena, Amaury of Chartres, Saint Doucine, and that admirable mystic, Joachim of Floris. This was the belief throughout the Middle Ages, and I admit that it obsesses me and fills me with joy, that it responds to the most ardent of my yearnings. Indeed," he said, sitting down and crossing his legs, "if the third kingdom is an illusion, what consolation is left for Christians in face of the general disintegration of a world which charity requires us not to hate?"

"I am furthermore obliged to admit," said Des Hermies, "that in spite of the blood shed on Golgotha, I personally feel as if my ransom had not been quite effected."

"There are three kingdoms," the astrologer resumed, pressing down the ashes of his pipe with his finger. "Of the Old Testament, that of the Father, the kingdom of fear. Of the New Testament, that of the Son, the kingdom of expiation. Of the Johannite Gospel, that of the Holy Ghost, the kingdom of redemption and love. They are the past, present and future; winter, spring and summer. The first, says Joachim of Floris, gives us the blade, the second, the leaf, and the third, the ear. Two of the Persons of the Trinity have shown themselves. Logically the Third must appear."

"Yes, and the Biblical texts abound, conclusive, explicit, irrefutable," said Carhaix. "All the prophets, Isaiah, Ezekiel, Daniel, Zachariah, Malachi, speak of it. The Acts of the Apostles is very precise on this point. In the first chapter you will read these lines, 'This same Jesus, which is taken up from you into heaven shall so come in like manner as ye have seen him go into heaven.' Saint John also announces the tidings in the Apocalypse, which is the gospel of the second coming of Christ, 'Christ shall come and reign a thousand years.' Saint Paul is inexhaustible in revelations of this nature. In the epistle to Timothy he invokes the Lord 'who shall judge the quick and the dead at his appearance and his kingdom.' In the second epistle to the Thessalonians he writes, 'And then shall that Wicked be revealed, whom the Lord shall consume with the Spirit of his mouth, and shall destroy with the brightness of his coming.' Now, he declares that the Antichrist is not yet, so the coming which he prophesies is not that already realized by the birth of the Saviour at Bethlehem. In the Gospel according to Saint Matthew, Jesus responds to Caiaphas, who asks Him if He is the Christ, Son of God, 'Thou hast said, and nevertheless I say unto you, Hereafter shall ye see the Son of man sitting on the right hand of power and coming in the clouds of heaven.' And in another verse He says to His apostles, 'Watch, therefore, for ye know not what hour your Lord doth come.'

"And there are other texts I could put my finger on. No, there is no use in talking, the partisans of the glorious kingdom are supported with certitude by inspired passages, and can, under certain conditions and without fear of heresy, uphold this doctrine, which, Saint Jerome attests, was in the fourth century a dogma of faith recognized by all. But what say we taste a bit of this crême de céléri which Monsieur Durtal praises so highly?"

It was a thick liqueur, sirupy like anisette, but even sweeter and more feminine, only, when one had swallowed this inert semi-liquid, there lingered in the roots of the papillæ a faint taste of celery.

"It isn't bad," said the astrologer, "but there's no life to it," and he poured into his glass a stiff tot of rum.

"Come to think of it," said Durtal, "the third kingdom is also announced in the words of the Paternoster, 'Thy kingdom come.'"

"Certainly," said the bell-ringer.

"But you see," interjected Gévingey, "heresy would gain the upper hand and the whole belief would be turned into nonsense and absurdity if we admitted, as certain Paracletists do, an authentic fleshly incarnation. For instance, remember Fareinism, which has been rife, since the eighteenth century, in Fareins, a village of the Doubs, where Jansenism took refuge when driven out of Paris after the closing of the cemetery of Saint Médard. There a priest, François Bonjour, reproduced the 'convulsionist' orgies which, under the Regency, desecrated the tomb of Deacon Pâris. Then Bonjour had an affair with a woman and she claimed to be big with the prophet Elijah, who, according to the Apocalypse, is to precede the last arrival of Christ. This child came into the world, then there was a second who was none other than the Paraclete. The latter did business as a woolen merchant in Paris, was a colonel in the National Guard under Louis-Philippe, and died in easy circumstances in 1866. A tradesman Paraclete, a Redeemer with epaulettes and gold braid!

"In 1886 one Dame Brochard of Vouvray affirmed to whoever would listen that Jesus was reincarnate in her. In 1889 a pious madman named David published at Angers a brochure entitled *The Voice of God,* in which he assumed the modest appellation of 'only Messiah of the Creator Holy Ghost,' and informed the world that he was a sewer contractor and wore a beard a yard and a half long. At the present moment his throne is not empty for want of successors. An engineer named Pierre Jean rode all over the Mediterranean provinces on horseback announcing that he was the Holy Ghost. In Paris, Bérard, an omnibus conductor on the Panthéon-Courcelles line, likewise asserts that he incorporates the Paraclete, while a magazine article avers that the hope of Redemption has dawned in the person of the poet Jhouney. Finally, in America, from time to time, women claim to be Messiahs, and they recruit adherents among persons worked up to fever pitch by Advent revivals."

"They are no worse than the people who deny God and

Creation," said Carhaix. "God is immanent in His creatures. He is their Life principle, the source of movement, the foundation of existence, says Saint Paul. He has His personal existence, being the 'I AM,' as Moses says.

"The Holy Ghost, through Christ in glory, will be immanent in all beings. He will be the principle which transforms and regenerates them, but there is no need for him to be incarnate. The Holy Ghost proceeds from the Father through the Son. He is sent to act, not to materialize himself. It is downright madness to maintain the contrary, thus falling into the heresies of the Gnostics and the Fratricelli, into the errors of Dulcin de Novare and his wife Marguerite, into the filth of abbé Beccarelli, and the abominations of Segarelli of Parma, who, on pretext of becoming a child the better to symbolize the simple, naïf love of the Paraclete, had himself diapered and slept on the breast of a nurse."

"But," said Durtal, "you haven't made yourself quite clear to me. If I understand you, the Holy Ghost will act by an infusion into us. He will transmute us, renovate our souls by a sort of 'passive purgation'—to drop into the theological vernacular."

"Yes, he will purify us soul and body."

"How will he purify our bodies?"

"The action of the Paraclete," the astrologer struck in, "will extend to the principle of generation. The divine life will sanctify the organs which henceforth can procreate only elect creatures, exempt from original sin, creatures whom it will not be necessary to test in the fires of humiliation, as the Holy Bible says. This was the doctrine of the prophet Vintras, that extraordinary unlettered man who wrote such impressive and ardent pages. The doctrine has been continued and amplified, since Vintras's death, by his successor, Dr. Johannès."

"Then there is to be Paradise on earth," said Des Hermies.

"Yes, the kingdom of liberty, goodness, and love."

"You've got me all mixed up," said Durtal. "Now you

announce the arrival of the Holy Ghost, now the glorious advent of Christ. Are these kingdoms identical or is one to follow the other?"

"There is a distinction," answered Gévingey, "between the coming of the Paraclete and the victorious return of Christ. They occur in the order named. First a society must be recreated, embraced by the third Hypostasis, by Love, in order that Jesus may descend, as He has promised, from the clouds and reign over the people formed in His image."

"What rôle is the Pope to play?"

"Ah, that is one of the most curious points of the Johannite doctrine. Time, since the first appearance of the Messiah, is divided, as you know, into two periods, the period of the Victim, of the expiant Saviour, the period in which we now are, and the other, that which we await, the period of Christ bathed in the spittle of mockery but radiant with the superadorable splendour of His person. Well, there is a different pope for each of these eras. The Scriptures announce these two sovereign pontificates—and so do my horoscopes, for that matter.

"It is an axiom of theology that the spirit of Peter lives in his successors. It will live in them, more or less hidden, until the longed-for expansion of the Holy Ghost. Then John, who has been held in reserve, as the Gospel says, will begin his ministry of love and will live in the souls of the new popes."

"I don't understand the utility of a pope when Jesus is to be visible," said Des Hermies.

"To tell the truth, there is no use in having one, and the papacy is to exist only during the epoch reserved for the effluence of the divine Paraclete. The day on which, in a shower of meteors, Jesus appears, the pontificate of Rome ceases."

"Without going more deeply into questions which we could discuss the rest of our lives," said Durtal, "I marvel at the placidity of the utopian who imagines that man is perfectible. There is no denying that the human creature is born selfish, abusive, vile. Just look around you and see. Society cynical and ferocious, the humble heckled and pillaged by the rich traffickers in necessities. Everywhere the triumph of the mediocre and unscrupulous, everywhere the apotheosis of crooked politics and finance. And you think you can make any progress against a stream like that? No, man has never changed. His soul was corrupt in the days of Genesis and is not less rotten at present. Only the form of his sins varies. Progress is the hypocrisy which refines the vices."

"All the more reaon," Carhaix rejoined, "why society— if it is as you have described it—should fall to pieces. I, too, think it is putrefied, its bones ulcerated, its flesh dropping off. It can neither be poulticed nor cured, it must be interred and a new one born. And who but God can accomplish such a miracle?"

"If we admit," said Des Hermies, "that the infamousness of the times is transitory, it is self-evident that only the intervention of a God can wash it away; for neither socialism nor any other chimera of the ignorant and hate-filled workers will modify human nature and reform the peoples. These tasks are above human forces."

"And the time awaited by Johannès is at hand," Gévingey proclaimed. "Here are some of the manifest proofs. Raymond Lully asserted that the end of the old world would be announced by the diffusion of the doctrines of Antichrist. He defined these doctrines. They are materialism and the monstrous revival of magic. This prediction applies to our age, I think. On the other hand, the good tidings was to be realized, according to Our Lord, as reported by Saint Matthew, 'When ye shall see the abomination of desolation . . . stand in the holy place.' And isn't it standing in the holy place now? Look at our timorous, skeptical Pope, lukewarm and politic, our episcopate of simonists and cowards, our flabby, indulgent clergy. See how they are ravaged by Satanism, then tell me if the Church can fall any lower."

"The promises are explicit and cannot fail," and with his elbows on the table, his chin in his hands, and his eyes to heaven, the bell-ringer murmured, "Our father—thy kingdom come!"

"It's getting late," said Des Hermies, "time we were going."

While they were putting on their coats, Carhaix questioned Durtal. "What do you hope for if you have no faith in the coming of Christ?"

"I hope for nothing at all."

"I pity you. Really, you believe in no future amelioration?"

"I believe, alas, that a dotard Heaven maunders over an exhausted Earth."

The bell-ringer raised his hands and sadly shook his head.

When they had left Gévingey, Des Hermies, after walking in silence for some time, said, "You are not astonished that all the events spoken of tonight happened at Lyons." And as Durtal looked at him inquiringly, he continued, "You see I am well acquainted with Lyons. People's brains there are as foggy as the streets when the morning mists roll up from the Rhone. That city looks magnificent to travellers who like the long avenues, wide boulevards, green grass, and penitentiary architecture of modern cities. But Lyons is also the refuge of mysticism, the haven of preternatural ideas and doubtful creeds. That's where Vintras died, the one in whom, it seems, the soul of the prophet Elijah was incarnate. That's where Naundorff found his last partisans. That is where enchantment is rampant, because in the suburb of La Guillotière you can have a person bewitched for a louis. Add that it is likewise, in spite of its swarms of radicals and anarchists, an opulent market for a dour Protestant Catholicism; a Jansenist factory, richly productive of bourgeois bigotry.

"Lyons is celebrated for delicatessen, silk, and churches. At the top of every hill—and there's a hill every block—is a chapel or a convent, and Notre Dame de Fourvière dominates them all. From a distance this pile looks like an eighteenth century dresser turned upside down, but the interior, which is in process of completion, is amazing. You ought to go and take a look at it some day. You will see the most extraordinary jumble of Assyrian, Roman, Gothic, and God knows what, jacked together by Bossan, the only architect for a century who has known how to create a cathedral interior. The nave glitters with inlays and marble, with bronze and gold. Statues of angels diversify the rows of columns and break up, with impressive grace, the known harmonies of line. It's Asiatic and barbarous, and reminds one of the architecture shown in Gustave Moreau's Hérodiade.

"And there is an endless stream of pilgrims. They strike bargains with Our Lady. They pray for an extension of markets, new outlets for sausages and silks. They consult her on ways and means of getting rid of spoiled vegetables and pushing off their shoddy. In the centre of the city, in the church of Saint Boniface, I found a placard requesting the faithful, out of respect for the holy place, not to give alms. It was not seemly, you see, that the commercial orisons be disturbed by the ridiculous plaints of the indigent."

"Well," said Durtal, "it's a strange thing, but democracy is the most implacable of the enemies of the poor. The Revolution, which, you would think, ought to have protected them, proved for them the most cruel of régimes. I will show you some day a decree of the Year II, pronouncing penalties not only for those who begged but for those who gave."

"And yet democracy is the panacea which is going to cure every ill," said Des Hermies, laughing. And he pointed to enormous posters everywhere in which General Boulanger peremptorily demanded that the people of Paris vote for him in the coming election.

Durtal shrugged his shoulders. "Quite true. The people are very sick. Carhaix and Gévingey are perhaps right in maintaining that no human agency is powerful enough to effect a cure."

CHAPTER XXI

Durtal had resolved not to answer Mme. Chantelouve's letters. Every day, since their rupture, she had sent him an inflamed missive, but, as he soon noticed, her Mænad cries were subsiding into plaints and reproaches. She now accused him of ingratitude, and repented having listened to him and having permitted him to participate in sacrileges for which she would have to answer before the heavenly tribunal. She pleaded to see him once more. Then she was silent for a while week. Finally, tired, no doubt, of writing unanswered letters, she admitted, in a last epistle, that all was over.

After agreeing with him that their temperaments were incompatible, she ended:

"Thanks for the trig little love, ruled like music-paper, that you gave me. My heart cannot be so straitly measured, it requires more latitude——"

"Her heart!" he laughed, then he continued to read:

"I understand that it is not your earthly mission to satisfy my heart but you might at least have conceded me a frank comradeship which would have permitted me to leave my sex at home and to come and spend an evening with you now and then. This, seemingly, so simple, you have rendered impossible. Farewell forever. I have only to renew my pact with Solitude, to which I have tried to be unfaithful——"

"With solitude! and that complaisant and paternal cuck-old, her husband! Well, he is the one most to be pitied now. Thanks to me, he had evenings of quiet. I restored his wife,

270

pliant and satisfied. He profited by my fatigues, that sacristan. Ah, when I think of it, his sly, hypocritical eyes, when he looked at me, told me a great deal.

"Well, the little romance is over. It's a good thing to have your heart on strike. In my brain I still have a house of ill fame, which sometimes catches fire, but the hired myrmidons will stamp out the blaze in a hurry.

"When I was young and ardent the women laughed at me. Now that I am old and stale I laugh at them. That's more in my character, old fellow," he said to the cat, which, with ears pricked up, was listening to the soliloquy. "Truly, Gilles de Rais is a great deal more interesting than Mme. Chantelouve. Unfortunately, my relations with him are also drawing to a close. Only a few more pages and the book is done. Oh, Lord! Here comes Rateau to knock my house to pieces."

Sure enough, the concierge entered, made an excuse for being late, took off his vest, and cast a look of defiance at the furniture. Then he hurled himself at the bed, grappled with the mattress, got a half-Nelson on it, and balancing himself, turning half around, hurled it onto the springs.

Durtal, followed by his cat, went into the other room, but suddenly Rateau ceased wrestling and came and stood before Durtal.

"Monsieur, do you know what has happened?" he blubbered.

"Why, no."

"My wife has left me."

"Left you! but she must be over sixty."

Rateau raised his eyes to heaven.

"And she ran off with another man?"

Rateau, disconsolate, let the feather duster fall from his listless hand.

"The devil! Then, in spite of her age, your wife had needs which you were unable to satisfy?"

The concierge shook his head and finally succeeded in saying, "It was the other way around."

"Oh," said Durtal, considering the old caricature, shrivelled by bad air and "three-six," "but if she is tired of that sort of thing, why did she run off with a man?"

Rateau made a grimace of pitying contempt, "Oh, he's impotent. Good for nothing——"

"Ah!"

"It's my job I'm sore about. The landlord won't keep a concierge that hasn't a wife."

"Dear Lord," thought Durtal, "how hast thou answered my prayers!—Come on, let's go over to your place," he said to Des Hermies, who, finding Rateau's key in the door, had walked in.

"Righto! since your housecleaning isn't done yet, descend like a god from your clouds of dust, and come on over to the house."

On the way Durtal recounted his concierge's conjugal misadventure.

"Oh!" said Des Hermies, "many a woman would be happy to wreathe with laurel the occiput of so combustible a sexagenarian.—Look at that! Isn't it revolting?" pointing to the walls covered with posters.

It was a veritable debauch of placards. Everywhere on lurid coloured paper in box car letters were the names of Boulanger and Jacques.

"Thank God, this will be over tomorrow."

"There is one resource left," said Des Hermies. "To escape the horrors of present day life never raise your eyes. Look down at the sidewalk always, preserving the attitude of timid modesty. When you look only at the pavement you see the reflections of the sky signs in all sorts of fantastic shapes; alchemic symbols, talismanic characters, bizarre pantacles with suns, hammers, and anchors, and you can imagine yourself right in the midst of the Middle Ages."

"Yes, but to keep from seeing the disenchanting crowd you would have to wear a long-vizored cap like a jockey and blinkers like a horse."

Des Hermies sighed. "Come in," he said, opening the

door. They went in and sitting down in easy chairs they lighted their cigarettes.

"I haven't got over that conversation we had with Gévingey the other night at Carhaix's," said Durtal. "Strange man, that Dr. Johannès. I can't keep from thinking about him. Look here, do you sincerely believe in his miraculous cures?"

"I am obliged to. I didn't tell you all about him, for a physician can't lightly make these dangerous admissions. But you may as well know that this priest heals hopeless cases.

"I got acquainted with him when he was still a member of the Parisian clergy. It came about by one of those miracles of his which I don't pretend to understand.

"My mother's maid had a granddaughter who was paralyzed in her arms and legs and suffered death and destruction in her chest and howled when you touched her there. She had been in this condition two years. It had come on in one night, how produced nobody knows. She was sent away from the Lyons hospitals as incurable. She came to Paris, underwent treatment at La Salpetrière, and was discharged when nobody could find out what was the matter with her nor what medication would give her any relief. One day she spoke to me of this abbé Johannès, who, she said, had cured persons in as bad shape as she. I did not believe a word, but hearing that the priest refused to take any money for his services I did not dissuade her from visiting him, and out of curiosity I went along.

"They placed her in a chair. The ecclesiastic, little, active, energetic, took her hand and applied to it, one after the other, three precious stones. Then he said coolly, 'Mademoiselle, you are the victim of consanguineal sorcery.'

"I could hardly keep from laughing.

"'Remember,' he said, 'two years back, for that is when your paralytic stroke came on. You must have had a quarrel with a kinsman or kinswoman?'

"It was true. Poor Marie had been unjustly accused of

the theft of a watch which was an heirloom belonging to an aunt of hers. The aunt had sworn vengeance.

" 'Your aunt lives in Lyons?'

"She nodded.

" 'Nothing astonishing about that,' continued the priest. 'In Lyons, among the lower orders, there are witch doctors who know a little about the witchcraft practised in the country. But be reassured. These people are not powerful. They know little more than the A B C's of the art. Then, mademoiselle, you wish to be cured?'

"And after she replied that she did, he said gently, 'That is all. You may go.'

He did not touch her, did not prescribe any remedy. I came away persuaded that he was a mountebank. But when, three days later, the girl was able to raise her arms, and all her pain had left her, and when, at the end of a week, she could walk, I had to yield in face of the evidence. I went back to see him, had occasion to do him a service; and thus our relations began."

"But what are his methods?"

"He opens, like the curate of Ars, with prayer. Then he evokes the militant archangels, then he breaks the magic circles and chases—'classes,' as he says—the spirits of Evil. I know very well that this is confounding. Whenever I speak of this man's potency to my confrères they smile with a superior air or serve up to me the specious arguments which they have fabricated to explain the cures wrought by Christ and the Virgin. The method they have imagined consists in striking the patient's imagination, suggesting to him the will to be cured, persuading him that he is well, hypnotizing him in a waking state—so to speak. This done —say they—the twisted legs straighten, the sores disappear, the consumption-torn lungs are patched up, the cancers become benign pimples, and the blind eyes see. This procedure they attribute to miracle workers to explain away the supernatural—why don't they use the method themselves if it is so simple?"

"But haven't they tried?"

"After a fashion. I was present myself at an experiment attempted by Dr. Luys. Ah, it was inspiring! At the charity hospital there was a poor girl paralyzed in both legs. She was put to sleep and commanded to rise. She struggled in vain. Then two interns held her up in a standing posture, but her lifeless legs bent useless under her weight. Need I tell you that she could not walk, and that after they had held her up and pushed her along a few steps, they put her to bed again, having obtained no result whatever."

"But Dr. Johannès does not cure all sufferers, without discrimination?"

"No. He will not meddle with any ailments which are not the result of spells. He says he can do nothing with natural ills, which are the province of the physician. He is a specialist in Satanic affections. He has most to do with the possessed whose neuroses have proved obdurate to hydrotherapeutic treatment."

"What does he do with the precious stones you mentioned?"

"First, before answering your question, I must explain the significance and virtue of these stones. I shall be telling you nothing new when I say that Aristotle, Pliny, all the sages of antiquity, attributed medical and divine virtues to them. According to the pagans, agate and carnelian stimulate, topaz consoles, jasper cures languor, hyacinth drives away insomnia, turquoise prevents falls or lightens the shock, amethyst combats drunkenness.

"Catholic symbolism, in its turn, takes over the precious stones and sees in them emblems of the Christian virtues. Then, sapphire represents the lofty aspirations of the soul, chalcedony charity, sard and onyx candor, beryl allegorizes theological science, hyacinthe humility, while the ruby appeases wrath, and emerald 'lapidifies' incorruptible faith.

"Now in magic," Des Hermies rose and took from a shelf a very small volume bound like a prayer book. He showed Durtal the title: *Natural magic, or: The secrets and miracles of nature, in four volumes, by Giambàttista Porta of Naples.*

Paris. Nicolas Bonfour, rue Neuve Nostre Dame at the sign Saint Nicolas. 1584.

"Natural magic," said Des Hermies, "which was merely the medicine of the time, ascribes a new meaning to gems. Listen to this. After first celebrating an unknown stone, the Alectorius, which renders its possessor invincible if it has been taken out of the stomach of a cock caponized four years before or if it has been ripped out of the ventricle of a hen, Porta informs us that chalcedony wins law suits, that carnelian stops bloody flux 'and is exceeding useful to women who are sick of their flower,' that hyacinth protects against lightning and keeps away pestilence and poison, that topaz quells 'lunatic' passions, that turquoise is of advantage against melancholy, quartan fever, and heart failure. He attests finally that sapphire preserves courage and keeps the members vigorous, while emerald, hung about one's neck, keeps away Saint John's evil and breaks when the wearer is unchaste.

"You see, antique philosophy, mediæval Christianity, and sixteenth century magic do not agree on the specific virtues of every stone. Almost in every case the significations, more or less far-fetched, differ. "Dr. Johannès has revised these beliefs, adopted and rejected great numbers of them, finally he has, on his own authority, admitted new acceptations. According to him, amethyst does cure drunkenness; but moral drunkenness, pride; ruby relieves sex pressure; beryl fortifies the will; sapphire elevates the thoughts and turns them toward God.

"In brief, he believes that every stone corresponds to a species of malady, and also to a class of sins; and he affirms that when we have chemically got possession of the active principle of gems we shall have not only antidotes but preventatives. While waiting for this chimerical dream to be realized and for our medicine to become the mock of lapidary chemists, he uses precious stones to formulate diagnoses of illnesses produced by sorcery."

"How?"

"He claims that when such or such a stone is placed in the hand or on the affected part of the bewitched a fluid escapes from the stone into his hands, and that by examining this fluid he can tell what is the matter. In this connection he told me that a woman whom he did not know came to him one day to consult him about a malady, pronounced incurable, from which she had suffered since childhood. He could not get any precise answers to his questions. He saw no signs of venefice. After trying out his whole array of stones he placed in her hand lapis lazuli, which, he says, corresponds to the sin of incest. He examined the stone.

" 'Your malady,' he said, 'is the consequence of an act of incest.'

" 'Well,' she said, 'I did not come here to confessional,' but she finally admitted that her father had violated her before she attained the age of puberty.

"That, of course, is against reason and contrary to all accepted ideas, but there is no getting around the fact that this priest cures patients whom we physicians have given up for lost."

"Such as the only astrologer Paris now can boast, the astounding Gévingey, who would have been dead without his aid. I wonder how Gévingey came to cast the Empress Eugénie's horoscope."

"Oh, I told you. Under the Empire the Tuileries was a hotbed of magic. Home, the American, was revered as the equal of a god. In addition to spiritualistic séances he evoked demons at court. One evocation had fatal consequences. A certain marquis, whose wife had died, implored Home to let him see her again. Home took him to a room, put him in bed, and left him. What ensued? What dreadful phantom rose from the tomb? Was the story of Ligeia re-enacted? At any rate, the marquis was found dead at the foot of the bed. This story has recently been reported by *Le Figaro* from unimpeachable documents.

"You see it won't do to play with the world spirits of Evil.

I used to know a rich bachelor who had a mania for the occult sciences. He was president of a theosophic society and he even wrote a little book on the esoteric doctrine, in the Isis series. Well, he could not, like the Péladan and Papus tribe, be content with knowing nothing, so he went to Scotland, where Diabolism is rampant. There he got in touch with the man who, if you stake him, will initiate you into the Satanic arcana. My friend made the experiment. Did he see him whom Bulwer Lytton in *Zanoni* calls 'the dweller of the threshold'? I don't know, but certain it is that he fainted from horror and returned to France exhausted, half dead."

"Evidently all is not rosy in that line of work," said Durtal. "But it is only spirits of Evil that can be evoked?"

"Do you suppose that the Angels, who, of earth, obey only the saints, would ever consent to take orders from the first comer?"

"But there must be an intermediate order of angels, who are neither celestial nor infernal, who, for instance, commit the well-known asininities in the spiritist séances."

"A priest told me one day that the neuter larvæ inhabit an invisible, neutral territory, something like a little island, which is beseiged on all sides by the good and evil spirits. The larvæ cannot long hold out and are soon forced into one or the other camp. Now, because it is these larvæ they evoke, the occultists, who cannot, of course, draw down the angels, always get the ones who have joined the party of Evil, so unconsciously and probably involuntarily the spiritist is always diabolizing."

"Yes, and if one admits the disgusting idea that an imbecile medium can bring back the dead, one must, in reason, recognize the stamp of Satan on these practises."

"However viewed, Spiritism is an abomination."

"So you don't believe in theurgy, white magic?"

"It's a joke. Only a Rosicrucian who wants to hide his more repulsive essays at black magic ever hints at such a thing. No one dare confess that he satanizes. The Church, not duped by these hair-splitting distinctions, condemns black and white magic indifferently."

"Well," said Durtal, lighting a cigarette, after a silence, "this is a better topic of conversation than politics or the races, but where does it get us? Half of these doctrines are absurd, the other half so mysterious as to produce only bewilderment. Shall we grant Satanism? Well, gross as it is, it seems a sure thing. And if it is, and one is consistent, one must also grant Catholicism—for Buddhism and the like are not big enough to be substituted for the religion of Christ."

"All right. Believe."

"I can't. There are so many discouraging and revolting dogmas in Christianity——"

"I am uncertain about a good many things, myself," said Des Hermies, "and yet there are moments when I feel that the obstacles are giving way, that I almost believe. Of one thing I *am* sure. The supernatural does exist, Christian or not. To deny it is to deny evidence—and who wants to be a materialist, one of these silly freethinkers?"

"It is mighty tiresome to be vacillating forever. How I envy Carhaix his robust faith!"

"You don't want much!" said Des Hermies. "Faith is the breakwater of the soul, affording the only haven in which dismasted man can glide along in peace."

CHAPTER XXII

"You like that?" asked Mme. Carhaix. "For a change I served the broth yesterday and kept the beef for tonight. So we'll have vermicelli soup, a salad of cold meat with pickled herring and celery, some nice mashed potatoes *au gratin,* and a dessert. And then you shall taste the new cider we just got."

"Oh!" and "Ah!" exclaimed Des Hermies and Durtal, who, while waiting for dinner, were sipping the elixir of life. "Do you know, Mme. Carhaix, your cooking tempts us to the sin of gluttony—If you keep on you will make perfect pigs of us."

"Oh, you are joking. I wonder what is keeping Louis."

"Somebody is coming upstairs," said Durtal, hearing the creaking of shoes in the tower.

"No, it isn't his step," and she went and opened the door. "It's Monsieur Gévingey."

And indeed, clad in his blue cape, with his soft black hat on his head, the astrologer entered, made a bow, like an actor taking a curtain call, rubbed his great knuckles against his massive rings, and asked where the bell-ringer was.

"He is at the carpenter's. The oak beams holding up the big bell are cracked and Louis is afraid they will break down."

"Any news of the election?" and Gévingey took out his pipe and filled it.

"No. In this quarter we shan't know the results until nearly ten o'clock. There's no doubt about the outcome, though, because Paris is strong for this democratic stuff. General Boulanger will win hands down."

"This certainly is the age of universal imbecility."

Carhaix entered and apologized for being so late. While his wife brought in the soup he took off his goloshes and said, in answer to his friends' questions, "Yes; the dampness had rusted the frets and warped the beams. It was time for the carpenter to intervene. He finally promised that he would be here tomorrow and bring his men without fail. Well, I am mighty glad to get back. In the streets everything whirls in front of my eyes. I am dizzy. I don't know what to do. The only places where I am at home are the belfry and this room. Here, wife, let me do that," and he pushed her aside and began to stir the salad.

"How good it smells!" said Durtal, drinking in the incisive tang of the herring. "Do you know what this perfume suggests? A basket funnelled fireplace, twigs of juniper snapping in it, in a ground-floor room opening on to a great harbour. It seems to me there is a sort of salt water halo around these little rings of gold and rusted iron.— Exquisite," he said as he tasted the salad.

"We'll make it again for you, Monsieur Durtal," said Mme. Carhaix, "you are not hard to please."

"Alas!" said her husband, "his palate isn't, but his soul is. When I think of his despairing aphorisms of the other night! However, we are praying God to enlighten him. I'll tell you," he said to his wife, "we will invoke Saint Nolasque and Saint Theodulus, who are always represented with bells. They sort of belong to the family, and they will certainly be glad to intercede for people who revere them and their emblems."

"It would take a stunning miracle to convince Durtal," said Des Hermies.

"Bells have been known to perform them," said the astrologer. "I remember to have read, though I forget where, that angels tolled the knell when Saint Isidro of Madrid was dying."

"And there are many other cases,' said Carhaix. "Of

their own accord the bells chimed when Saint Sigisbert chanted the De Profundis over the corpse of the martyr Placidus, and when the body of Saint Ennemond, Bishop of Lyons, was thrown by his murderers into a boat without oars or sails, the bells rang out, though nobody set them in motion, as the boat passed down the Saône."

"Do you know what I think?" asked Des Hermies, looking at Carhaix. "I think you ought to prepare a compendium of hagiography or a really informative work on heraldry."

"What makes you think that?"

"Well, you are, thank God, remote from this epoch and fond of things which it knows nothing about or execrates, and a work of that kind would take you still further away. My good friend, you are the man forever unintelligible to the coming generations. To ring bells because you love them, to give yourself over to the abandoned study of feudal art or monasticism would make you complete—take you clear out of Paris, out of the world, back into the Middle Ages."

"Alas," said Carhaix, "I am only a poor ignorant man. But the type you speak of does exist. In Switzerland, I believe, a bell-ringer has for years been collecting material for a heraldic memorial. I should think," he continued, laughing, "that his avocation would interfere with his vocation."

"And do you think," said Gévingey bitterly, "that the profession of astrologer is less decried, less neglected?"

"How do you like our cider?" asked the bell-ringer's wife. "Do you find it a bit raw?"

"No, it's tart if you sip it, but sweet if you take a good mouthful," answered Durtal.

"Wife, serve the potatoes. Don't wait for me. I delayed so long getting my business done that it's time for the angelus. Don't bother about me. Go on eating. I shall catch up with you when I get back."

And as her husband lighted his lantern and left the room the woman brought in on a plate what looked to be a cake covered with golden brown caramel icing.

"Mashed potatoes, I thought you said!"

"*Au gratin*. Browned in the oven. Taste it. I put in everything that ought to make it very good."

All exclaimed over it.

Then it became impossible to hear oneself. Tonight the bell boomed out with unusual clarity and power. Durtal tried to analyze the sound which seemed to rock the room. There was a sort of flux and reflux of sound. First, the formidable shock of the clapper against the vase, then a sort of crushing and scattering of the sounds as if ground fine with the pestle, then a rounding of the reverberation; then the recoil of the clapper, adding, in the bronze mortar, other sonorous vibrations which it ground up and cast out and dispersed through the sounding shutters.

Then the bell strokes came further apart. Now there was only the whirring as of a spinning wheel; a few crumbs were slow about falling. And now Carhaix returned.

"It's a two-sided age," said Gévingey, pensive. "People believe nothing, yet gobble everything. Every day a new science is invented. Nobody reads that admirable Paracelsus who rediscovered all that had ever been found and created everything that had not. Say now to your congress of scientists that, according to this great master, life is a drop of the essence of the stars, that each of our organs corresponds to a planet and depends upon it; that we are, in consequence, a foreshortening of the divine sphere. Tell them—and this, experience attests—that every man born under the sign of Saturn is melancholy and pituitous, taciturn and solitary, poor and vain; that that sluggish star predisposes to superstition and fraud, directs epilepsies and varices, hemorrhoids and leprosies; that it is, alas! the great purveyor to hospital and prison—and the scientists will shrug their shoulders and laugh at you. The glorified pedants and homiletic asses!"

"Paracelsus," said Des Hermies, "was one of the most extraordinary practitioners of occult medicine. He knew the now forgotten mysteries of the blood, the still unknown medical effects of light. Professing—as did also the cabalists, for that matter—that the human being is composed of three parts, a material body, a soul, and a perispirit called also an astral body, he attended this last especially and produced reactions on the carnal envelope by procedures which are either incomprehensible or fallen into disuse. He cared for wounds by treating not the tissues, but the blood which came out of them. However, we are assured that he healed certain ailments."

"Thanks to his profound knowledge of astrology," said Gévingey.

"But if the study of the sidereal influence is so important," said Durtal, "why don't you take pupils?"

"I can't get them. Where will you unearth people willing to study twenty years without glory or profit? Because, to be able to establish a horoscope one must be an astronomer of the first order, know mathematics from top to bottom, and one must have put in long hours tussling with the obscure Latin of the old masters. Besides, you must have the vocation and the faith, and they are lost."

"Just the way it is with bell ringing," said Carhaix.

"No, you see, messieurs," Gévingey went on, "the day when the grand sciences of the Middle Ages fell foul of the systematic and hostile indifference of an impious people was the death-day of the soul in France. All we can do now is fold our arms and listen to the wild vagaries of society, which by turns shrieks with farcical joy and bitter grief."

"We must not despair. A better time is coming," said Mme. Carhaix in a conciliating tone, and before she retired she shook hands with all her guests.

"The people," said Des Hermies, pouring the water into the coffee-pot, "instead of being ameliorated with time, grow, from century to century, more avaricious, abject, and stupid. Remember the Siege, the Commune; the unreasonable infatuations, the tumultuous hatreds, all the dementia of a deteriorated, malnourished people in arms. They certainly cannot compare with the naïf and tender-hearted plebes of the Middle Ages. Tell us, Durtal, how the people acted when Gilles de Rais was conducted to the stake."

"Yes, tell us," said Carhaix, his great eyes made watery by the smoke of his pipe.

"Well, you know, as a consequence of unheard-of crimes, the Marshal de Rais was condemned to be hanged and burned alive. After the sentence was passed, when he was brought back to his dungeon, he addressed a last appeal to the Bishop, Jean de Malestroit, beseeching the Bishop to intercede for him with the fathers and mothers of the children Gilles had so ferociously violated and put to death, to be present when he suffered.

"The people whose hearts he had lacerated wept with pity. They now saw in this demoniac noble only a poor man who lamented his crimes and was about to confront the Divine Wrath. The day of execution, by nine o'clock they were marching through the city in processional. They chanted psalms in the streets and took vows in the churches to fast three days in order to help assure the repose of the Marshal's soul."

"Pretty far, as you see, from American lynch law," said Des Hermies.

"Then," resumed Durtal, "at eleven they went to the prison to get Gilles de Rais and accompanied him to the prairie of Las Biesse, where tall stakes stood, surmounted by gibbets.

"The Marshal supported his accomplices, embraced them, adjured them to have 'great displeasure and contrition of their ill deeds' and, beating his breast, he supplicated the Virgin to spare them, while the clergy, the peasants, and the people joined in the psalmody, intoning the sinister and imploring strophes of the chant for the departed:

" 'Nos timemus diem judicii
  Quia mali et nobis conscii.
  Sed tu, Mater summi concilii,
  Para nobis locum refugii,
      O Maria.

" 'Tunc iratus Judex——"

"Hurrah for Boulanger!"

The noise as of a stormy sea mounted from the Place Saint Sulpice, and a hubbub of cries floated up to the tower room. "Boulange—Lange—" Then an enormous, raucous voice, the voice of an oyster woman, a push-cart peddler, rose, dominating all others, howling, "Hurrah for Boulanger!"

"The people are cheering the election returns in front of the city hall," said Carhaix disdainfully.

They looked at each other.

"The people of today!" exclaimed Des Hermies.

"Ah," grumbled Gévingey, "they wouldn't acclaim a sage, an artist, that way, even—if such were conceivable now—a saint."

"And they did in the Middle Ages."

"Well, they were more naïf and not so stupid then," said Des Hermies. "And as Gévingey says, where now are the saints who directed them? You cannot too often repeat it, the spiritual councillors of today have tainted hearts, dysenteric souls, and slovenly minds. Or they are worse. They corrupt their flock. They are of the Docre order and Satanize."

"To think that a century of positivism and atheism has been able to overthrow everything but Satanism, and it cannot make Satanism yield an inch."

"Easily explained!" cried Carhaix. "Satan is forgotten by the great majority. Now it was Father Ravignan, I believe, who proved that the wiliest thing the Devil can do is to get people to deny his existence."

"Oh, God!" murmured Durtal forlornly, "what whirl-winds of ordure I see on the horizon!"

"No," said Carhaix, "don't say that. On earth all is dead and decomposed. But in heaven! Ah, I admit that the Paraclete is keeping us waiting. But the texts announcing his coming are inspired. The future is certain. There will be light," and with bowed head he prayed fervently.

Des Hermies rose and paced the room. "All that is very well," he groaned, "but this century laughs the glorified Christ to scorn. It contaminates the supernatural and vomits on the Beyond. Well, how can we hope that in the future the offspring of the fetid tradesmen of today will be decent? Brought up as they are, what will they do in Life?"

"They will do," replied Durtal, "as their fathers and mothers do now. They will stuff their guts and crowd out their souls through their alimentary canals."

FINIS

CHRONOLOGY

1847	Huysmans born and christened Charles-Marie-George.
1852	Berthe Courrière born.
1856	Abbé Boullan begins affair with Adèle Chevalier. Death of Huysmans's lithographer father.
1857	Huysmans's mother remarries.
1860	Abbé Boullan allegedly sacrifices his illegitimate child on the altar.
1861	Abbé Boullan tried for fraud and indecency and spends three years in prison.
1863	Huysmans's first visit to a brothel.
1866	Huysmans finds a job as a small time civil servant in the Ministry of the Interior.
1867	**La Revue Mensuelle** publishes Huysmans's first articles.
1869	Abbé Boullan imprisoned again, this time by the Holy Office in Rome, and he writes a confession of his crimes.
1870	Huymans called up for Franco-Prussian War, but invalided out because of dysentry.
1874	Publication of **Drageoir aux Epices** (prose poems and short sketches).
1875	Death of the prophet and miracle worker Vintras. Abbé Boullan leaves the Church and takes over the leadership of part of Vintras's movement. Death of the occultist Eliphas Levi.

1876	Huysmans visits Zola for the first time and meets Maupassant. Publication of **Marthe**.
1877	Arranges famous literary dinner attended by Zola, Edmond de Goncourt and Flaubert.
1879	Publication of **Les Soeurs Vatard** (a realistic novel about two girls working in a book-binders).
1880	Publication of **Les Soirées de Medan**.
1882	Publication of **A Vau L'Eau,** (a novel about the miseries of a small time clerk).
1884	Beginning of friendship with extreme right-wing Catholic writer Leon Bloy. Publication of **A Rebours** (or 'Against Nature', his masterly novel about artificiality and decadent taste. Its hero is partly modelled on Comte Robert de Montesquiou and partly on Huysmans himself).
1886	Publication of **En Rade.** E. Bossard and R. de Maulde publish their life of Gilles de Rais.
1887	Begins to frequent Naundorffist circles. Oswald Wirth and Stanislas de Guaita condemn the occult activities of Abbé Boullan.
1888	Huysmans's trip to Germany. Paintings by Grunewald and by Roger van der Weyden make a powerful impression on him. Has an affair with Henriette Maillat (an ex-mistress of the flamboyant occultist Péladan).
1889	Meets Berthe Courrière and Sar Péladan. General Boulanger threatens a military coup in Paris but then flees to Brussels. The Exposition Universel is held in Paris. The Eiffel Tower is its leading attraction. Huysmans visits Tiffauges (the castle of Gilles de Rais). Gilbert and Sullivan produce **The Gondoliers**.

1890   Berthe Courrière certified insane in Bruges. Péladan founds the Order of the Rose Croix of the Temple and the Grail. Huysmans begins corresponding with Abbé Boullan. In October **Là-Bas** is finished.

1891   In February **Là-Bas** starts appearing in the **Echo de Paris**. In the summer Huysmans visits Boullan and Julie Thibault for the first time. Boullan sends exorcism paste to Huysmans, but Huysmans is psychically attacked anyway. Oscar Wilde's **The Picture of Dorian Gray** is also published in this year.

1893   Boullan dies. French press accuses Guaita of having murdered Boullan by occult means. Julie Thibault (ex-priestess of Carmel and Apostolic Woman) becomes Huysmans's housekeeper. Stanislas de Guaita challenges Huysmans to a duel after Huysmans had written in the press about their alleged murder of Boullan by psychic means.

1895   Publication of **En Route** (novel in which Durtal retires to a Trappist monastery). Publication of **Satanisme et Magie.**

1897   Stanislas de Guaita dies of a drugs overdose.

1898   Publication of **La Cathédrale** (novel in which Durtal retires to Chartres). Huysmans retires from civil service.

1899   Huysmans becomes an oblate in a Benedictine monastery.

1900   Louis Massignon visits Huysmans for the first time.

1903   Publication of **L'Oblat.**

1907   May 12 Huysmans dies.

Titles in the Decadence from Dedalus Series include:

The Child of Pleasure - Gabriele D'Annunzio £7.99
Triumph of Death - Gabriele D'Annunzio £6.99
L'Innocente (the Victim) - Gabriele D'Annunzio £7.99
Senso (and other stories) - Camillo Boito £6.99
Angels of Perversity - Remy de Gourmont £6.99
La -Bas - J.K. Huysmans £6.99
The Green Face - Gustav Meyrink £7.99
Torture Garden - Octave Mirbeau £6.99
The Diary of A Chambermaid - Octave Mirbeau £7.99
Le Calvaire - Octave Mirbeau £7.99
The Dedalus Book of Decadence -
  editor Brian Stableford £7.99
The Second Dedalus Book of Decadence -
  editor Brian Stableford £8.99

forthcoming:

The Dedalus Book of Russian Decadence -
  editor Natalia Rubenstein
The Dedalus Book of Chinese Decadence -
  editor Richard Ings

All these titles can be obtained from your local bookshop or newsagent, or directly from Dedalus by writing to :
Cash sales, Dedalus Ltd, Langford Lodge, St Judith'sLane, Sawtry, Cambs, PE17 5XE.
Please enclose a cheque to the value of the books ordered +75p pp for the first book, 50p for the second and subsequent books up to a maximum of £2.

En Route - *J.K. Huysmans*

En Route continues the story of Durtal from *La-Bas*, a modern anti-hero; solitary, agonised and alienated. Robbed of religion and plunged into decadence by the pressure of modern life, Durtal discovers a new road to Rome .

Art, architecture and music light his way back to God . For Durtal, God's death is a temporary demise, and by the end of the novel, he is morally mended and spiritually healed.

First published in 1895, *En Route* earned the hostility of the Catholic Church and was condemned for obscenity.

£6.95   ISBN 0 946626 56 1   B. Format Paperback

The Cathedral - *J.K.Huysmans*

The Cathedral is the most ambitious and controversial of Huysmans novels . Durtal's conversion from satanism (*La-Bas*) to Roman Catholicism incensed French catholics who tried to get the novel banned. The symbolists defended *The Cathedral* as a major step forward in the development of the novel.

All the various facets of Huysmans' writing -aestheticism, decadence, spirituality, art and architecture -come together in *The Cathedral* to produce his masterpiece.

"A wonderful picture of the inner meaning of Gothic architecture" - *Daily Telegraph*

" a most astonishing piece of fiction." - *The Bookman*

£6.95 ISBN 0 946626 49 9 B.Format Paperback